Praise for Laura Frantz

"Frantz infuses color and life into a multifaceted story of liberty featuring unexpected twists and transforming history."

Booklist on *The Indigo Heiress*

"Frantz's characters leap off the page, propelling an ambitious, twisty plot that draws energy from the tensions of the Revolutionary era. The results are captivating."

Publishers Weekly on *The Indigo Heiress*

"Frantz is a wordsmith extraordinaire who makes readers care about little-known episodes of history through her characters."

Library Journal on *The Seamstress of Acadie*

"An epic journey of faith and love wrought through hardship. Laura Frantz is a gifted writer."

Julie Klassen, bestselling author, on *A Bound Heart*

"Make a spot on your keeper shelf, because this is one story you'll want to reread! Classic Laura Frantz stellar writing, weaving in history and a solid biblical message."

Michelle Griep, bestselling author, on *A Bound Heart*

"An enlightening tale of the dangerous days of our country's revolution and struggle for freedom, and a heart-tugging romance made even more poignant as it is intertwined with courage and tenacity. A great story!"

Melanie Dickerson, *New York Times* bestselling author, on *The Lacemaker*

The Belle of Chatham

Books by Laura Frantz

The Frontiersman's Daughter
Courting Morrow Little
The Colonel's Lady
The Mistress of Tall Acre
A Moonbow Night
The Lacemaker
A Bound Heart
An Uncommon Woman
Tidewater Bride
A Heart Adrift
The Rose and the Thistle
The Seamstress of Acadie
The Indigo Heiress
The Belle of Chatham

THE BALLANTYNE LEGACY

Love's Reckoning
Love's Awakening
Love's Fortune

The Belle of Chatham

LAURA FRANTZ

Revell

a division of Baker Publishing Group
Grand Rapids, Michigan

© 2026 by Laura Frantz

Published by Revell
a division of Baker Publishing Group
Grand Rapids, Michigan
RevellBooks.com

Printed in the United States of America

Library of Congress Cataloging-in-Publication Data
Names: Frantz, Laura, author.
Title: The belle of Chatham / Laura Frantz.
Description: Grand Rapids, Michigan : Revell, a division of Baker Publishing Group,
    2026.
Identifiers: LCCN 2025014435 | ISBN 9780800746568 paperback | ISBN 9780800747886
    casebound | ISBN 9781493452712 ebook
Subjects: LCGFT: Fiction | Christian fiction | Romance fiction | Novels
Classification: LCC PS3606.R4226 B45 2026 | DDC 813/.6—dc23/eng/20250602
LC record available at https://lccn.loc.gov/2025014435

Scripture quotations, whether quoted or paraphrased by the characters, are from the King James Version of the Bible.

Cover design by Laura Klynstra
Photograph of woman © Crow's Eye Productions / Arcangel

Published in association with Books & Such Literary Management, www.booksandsuch
.com.

Baker Publishing Group publications use paper produced from sustainable forestry practices and postconsumer waste whenever possible.

26 27 28 29 30 31 32   7 6 5 4 3 2 1

To American soldiers from 1776 forward—
heroes of immense courage and incalculable sacrifices.
And to my own Patriot line. You are not forgotten.

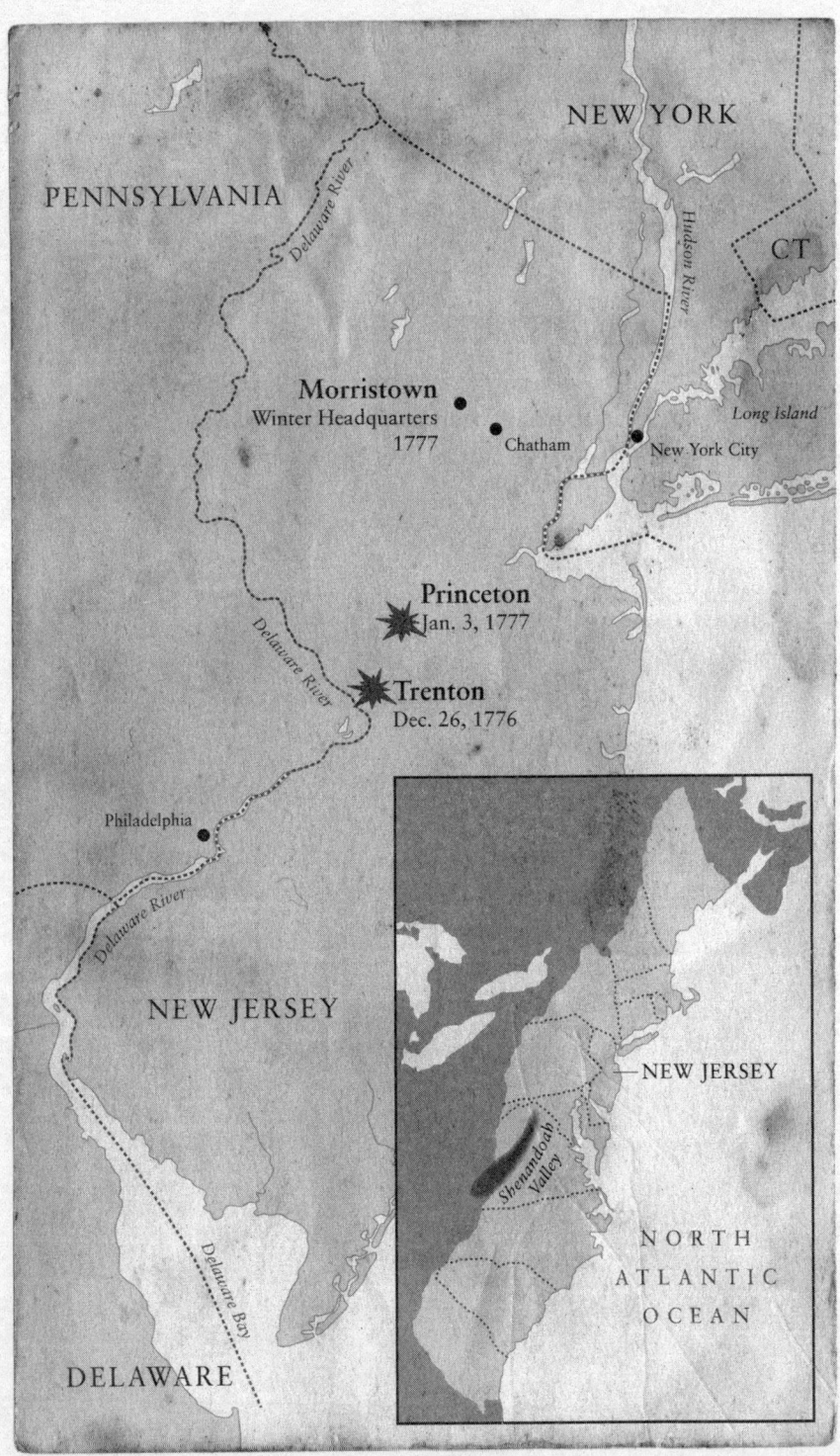

PENNSYLVANIA

NEW YORK

CT

Delaware River

Hudson River

Morristown
Winter Headquarters
1777

Chatham

New York City

Long Island

Princeton
Jan. 3, 1777

Delaware River

Trenton
Dec. 26, 1776

Philadelphia

Delaware River

NEW JERSEY

NEW JERSEY

Shenandoah Valley

NORTH

ATLANTIC

OCEAN

Delaware Bay

DELAWARE

Prologue

JANUARY 1777
CHATHAM, NEW JERSEY

Her four-poster bed seemed made for winter. With the curtains drawn, Mae felt snug as a she-bear in its den, far removed from the turmoil of their colonial world. But sleep of late was often elusive. It took time to disentangle oneself from the day's moods and happenings. Tonight, once she did drift away, she dreamed of a dance—and a violet silk gown in the French polonaise style. The sheen of the silk struck her. They'd not had such sumptuous fabric since 1774.

The candlelit ballroom of her dream smelled of wax . . . and war. War had a distinct smell and sound. She knew that all too well, caught in the thick of it these last months. Tonight, war had woken her up.

The tread on the wooden bridge across the Passaic River nearby, the crunch of ice and creak of harnesses, the shuffling steps of soldiers and the officers' more sure-footed horses, and the thunder of the baggage wagons violated the usually hushed night. Mae sat up, drawing her knees to her chest beneath the blankets. Which army could it be?

The Americans or the British?

Was Coralie awake? Her sister was a light sleeper, though no sound issued from the open door adjoining their rooms. Coralie's bedchamber faced Chatham's village green while hers overlooked the dependencies at the back.

Mae stifled a yawn, roused further by a sound just beyond her frigid windowpane. The creak of the smokehouse door? Pushing aside the bed linens, she lowered her bare feet to the floor. Her icy soles sent a shiver to her spine as she hurried to Coralie's room and stared out the front-facing window. Snow spun down, obscuring her view. Dark silhouettes moved in rapid succession over river and bridge in the scant moonlight. A menacing presence whether friend or foe.

She returned to her room and looked out her rear window onto the fenced area below. Kitchen garden and well, stable and necessary were snow-drifted and undisturbed. Shadows moved toward the smokehouse. Thieves? They hadn't an abundance of meat to steal.

Wrapping herself in a shawl, Mae crept downstairs, clutching the banister with one hand and a lantern in the other. She pulled on her father's boots, retrieved his pistol, and tugged open the back door. A blast of wind nearly snuffed the lantern she hung from a hook beneath the porch's eave. Eyes on the smokehouse, she gathered her courage and bypassed the winter-bitten kitchen garden, no longer seeing shadows but sensing a distinct presence.

Snow spat at her, and the distant sound of an army on the march almost muffled the sounds within the smokehouse as she pointed her pistol at the door left ajar.

"Show yourselves and stop your thieving." Her voice rose above the wind. "If it's victuals you want, I'll supply them honestly, but leave our meat alone."

The smokehouse door groaned open and turned Mae more skittish. Two figures appeared, a rasher of filched bacon in hand. They seemed little more than children—waifs—their clothes in tatters, their scarecrow figures startling. The snow's brightness and the lantern light illuminated more than she cared to see. Was that a drum the lad had slung about his neck? His bare feet, slashed by ice, left bloody footprints in the snow.

"We're sorry, miss." A woman's voice, trembling with contrition and the cold, reached her. "We mean no harm. We're half starved—worn down."

"Are you rebels?" Mae pocketed her pistol. "Or redcoats?"

"Rebels," the man said, his deep voice dispelling the notion he was a mere lad. "But General Washington don't hold with stealing, so we might as well desert."

Mae's simmering turned to sympathy. Coralie had always chided her for being soft. The gift of mercy, others said. "Come inside," she told them breathlessly, leading the way.

The pair followed somewhat reluctantly as if *she* were the enemy and they feared ambush. Once inside the low-beamed kitchen, where the hearth's fire crackled in welcome, they sat on a settle facing the flames while Mae served them warm stew and coffee left over from supper. As they ate, she hurriedly shoved bread and cheese and bacon into a knapsack, fearful that if they tarried by the fire, they might miss the army's route altogether. But given the numbers she'd spied coming over the river and bridge, the march was miles long.

Where was General Washington headed?

Once they'd eaten and more victuals were packed, Mae said, "Take these stockings and boots of my father's—and here's my mother's warmest woolen shawl." She draped the butter-colored wool around the young woman's bent shoulders while the boyish-faced man pulled on the woolen stockings and shoes.

Now far more moved than nettled, Mae watched her unexpected guests depart. The snow was whirling harder now. The bloody footprints would soon be naught but a harsh memory. Would these two beleaguered souls rejoin the army or run?

She'd forgotten to ask them their names.

one

We marched from Morristown at 3. PM, and arrived at Chatham at dark, in the suburbs of which we got very agreeable quarters. The young ladies here are very fond of the soldiers, but much more so of officers.

Lieutenant James McMichael's journal,
January 12, 1777

Drifted with snow, the village of Chatham was decidedly quaint. Tidy. Or once had been. Now it was infused with Patriots. Infested, some said. Countless rebel soldiers milled about, some of them almost leisurely, others purposefully. Since the Continental Army had no standardized uniform aside from the topmost officers, most of these Patriots were a ragtag, homespun sort, some even barefoot, reminding Mae of the couple she'd caught in the smokehouse.

Had it only been a fortnight ago she'd ushered them into the kitchen and supplied them? She'd told no one, not even Coralie. Try as she might, she couldn't scrub her mind clean of the bloody footprints in the snow. And she continued to wonder . . . Had the sad pair returned to the army? Or deserted?

Basket on one arm, Mae crossed the village green, her progress as slow as it was slippery, her scarlet cape furling and unfurling like a flag in the wintry wind. Few would guess British-occupied New York City with its hordes of redcoated soldiers was only twenty-five miles away.

"Morning, miss." One tattered soldier doffed his cocked hat to her in the middle of the green.

"Good morning to you, sir," she returned, hastening past.

Tattered and ragtag, aye. But these men were unified in spirit if not dress, and she sensed their resiliency and resolve from a distance. Wrestling with admiration and pity, she fixed her eye on the trade sign that waved in a north wind. The words "Old Town Apothecary" lettered a wooden board where clusters of lavender, rosemary, and mint grew in painted profusion. Her youngest brother's business, the shop was the handsomest building in Chatham save the Presbyterian church. Aaron Bohannon did them all proud.

If she'd expected an empty shop she was sorely mistaken. Winter's agues and miasmas laid many low. A line of villagers snaked out the front door, sending her round to the side entrance. After letting herself in, she made her way to a back chamber, a cozy bower lined with medical books that boasted Aaron's desk and an immense brick hearth roaring with heat.

She pulled off her mittens, extended cold fingers to the fire, and breathed in the earthy, medicinal scent while listening to the shop's chatter. In minutes, her sister-in-law Hanna appeared, her lovely face pinched with concern.

"Morning, dear Mae." She wiped her hands on her apron. "Is Coralie's cold worse?"

"No better," Mae replied. "And we've run out of herbs and simples."

"I do worry, as she's painfully thin."

As painfully thin as I am plump, Mae thought.

"I recommend a decoction of peppermint leaves, dried ginger, a pinch of yarrow, and lemon balm with a small piece of willow bark." Hanna disappeared again to fetch the needed ingredients before returning and advising, "Add all to hot water and let rest for fifteen minutes, then strain. Have Coralie inhale the steam as she drinks to help clear her head."

Thanking her, Mae turned her backside to the fire and took in her brother behind the counter as Hanna returned to help the next customer. Aaron bore a marked resemblance to their late father, though it was their mother she missed most.

Grief, still raw, pushed Mae out the door and past the First Presbyterian Church. Across the stone fence was her parents' grave marker, hidden by snow. If only she could do the same with her emotions. Bury them. Banish them.

Armed with a fresh remedy for Coralie, she allowed herself a last, less practical stop. Down a side street stood the dressmaker's shop, beckoning her inside with all its color and creature comforts. The pomaded, powdered owner was a French Huguenot, an independent woman of means who somehow seemed to be the only merchant immune to the war's blockades and barriers. Some suspected her of smuggling, but who knew?

"Ah, Mademoiselle Bohannon." Madame Jaquett's heavily accented English gave no hint she'd been in Chatham for a decade. "My shop is all too quiet on account of the snow, so it is good to see you venture forth."

Smiling and shivering, Mae set her market basket down. "I promised Coralie I'd ask about her gown."

"Of course. You'll be happy to know that I've nearly finished." Escorting her to the rear of the shop, Madame Jaquett pointed to a wickerwork mannequin bedecked in exotic Indian chintz. "Voilà!"

Awed, Mae eyed the gown and tried to put down the envy that needled her. "My sister will look lovely."

"Alors, mademoiselle! This dress is yours—her gift to you."

Mae stared at her.

"For a very special occasion, she said." Madame Jaquett smiled and lifted a lace sleeve ruffle made from the same delicate lace that lined the bodice. "Would you like a decorative ladder of bows at the front? A flounce at the hem?"

Mae smiled and shook her head, even more appreciative of the colorful fabric now that she'd come out of mourning. "Nothing more is needed, thank you."

"Then I shall finish it at once." Madame Jaquett went to a chest of drawers and took out a length of silk ribbon. "Please take this to your sister and tell her I am trimming her gown with such."

Mae took the ribbon, a marvel of embroidered flowers. "I can't thank you enough."

"I send my best wishes for her complete recovery"—she darted a wary look out the window, where snow masked the alley and surrounding structures—"and an end to all this inclement weather."

★ ★ ★ ★ ★

Mae let herself into their clapboard house quietly, removed her damp cape, and hung it on a peg to dry. The center hall was quiet, the staircase empty as it wound upward to several bedchambers and an attic. She darted a look into the parlor, where a fire burned in a large hearth, bookended by shelves. A red-nosed Coralie dozed in a Windsor chair nearest the blaze, eyes closed, a handkerchief fisted atop her quilted petticoat.

Tiptoeing, Mae took her basket into the kitchen and began to prepare the apothecary tea. Above her head, the room's oak beams, taken from a spice ship, held their own exotic scent and seemed to whisper of faraway ports. In summer the room hinted of pepper and mace, in winter cinnamon and cloves. Mae inhaled deeply, happy to be home.

When the kettle sang, she swung it off the fire and poured hot water over the herbals in a large stoneware mug. Mrs. Hurst, their longtime cook and housekeeper, had left a kettle of fish chowder in the ashes and a loaf of bread on the open door of the beehive oven. A widow, she lived across the alley behind their stable.

Night was falling fast, the wind rising.

"Mae?" Coralie's hoarse voice reached out from the adjoining room. "Is that you?"

"Finally home," Mae called, carrying in the aromatic, steaming mug.

"How I miss going out with you." Coralie sat up straighter, then sneezed into her handkerchief. "Surely this sickness will pass with a little help from Aaron and Hanna."

"They send their regards. Madame Jaquett too. I'd hug you if I could because of that lovely chintz gown." Mae smiled her thanks and passed her sister the tea.

"So you discovered my surprise." Coralie's wan face brightened. "Isn't it lush? Since you're to be my bridesmaid, I wanted something colorful."

"'Tis vibrant as a garden in full bloom. And the skill with which Madame sews! My stitches shame me."

"Seamstresses we are not." Coralie sighed. "Though we do manage petticoats and aprons and caps admirably."

Mae sat back in Father's worn chair, wishing she had Mother's warmest shawl to give Coralie. "Mrs. Hurst said she feels a blizzard in her bones."

"She's rarely wrong about the weather, but oh, what woe it brings." Coralie stifled a cough and took another sip. "I pray my beloved is warm and dry up north."

Coralie's betrothed seemed far away. Last they'd heard, Eben Gibbs was serving as a British lieutenant under General Burgoyne at a remote garrison in New York.

"Eben doesn't tell me much about his whereabouts or happenings. I suppose, being an officer, he fears anything he writes might be confiscated," her sister lamented. "This weather will prevent any post riders from coming, anyway."

"How long since you've had a letter?"

"Twenty-three days."

So she *was* counting? "Take heart—you have an amazing array of them to reread in the meantime." Mae's teasing was not far from the truth. She'd never seen a man pen so many letters. It made her wonder what officers did if they had the luxury of so much ink and pounce and paper.

"We must pray he gets leave to return this spring. After the wedding we hope to go to New York City to see his family, if they can rebuild after the terrible fire there. Then he'll return to the fray, wherever that is." Coralie sneezed again, jostling her tea. "Odd to think Eben might be fighting against our own brothers."

"Whom we haven't heard from in so long I'm beginning to wonder."

The moment turned melancholy. All they knew was that James had joined the Continental Army following the bloody debacle in Boston, and Jon was a militia captain somewhere along New York's Hudson River.

"Have you any fresh news from villagers?" Coralie pulled her shawl closer. "About the conflict?"

Conflict. Coralie refused to call it war, as if changing the wording would wish England's and America's ire away.

"There's talk that General Washington may winter in Jersey." Mae reached for her knitting, wanting to change the subject yet driven to keep abreast of matters as an older sister should.

"With all the Continental soldiers here lately being resupplied, I'm not surprised. Where, exactly?"

"Somewhere in the Watchung Mountains," Mae said, eyes on her yarn. "General Washington's troops need to recover after their recent victories at the battles of Trenton and Princeton."

"Hollow victories, you mean." Coralie made a face. "You're not sympathizing with that turncoat, I hope."

Turncoat? Mae tried to ignore her personal feelings and deal with facts. "How can I not sympathize with wounded soldiers on either side? A great many of Washington's men have been lost with expiring enlistments. The Continental Army has been whittled down to three thousand or less. Without fresh recruits I don't know how they'll continue."

"Eben's last letter indicated the British army's strength at five times that, given all the Hessians and Prussians, Brunswickers and Hanoverians coming to our shore in droves. They've even brought over a German general, if I recall."

"General Riedesel, yes. A fine commander, though German troops are said to be among the fastest deserters." All she'd heard and read crossed Mae's mind like buckshot. "I hardly blame them. Imagine being in a strange land with a different language and customs. It's not their battle to begin with, though I hear they're rewarded handsomely to fight—the officers, anyway."

"Heaven help us all. 'Tis so hopelessly complex and dangerous." Coralie dabbed her nose with her handkerchief. "How did it all go so wrong?"

"Matters have been coming to a head for years now with king and parliament. We just never thought it would amount to men taking up arms."

What they'd once considered a minor skirmish over tea and taxes had turned into something far more frightening and enduring. New Jersey seemed to be the very crossroads of the revolution. Lately most of the war's action seemed to play out on their very doorstep, making them wish themselves elsewhere.

"I want to be like Father and Mother, taking neither side," Mae told her. "Father always strove to keep the peace as pastor and stay far from any divisiveness."

Coralie breathed in the tonic's steam. "I'm glad they didn't live to see the conflict unfold and us in the midst of it."

"They certainly didn't want to leave us alone, two women rolling around this house like misplaced marbles."

"At least Aaron and Hanna are close at the apothecary. And Mrs. Hurst is near, as well as Adam."

Mrs. Hurst had been with them since their parents married. But aged and rheumatic as she was, how much longer could she keep at her tasks? And Adam, their hired lad, was at an age where he could enlist in the army.

"We're immensely blessed. The future is bright. Your future, anyway." Mae tried to summon some joy. "I'm not at all sure about mine."

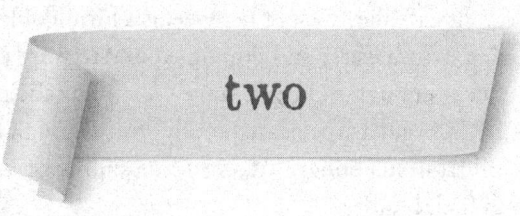

two

Rifle Men that for their number make the most formidable light infantry in the world. . . . Men who from their amazing hardihood, their method of living so long in the woods without carrying provisions with them, the exceeding quickness with which they can march to distant parts, and above all, the dexterity to which they have arrived in the use of the Rifle Gun. . . . Every shot is fatal.

The Virginia Gazette

Within the smoky, dimly lit Day's Bridge Tavern along the Passaic River, General Rhys Harlow sat at a corner table. Spread over the spacious taproom were his company of riflemen—eighty enlisted men and sixteen officers. The slim profiles of ninety-six long rifles turned the tavern into a military garrison.

On the table before him lay a letter from General Washington, recommending him to the particular notice of Congress as a good and valuable officer. He'd been promoted to the rank of brigadier general in the Continental Army after being a prisoner of war in Quebec till recently. His time among the British was finally finished, at least in their custody. He'd far rather face them on the field.

"Here's to the Canadian expedition officially coming to a close." Major James Bohannon, his adjutant, raised his pint of ale. "I never thought we'd escape the far north, but here we are, a stone's throw from my very home."

Captain Casper Sperry reached for a worn copy of *The New Jersey Gazette*. "So, General, bets are being placed on where the American army should winter. What's your preference?"

"The Lowantica Valley west of here seems a formidable defense with a brook for fresh water and sloping ground to ward off north winds. And near enough to keep a wary eye on Philadelphia and New York," Rhys said as the heated toddy stole through him and took the chill from his bones. "We've a fair supply of wood for covering and fuel, besides."

Bohannon nodded. "The enlisted men will winter in tents, God help them, though there's talk of building log huts. General Washington will likely headquarter at Jacob Arnold's Tavern on Morristown Green, large enough to hold his aides-de-camp, servants, and guard. Even Mrs. Washington, should she visit."

"Imagine that." Sperry grinned as a harried maidservant plopped down heaping pewter plates. "A little feminine company would be most welcome."

Bohannon surveyed the fried eggs and bacon and toast with obvious approval after months of scant rations. "I heard tell of a promised dance or two hosted by none other than the general himself."

"As for us officers, we're billeting here in Chatham, aye?" Sperry asked. "Or riding on to Morristown if it proves more accommodating?"

"New Jersey declared for independence last year, so hopefully the villagers will be obliging. Chatham's liberty pole marks them as firm Patriots," Rhys said. "Much like Morristown."

Nodding, Bohannon picked up a fork. "My parents, God rest them, left a large house on Chatham Green. There's room enough for a few of us officers . . . if my sisters are willing."

Rhys listened, hopeful. For a soldier on the run, a canvas tent seemed the best to be had, but a house? Though the winter had been mild and muddy thus far aside from a spate of snow, he sensed it would soon turn brutal, as northeast winters often were.

Bohannon continued, "My brother is a staunch Patriot and apothecary and lives in his shop. He'd be a valuable resource should there be medical needs among the troops."

Sperry winked. "I'd rather talk about your sisters."

Bohannon grinned. "Well, they're not yet married, nor are they spinsters. One is known as the belle of Chatham."

Sperry's interest sharpened. "The *belle*? That bodes well."

"But can they cook?" Rhys asked wryly.

Sperry chuckled, but Bohannon turned sheepish. "Pampered pastor's daughters? A hired woman helps—and a lad who tends the horses and brings in wood and whatnot."

Rhys forked another bite. Pampered? Unable to do the most basic of tasks? He thought of his own mother and sister, the ordinary he was raised in, and the lack of the smallest luxuries at first. A few of his officers had been born and bred with a silver spoon while his was a humble wooden ladle. Yet they all were proven marksmen, having survived conditions most snuff-snorting men couldn't. All for the cause of liberty.

"I should like to meet these sisters of yours," Sperry said, taking a pinch of snuff, which was, to Rhys's reckoning, his only fault. "And billet with you Bohannons for the winter."

★ ★ ★ ★ ★

Leaving the tavern, Rhys surveyed the Bohannon home from a distance. Situated on Chatham's village green, it was a handsome house with a red sandstone foundation, pitched roof, puffing chimneys—four, to be exact—and large, elegantly proportioned windows. His own newly finished home in Virginia, though smaller, mirrored these sturdy Yankee dwellings.

Bohannon led them across the snow-slick green, avoiding the wagons, carts, and horses on the main streets. Sperry seemed high-spirited, confident the Bohannons would be their host. Rhys could hardly believe their good fortune after so long and harsh a campaign. Would they really sleep atop a bed out of the weather? Sit down for a meal of something other than hardtack and dried peas? He craved coffee. Cake. Even chocolate.

As they came closer, he was suddenly mindful of how ragged he looked. An icy dawn plunge into the Passaic had cleansed him bodily, but his buckskins and linens could stand some mending. Did Bohannon's sisters sew? Or did the hired help do that too?

Hat in hand, Bohannon knocked on the door of his own house. An unfavorable sign? Rhys stood behind him with Sperry on the wide stone steps. Soon the well-made oak door swung open and a young woman stood before them, her mouth a perfect O. In a trice he took her in. Her indigo gown was edged with delicate lace. Her flaxen hair seemed a shade lighter than her paleness, which heightened her piercing eyes.

"Brother, can it be you?" Her shock led to an exuberant embrace that sent Bohannon backward on the slippery steps.

Amused, Rhys looked to his boots to allow them a moment's privacy, though Sperry continued his gawking. With good reason. Bohannon's sister was as comely as winter was long. Surely this was Chatham's belle. There couldn't be a prettier sister.

"Your Patriot brother, at long last, aye," Bohannon finally said. "I've returned from Canada to winter over with General Washington and troops. Me and my two, um, compatriots."

"Welcome, gentlemen." Her eyes widened again as she took in all three of them. "Do come in out of the cold."

"Gentlemen" was a stretch, but they all removed their cocked hats just the same.

"This is my oldest sister, Maebel—we call her Mae. Miss Bohannon to you," Bohannon half jested, darting a look at Sperry. "And this is Captain Sperry and my commanding officer, General Harlow, of Harlow's Rifle Corps."

"Honored." She smiled at Sperry and then Rhys, a wide, dimpled smile as beguiling as her lively eyes.

They stood in the hall of the house now, midday light streaming through the open door behind them.

"And this is Coralie, the youngest of the clan." Bohannon gestured toward the staircase another young woman was descending.

She was as plain as Maebel Bohannon was pretty. Or mayhap the stark black she wore made her seem so. Seemingly flustered by so many men, she uttered nothing in reply. Or did she simply rely on her sister to speak for her? Flushing, she gave Bohannon a quick peck on his cheek.

"Your timing is excellent." Again, Mae smiled and gestured to the dining room, where a dozen different dishes sat upon the table. "Perhaps you can even guess what we're having for dinner."

Rhys held her gaze in question, hardly believing his good fortune. There was no mistaking that distinct scent. "Virginia ham?"

"You have a discerning palate, General Harlow." Pleasure lit her pale features. "There's also corn chowder, codfish, and gravy. Potatoes, bread, pickles, and preserves. Even molasses dumplings."

His mouth watered as it hadn't done for months.

"We don't normally feast like this." The younger Miss Bohannon's hoarse voice bespoke a cold. "'Tis our brother Aaron's birthday."

"If you'd like to wash up first, James can show you the way." With that, Mae disappeared into what Rhys guessed was the kitchen to likely tell the hired help there'd be more guests at table. When she reappeared she said, "You'll stay the night, of course, all three of you."

"Nay, all the winter," Bohannon corrected with a smile.

"Oh my, a billet of invitation, then." Coralie Bohannon's brow tightened. For a fleeting moment, Rhys detected resistance in her gaze. Then she pursed her lips and looked upstairs as if trying to parcel out bedchambers.

Mae took charge again. "We've unused beds that shall do nicely."

"I'll take my old attic room," Bohannon told her. "The guest rooms should suit the general and captain."

For now, his rifle stowed in the hall, Rhys became acquainted with the washbowl and linen towels in a small room adjoining the kitchen while Mae held court in the dining room. She signaled him and her brother to take the table's ends. The sisters sat opposite Sperry, who seemed none too troubled by the view.

Coralie placed a napkin in her lap. "Despite it being his birthday, our apothecary brother has been called away on an emergency."

Aaron Bohannon. Rhys tried to track the names. An elderly woman appeared, her white mobcap covering silvered hair, more dishes in each hand. The housekeeper?

"Good to see you again, Major James," she said briskly. "For a moment I mistook you for your brother, Colonel Jon."

"Understandable, Mrs. Hurst," Bohannon replied. "I may encounter him and the Albany County Militia in future should we move into New York."

"Then you must tell him he's missed here in Chatham." Eyes down, Mrs. Hurst poured them all cider, commencing the meal.

Nearly speechless at the bounty in wartime, Rhys counted eleven temptations adorning the linen tablecloth, serving spoons at the ready.

Folding her hands, Mae looked at Rhys. "Will you do us the honor of a mealtime prayer, General Harlow, given you're the foremost officer here?"

With a nod, Rhys obliged. "Grant, O God, Your protection, strength, understanding, knowledge, justice, our very existence, but foremost the love of God and all goodness."

At his "amen," not a person moved. Coralie looked perplexed while Mae regarded him with something he couldn't name. Were they Anglican? He thought Bohannon had told him Presbyterian.

"A Welsh prayer," Rhys said.

"General Harlow is from Virginia," Bohannon said by way of explanation. "His father is an English Quaker, his mother Welsh."

"I've read of the Welsh revivals, General Harlow." Mae sent Rhys a look of appreciation. "My late father kept abreast of spiritual matters in Britain and often exchanged letters with ministers there."

"I'm sorry to hear of your parents," Rhys said, serving himself bread.

"Do you have family, General?" Coralie asked, helping pass dishes.

"My father and sister are in the Shenandoah Valley. My mother's been buried three years now."

Murmured condolences went round the table.

"I've never been further than Chatham," Coralie said. "You're a long ways from home, General."

"And you, Captain Sperry?" Mae asked. "Where are you from?"

"Eastern Virginia. But I have my eye on New York's Champlain Valley or even further southwest at Cherry Valley."

"Indian lands," Mae said. "Those in league with the British."

Surprised, Rhys kept his eyes on his plate and continued eating. Miss Bohannon obviously kept abreast of the conflict. Not all women did.

"If we win the war, we'll receive land grants for our service from the new American government," Sperry told her. "Two hundred acres or more per man."

"Our oldest brother, Colonel Jon, lives in New York," Mae said. "After our parents passed last year he asked us to visit him along the Hudson River, where he's farmed for almost a decade. But now with the war on . . ."

"As soon as peace is restored, perhaps." Coralie smiled for the first time all evening. "I'm sure order will soon reign in all thirteen of His Majesty's colonies."

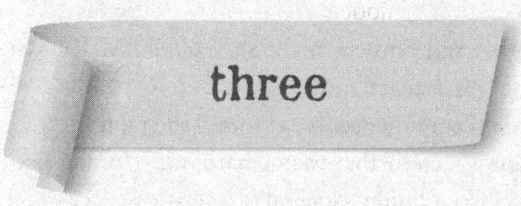

three

Should there still be soldiers without accommodation after all such publick houses were filled, the colonies were then required to take, hire and make fit for the reception of his Majesty's forces, such and so many uninhabited houses, outhouses, barns, or other buildings as shall be necessary.

The Quartering Act of 1765

Mae could hardly keep her mind on the meal, given their unexpected guests. Though she longed to have James to herself for a heartfelt talk, his fellow officers deserved all the graciousness she could muster. These three, all deemed traitors to the Crown, were men of merit and distinction. She'd heard of General Harlow and his Rifle Corps, even read about them in the newspapers, but had never imagined he'd be sitting at their very table, her brother among them.

Given their rank, she'd expected a uniform, but all three men dressed like humble woodsmen—a blend of fringed linen, buckskin, and leather offset by the black straps and belts of their weapons, which they'd left in the hall. James's and Captain Sperry's tricornes looked worn, but General Harlow sported a new cocked hat with a black ribbon cockade held by a cord and button.

None were gentlemen like so many British officers, nor were these rebels the ruffians and convicts that newspapers and broadsheets wailed about. Though quieter than her brother and the captain, General Harlow had more of a presence. Nothing, she wagered, escaped his notice, including Coralie's obvious unease and her own barely hidden awe.

Whittled down by the wilderness, the foremost officer at table's end was all whipcord. The mother hen in her wanted to mend his worn garments and insist he sleep undisturbed for a week—and fatten him with endless dishes and drinks. James was leaner than he'd once been, though the captain was more fleshed out and the shortest of the three. General Harlow had to duck beneath the lintel to enter their kitchen to wash. He had a healthy appetite, and she detected a deep, unspoken appreciation for the bounty before him.

"Please, have more," she said, passing him seconds of the heartiest dishes. "And if you're wondering why there's Virginia ham, we've Tidewater friends who keep us supplied, though this is the last in our smokehouse."

James chuckled. "Billeting here should come with a warning. My sister seems determined to reverse our soldierly starvation and make us fleshy, indolent men."

"Here's to dessert." General Harlow's lift of his cider glass told Mae he hadn't forgotten what was to come.

Looking at him again, she lifted her glass in turn, the sudden swirl to her middle as silly as it was rash. There were a hundred Chatham men who didn't move her. How could one rough-hewn stranger do so with a mere half smile?

On the other hand, the general hardly gave her a glance. She acknowledged it with a bruised feeling. She wasn't a plain woman, but he made her feel quite undeserving of notice. He never met her eyes overlong, nor did he direct any comments to her.

"Save room, too, for Mrs. Hurst's excellent coffee," Mae said, noting Coralie's cold had stolen most of her appetite. Or was it their unexpected company? "We've a coffee mill in the kitchen that hails from Boston. And plenty of cream, even a hoarded sugar loaf."

"Or if you prefer cocoa," Coralie added, "there's hot chocolate."

"Chocolate?" Captain Sperry rolled his eyes in a sort of ecstasy. "Have you no shortages here in this part of Jersey?"

Talk turned to the dearth of supplies as a dozen questions beat between Mae's brows. Would these men truly winter here in their very home? An hour ago the house had echoed, and she'd been disappointed Aaron and Hanna weren't coming. How life could take an unexpected turn.

The next pressing thought lent a flush she felt from her hairline to her toes.

Had General Harlow a sweetheart?

When she stole another look at him, she saw his plate was empty. Rising from her chair, she helped Mrs. Hurst serve coffee, hot chocolate, and dessert. As the men lingered at table, she and Coralie withdrew to the parlor. No sooner were they in the paneled room across the hall than Coralie began her frantic whispering.

"What if Eben were to suddenly appear and find Patriots at our very table?"

"Then he'd be outnumbered," Mae replied wryly. "The only redcoat in the room."

Arms crossed, Coralie began pacing before the hearth. "I feel duplicitous, though I've done nothing but sit down with them."

"Chatham's support for the revolution is what sent your lieutenant away to begin with," Mae reminded her quietly, casting a look at the dining room where talk continued robust. "Have you not told him that Jon joined the militia and James is an American officer too? Aaron has made no secret of his allegiance either."

"I've told him nothing of the sort. Suppose Eben doubts his feelings for me due to my family's loyalties—or rather the lack of them?" Her acrid tone turned plaintive. "Suppose he changes his mind about our marriage?"

"Then he's not worth a pittance." Mae took up an iron poker

and jabbed at the fiery logs as if adding an exclamation point to her words.

"Worse, are we ready to billet them all winter? When Eben arrives I won't be able to keep our engagement secret any longer."

"'Tis time to tell our family your plans, then."

"But what if it creates more division? James never cared for Eben to begin with, and now we're to be married. What are we to do?"

"Deal with that on the day." Mae, used to Coralie's worrying, now found it especially exasperating. "Can we not rejoice that James is home after not hearing from him for months?"

Chastised, her sister finally settled, hunkering down in the wingback chair that had been their mother's. "I've heard the Rifle Corps are a favorite of General Washington, given they scare the British to death. I can't believe our brother is now one of them."

"James was always an excellent shot." Mae felt a beat of pride. Her brother with an esteemed company of riflemen. Who would have thought?

"He seems much changed." Coralie darted a look toward the open door. "Captain Sperry is amiable enough, but General Harlow seems rather dangerous."

"Their weapons are certainly dangerous," Mae said. She'd been struck by the length of their long rifles as soon as she set eyes on them. No doubt they weighed ten pounds apiece.

"He says very little and seems to be weighing every window and door for the enemy, and us too, as if testing our allegiance."

"Being quiet and observant are the hallmarks of an officer, I would think. General Washington is said to be the same."

Coralie grimaced. "And all three are dressed like the worst of backwoodsmen—hardly the equal of respectable British officers. I'd expected decent uniforms, at least."

"You can hardly expect a new fighting force of thirteen colonies—now states—to wear the same garb, especially with British blockades depriving us of cloth."

A noise in the hall quieted them as the men crossed over to the parlor. Mae's pleasure rivaled her sister's pain. Could Coralie not, as she'd said, rejoice in James's return?

Their long-lost brother stifled a yawn as he looked around the room rather mournfully. "Little has changed except Mother and Father aren't here." He began rummaging in a rucksack while General Harlow and Captain Sperry stood by the parlor's two windows and looked out on the snowy green.

Finished digging, James stood, holding something behind his back, and Coralie's sternness eased.

"You remind me of our mischievous brother of old," she said, "who used to scare Mae and me to death with spiders and snakes."

"Hopefully you'll like this much better." He presented large twin balls of fur. "Two Canadian gray marten hats to keep you warm this winter."

"A replica of Benjamin Franklin's?" Mae took hers, marveling. "I'd heard of the coiffure à la Franklin—all the rage in Paris—but I never expected to own one."

James smiled. "Try it on, the both of you."

Mae did so, catching the eye of General Harlow when he turned away from the window. His admiration—or was it amusement?—didn't escape her. Flushing, she turned her back on him to peer into a looking glass. The fur had the feel of silk and instantly warmed her head like a wig.

"Thank you, James. A very thoughtful gift."

Coralie still held hers askance, staring at the fur as if it might bite.

"It doesn't have teeth, Sister," James said as if reading her mind. "Cured and fashioned by a Quebec hatter at my request. If the esteemed Dr. Franklin approves, surely you must."

Coralie relented, donning the creation with obvious distaste. "I shall get used to it, I suppose."

"You Continental officers would be warmer in these than your cocked hats." Mae removed hers, admiring the silver-gray fur. "I'm not a hatter, but I can sew shirts and breeches or knit stockings for any soldiers who need them."

"Obliged." General Harlow met her eyes as if holding her to it. "Many of the troops lack proper garments, even shoes. Some are reduced to rags on their feet."

"Bloodied snow is a frightful sight." Captain Sperry winced. "Several died on the march into northern Jersey." At Coralie's gasp, he apologized. "My manners suffer, I'm afraid. I know better than to talk war and wounds in feminine company."

"I would rather hear the truth and be of help than have matters hidden." Mae's thoughts returned to her smokehouse guests. "We heard the battles of Trenton and Princeton took a frightful toll."

"Washington fought like a lion. If the Americans hadn't won there'd be no continuing now." James took a seat on the sofa. "As it was, we lost some of our best, including General Mercer, a first-rate commander and Scot."

"I pray there's no more fighting this winter," Mae said, turning her hat into a muff to warm her hands. Even a roaring fire failed to reach the parlor's corners. Noting Captain Sperry's stifled yawn, she said, "You men are understandably weary. Let me show you to your rooms upstairs."

Coralie stayed behind as Mae climbed the steps ahead of their guests. Thankfully the rooms were kept in readiness for visitors. Her parents had always practiced hospitality, and that hadn't ended. Mrs. Hurst had even lit the hearths, their fires casting a comforting glow on paneled walls.

Which bedchamber would General Harlow choose?

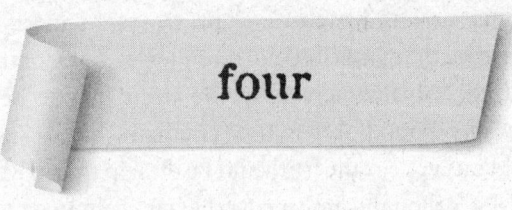

four

What a glorious morning for America!

Samuel Adams, on hearing of the battle of Lexington

Over the next days, Mae saw little of their unexpected lodgers. The officers left before first light and returned well after dark, once she and Coralie were in bed, though Aaron and Hanna told her James had come by the apothecary to speak with them. Something about Washington needing smallpox inoculations for his troops.

"Just when we think we have James safely home, he's elusive as a fox," Coralie said as she stifled a cough.

"I imagine they're preparing winter quarters in the foothills. Regular soldiers don't billet like officers here in the village but camp in tents, he said—and undergo winter training and such."

"This bitter cold is an enemy too." Coralie looked toward the sofa where she'd discarded her fur hat. "I'd gladly return that bushy monstrosity to James if he'd wear it."

"I'm going to wear mine when I go out this afternoon." Mae's glee matched Coralie's revulsion. "Perhaps all of Chatham will soon be donning Mr. Franklin's hats."

In a quarter of an hour she ventured outside. A great many Continental soldiers remained in the village, some wearing wool overalls. A few gawked at her, one of them even asking where she'd gotten her unusual hat. The question sent her into the butcher shop with more eagerness than usual.

Bypassing the mostly empty window display, she called out a greeting upon entering. "Good morning, Mr. Vanderpoel."

"Is it, Miss Bohannon?" The Dutch butcher's florid face tempted her to flee outside again.

Villagers stood about, not bemoaning a lack of meat as much as sharing news. A few nodded and greeted her as she returned her attention to the man behind the counter.

"I suppose 'tis futile to ask for red meat," she began.

"Ja, all the beeves are provisioning fighting men."

She withheld a sigh. James and the officers needed meat—lots of it. She was especially determined to flesh out General Harlow's striking leanness.

"And I'll save you traipsing out to the mill, for there's little flour and salt to be had either since the army moved in." Mr. Vanderpoel continued whacking mutton with a cleaver. "Scarce as Spanish dollars and Dutch guilders."

Thanking him, she left the shop and pondered Chatham's noticeably bare shelves, its residents uneasy. Their own personal larder and root cellar contained enough pickles, preserves, potatoes, and apples to last till spring, or so she hoped. But meat was another matter entirely.

Once she was home, Mrs. Hurst promised to make another fish chowder. "Major James left this morn, saying he and the other officers would return to dine here this evening."

Mae suppressed her delight, knowing Coralie wouldn't be pleased and unsure how Mrs. Hurst felt about their extra guests, James aside.

As dusk fell, supper preparations were well underway, given they had cod. As she came downstairs, Mrs. Hurst met her, wonder on her face. "We've something out back, Miss Mae."

Together they retreated to the rear door overlooking the frozen kitchen garden to find a dressed deer hanging. Mae's surprise equaled that of Mrs. Hurst, who exclaimed, "I've not had venison in an age!"

Shivering, Mae shut the door. "Father always had a fondness for wild game."

"Who on earth could have brought it?" Mrs. Hurst asked, returning to the hearth in higher spirits.

Mae followed her into the kitchen, hearing a noise at the front door. Their supper guests already? James's familiar voice rang out. Was General Harlow with him? Never mind the amiable Captain Sperry. He wasn't quite so intriguing and couldn't be guilty of bringing them venison, she felt certain. She continued to the hall, where they were hanging hats and matchcoats on a pegged wall. The hired lad, Adam, had taken their horses to the stable.

"I'm guessing we have you, General Harlow, to thank for the back door gift," Mae said.

He turned toward her with a smile. "Only if you prefer venison."

"And if I don't?"

"I'll bring down an elk, then."

Mae grew tongue-tied, realizing they were the only two in the hall. Coralie and James had already passed into the parlor with Captain Sperry, who was running a hand over the veneered spinet after exclaiming his pleasure over the cello in the corner.

"Whose instrument?" he asked.

"My late mother's and now my sisters'," James replied. "The cello is my poor attempt to join them."

"Have you a violin?" Captain Sperry asked with a quick look at General Harlow as he entered the room. "One of us plays rather admirably. And he's been trying to teach me when we're not on the march."

Mae masked her surprise. A sharpshooting violinist? She went to a corner cupboard and withdrew a cracked leather case. Of all the things she missed about her parents, their music was foremost.

Turning back around, she handed it over to the general. "Our father's."

He opened the case with a thoughtfulness that touched her. "Maple and spruce. A fetching fiddle. Mine was lost at Quebec."

Lost? A story there, she thought, her curiosity at fever pitch. She watched him rosin the bow and tune the strings while James sat down with the cello and Coralie at the spinet. Not quite a quartet . . .

The general, still tuning, already had her on the edge of her seat. "My mother taught me when I was small. Her family had a long fiddling tradition in Wales."

Mae could no longer hide her surprise. A female fiddler?

He paused his tuning to look up at her. "Being a pastor's daughter, you don't associate the fiddle with drinking, dancing, and the devil?"

She smiled. "Heaven's music, rather, Father often said."

"Aye." He struck a string. "Music has gotten me past many a hard place."

His intriguing words gave her pause as he launched into a tune that began slowly but soon had her pinned to her chair, mouth half open. His fingers flew on the fingerboard, infusing emotion into every skillful stroke. Some of his notes resembled chirps—birdsong—so lifelike she almost looked out the window to the nearest tree. She wasn't the only one transfixed as he finished and his bow slid from the strings.

"See what we have to endure in camp some evenings?" James jested.

"Well, I've never . . ." Coralie said from her seat at the spinet as General Harlow returned the borrowed fiddle to its case. "I hardly feel capable of following such a musical feat."

"I shall limp along with you," James said, taking up his own bow.

In seconds the parlor was filled with the cello's rich resonance, a harmonious balance to the spinet's delicate notes. But Mae was wanting more of the violin—more of General Harlow himself. He sat near her on the sofa facing the hearth. Firelight flickered over his strong features, shadowing his whiskered jaw and dark brows, the slant of his nose and cheekbones. He was as rugged as he was handsome. His presence, like his violin playing, seemed to overflow the parlor.

Or had he made such a bold impression because masculine company was a rarity?

"I meant what I said about sewing for the army," she told him during a lull in the music. "Your men must have many material needs. I'm a lone woman, but I can make a small difference."

Finally he looked at her. "What have you in mind?"

"Shirts. Blankets. Hats and scarves and stockings. Whatever is needed most." If he'd asked for the moon she might have agreed to it, given her fledgling infatuation.

There, she'd admitted it. Though it was clearly one-sided, her attraction to him was undeniable. She prayed it wasn't apparent.

He mulled her offer for a moment. "Do you have friends willing to do the same?"

"Of course." Why had she not thought of that herself? Proof he could make an addled mess of a reasonably intelligent woman. "I'll send word round and gather a sewing circle. Plenty of Chatham women spin their own cloth or have the means to procure some. We'll do what we can."

She had General Harlow's undivided attention at last. Shame flushed her face. Why would she want it? He was as different from her as night and day. A Virginian and a soldier she'd never see again once the army moved on. And certainly nothing like the man her father hoped she'd wed. Mulling the matter, she fisted her hands in her lap, hardly hearing the music as Coralie and James finished the piece.

Mrs. Hurst appeared at the parlor doorway. "Supper shall be served at seven o'clock."

"We'll make a little more music till then," Coralie said, exchanging her spinet bench for a Windsor chair.

James took a seat beside Mae. "My sisters may well ruin me. I'm growing too used to the comforts of home."

"Nonsense." Mae smiled at him fondly. "You're in need of some spoiling, given you've been away from home so long."

She'd still not had time with James like she'd hoped, nor been able to ask him the questions she'd been saving since he left. Coralie was right. James seemed changed in ways she couldn't fathom. Hardship and death did that to a man. He'd no doubt fought in brutal, bloody battles that felled men he knew well. Yet for a short interlude, at least, he was well-fed and warm and removed from the turmoil.

"I, for one, have no complaint about billeting here," Captain Sperry said as he stood to one side of the crackling hearth.

Mae looked at James. "You've told us little about the hardships you've endured with the Continental Army, but I can tell they've taken a toll."

His narrow face darkened. "War is a brutal business, though we're led by the most fearless of men."

Coralie lifted a newspaper resting on a side table. "Is it true Mrs. Washington will join the general at headquarters in Morristown?"

Captain Sperry took the paper from her. "Probably not till March when the weather warms. Would you ladies care to attend a dance at Arnold Tavern on the Green?"

Lowering her eyes, Coralie didn't answer, her resistance plain.

Mae hadn't reckoned with a ball. Since the war's start, all merriment had seemed to stop. "I would," she said, "if only to meet your commander in chief. I've heard so much about him."

Coralie's gaze rose and fixed on their brother. "What is Washington like?"

"Tall." James seemed a bit flummoxed, as if Washington defied description. "Slightly scarred by smallpox. His hair is reddish-brown when unpowdered, and he rarely smiles on account of his terrible teeth."

"Poor man," Mae breathed.

"He doesn't play the peacock like some officers and has a general's bearing," Captain Sperry added. "Commanding. Stern. He's the most superb horseman I've ever seen."

"I've heard he dances upwards of three hours without sitting down." Mae had long heard accounts of his prowess in the ballroom. "He's even mastered the cotillion."

"Ah, the latest dancing craze." Captain Sperry chuckled. "You'll see it for yourself if you come to headquarters."

Mae smiled. "If invited, we could stay with our Morristown aunt."

"I'm sure the captain will keep you duly informed," James said. "He's as fond of dancing as Washington."

Mae stole a look at General Harlow. Did he not care to dance? He seemed to prefer to let the rest of them carry the conversation. Maddeningly so.

They went in to dinner before returning to the parlor, where Mrs. Hurst served dessert along with coffee and cocoa.

"Ah, the aroma," came a boisterous voice from the parlor doorway. "Are you drinking the last of my chocolate?" Aaron stood there, Hanna on his arm, the both of them smiling as if delighted to find it so.

"Guilty," Mae told them as they entered the parlor. Mrs. Hurst hurried away to bring more chocolate cups, and James more chairs. "My favorite apothecary and his wife highly recommend it."

"Cocoa aids digestion and is even thought to promote longevity, among other things," Aaron told them. "We certainly do a brisk business selling it at the shop, though it's hard to come by of late."

"Enough about chocolate," Hanna teased. "We nearly have enough numbers here for a dance."

"We were just discussing a future frolic hosted by General Washington and his officers," Mae told her, warming her hands around her chocolate cup. "I've never attended any function in Morristown."

"Arnold Tavern has a large ballroom on the second floor," James said. "Some would say this isn't the time for dancing, but I think otherwise."

Captain Sperry cleared his throat. "We've seen so much misery that any mirth is most welcome."

"Speaking of that, I need to confer with your commander." Aaron turned to General Harlow. "Washington said I should speak with your Rifle Corps soon since they're among the first to be quarantined in camp. I also have questions about the smallpox inoculation you had in Quebec."

"At your convenience."

"I have surgeries scheduled for tomorrow with the doctors, but after that . . ."

The general nodded. "I can ride out with you to camp day after tomorrow then."

five

Don't fire until you see the whites of their eyes!
William Prescott, Battle of Bunker Hill

The next morning dawned clement if bitterly cold. Wearing her beloved Franklin hat, Mae ignored her sister's chiding as she saddled Orion.

"What's come over you?" Arms akimbo, Coralie stood in the stable's open doorway. "Where's Adam? He always saddles Orion for you."

"He's away getting wood." Mae adjusted the girth, not wanting to make a mockery of her next words. "I'm perfectly capable of helping myself."

Coralie took a frosted breath. "Ever since James returned with our lodgers you seem a different person."

"I'm simply interested in the outside world and those who people it."

"*One* in particular," Coralie replied, her disapproval plain. "And something tells me your sudden urge to go riding is all about that."

Mae stepped onto a mounting block to lift herself to the saddle. "Please hold Orion's head still."

Coralie did as she bade, albeit reluctantly. Once seated, Mae put a foot on the stirrup and a knee over the pommel.

"Well, I must say you cut a fine figure in Mother's remade riding habit despite that ridiculous fur hat," Coralie said. "I don't need to remind you your jaunt will be cold and dangerously slippery. And you may well come down with a horrid cold like me." She shook her head in disgust. "I shan't rest till you return."

"I'm quite warm and I'll be careful," Mae told her in the tone of an older, wiser sister. "You mustn't fret. Life is beset with difficulties. Worrying only worsens them."

Mae pressed Orion's warm sides and left the stable. If she didn't hurry she'd lose sight of James and General Harlow altogether. She took a back lane and caught up with the men at the edge of the village before they disappeared into a wall of woods.

She knew the deer trail they took, worn down over countless years, by heart. Soon they traversed the foothills where snow clung to dense stands of evergreens and barren oaks and elms. January's end was always bleak, though today's cannonball clouds kept the temperatures from plummeting further.

James and the general rode ahead of her a quarter mile or so, unaware of her following, or so she thought. She slowed as Orion picked his way across a stream that burbled faintly beneath a skim of ice. For a moment she was so focused on the forest floor she failed to look ahead, until a voice cut through the cold and brought her chin up.

"Miss Bohannon."

Found out.

Astride his handsome horse, General Harlow faced her. "Do you often ride in the dead of winter in risky conditions?"

"I'm curious about the winter encampment," she confessed. "And 'tis safer to follow you and James than venture out by myself."

"Your brother has gone ahead to deliver a message to headquarters." He motioned her forward. "I'll show you where troops are cutting trees to build huts south of Morristown."

"Thank you." Relieved, she prodded Orion on.

He eyed her specially made saddle for riding aside. "You're an able horsewoman."

"I prefer astride, but that would be—"

"The scandal of Chatham."

"Not fitting for a pastor's daughter, nay." She flushed so hotly her ears warmed. "Father always kept horses, and we learned to ride young."

She kept pace with him, wondering his chestnut gelding's name. James had mentioned what an excellent horseman General Harlow was, and now she saw it firsthand. But in truth, he would make a weathered nag look good. She'd heard some horses were battle-trained by standing near cannon fire. Many officers had their mounts shot from under them. A travesty she tried not to dwell on.

"Can you outrun the enemy?" he asked, his breath pluming in the bitter air.

"British patrols, you mean?"

"I'm thinking more of thieves and vagabonds. Marauding murderous soldiers and citizens like the Pine Banditti of Monmouth County."

"An unlikely concern, given I have an officer escort." She darted another look at him. "Though I hope I'm not keeping you from your duties."

"Nay, but I'm about to go hunting as rations need rounding out."

"Well, your clothing shortage is soon to ebb, at least."

His attention was on her again, as intently as when they'd first broached the subject in the parlor. He clearly cared for his fellow soldiers and their well-being. Not all officers did.

"We're gathering to sew at my sister-in-law's this afternoon. Our only point of contention is what to call ourselves." She smiled, still mulling the fanciful names suggested. "Red, White, and Sew? Needle Rebels?"

He chuckled. "You'll be branded angels once you deliver any goods."

He led her to the top of a ridge overlooking Lowantica Valley, an exhilarating climb that left her slightly winded if only because of his company. She'd not been far from the village in so long it felt especially thrilling. Up so high, the whole world seemed to lie at their feet. To her astonishment the valley floor held hundreds of soldiers, perhaps a few thousand, moving about makeshift dwellings, both log huts and tents. Smoke from countless fires wafted upward, hazing the view and scattering ash.

Were her midnight visitors among them? She'd not stopped thinking about them, the young woman especially. Were they here?

"A beautiful valley like this seems made for an encampment, though our New Jersey winters are bitter," she said. She spied a parade ground for drilling and numerous sheds for horses that had hauled cannon. Even a commissary south of the huts and a makeshift hospital.

"A third here in the valley are ill or unfit for service but should be on their feet come spring," he told her. "We've commandeered your church in Chatham as well as Morristown for the worst of the suffering."

Her heart went out to them in such dire conditions, and she didn't miss the graveyard marked with crosses in the distance. If only she was an able nurse like Hanna. The least she could do was sew.

"I won't keep you any longer." Her gaze traveled from the encampment to his rifle secured in a leather holder. "My sister will be wondering about me too."

"Since you know the area well, where would you recommend I hunt?"

She gestured north. "Follow the Passaic as it bends and you'll find a big meadow where deer and elk flock."

"After I return you home, aye."

"No need." She fisted her riding whip. "'Tis broad daylight and I can fend for myself."

"Mayhap. But I don't want to take any chances and have to fend for my supper."

She laughed, reluctant to admit her kitchen skills were lacking. "Mrs. Hurst deserves any praise."

"So I heard." He smiled, that rare smile that eased the lines in his lean face and turned him more handsome—and she more smitten.

Mercy, what's befallen me?

She, the sensible older sister, who rarely let a man turn her head. She refused to look at him again as they turned back, just bade him a ladylike goodbye at the edge of Chatham while counting the hours till evening.

When he'd make another impression on her soft-as-wax heart.

★ ★ ★ ★ ★

"Mercy, Mae!" A relieved Hanna met her at the private entrance to her home behind the apothecary shop. "Coralie said you'd gone out, and I feared you'd miss our first gathering completely."

Clutching a stack of linen and her sewing kit, Mae joined a dozen women in the parlor already busily employed in shirt making while others knitted stockings and hats, even blankets.

"A robust beginning," Mae exclaimed, still exhilarated from her ride.

"I'm about to make some independence tea for our ladies." Hanna moved toward the kitchen. "And I baked your favorite jumbles too."

Widow Watt looked up from her knitting as Mae took an empty chair beside her longtime friend Samantha Heath. "Won't Coralie be joining us?"

Mae schooled her reaction. Coralie adamantly refused to sew for the Continental Army, but how could she communicate that? Rather, how long would she make excuses for her? Her sister seemed the only Loyalist left in Chatham. "My sister is overcoming a cold."

"Dreadful." The widow fixed her with an appraising eye. "You're looking quite robust yourself."

Robust? Were her cheeks still ruddy from her ride? Without a word, Mae dug in her sewing basket for needle and thread, continuing the shirt she'd begun. Outfitting men who sorely needed it filled her with renewed purpose. She'd even begun embroidering her initials in the hem of the garments she made. A small embellishment with much meaning, at least to her.

"Your cheeks *are* quite rosy," Samantha whispered. "Mightn't that have to do with the Continental company you're keeping?"

Mae's smile was sheepish. "I don't deny it." Word had quickly flown round the village about which officers were lodging where. Samantha and her pastor brother billeted soldiers too. "This morning I went to overlook the winter encampment. What a sight!"

"So much soldiery, many of them unwell." Samantha's knitting continued apace. "Half starved, even."

"Not only the men but a large following of women. James said many are wives who cook and launder for each mess of twelve soldiers."

"I can't imagine living in such dire conditions, though Chatham has become a military encampment all its own."

"I scarcely recognize our village," another woman murmured as she finished a pair of stockings. "Fifes and drums seem our continual music. Soldiers come and go, the alarm gun is continually firing, and the beacon light is burning atop Prospect Hill."

"I'm more afraid of smallpox than the British," said another.

Hanna soon returned and began serving tea. "As for the pox, my husband is helping inoculate the army, given General Washington's recent mandate."

"Unprecedented for a commander in chief to enforce such an order, is it not?" Widow Watt seemed to wear a perpetual frown, though she was a Patriot, at least.

"'Tis for our benefit as well as his troops," Hanna said quickly. "Winter camps are harsh places, and disease is sure to spread if not countered quickly."

A small hubbub ensued as each woman expressed her opinion about the matter.

"I never thought I'd be glad of smallpox scars, but I am." Samantha took out more yarn dyed a pleasing blue. "I'm quite concerned about you not having had the pox," she said to Mae.

"Both Coralie and I need to brave the inoculation." Mae continued stitching, a sleeve taking shape. "I recently read in the papers that Mrs. Washington was inoculated in Philadelphia not long ago. She weathered it well, and I hope and pray we do the same."

"The sooner the better." Samantha took a sip of tea, her knitting in her lap. She could fashion a scarf or sock faster than any other woman in the room.

Mae's thoughts veered another direction. Had General Harlow survived the pox? She'd not detected any scars. Yet another unknown that added to his intrigue.

"I miss seeing you at Sabbath service, Mae, given the church has become an army hospital."

"Father would have welcomed the chance to house sick and wounded soldiers in his tenure as pastor. That's akin to preaching a daily sermon right where you are." Mae studied her stitches in the window's light. "Providential too, being so near the apothecary."

"Once the weather warms, Sabbath services will be held on the village green," Samantha said. "Why don't you and Coralie join us for dinner in future? You always bring such cheer. The officers we're billeting are often away in Morristown. Besides"—she darted a glance at Mae—"Phineas has been asking about you."

Had he? She'd sensed Pastor Heath's interest, though he'd never stated his intentions. But he was a busy pastor, and never busier than now.

"Of course we'll come," Mae replied, trying to rein in her thoughts lest they gallop toward General Harlow again. "James and his fellow officers are headed to Morristown too. They have army chaplains they speak highly of."

"I sometimes think my brother might become one of them." She sighed and smiled all at once. "But perhaps he's most needed right here."

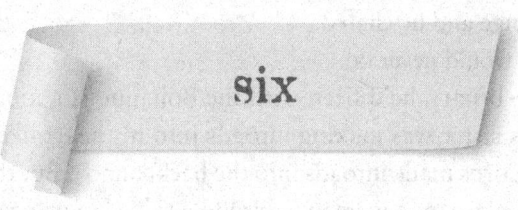

six

I luckily escap'd with't a wound, tho' I had four Bullets through my Coat, and two Horses shot under me.

George Washington, after the Battle of Monongahela

Rhys walked away from the Day's Bridge Tavern once he'd checked the post. Exhaling a frosty breath, he looked toward the frozen Passaic. Children and adults hugged the river's edges on both sides, undeterred by the cold, their happy chatter and laughter welcome after so many military matters.

"Afternoon, sir," an elderly gentleman said in passing, touching the brim of his hat.

Belatedly, Rhys raised a hand to his own hat in return. He'd never been so . . . distracted. Miss Mae Bohannon had a great many charms—and they'd never been so apparent as on ice.

Unaware of him, she cut a comely figure in her fluttering crimson cape as she circled midriver and made figure eights. Her mittened hands were outstretched as if to maintain her balance, and she wore the Franklin fur hat. He slowed to a complete stop along the ice-encrusted bank. Not too near as to draw attention to his gawking at her but near enough to admire her more closely. She was as adept a skater as she was a rider.

A young girl skated after her in mimicry. When she fell down, Mae hurried to her side and helped her stand again before flying away farther downriver. He'd never tried ice-skating, but she made him want to. A few other villagers had strapped blades to their boots, but none of them had her grace or speed. She skated out of rifle range and he chafed.

Which would never do.

Now February, he'd been with the Bohannons a month. His adjutant's sister was making inroads into his heart like he and his Rifle Corps made inroads into the backcountry. But there was simply no place for a woman in his life, wedded to war as he was. His head accepted the fact even as all the rest of him craved more. And it seemed she felt that same irresistible pull. He sensed it every time she looked at him or spoke to him. When she'd touched his arm he felt lightning-struck. She'd earned the distinction of being the first to have that sort of hold on him.

Did she not understand all that was at stake?

He was the worst sort of suitor. The British hated his kind. Feared them for fighting like Indians with an utter disregard for military conduct. As an officer, he was a sought-after target, not just a marksman but a marked man. A man who might well not return once the fighting was done. Some women, looking for a short-lived affair, wouldn't care.

But Maebel Bohannon wasn't that sort of woman.

He climbed the steps to the Bohannon home, and his knock brought Mrs. Hurst. She led him to the parlor, where a robust fire chased the chill from the room. Unlike some who billeted soldiers, she showed no displeasure at his presence.

"I'll bring you a toddy, General." She smiled, her spiderweb of wrinkles softening. "Surely that will warm you better than the hearth."

He thanked her heartily. Patriot to the bone, he'd wager.

Steaming toddy brought, she returned to the kitchen while he prowled the parlor, wondering when Mae would return. Coralie he rarely wondered about. She was mostly inward and absent. When he came round, she seemed inclined to go elsewhere.

He traded the window for a wall, drawn to a black-cut shadow portrait. Encased in an oval gilt frame, it bore a startling likeness to the woman who rarely left his head. He was still standing there when the front door opened and shut, Mae's voice carrying across the hall. Feeling he'd won some sort of victory, he waited for her to join him. Did his pleasure at seeing her show? He tamped it down as hard as the ball in his rifle's barrel when reloading.

Her lively eyes danced. "General Harlow, are you all alone?"

"Not anymore."

She smiled, removed her wraps, and hung them on a peg in the hall. The sharpness of wind and weather called out her lovely features, her cheeks apple red. He felt quite undone as she came nearer, only the two of them in the room.

She eyed his mug as she held her hands out to the fire. "I'm glad Mrs. Hurst gave you something warm to drink."

"You're more in need of it than I am, being on the ice."

Surprise shone in her eyes. "You saw me on the river."

"I did."

"Have you ever skated?"

"Virginia's waters rarely freeze."

"I sometimes forget where you're from. A brighter, milder place. I've heard the southern colonies are beautiful."

"The Shenandoah especially."

Mrs. Hurst appeared with another toddy. Taking hers with thanks, Mae seemed not to mind when the housekeeper closed the parlor door. To keep in the heat? These northerners constantly battled the cold.

He stood to one side of the hearth while his whole being urged him otherwise. *Flee, man.* But if he made no promises, formed no attachments, what would a little tarrying hurt?

She looked up at him, a question in her eyes. "I suppose I should ask you where James and the captain are."

"Your brother is in Morristown recording new regulations and general orders as Washington reorganizes the army." He glanced at the window. "Sperry is in Lowantica Valley overseeing the barracks building."

"Are you absent without leave, sir?" Her playful banter didn't help matters. Nor did her nearness, close enough for him to catch her herbal scent.

For a trice he forgot where he'd been. "I spent the forenoon at a tavern meeting and the church hospital, visiting my ailing riflemen."

"My heart goes out to your men. Being ill and far from home is hard enough. James said General Washington has been sick for a fortnight himself."

He took another drink of the spicy toddy. "He's recovering well."

"I'm relieved to hear it. What on earth would we do if he succumbed?" Her barely masked horror echoed his own.

All would be lost and we'd all be hung.

He settled on a less treasonous answer. "General Washington is remarkable for many reasons, one of them being he stays alive. More than a few horses have been shot out from under him, his uniform torn by bullets. In battle he's utterly fearless."

"A lion among men, James said."

"There's none like him."

"Is it true about the Indian prophecy?" She studied him for confirmation. "That a great chief foretold Washington has special protection and will live to lead a great nation?"

"So a sachem said along the Monongahela years back after Braddock's defeat."

She looked down pensively at her toddy. "I suppose should he fall, the next in rank would take his place. General Charles Lee?"

"Aye, Lee." He reined in his disgust. "Boiling Water, the Mohawk call him."

"On account of his temper, I suppose. Is it true he was recently captured by the British at Widow White's Tavern some twelve miles from here? If so, I can only hope they hold on to him."

He chuckled, but it was no laughing matter. Lee was another nettle in a whole field of them. Did Mae realize the continuation of the entire Continental Army was in question, weakened and poorly supplied as they were? He didn't let himself think too far into the future lest he lose heart altogether.

"I'm sorry if I'm carrying on about the very things you need to forget about, if only momentarily." She smoothed a wrinkle in her petticoat with a pale hand. "My brother Jon is particularly concerned we may come to harm in Chatham should the British strike here. He's not near enough to help us since he's serving in New York."

He nodded and set aside his empty mug. "Washington's made mention of his defense of the Hudson Valley. He distinguished himself at the battle of Long Island last August. As far as enemies here in Chatham, smallpox is more a threat than the British."

She looked so dismayed he was half sorry he'd said it. But her brother had told him she wasn't inoculated, and that concerned him more than redcoats. "I had the pox in Quebec while a prisoner there last year. A brutal experience. I'd spare you the same."

"Your marks are few." She looked at him searchingly, the toddy cupped in her hands. "I've almost convinced my sister to take the inoculation. Aaron won't rest till we do."

"Wise."

"Is it true Washington is recruiting women who've been inoculated as nurses to tend the sick in private homes and makeshift hospitals?"

"For eight dollars a month, aye." He added another log to the dwindling fire. "But sewing seems good enough."

"I would make a poor nurse, though I might visit the sick at the church."

"Your father was pastor there?"

"For almost thirty years. 'Tis odd to find the pews removed after a lifetime of sitting in them and hearing my father preach. A year ago he took a fever." Her face grew shadowed. "My mother nursed him, fell ill herself, and then they died within a day of each other. Coralie is still wearing mourning, but I felt the need for brighter colors."

He tried to picture her in black. A stark contrast given her flaxen hair and fair skin. Her unusual eyes could stop a man mid-sentence. He'd been trying to place their hue. All he came up with was wild chicory blue.

A sudden knock ended his musings. Coralie appeared after pushing the door open, a scolding in her expression. Sensing a confrontation brewing, Rhys excused himself and went upstairs to his bedchamber, certain that didn't please her either.

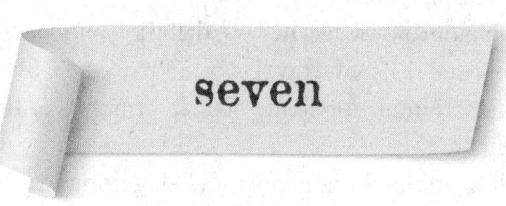

seven

In the name of the great Jehovah and the Continental Congress.

Attributed to Ethan Allen at Fort Ticonderoga

"I've a letter from Eben." Coralie's sternness faded as soon as General Harlow went upstairs. "A post rider finally arrived at the tavern. I could hardly wait for the general to leave to tell you. He seemed to hold you captive forever."

"Captive?" Mae laughed. She'd missed his company the moment he left the parlor. "I'm hardly a bird in a cage, Coralie. I just skated the river."

Coralie made a face and brought the letter from her pocket. "Eben is insisting I take the inoculation right away."

"As soon as possible, yes, though we've delayed so long Aaron has his hands full inoculating American troops."

Taking a seat beside Mae on the sofa, Coralie unfolded the paper, the red wax seal bright. "As for Eben, he's well and sends news from New York but doesn't say just where."

The ever-elusive Eben. He'd always had a furtive quality about him. There were many forts along those New York waterways, some British occupied and some American, all of them in dispute.

Jon was on the west bank of the Hudson River at a place called Highland Falls near Fort Montgomery.

"He writes that he desires to be led directly to action, in resentment of the atrocious insults to king and country."

Grandiloquent Eben. Mae held her tongue, though it was becoming increasingly difficult to do so.

"'Tis common knowledge, he says, that the Continental Army is near collapse and the conflict will soon be at an end." She scanned the letter, her triumph apparent. "Which brings us to the matter of our nuptials."

Mae felt a sinking in her spirit. "Is he getting leave to come here?"

Coralie looked up, holding Mae's gaze. "Promise me you won't breathe a word of our plans till the deed is done."

Plans? Eben didn't seem to have any. Patience wearing thin, Mae sent a silent prayer heavenward. "Will you elope and leave for your honeymoon in New York City without a word to anyone?"

"Why wouldn't I? I don't think anyone here would take kindly to Eben's return or our marriage."

"No matter what happens, we're still family. You still have friends here."

"Then why do I want to flee?" Coralie folded up the letter and stood. "Our village is nothing like it once was prior to the conflict. I fear Chatham will never be the same."

Nor will I, Mae thought. General Harlow had seen to that.

★ ★ ★ ★ ★

The new parsonage, home to the Heaths, sat beside the Presbyterian church. Samantha and Phineas welcomed Mae and Coralie the next Sabbath with cups of mulled cider that spiced the air and raised Mae's spirits. Soon the four of them were gathered round the table for a filling if simple meal.

"I've not seen you Bohannons in an age," Phineas told them as he carved roasted mutton at the head of the table. He was nearly as gaunt as General Harlow. "What with the church becoming a hospital, I've not stopped ministering all day and sometimes all night."

"How many men are in your care there?" Coralie asked.

"Two and forty at present, though the number varies daily. We've just buried two soldiers from the First Connecticut Brigade." His mournful look said much. "We need a larger building, given the number who've fallen ill and require surgery and a lengthy recovery." He looked toward Mae. "I don't suppose you want to join the village's nurses like Samantha instead of sewing?"

Coralie laughed outright. "My sister is much better at smiling coyly and handing out sweetmeats and kind words."

Mae winced. "Samantha is made of heartier stuff, I confess."

"We each have our talents and our shortfalls," he said amiably. "So tell me, how fares your brother James? I hear he's billeting at your house with two fellow officers."

Mae nodded and passed a bread basket. "They travel between Lowantica Valley and Morristown most of the time, though they do manage to join us for supper on occasion and stay the night."

Samantha managed a rueful smile. "I regret I've not seen James as much as I'd like, though he's oft in my thoughts and always in my prayers."

She looked so troubled that Mae wished she could offer some encouragement. Before James declared as a Patriot, he'd been a frequent visitor at the Heath residence. But time and distance seemed to have come between them and snuffed Mae's hope to have another sister-in-law.

"Your father's last wish was to see him again," Phineas said. "I regret James's service kept him from it."

Did James regret it too? Or did serving his country trump being by his dying parents' side?

Mae met his intent gaze somewhat uncomfortably. She read more into his words than what was said. Had her father voiced a hope that they'd marry? Phineas had attended him at the last. Though she and Phineas had no understanding betwixt them,

Samantha had hinted of his interest. Mae shied from the role of pastor's wife but hadn't naysayed the notion—until Rhys Harlow wiped him from her mind at first meeting.

"So many Chatham men have enlisted," Samantha said. "The village seemed to empty at the start of the war and now leaves me wondering who will make it back." She turned to Coralie. "What do you hear from your British officer?"

"Lieutenant Gibbs? We exchange letters on occasion." Coralie darted a glance at Mae as if to shush her from saying otherwise. "He may return here, though given his loyalties I fear he won't get a warm welcome."

"His parents moved to New York City at the outset of the rebellion to be with their Loyalist kin, if I remember right." Phineas frowned. "It might be wise if he steered clear of Chatham, given that last tarring and feathering incident."

"Please, say no more," Coralie murmured. "'Tis terribly upsetting."

Samantha eyed her sympathetically. "I remember your eldest brother is with the New York militia now."

"Colonel Jon Bohannon." Mae felt a particular pride in all he'd accomplished away from Jersey. "He's missed."

"He's been back to Chatham but twice," Coralie told them. "We've met his wife and oldest children but not the youngest."

"He's along the Great Warpath, if I recall." Phineas grimaced. "As it stands, I'd rather encounter smallpox than a Huron warrior. We're not just fighting the British but their Indian allies."

"The Americans have the Oneida on their side," Mae said quietly. "The Tuscarora too."

Had they read the newspaper accounts of the worst of the violence in New York? Settlements and towns set on fire, families burned out, many displaced or killed. Both sides were guilty of untold brutality and bloodshed.

"Heaven help us all." Samantha looked more distressed than Mae had ever seen her.

"I pray for peace." Phineas poured them all more cider. "I've heard firsthand that most of the Continental Army's enlistments have ended and many men have returned home, thus General Washington has no substantial fighting force despite his latest victories."

"What a waste war is." Coralie shook her head. "Imagine the men taken away from their families and their women and children left to fend for themselves. And now many of those fallen soldiers won't return home or see their loved ones again. I feel helpless in the face of it."

Mae had prayed for peace when the fighting raged in Princeton and Trenton, almost on their doorstep. And then came a January lull. "I admire General Washington calling for prayer and fasting so frequently."

Prayer, fasting, and spring would bring a great many changes. The army, if not disbanded, would move on and Lowantica Valley would return to fertile fields, Chatham and Morristown to soldierless hamlets. James would leave, as would Captain Sperry—and General Harlow.

That she wasn't ready to wrestle with. Not yet.

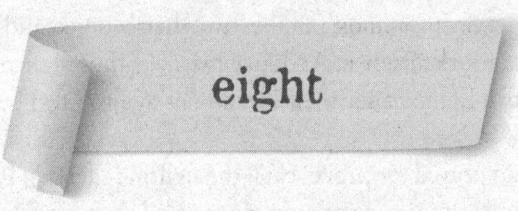

eight

Don't tread on me.

Gadsden Flag

Mae returned home with Coralie in a state of high if hidden anticipation. But by full dark neither James nor the officers appeared, turning her sister as relieved as Mae was disappointed.

"One never knows when they'll darken our door," Coralie said as they huddled by the hearth on the sofa. "How weary I am of the unpredictability of it all—and feeling my brothers are the enemy."

"Our brothers have admirable convictions." Mae's tone held a rare rebuke. "Hardly a summer soldier or sunshine patriot, shrinking from service to his country, but deserving of the love and thanks of man and woman."

"You quote the rebel Thomas Paine." Coralie pulled her shawl closer as the evening chill deepened. "How almighty and glorious he makes violence and bloodshed sound."

"Wars have been fought for less noble reasons."

"Noble? Then why are these Americans deemed traitors to the Crown? You well know they'll be hung along with General Washington himself once the army is disbanded."

"No matter the outcome, they're honorable men who've taken a stand against oppression and tyranny."

"Oppression and tyranny, my eye!" Coralie looked aghast. "'Tis bad enough you're sewing with the Liberty Ladies. Are you now a Patriot too?"

"I desire peace foremost." Mae felt it to her soul, but how did anyone stay objective or impartial? "Can you honestly say you're neutral, given you're affianced to a British officer? Doesn't his allegiance sway you?"

"I believe *he* is on the right side, the winning side. I feel a loyalty to king and country you obviously don't." Coralie stood, her skirts swirling as she turned rapidly aside. "I'm sick to death of this conflict and all the fury it incites. I can only pray all this madness and bloodshed soon come to an end."

She hurried upstairs, her irate words lingering. Dispirited, Mae pondered whether to read or sew or follow her sister to bed. The tall case clock in the hall struck ten, but the officers were still away. Numerous scenarios besieged her. Had General Washington received dire news? Had he made the decision to abandon the war? Or had someone betrayed him? Spies were everywhere, 'twas said . . .

Mae climbed the stairs to find the door between her and Coralie's bedchambers shut. Bending, Mae looked through the keyhole. Coralie sat at her candlelit desk, scratching out a letter. To Eben? Pouring out her turmoil?

Mae readied for bed with a heavy heart. Not even a shallow bath in the copper hip tub helped. Brushing and braiding her hair at her dressing table found her staring back at the frowning, shivering woman in the looking glass. Clad in her warmest nightgown, she closed the bed curtains, her feet seeking the heated brick wrapped in flannel at her feet. By morning the water in the ewer atop her washstand would be ice and she'd need her quilted petticoat lined with eiderdown.

"Sometimes only another warm body will do," Mama had often

said in winter. Growing up, Mae and Coralie had shared a bed from the first frost to spring's thaw.

Yawning, Mae hoped Mrs. Hurst would be snug in her two-room cottage. Her thoughts trailed to General Harlow, who seemed impervious to the cold. James slept with five blankets beneath the eave, but thus far she'd not heard his commander ask for more.

Pulling her nightcap more snugly about her head, she burrowed beneath the covers. Had Adam gotten enough wood for their guests should they reappear? She'd forgotten to check as she usually did, her earlier conversation with Coralie upsetting enough to thwart her usual nighttime routine.

The thought of the officers returning to frigid rooms brought her to her feet again. Was Coralie warm enough? She heard her sister's soft snores in her bedchamber.

She opened the adjoining door and tiptoed through Coralie's room, the letter her sister had been writing on the table. Curiosity got the better of her. She took the paper in hand and stood by the fire to confirm the recipient.

Dearest Eben,

We are now forced to billet my brother James and his commanding officer, General Rhys Harlow, and a Captain Casper Sperry beneath our very roof. No doubt you are well aware of Harlow's Rifle Corps, said to terrorize British officers foremost, unseating them from their saddles at long range with their rifles. Take heed. I abhor this savage conduct and am entirely with you in your loyalty to king and country.

I now consider Maebel an outright rebel, though she pleads peace and neutrality so prettily. Given these treasonous times I have decided to take action and tell you of all that conspires beneath our roof. It is the least I can do for this glorious cause of which you play such a noble part. I trust no one here in Chatham.

The sooner I'm removed from this volatile situation, the

better. I loathe being amongst those who are so blatantly disloyal and treasonous.

Stung, Mae returned the unfinished letter to the desk. Coralie's prose bordered on hysterical, sure to incite Eben—and all the rest of the family if read. Being cast in the role of enemy, not sister, cut especially deep. Since the war began Coralie seemed to have erected a wall, a breastwork of her own making, distancing herself from them all. Would their family recover from these divisions in time?

As quietly as she could, Mae laid another log on Coralie's fire before venturing to the room used by Captain Sperry. Adam hadn't shirked his duties. The hearth was brilliantly lit, seasoned oak and hickory burning brightly. She checked General Harlow's next— needlessly. His was crackling merrily too, a terrible waste of wood for unoccupied rooms.

She saw three books on his nightstand and remembered his penchant for reading. He was self-taught, James had said. What he lacked in formal education he made up for in life experience. She started for the books, wanting to know what filled his mind of late, but hearing a creak in the floorboards, she whirled around. The tall shadow in the open doorway shocked then sent a shiver through her. None other than General Harlow himself.

"You're stealthy as a fox," she told him, as rattled by his sudden appearing as her own racing heart.

He entered the room and walked to the hearth as the thought crossed her mind to excuse herself, but her fascination fixed her to the floor.

"You're to be thanked for tending my fire." He extended his hands to the heat as leaping light gilded him. "I'm tempted to bed down right here."

"You're used to sleeping on the ground, then."

"Mostly in the open, aye. Or atop a cot in a tent."

She couldn't imagine, not in Jersey. "The stories you could tell . . ."

"They'd fill more than one book, aye." He took the poker from her. "You need to be abed, Miss Bohannon. Your hospitality borders on frostbite."

Smiling, she simply pulled her quilted wrapping gown closer. "Are my brother and Captain Sperry here too?"

"Morristown."

She was growing used to his one-word answers. "You officers are in Morristown so much it's a wonder why you don't stay there."

"Chatham has its own charms."

She refused to think herself among them, yet heat warmed her neck and ears at his words. Surely he meant the ongoing competition between the two villages. Comely Chatham usually won, being on the river with the surrounding foothills.

On second thought, why was *he* here? Did the thought of a hot fire and feather bed lure him? Or was it something more? He was, she decided, a very practical man, so she shrugged aside the romantic for the mundane.

"The eggs and milk will be frozen by morning, so I can't promise you a decent breakfast, General Harlow."

"Breakfast is the farthest thing from my mind, Miss Bohannon."

Her breath suspended as he turned toward her. Though he hadn't touched her, his nearness wrapped round her, as warm as a coverlet. She didn't care a whit about her bare toes peeking out beneath the hem of her nightclothes or the disheveled state of her braid. His company was all that mattered.

The light called out all the fine lines in his striking face. She'd missed him in the short time he'd been away, forever wondering where and how he'd been. Since he'd first appeared at their door, the wind and weather didn't seem so bitter, the pinch of supplies less vexing. She seemed above so many earthly things when he came round . . . which wasn't often enough.

As she thought it, he pulled something from beneath his wool coat and held it out to her. The sight of the small heart-shaped pendant dangling on a pale blue ribbon sent her emotions swirling anew.

"Mother-of-pearl," he said when she took it. "I found it in the snow coming here in January. A pretty trinket."

"Pretty, yes." The firelight reflected pale pink and green hues.

"It belongs to someone like you." His voice struck a chord she'd not heard before. "Refined. Deserving of genteel things."

Heart overfull, she thanked him and studied it, the cold pearl becoming warm beneath her touch.

★ ★ ★ ★ ★

Rhys took Mae in, her presence filling him with a pleasure he hadn't reckoned possible, at least in wartime. He'd never expected to find her in his very chamber, tending his fire and turning his thoughts to his own future home and the woman who'd be waiting.

She made him forget, for a few moments, war and wounds and enlistment numbers and desertions. He was weary of the war. Weary, too, of fighting his feelings for her. Could she sense that? Standing alone with her made a man lose all reason. All his reserve and self-control were felled like a tree before her.

No woman had held any sway over him before. He was having a hard time pushing past his need of her, past the innocent seduction of her softness and scent, the silken strand of hair that fell against her left cheek with a maddening twirl, as curvaceous as all the rest of her.

I wish this was our home, our only world, and we didn't need to say good night.

There was nothing more he wanted than to speak those words, make her his, cradle her against him till dawn intruded. As it was, the clock belowstairs chimed the late hour and reminded him they both needed rest.

"Good night, Miss Bohannon."

"Good night, General Harlow."

nine

I am satisfied that one active campaign, . . . burning two or three of their towns, will set everything to rights.

John Pitcairn, British major

The dreaded hour had come. Mae approached the apothecary shop with lead in her steps, Coralie following. It didn't help that Aaron was to give the inoculation, though he would administer it with the same skill and wisdom with which he did everything else. None knew the ultimate outcome, and the risky procedure was still shunned by many.

Coralie had spent the morning crying and penning another letter. From the look on her wan face, she might have been finalizing her will instead. Mae prayed privately, asking the Lord to spare them both.

"I'm sorry we waited this long," Mae told her as they entered the apothecary through the side door. "We might have caught the pox by now with so many soldiers sick right here in Chatham."

"I pray we're not horribly ill from the inoculation alone."

Hanna greeted them, concern in her eyes as she helped prepare them. "Aaron will be with us shortly as he's seeing an infected patient ahead of your procedure. For now, remove your sleeve ruffles."

Doing so, Mae overheard Aaron return and tell his apprentice to man the shop while he tended to them. His steady smile was reassuring as he opened his surgery kit. "Well, sisters, are you ready?"

Coralie's distress mounted. "I prefer not to hear about it nor watch you whilst it's done."

"I shall go first." Mae watched unwillingly, trying to maintain her composure and not snatch her arm away when her skin was cut with a small razor blade and a smallpox pustule from the infected patient applied.

Aaron's calm competence made little of the matter. "As far as this variolation, I've now performed it on hundreds of soldiers and civilians, mayhap a few thousand. Hopefully your lesions will be few."

"Few?" Coralie turned her face away. "We might die."

"Your chances are better than if you contract the disease," he replied patiently.

Mae watched him dab the blood from her forearm and bind it with a linen strip. "Is it true variolation is outlawed in Virginia?"

"Aye, the irony. General Washington's very colony—state, rather. Yet he has saved the lives of thousands with so bold an inoculation order."

Mae vacated her chair for Coralie, who seemed more upset by the minute. "I fear I'll cast up accounts undergoing this. 'Tis *that* revolting."

Hanna brought a bucket just in case as Aaron took hold of Coralie's arm.

"Summon to mind a hymn or Scripture," he said without slowing his work. "Think on what is true, honorable, of good report, and so forth."

"How like Father you sound." Coralie sighed. "Perhaps you missed your true calling."

"Nay, preacher I am not. Nor soldier. I'm quite content as an apothecary treating any who come my way."

"Even rebel soldiers." Coralie's tone held a bitter taint that made

Mae squirm, but their brother seemed to take no notice—or no offense if he did.

Aaron closed his surgery kit. "You should expect to feel no different at first. A fortnight might bring a fever or rash. Hopefully any symptoms will be mild. I've already told Mrs. Hurst to send for me immediately if either of you worsen."

"Thank heavens Mrs. Hurst has survived the pox twice herself," Hanna said. "Though 'tis rare anyone suffers a second time."

"Washington calls smallpox more destructive than the sword. He's inoculating most of his men in secret. If word leaks to the British that most of his men are in quarantine and recovering, the British might well strike."

"Strike here in Chatham and Morristown?" Coralie looked at him. "Just like Jon warned might happen."

Mae's bare arms turned to gooseflesh as he continued.

"You'll both need to quarantine for three weeks. Of course the officers billeting with you have either had the disease or the inoculation, so they can come and go freely."

Mae moved to a window, her back to them all. Three weeks. She could make a great many garments and such as she'd already laid up supplies with that in mind.

"I pray there's no scarring." Coralie touched her cheek. "I wouldn't be able to face anyone if the pockmarks are as hideous as some I've seen. Heaven forbid I be blinded."

"Whatsoever things are true, honest, just . . ." Mae said over her shoulder, fingering the mother-of-pearl heart hidden in her pocket.

"All finished. I commend you both." Aaron began washing his hands in a basin. "Now go home. Have plenty of tea and molasses bread, read and rest, and think no more about what we've just done."

Bundled up again, they left the apothecary and made none of the usual stops to the booksellers or dressmaker or butcher. In early morn, few of Chatham's citizens were out, just an abundance of soldiers.

"I wonder why there are so many Continentals about." Coralie voiced Mae's concern aloud.

"Perhaps the lobsterbacks are near." She ignored the vexed look Coralie sent her. "Look, they've doubled the sentries on the bridge and atop the hill."

"So we're to be raided by the British or endure twenty-one days of isolation instead," Coralie grumbled. "I do wonder what's in store for us."

★ ★ ★ ★ ★

Mae settled in, finding life not much different after inoculation. Winters always kept them close to the hearth, and this was no different except they couldn't venture beyond the front or back door. Sewing and knitting became her mainstay. She fancied she was becoming better at it as the stacks of shirts and tangle of stockings grew.

Coralie returned to writing letters. Since Mae had snuck a look at her letter to Eben, she couldn't help but feel their sisterly relationship had severed. Forever changed. Coralie had vowed to report to him all that she observed. Her possible perfidy taunted Mae, and Eben Gibbs became the worst of blackguards in her mind. Would Coralie inform him of what General Washington hoped to keep secret—the weakened condition of Continental troops?

As she stitched till her fingers grew sore, Mae prayed and tried to ignore the thickening ill feeling betwixt them. It didn't help that there'd been no sign of James or the officers. What was happening in Lowantica Valley and Morristown? Teetering between suspicion, hurt, and fear made her especially low-spirited, but she forced herself to remain amiable.

Almost two weeks passed and they seemed to have weathered the inoculation well, and then . . .

"There's a faint mark on my chin. A pimple, I hope, nothing more." Coralie held a hand mirror, examining her face for any marks, then looked back at Mae. "You're rather flushed."

Mae continued to sew. "Only a headache."

"Let's have a last cup of hot chocolate since you favor that." Coralie set down the mirror. "We've just enough for another serving for us both. I overheard Aaron say that there'll likely be no more cocoa unless it's smuggled or the war ends."

Hot chocolate sounded nauseating, but Mae was too weary to naysay her sister. When she disappeared to the kitchen, Mae felt stark relief. She was weary of Coralie's company. Weary of her sore arm and this chair and her benumbed backside, all the while wondering about the general, whom she hadn't seen for days. So many days that it seemed callous—uncaring—if not outright rejection. Or was he simply so busy with military matters he hadn't time for anything else? Putting her sewing away, she shut her eyes to ease the strain.

Coralie brought a tray, not the usual tall porcelain chocolate pot but two cups. "Are you all right?"

"Well enough. I simply need to read or do something else."

She passed Mae a cup. "You're certainly not your usually cheery self."

"I'm a bit melancholy as I'm missing Mother and Father. Mother, especially, when I'm less than well."

"A headache, is it?"

Taking a sip of the unappetizing drink, Mae burned her tongue. The chocolate tasted especially bitter. Were they low on sugar? What she craved was cold well water—and a reprieve from Coralie's sudden scrutiny.

Coralie reached out and felt Mae's forehead with her palm. "Sister, you're on fire!"

Was she? Mae closed her eyes as if to stop the blinding pain at her brow. Coralie continued to talk, her voice indistinct. Mae fought a tide of nausea as the parlor walls closed in and grew shadowed. Panic scattered her thoughts as she lost her hold on the cup. It slipped from her hands and spattered her quilted petticoat before it rolled to the rug.

"Mae!"

Suddenly so ill she couldn't stay upright, Mae slumped sideways and slid from the sofa.

★ ★ ★ ★ ★

"Here's the latest tally, sir."

Rhys looked up from his makeshift desk by a window on Arnold Tavern's second floor as Bohannon handed him the muster rolls.

"They're the first taken since Fort Washington, sir."

"The debacle at Fort Washington," Rhys said beneath his breath. The battle that had ended their disastrous New York campaign. It seemed an eternity ago, not mere months.

"I've dated it today's date. Both units comprise no more than one hundred ten officers and enlisted men on active duty currently, taking into account the men lost last winter to desertion and death."

"How many to desertion?" he asked, though he well knew the number. Confirmation was what he sought.

"Four, sir."

"Death?"

"Thirteen succumbed, being gravely wounded or ill, sir. Their names are listed in separate columns."

"I tallied fifteen wounded or ill. You forgot Sullivan and Mc-Tavish."

"My apologies for the oversight, sir."

Rhys took the list, giving it a cursory glance. Some losses grieved him, but others, like deserters, he was glad to be rid of. "I don't see prisoners of war."

A sudden lull ensued, long enough that Rhys looked from the list to his adjutant. Bohannon didn't look forgetful or flummoxed. He looked distressed.

"My apologies, sir," he repeated.

"Hartman and Paine were taken at Fort Lee." Rhys inked a quill and added the missing men. "Kersey, Randolph, and Barker captive at Princeton."

71

"Aye, sir."

Rhys continued his scribbling. "Why do you seem unusually addled?"

Bohannon hesitated yet again. "My sister is ill, sir—and my mind is elsewhere."

Rhys stopped writing. "Which sister?"

"Maebel."

Lists and ledgers fled Rhys's head. "What's the matter?"

"Day before yesterday she literally fell to the floor. There's concern the inoculation may have been botched or she's caught the pox severely in spite of it."

Rhys stood, almost upsetting his desk. "Why didn't you tell me?"

Bohannon looked more distressed. "With all due respect, sir, why would I?"

Why, indeed. Rhys held back an oath and reached for his matchcoat as Bohannon switched from being upset to surprised.

"Where are you going, sir?"

"To see your sister."

Though the road was slick with mud and ice, Rhys had rarely ridden faster. Both he and Copper were winded by the time they arrived in Chatham. Bohannon followed at a distance as if still grappling with the day's disruption. Rhys wasted no time taking the lane behind the Bohannon house to where the stable stood. He rode Copper straight through the open door, then dismounted, his need to see Mae making his movements sharp with haste.

His knock on the back door summoned Mrs. Hurst, whose grieved look told him more than he wanted. "I've come to see Miss Bohannon who's ill."

"Yes, sir." She stepped aside, holding the door open. "Mr. Aaron will be here soon with more medicine."

Rhys brushed past her, passed from the kitchen into the entry hall, and rounded the newel post. On the stair landing stood Coralie, arms crossed. She still wore the black of mourning, jarring him further.

"Pardon, General Harlow, what are you doing?"

"I've come to see your sister."

"She's not fit to be seen."

He removed his cocked hat, her bristling resistance like a wall. "I'll make that determination."

He moved past her with haste. Mae's door was closed. He turned the knob and took a deep breath as he opened it, slowing himself lest he startle her.

Coralie hurried after him as if determined to keep him out. "How unseemly for an officer to force his way in here and demand to see—"

He shut Mae's door on her heated words when what he wanted was to lock it. Would she follow and make a scene?

Though it was midday, little light crept past the closed shutters. The four-poster bed seemed immense, the form beneath the linens too still. Mae was turned away from him. Somehow that reached inside and wrung him hard, as if her back to him was a personal slight.

"Mae." He spoke her name softly as he pulled up a chair by the edge of the bed.

Beyond the door he could hear heated voices. Coralie and Bohannon? His eyes roamed over the woman before him, tip to toe beneath the sheet. Her hair, that halo of yellow silk, was no longer worn up but bound in a braid. Her eyes were closed, her lips parted. His gaze hung on the lace trim of her nightgown. A thin blue ribbon hung about her neck, something tucked beneath the fabric. The mother-of-pearl heart?

That wrung him too. Did it mean that much to her, this lost, retrieved . . . nothing? He resisted the urge to tug on the ribbon to free it. Instead he took her limp hand as it lay palm up on the sheet.

"Mae." He brought her fingers to his lips and kissed them, eyes never leaving her face. It was the first time he'd used her forename, though he'd called her that in his head and heart from the moment they'd met. Throat tight, he repeated it. "*Mae.*"

She didn't stir, but he saw the reassuring rise and fall of her chest—still far too shallow for his liking.

The arguing in the hall grew more fraught. His gaze shot to the closed door, and he clenched his jaw lest he yell and silence them. When he turned back, Mae opened her eyes and he forgot to breathe.

"General . . . ?" Her voice was faint. Too faint. As if it took every bit of her to form just one word.

"Nay, Mae. *Rhys.*"

A slight smile. Her eyes closed again and he sensed her leaving, pulling away like an ebb tide. Out of reach, beyond his control.

"Stay with me, Mae." He kissed her fingers again when what he wanted was to kiss her parted lips.

She grew more still. Was she breathing? He fought down the fear she would die in his presence. He'd seen so much death. Too many good men cut down in battle or by disease, their lives shriveled and spent. The pox was just as merciless.

"Mae, I beg you—"

The door opened with a creak of hinges. Aaron stood there, his expression as concerned as Coralie's had been surly. Rhys stood and realized the arguing beyond the door had stopped.

"She opened her eyes briefly," he said hoarsely.

Aaron came nearer the bed, a leather bag in hand. "A favorable sign, perhaps."

"What more can be done?"

"I don't know, General Harlow." Aaron sighed. "I wish I did."

Rhys's attention returned to Mae, his pressing need to take in as much of her as he could. One never knew—

"Her fever has been quite high, though she's not as flushed as when I saw her earlier. She has no lesions yet, though they might appear at any time. It's been a fortnight since she took the inoculation."

Rhys let go of Mae's hand. "I'll leave you with her, then."

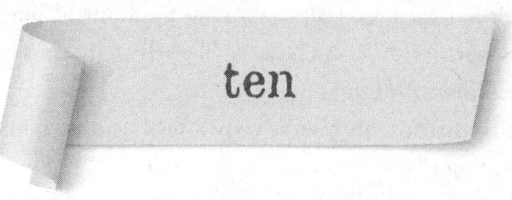

ten

*Yonder are the Hessians. They were bought for seven pounds and
tenpence a man. Are you worth more? Prove it. Tonight the American
flag floats from yonder hill or Molly Stark sleeps a widow!*

John Stark at the Battle of Bennington

Mae opened her eyes and remembered General Harlow sitting
beside her. *Rhys.* Now her bedchamber was empty. Doubly empty
since he had gone. Had she only dreamed it? The intensity in his
expression? The way he'd said her name and kissed her fingers?

Only a dream.

The chair where he'd sat seemed lonesome. A cup of water
rested on the table beside it. Her parched throat craved a long, cold
drink, but her arm was leaden. She could only stare at the cup as
she slid back into the uncomfortable cocoon of sleep.

Hanna's soothing voice intruded. "Mae?"

Her eyes came open again briefly, long enough to make out her
sister-in-law's anxious face.

"General Harlow is here. In fact, he stayed the night. He's working downstairs in the parlor right now. He said he won't leave till
you rouse yourself and convince him you're still among the living.

In fact, he's never left your side except when your fever climbed and we needed to undress you and pack you in snow."

Mae gave a slow, drowsy smile as Hanna continued talking. Her hand crept to the pearl heart. Had he noticed she wore it?

"James has brought him his traveling desk and papers. I've never seen a man so intent upon his work . . . or your recovery."

Mae felt her face, and all the joy leeched out of her. Beneath her fingers were hard, round bumps. Slightly itchy, they hurt when she touched them. "Hanna . . ."

"Don't be distraught. You've only a few lesions so far."

"And Coralie?"

"Coralie is fine. Well enough to protest General Harlow."

"What?"

"She's none too pleased to have him here, but he's put her in her place."

A twinge of alarm pierced her distress. Had Coralie gleaned anything more to pass on to Eben? If the general's lap desk and papers were near . . .

"You need to eat and drink." Ever the nurse, Hanna plumped the pillows. "Let me help you sit up first."

★ ★ ★ ★ ★

Her recovery was slow. But the fact they could be burying her instead checked her impatience. The graveyard behind the Presbyterian meetinghouse had never been busier. On the afternoon she finally roused herself, no one else was in the house save Mrs. Hurst, who had last checked on her half an hour ago and thought her sleeping.

Hanging her bare legs over the bed's edge, Mae tried to stand by holding on to a bedpost. The effort drenched her in a most unladylike sweat. The odor of illness still clung to both her and the bed linens. Though they'd been changed frequently, they still smelled of medicine and all the unsavory things she wanted to forget.

She spied a glass of water and downed it in a few gulps, though what she craved was herb tea. Her dressing table seemed a world away, its looking glass a hurdle she must reckon with. Lightheaded, she sank to the rug and hung her head till it cleared again, then crawled across the carpet.

Another burst of sweat, a blinding pain in her temples, and a weakness that turned her limbs to jelly resulted in a fierce struggle that finally landed her atop the dressing table's low seat. For a few moments she just sat, head in her hands, unable to peer in the looking glass. She could feel the hated lesions on her face.

Straightening, she took her hands away and forced herself to confront her fears. Her skin, once pale as milk, bore cranberry-red sores. She looked in horror at her arms, where especially vicious lesions welled. Grabbing at her linen shift, she raised it and saw other lesions marring her legs.

Never had she considered herself a vain woman—till now. Her disgust led to a shallow sob. She was too weak to push away from the dressing table. She could only hang her head again, tears making the sores sting like fire, reminding her of the time she'd fallen into a bees' nest as a child.

She reached up a welted hand and yanked at the ivory heart so hard she tore the silk ribbon. Free of her neck, it lay small in her palm. She opened the dressing table and shut up the trinket inside. She had no idea what Rhys had meant by the gift. He'd stumbled upon it, after all. It had cost him nothing. All she knew was what it had meant to her.

Slowly, she crawled back to the bed and lay face down atop the mattress, spent. She couldn't bear to be looked at by him. Her shame went soul deep. All her vanity rose up, and she sobbed like a child.

★ ★ ★ ★ ★

"Miss Maebel." A soft rap at her door signaled Mrs. Hurst. "General Harlow is here to see you."

Mae rolled over to face the door, glad she had locked it. "Send him away, please. I can't be seen."

At Mrs. Hurst's retreat, she realized she'd not locked the adjoining door to Coralie's room. Her sister rushed in, relief on her flawless face.

"I'm rejoicing you've come to your senses and refused him!" She dropped onto the mattress, taking Mae's hand. "He upset me greatly when he forced his way in when you were so ill. It proves how ungentlemanly he is, hardly a gallant officer, more bully—"

"Don't belittle him to me." Mae snatched her hand away. "Who else came round when I was ill?"

"Pastor Heath sent his regards."

"At least the general made an appearance. Ungentlemanly he is not, but brave. Bold, perhaps, as befits an officer."

Coralie stood, fury replacing her relief. "Then why did you send him packing?"

"Are you blind? What woman in her right mind would show herself in such a condition?"

Coralie began backing away. "Your body bears the brunt of the lesions, not your face."

"Easy for you to say, untouched as you are," Mae all but shouted. "I look nothing like before!"

Coralie went out and slammed the door, locking it behind her like Mae wished she had done.

★ ★ ★ ★ ★

Mae lost track of hours. Days. Finally she was well enough to travel. She perched precariously on the box seat of an overfull wagon as it rumbled up the rutted road to Lowantica Valley, the bed filled with blankets and garments, even bushels of wheat. James held the reins, Mae beside him, the team pulling them over the frozen ground. She gave thanks it wasn't mud. But it continued to be bitterly cold, their breath pluming along with the horses'.

"I feel like a fool allowing you to accompany me as you're still quite weak." James shook his head. "I'll likely get set down by Harlow himself."

"I'll do it or die. And I'll handle the general." She bit her lip, unsure of how she'd go about it. No matter how she looked, she needed to ask his forgiveness. "I owe him an apology."

"For refusing to see him? A first, I'm sure." He winked. "A great many more obliging ladies in Morristown and beyond thank you."

"James!" she blurted. "I hardly need the reminder that he's hand-some and unwed." Smallpox had sharpened her temper. Sometimes she sounded like Coralie. "I'm heartily sick of being indoors. As it is, I missed the sleighing you officers enjoyed with local ladies."

"General Harlow didn't go."

Oh? Relief lightened her mood only slightly. "'Tis nearly spring. It seems I've been ill half the winter."

"Well, I'm heartily glad of your company, for it means you're on the mend."

Near the foothills the wagon slowed, and then came the valley that resembled a village. Smoke from dozens of chimneys and campfires hazed the broad encampment. Surely General Washing-ton was more comfortable in Arnold Tavern on the Green.

"Three thousand souls right here," James said. "All those not billeting in Morristown and Chatham, anyway. I wish they had better conditions. But far superior to the HMS *Jersey*, where many of our captured Patriots lay destitute and dying."

"Off the shore of Long Island." She'd heard of the notorious prison ship. It kept her awake nights. "The Wallabout mud flats, specifically."

"Aye, the reeking mud flats in British-occupied New York. Six or more dead a day amid deplorable conditions. Their Scots Highland guards are said to be among the most savage."

Mae wanted to close her ears to the horrors that made her scar-ring seem so small. Sometimes her prayers seemed to no avail for these all-but-forgotten prisoners who'd sacrificed everything for liberty. For now, she returned to the misery of Lowantica Valley.

All looked bare bones. Frigid. She spied more than a few women among the melee.

"How are the camp followers faring?" she asked as James rolled to a stop and set the wagon brake.

"They're invaluable, in my opinion, though they're the bane of General Washington and a drain on the army's limited provisions. But what would we do without their service as laundresses, cooks, and nurses, helping with camp work?"

"Some are clad in rags." She blinked back tears, her emotional state as fragile as her physical. "We must sew for them too."

She looked down at her scarlet cape, her gloved hands fisted in her lap. A black lace veil fell from the hat she wore, obscuring her face. What would General Har—*Rhys's*—response be if he saw her unveiled? Revulsion? Even now her gaze scanned the far-flung camp for him, wanting a meeting, wanting to put whatever the moment held behind them and move on with a clear conscience if not an intact heart.

James helped her down as Captain Sperry appeared with a few men she guessed were among the Rifle Corps. At James's direction, they began unloading the wagon, all of them expressing sincere thanks.

"My Patriot sister and the Liberty Ladies do what they can in Chatham," James replied as Mae stood by.

But not Coralie.

Mae bit her lip at the flare of resentment over her sister's Loyalist stance—and then quickly forgot it when a flash of gold caught her eye. Mama's shawl? She knew it by heart, if not the russet braid snaking down the wearer's back. The woman's brilliant hair hadn't been so apparent that night in the smokehouse and kitchen.

Arms full of firewood, the woman looked back at Mae sharply, recognition dawning on her flushed, befreckled face. "Mercy, I almost didn't recognize you veiled. I never expected to see you here, Miss . . ."

"Maebel Bohannon."

A slight pause. "I'm Lucy Hawkes."

James looked at them bemusedly as he helped unload blankets. Did he not recognize their mother's favorite shawl?

Curiosity pushed Mae toward Lucy and out of hearing. "Are you the wife of a soldier?"

"Aye, the one you done met." Humor sparked in her amber eyes, her smile showing tea-stained teeth. "Most ladies would give me the back of their hand after that."

"If I was hungry," Mae said quietly, "I'd head for the first smokehouse too."

"Why are you hiding?" Lucy asked, concern etched across her features.

Mae hesitated, struck by her forthright question. Lucy was as quick as she was ragged. "I've been ill from smallpox . . . and am scarred." The honest admission brought no relief, only continued shame. Sometimes she wished she'd died instead. *That* was the extent of her vanity.

"Take care, Miss Bohannon," Lucy said with obvious sympathy as she started to walk away. "There are a great many ailing here the infirmary has no room for."

"I'm safe from the pox, thankfully." Mae followed Lucy and held her hem above the mud with one hand while she balanced her hat with the other in the cutting wind.

To her astonishment, ragged, dirty children ran in and out among the temporary shelters, as well as an assortment of dogs, large and small. A tent nearby was Lucy's abode, a growling mongrel at the entrance in need of a meaty bone.

"Petey won't hurt you none," his mistress said. "He's good company."

Mae reached out a gloved hand to the little dog as a sudden boom shook the camp and turned their eyes to a smoky ridge.

"Harlow's Riflemen," Lucy told her. "Target practice, likely."

Mae's heart quickened. Rhys was right there, surely. James was heading uphill, as drawn to the commotion as she was. Mae bid

Lucy goodbye and began the arduous climb, petticoats catching on brush and brambles as she wound her way over dead wood and uneven ground amid stands of trees, thick and thin.

Looking back as if he'd momentarily forgotten her, James hastened downhill and put a steadying hand on her elbow beneath her cape. "Prepare to be deafened."

"You said powder is low," she said, already breathless and weak-kneed from the exertion. "Isn't this a waste of ammunition?"

"Just one round each, to test supplies and keep the men sharp."

As they crested the hill the landscape flattened, revealing a firing line. Rhys stood amid men flanking him as he fired at a three-hundred-yard target. Smoke rolled around them as the rifle cracked. Dead center. Instead of applause there was complete silence as he took off as fleet-footed as a deer, the rifle clutched in his right hand.

"What on earth . . ." she wondered aloud as they watched him disappear.

"The general regularly runs the men through one-mile contests of speed as well as marksmanship, demonstrating how it's done. Reloading three times in under a minute is the goal."

Her brows rose. An astonishing feat. "What's the prize?"

"Extra rations and a second gill of rum."

Before she had time to catch her breath, Rhys reappeared through the trees and the next man in the corps took his place, sending Mae back down the hill. Resisting the urge to cover her ears, the smoke still stinging her senses, she flinched as more rifle fire burst from above. The immensity of war settled around her with an almost crushing weight.

Rhys had seen her. Looked straight at her, his cocked hat pulled low. But a private moment with him as she'd hoped was not to be had. She almost tripped in her haste, her veil billowing as she made for the wagon, hoping James was on her heels and they could depart. She drew up short and looked back, trying to catch her breath as she waited for him.

Over the rise came Rhys, not James. He overtook her before she could go another step. They faced off, his concern obvious. She put a hand atop her hat that the wind seemed determined to pick free, making her equally determined to stay veiled.

"I owe you an apology." She swallowed, feeling as fragile as when she'd dragged herself to her dressing table. "For refusing you when you last came to Chatham. I behaved abominably because I was ashamed to be seen."

"No apology needed."

"But—"

"I understand, Mae."

His use of her forename tore a rent in the wall she'd built between them. *Mae.* He said it so gruffly but with such feeling it turned her heart over.

"I-I couldn't be seen that day." Her voice warbled. She hated her weakness. "I still can't."

His reply was lost to her. The incessant firing on the hill continued and drowned out their voices. He reached out and took her hand. Her eyes went wide at the strength of his grip.

He led her inside a crude, unfinished cabin that was clearly his. Wind whistled through the cracks in a less than merry tune. The lap desk she remembered sat atop a rough-hewn table, papers scattered hither and yon. Inkpots and quills stood like sentinels alongside books piled high. How did he keep the ink from freezing? A fire burned in the rock hearth but held little warmth.

Her attention swiveled back to him. "This is your headquarters?"

"Such as it is, aye, when I'm not at Arnold Tavern." He regarded her as if he wanted to remove her hat.

She took a step back. "I'm . . . unsightly. I can't even bear to look at myself. That's why I came here today—to tell you I won't see you again after this."

"Mae." He took a step toward her, and she fought the urge to flee. The man she wanted to be beautiful for stared back at her, only she couldn't fully see him. Her tears and her veil saw to that.

She shook her head, her scant hold on her composure crumbling. "You don't understand."

"But I do. All of us have wounds. Some scarring you simply don't see."

He removed his coat. After draping it across the back of a chair, he unbuttoned the collar of his shirt. Her pulse picked up as he pulled the shirt over his head and the garment lifted to reveal his bare chest, as well-muscled as all the rest of him. And then he turned his back to her.

Her gasp was heard in the sudden lull of firing on the hill. Despite her veil she could see the savage welts that crisscrossed him from shoulders to waist. His back resembled a freshly plowed field, dark ridges and furrows of flesh in varying shades of reddish-brown, a strange sheen over all that told her they'd healed but still caused pain.

Forgetting herself, she stood behind him and lay a tentative hand on his bare skin. Tears coursed to her chin as she leaned in and pressed her lips to the worst of his scarring, the veil between them. Slowly he turned, taking her hands in his. She stayed still as he released her long enough to lift her veil, then encircled her with his embrace.

She met his eyes. "What happened to you?"

"I had some choice words for a British officer when a prisoner in Canada."

"You were whipped—brutally." She was crying openly now, her cheek against his smooth chest, which bore no resemblance to his torn back.

"It's over now." He stroked her hair. "It's over now for you too. Yours are simply beauty marks. I prayed God would spare you when I sat by your bed."

"I felt you, heard you. I was too weak to speak, but I knew the moment you left my side."

"I didn't want to leave. I would have stayed on if I could have. At the very least, I didn't return to camp till Aaron said you were no longer in danger." He looked toward a window as if he heard a passerby before letting go of her and pulling on his shirt.

When he'd buttoned the collar and shrugged on his coat, he gestured to the door, then followed her out. James waited a bit farther downhill by the wagon. Their disappearance inside what was little more than a shack might raise more than her brother's brows. But in light of what she'd just seen, she didn't care. All else paled.

"What brings you to camp, Major?" Rhys looked to James as if holding him responsible for taking Mae out when she was recovering.

"Delivery of goods, General." James turned deferential. "All have been distributed."

Rhys smiled his thanks at Mae, his eyes holding hers for a telling moment longer than necessary. She could hardly look away.

"I'll return my sister home, then ride to Morristown for this afternoon's meeting."

"Sperry will join you, then we'll meet up for supper in Chatham," Rhys replied.

Supper? Mae felt another qualm. "I must warn you both that Mrs. Hurst's rheumatism has her in bed, leaving the kitchen to myself and Coralie."

James chuckled. "In other words, perhaps we should tarry at Arnold Tavern."

Mae tried to make the best of it. "Supper will still be served, though I can't vouch for the quality. I might well be providing ground orange peel and calcium carbonate from the apothecary afterwards."

"I'll take my chances with any indigestion," Rhys said. "And hope Mrs. Hurst is on her feet again soon."

She took another look at him, feeling doubly undone. Their brief time together had left her as empty and grieved as she was elated, and all the more besotted. A thousand other things needed saying, but there seemed never enough time. Never enough words. Only insurmountable circumstances . . . and feelings.

Rhys handed her up into the wagon. On the seat lay a pale green pincushion. Made of embroidered silk damask, it was astonishing in design, with ombré ribbon, fly fringe, and lace. Mae's thoughts swerved to Lucy Hawkes before she slipped the pincushion into her pocket, eyes returning to Rhys.

The harsh winter light brought out a scar on his temple she'd not noticed before. She completely forgot the cold, lost in the sheen of his dark hair beneath his hat brim and the ruddy color in his cheeks as he said a few last words to James.

Look away, Mae, lest you lose your bearings all over again.

She and James rumbled off after a hasty goodbye, and she resisted the urge to look back. How long before the entire family knew of their regard for each other? And all the rest of the world besides?

eleven

If you were lost for America, there is nobody who could keep the army and the revolution [going] for six months.

Marquis de Lafayette to George Washington

Mae bent over the hearth, stirring a pot of venison stew with a long-handled spoon. Mrs. Hurst's apron was wrapped round her twice, reminding her she had no business being in the kitchen. Why hadn't Mother taught them to cook? Such a lack seemed a severe hindrance when the man she wanted most to impress was expected—and could likely cook better than she.

"I hear them in the hall," Coralie said, taking blackened bread out of the bake oven.

Mae looked on with dismay, singeing her petticoat's hem as she stepped too near the fire. "What a memorable meal this will be."

"The butter is no better," Coralie murmured. "It didn't set well once I churned it, though I put it outside to firm up."

Sighing, Mae poured applesauce into a dish. "Mrs. Hurst best recover soon or we'll all be thin as rail fencing."

"Surely this meal is better than camp rations."

"At least we have ample spirits in the cellar, though these particular officers don't seem overfond of drink, just victuals."

Coralie eyed her with concern, still shaken by Mae's falling so ill, or so she said. "I'm thankful you're up and about and don't seem so . . . shamefaced."

"Of my appearance?" Mae reached for more serving spoons. "I can do nothing about it."

And my scars are as nothing to his.

She reached for the tureen of stew while Coralie gathered up applesauce and bread. Together they served the three hungry men seated at table. Mae kept her eyes down as the dishes were passed. If only she was as competent a cook as he was a marksman. Rhys Harlow deserved a woman—a wife—who knew her way around the kitchen and larder.

"I apologize that we have no salt," Coralie said, seating herself. "Everything seems tasteless without it."

"Enjoy the peach preserves," Mae said, taking her usual place. "Mrs. Hurst's fruit is without fail, at least."

Rhys said grace, then met Mae's eyes across the table at their combined "amen." Still self-conscious, she resisted the urge to look to her lap, given she had no veil to hide behind. But his heartfelt words to her in Lowantica Valley stayed uppermost. The memory in the cabin—hours old—bolstered her even as the sight of his whipped back wrenched her. So private a moment, even intimate. And not long enough.

Tonight the men seemed especially subdued. *Lord, let it not be about the food.* James had mentioned a meeting in Morristown this afternoon. Had it gone awry?

When she could stand the silence no longer, Mae said, "I heard news in the village that General Washington's lady has arrived."

Coralie stared at her in disbelief. "Whyever would a woman of quality come so far in winter conditions?"

"She likely wants to make sure the general is recovering from his latest illness," Captain Sperry said. "For a time the entirety of the Continental forces seemed to hold its breath."

"There was even some discussion as to who would command

in his stead should the worst happen," James added. "It won't be General Lee, now a British prisoner."

"Oh?" Coralie asked, spoon suspended. "Who, then?"

Captain Sperry took another slice of bread. "General Henry Knox."

"The Boston bookseller?" she replied with a hint of disdain, spooning preserves.

"He's just returned to Massachusetts to raise an additional battalion of artillerymen. He's establishing an armory there."

Mae caught Rhys silencing Sperry with a glance. The captain returned to his meal and said nothing more. Why was her sister so garrulous? Because she was gathering information to pass to Eben Gibbs? The certainty set Mae asimmer.

"So the war shall continue?" Coralie said, looking around the table.

"I'd rather talk of Mrs. Washington and the coming ball." Mae smiled despite her ire. "I hope she's settling in well and raising spirits."

"The general's foremost," Rhys said, pouring himself cider.

"The ball is set for later this spring. Time is needed to prepare for such a function." James seemed well-versed on matters. "Tickets are three hundred dollars in Continental currency."

Coralie's gasp resounded to the room's corners. "For a poverty-stricken army? I've seen the rags recruits wear. They resemble beggars—"

"Only the officers and ladies will be in attendance, not the regulars," James told her. "And General Washington has good reason to host, much of it at his own personal expense."

Coralie shook her head in indignation as Mae said, "Gracious of him."

Captain Sperry winked as if suspecting Coralie would shun such a function. "Of course, you're both invited, as sisters of an officer, that is."

Coralie's frown deepened, but Mae took the notion to heart.

To attend a function with the general and his officers—a historic moment, truly. She stole a discreet look at Rhys. Would he go?

As the men discussed the weather and more banal matters, Mae backtracked to the kitchen to serve a rich custard made with molasses, eggs, and milk, the one dessert that never failed. She'd brewed a pot of coffee and poured that into treenware cups on a tray while her sister hovered.

"I'm weary tonight." Yawning, Coralie hung her apron from a peg. "I think I'll retire early."

Mae bit her tongue as she eyed the stack of unwashed dishes. "Good night, then."

The hall clock struck nine as Mae returned to the dining room to pour more coffee and remove the empty dessert dishes. Rhys had lit a pipe, the fragrant smoke reminding her of her father's favored Tidewater tobacco. The men continued talking in low voices that had turned quite serious in tone.

Wishing Rhys would take up her father's fiddle like he had at first, she took up her knitting by the parlor fire but soon found herself weary. She'd still not gotten her strength back. Aaron said it might be months till she felt herself again.

Going upstairs, she saw light under Coralie's door. Was she writing Eben again? She spoke her sister's name, to no answer. Opening the door, she found both bed and desk empty.

Where was she?

Flummoxed, Mae had almost forgotten the seldom-used stair accessed from Coralie's bedchamber. It led below to the hidden closet their grandparents had used when Chatham was still frontier and under attack. Had Coralie gone there?

Suspicions aroused, Mae tiptoed down the narrow steps. A single candle burned on the floor beside Coralie's stool. She sat with her back to Mae, head near the wall. The men's voices in the dining room were distinct—and they'd returned to discussing the war.

Mae froze, hardly breathing lest her sister suspect she was being watched. She turned slowly, her tread light upon the stair. Once in her own room she let out a pent-up breath, her stomach churning like the failed butter. Surely her sister didn't glean anything worth passing on to Eben and his superiors.

But if she did, wasn't it tantamount to . . . spying?

Did James realize everything he said was likely to be sent north to the British in New York? He and Captain Sperry, when they'd had more than a glass or two of spirits, could be too garrulous. Rhys, never. Often they were here without their commander, discussing matters. The hidden room was the perfect place to obtain information.

Returning downstairs, Mae heard the scrape of chairs against the plank floor as the men left the dining room. Had Coralie returned to her bedchamber?

Heartsick, Mae stood by the hearth where the coals glowered scarlet. She stirred the ashes, then added several pieces of seasoned hickory. The wood caught and sparked, mirroring the ire she felt over Coralie's perfidy. She gave the wood a vicious jab with the poker.

"Mae."

Rhys stood in the kitchen doorway, watching her. Returning the iron poker to its place, she faced him, sparks in her middle now.

"We need to talk." His voice was low but still heard above the men's footsteps as they went upstairs to their rooms.

Alone again. "Speak freely, then," she said quietly.

Would he ask her to marry him?

Her emotions seemed to run ahead of her, leaping over realities, bypassing flags of warning. Something about this moment seemed . . . awry.

He came to stand by her at the hearth, much like they'd done at Lowantica Valley. Only he didn't touch her. She felt the divide almost painfully. Her need of him made her ache. She clasped her hands together to keep from reaching for him.

"I don't know how to say what needs saying." His tone, usually tender when he was alone with her, held a determined edge.

91

She braced herself, sensing something hurtful ahead. He'd brightened her days so much since his coming. His steady, quiet presence. His fiddle music. His wisdom. The way he weighed his words before speaking. Even his wry teasing. She sensed him withdrawing now before he'd uttered a word.

"Mae, you know how I feel about you." He looked down at her, and she read deep concern and hurt in his own eyes. "Let there be no doubt."

She swallowed hard. "But . . ."

"I'm in the midst of a war without any certainty of the outcome. I have a British target on my back. To entangle you in all that is wrong, even foolish, and I'm not a foolish man."

Nay, he was far from foolish. He was levelheaded. Wise. But . . . "Not even a war should keep you from planning or hoping for the future, Rhys. Some would even say that hope keeps them going, keeps them sane."

"My concern is that it gives you false hope. I'm to march when it thaws. I have my orders . . ." He hesitated, frustration flaring in his eyes. "But all I can think about is you."

"Is that wrong?"

"It puts me and my men at a decided disadvantage."

She understood this too, and she hated that she'd become a distraction.

"After tonight I'm moving to Lowantica Valley, where I'll be till we break camp."

After tonight. She bit her lip. Already his absence loomed large. "Wouldn't continuing here in the comfort and care of a home benefit you for that next foray? Camp conditions are harsh—"

"Being here means being with you—raising your hopes and mine—and that I cannot conscience."

The pearl heart she'd taken from her dressing table and tucked inside her bodice seemed heavy. "You're sure?"

"Nay—and aye."

She sensed his dilemma and vowed not to make it harder for

him. She reached for the broken silk ribbon attached to the heart pendant and pulled it free of her bodice. Taking his hand, she placed it there and folded his fingers about it.

"Mae—" he protested.

"I don't need a reminder, especially if our tie is broken." Her voice held no rebuke, just a flat acceptance of what he'd obviously given considerable thought.

"You're not angry with me?"

"I'm angry with a king and parliament who can't make peace, who cause good men to suffer and die on both sides when far better things await."

She took a step back, turning away from him toward the warmth of the fire. He stayed where he was, all their feelings roiling in the silence between them.

"There's much that you don't know about me, Mae. You might not hold me in the same regard if you did."

His low words sent her thoughts spinning. She kept her eyes on the flames. "You have no sweetheart in Virginia?"

"None. The only woman I care about is right here."

"Then remember, should you stay alive, right here is where I'll be."

"Then take the gift back."

"Why?"

"Because you're meant to have it. Because it means something, even if I stumbled across it in the snow coming here."

They were dallying, if only to delay their inevitable parting. He knew it and she knew it, but time ticked on, the hall clock's shuddering toll detested. Her concern over Coralie only added to her angst. She was crying again despite biting her lip till it nearly bled.

Was this what heartbroken felt like?

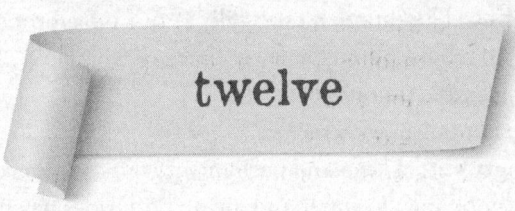

twelve

These are not troops. These are skeletons.

Baron Friedrich Wilhelm von Steuben,
on arriving at Valley Forge

Maebel Bohannon melted his iron resolve. He'd never been able to endure a woman's tears, especially given he was the cause of them. Reaching out, Rhys took her in his arms, and that inexplicable sense of homecoming swept through him again, that completeness he felt in her company. He'd steeled himself against this happening, but she was his weakness and he wanted to comfort her.

Kiss her.

Chin resting atop her head, he savored her warmth and softness and that indefinable herbal-honey scent that marked her. Her silent tears dampened his linen shirt as he held her and stroked her silky hair caught up in pins beneath her cap, its lace edge tickling his rough fingers. He'd wanted this from the moment he'd met her. The strength of that first impression at her front door still shook him. Somehow he'd lost his heart to her the moment he'd first seen and spoken to her. The suddenness of their mutual attraction astonished him still.

Was he a fool for turning away from her?

"Mae, forgive me . . . please."

"There's nothing to forgive. We're just two people caught up in circumstances beyond our control. Our feelings aren't wrong. The war is."

"I won't leave you heartbroken—or a widow."

"I'm already heartbroken, Rhys. And I'd marry you tonight if you'd agree. I'd even follow the army for you."

"Ladies don't follow armies."

"Martha Washington does."

He chuckled. "Don't say that in the general's hearing."

"I'm made of sterner stuff than you think."

"I agree, but it would be an everlasting punishment to see you suffer in the cold and damp, hungry, mayhap even afraid. And always in danger."

"Yet you do the same."

"I'm a soldier, not a civilian." He returned the pendant to her, tying the ribbon clumsily around her neck before leaving it dangling on her bodice. "You have my heart if not all the rest of me. Let that be enough."

Stepping back, he fisted his hands lest he reach for her again. Her chin came up, and they regarded each other in the firelight, waging a stoic battle of wills, unable to disguise or deny their bond.

"Good night," she finally whispered.

★ ★ ★ ★ ★

His return to camp was bleak, the hole inside him worsened by the fact Mae hadn't appeared at breakfast when he'd gathered his belongings and left. He didn't blame her. They'd said their goodbyes the night before in the firelit kitchen. For now, he needed to expend his remorse completing the Lowantica Valley hut that bore no resemblance to the Bohannons' house.

He took up an ax and finished splitting shingles for the crude gable roof before climbing up a makeshift ladder and hammering them on. Chinking the cracks in the logs came next once the roof was weathertight. Glad he was of the hefty supply of firewood beneath one eave. The fireplace wasn't sufficient to heat even so small a room, but it raised his men's morale that he was among them . . . even if it removed him from Mae.

The irony wasn't lost on him. He may have distanced himself, but she remained ever present. Winter gave way to a certain idleness that a march and a fight never did. As he wrestled with the winsome image of her in the firelit kitchen, a Scripture lanced his thoughts.

He that hath no rule over his own spirit is like a city that is broken down and without walls.

A northeasterly wind buffeted him, foretelling a change of weather. He continued working—trying to push Mae from his mind. A far less bloody battle but a battle nevertheless.

In midafternoon, Bohannon appeared, a hamper in arm. "You may have left Chatham, but it hasn't left you, General."

Rhys descended the ladder, belly rumbling, and invited him inside.

"Blast but 'tis frigid!" Setting the hamper on the crude table that also served as a desk, Bohannon took a look around. "Did you shove enough clay in those cracks, sir?"

"There's never enough of anything," Rhys said matter-of-factly, wondering what delights the hamper held. "Though I've a good supply of furs for my bedding. I've a mind to put that bearskin up on the wall."

Bohannon added another log to the fire. "You'd need wall-to-wall skins to help with that draft."

"In other words, only a bear wintering in his den would weather this well."

Bohannon nodded. "Your returning here is good for the men—provided you don't freeze to death."

With a rueful smile, Rhys opened the hamper. Mae's goodwill had obviously withstood his repulse. Bread. Butter. Preserves. Maple syrup. A rasher of bacon. Sausages. A knitted hat. Shirts and stockings neatly folded. Even a striped blanket. What hadn't she thought of?

Her brother's next bold words caught him off guard. "I had hoped to have you as more than a commanding officer, but I seem to have been mistaken."

A brother-in-law? Rhys stanched his surprise. "For now, aye."

"Mae said nothing, just to be clear. I surmised the rest. For now, I'll leave you to your hamper as I'm due home before dark."

"Thank her for me."

"Aye. I'll return for morning drill."

Bohannon left, leaving Rhys alone. Fresh memories of the Chatham parlor and dining room, the fine dishes and spirits, but most of all the companionship, turned the hollow space all the emptier.

Curse the war. Curse the winter.

Shoving comparisons aside, he put the empty hamper away.

While he was here in the foothills, would someone else take first place in Mae's affections? He'd heard something about the Presbyterian pastor setting his sights on her. She'd make a fine pastor's wife, serving in the meetinghouse that had been her father's. Having a family and continuing in the place she'd spent her entire life.

The possibility sat like gravel in his gut. Yet hadn't he forfeited that right, given he'd stepped back? No matter his feelings for her, the coming confrontation with the British scuttled the most pined-for plans.

If he lived through it, he would return to Virginia. His acreage waited. His new house had barely been finished before he'd been commissioned, and he prayed the British hadn't burned it down. His father and sister would welcome him home, a war veteran, and he'd return to his crops and fields and farm. Only that peaceful prospect didn't hold the appeal it once did.

Not without Mae.

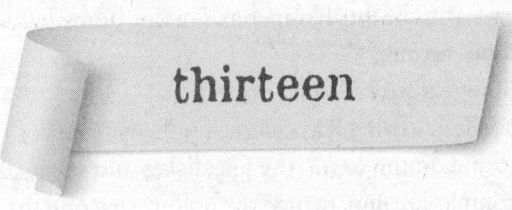

thirteen

*The men are literally naked, some of them of every color and make.
. . . Saw officers mounting guard in sort of a dressing gown made
of an old blanket or bed cover.*

Baron Friedrich Wilhelm von Steuben

The next week, Rhys's place at table yawned empty. Mae sat in her usual place across from his empty chair, recalling all the little things she missed about him. His thoughtful presence. The half smiles he sent her when no one else was watching. How his queued hair refused to be confined to a ribbon, coffee-colored strands falling free to his wide shoulders. His mesmerizing gray eyes, intent in his gaze.

"More peppermint tea?" Mrs. Hurst offered, coming from the kitchen with the pot.

Thankfully their housekeeper was back on her feet, bemoaning the ongoing lack of salt and disappointed General Harlow had returned to the winter encampment and wouldn't lodge with them again. Coralie looked rather smug, as if she'd overheard their kitchen conversation and knew he'd distanced himself. Might she have been spying on her and Rhys too?

Now, as they finished two o'clock dinner with just Coralie,

James, and Captain Sperry, Mae felt increasingly uneasy. Having had several glasses of wine, James and the captain were even more talkative than usual. And, as usual, Coralie excused herself under the pretense of writing another letter.

Mae's relief was tinged with alarm. Coralie's company was a continual thorn. Wondering if her sister would sneak down the stair to the secret room, Mae listened absently as the men discussed winter encampment woes, even the coming ball.

"You've been invited." James pulled a paper from his pocket.

Setting her coffee cup down, Mae took the invitation and read aloud.

Pleasure Ball
The Misses Bohannon are expected to attend the ball at Arnold Tavern on the Green on Friday, 28th of March current, at 7 o'clock PM.

She felt a bit awed at the fine script. The general and Mrs. Washington's names were penned beneath though likely signed by a secretary or aide-de-camp.

"Will you attend?" James asked as she pocketed the invitation.

"Should I? There seems to be so much . . . need. I'm afraid I would feel a bit hypocritical to make merry in the midst of it."

Captain Sperry winked. "The ball is part ruse, remember. Meant to outfox the British into thinking we're a more well-supplied enemy than we actually are. What better way to assert a show of strength than an expensive fete at winter's end?"

"Granted," James added, "more than a few officers might attend looking threadbare, but we shall have a grand time of it if only to flummox the British."

"We need ladies like you to raise the men's spirits," Captain Sperry said. "Make them forget the woes of war for a few hours."

There was only one man for whom she was interested in doing that. Would Rhys be there? As an officer, could he refuse? If he danced as well as he handled a rifle and played the violin, she'd be smitten all over again.

For now, Coralie was uppermost in her thoughts, likely hiding behind the wall and listening, casting a dark cloud over everything. Mae felt up for a little ruse of her own.

"Have you heard the news?" she asked conspiratorially, toying with her empty cup.

James and the captain looked at her.

"Of course, 'tis somewhat secretive thus far"—she raised her voice rather than lowering it—"but I have it on good authority that the French are to provide a great quantity of weapons, equipment, and uniforms to you Patriots. French arms and French gunpowder should put the British at a decided disadvantage. Spain and the Dutch aren't far behind to join the alliance."

A lengthy pause.

"Where are you getting your information?" James asked, his expression difficult to read.

"I have my sources." She smiled in a show of confidence. "Corresponding regularly with a former Chatham friend who lives near the Franklins in Philadelphia helps."

"The same Franklin who sailed to Europe recently for unknown reasons?" Captain Sperry said.

"The same." She all but glared at the wall and the secret room behind it.

Subterfuge did not come easily to her, but let that bit of news be passed on to the British. She *had* heard the French were anxious to deal a blow to their longtime enemies after suffering such a stinging defeat in the Seven Years' War.

She said with relish, "Britain shall soon find themselves the loser in a very costly international war."

James knelt by the fire to light his pipe. "We've been hearing of a great many Frenchmen enlisting of late."

She nodded. "The French rather fancy our republican notions of independence."

Captain Sperry blew out a breath. "All I've been hearing about are Britian's formidable Hessians and hired mercenaries."

"Who are deserting in spades?" Mae couldn't hide her triumph.

James nodded as he returned to his seat. "What a bundle of confliction a war is when men are hired to fight battles they didn't start. Not even their esteemed general, Friedrich Adolph, Baron Riedesel, can stop the tide of German desertions."

Captain Sperry looked to Mae. "Did you also hear that his baroness will soon join him?"

"Tell me more."

"Baroness Riedesel has decided to brave the Atlantic voyage and even bring their small children."

"As camp followers?" Suddenly Martha Washington's journey from Virginia seemed a small matter indeed.

"That remains to be seen, but if she does follow the British army it will be in a chariot with a retinue of servants in tow."

"Perhaps she's a spy." James looked disgruntled. "Why else would a noblewoman cross an ocean and risk her own life and that of her children?"

"To think a great many men and women are spying on both sides." Mae spoke slowly, recalling something she'd read in *The New York Journal*. "Is it true those Americans who unmask enemy spies are to be awarded large pensions, land, and medals?"

James stared at her through his haze of pipe smoke. "Sister, you've always had an active mind and appetite for news, but you seem to be particularly zealous regarding wartime matters."

"On a lighter note"—she smiled at him—"I want you to take Father's violin to General Harlow. None of us play it, and he can put it to good use in camp amongst his men. Nothing like music to lighten hearts."

"Generous of you. Is this a loan or a gift?"

"A gift, to remember us by once he leaves Jersey."

"Shouldn't you ask Coralie first?"

She lifted her shoulders slightly. "I'm invoking my right as the senior musician and sister."

Chuckling, Captain Sperry took out his pipe. "I sense a family feud."

"Nonsense," Mae said. "Betimes it's better to ask for forgiveness than permission."

"Violin aside, I doubt she'll be joining us at the ball," James mused.

A footfall drew their eyes to Coralie, who carried a tray with cups and a chocolate pot. "Aaron brought more cocoa by earlier, and I decided not to be a sleepyhead."

"We were just discussing"—Captain Sperry shot a look at Mae—"the coming ball."

"At Arnold Tavern?" Coralie sat down and began pouring the fragrant chocolate into cups. "I've decided to go."

What? Mae barely masked her dismay. "I thought it would be of no interest to you whatsoever, given your tie to Lieutenant Gibbs."

Coralie sent her a venomous look.

"Eben Gibbs?" James's attention swung to Coralie. "What means you?"

With a frown, Coralie passed Mae a brimming cup. "Oh, you know . . . he and I are longtime friends. We exchange letters on occasion."

James sat back, pipe in hand. "Where is he?"

"Somewhere in New York." She yawned as if the mention bored her. "I'd rather talk about the coming ball."

"I didn't think you were interested." James set down his smoking pipe to drink the chocolate. "I was going to ask Samantha Heath in your stead."

"I hope you do," Mae told him earnestly.

"Well, Mae and Samantha can't be having all the fun." With a little laugh, Coralie poured herself a cup. "Besides, Aunt Verity will feel snubbed by my absence if I don't accompany you to Morristown."

"Will you be wearing your new"—Mae almost said *wedding*—"gown?"

Coralie took a sip. "Tomorrow I'll visit Madame Jaquett to see if she's finished with the final alterations."

"I'll go with you," Mae told her with an enthusiasm she was far from feeling.

★ ★ ★ ★ ★

"Bienvenue, mademoiselles!" Madame Jaquett welcomed them effusively into her shop as the ball approached. "I have finished both gowns. All that remains is for you both to try them on a final time."

Mae donned hers, which was deemed a perfect fit. Next came Coralie. Standing before them in what was to be her wedding finery, she looked every inch a bride. Her trim waist and height accented the crimson silk damask with blond lace sleeve ruffles and fichu.

"Alors, the hem still needs to be altered a half inch." Madame Jaquett knelt, examining where it touched the floor. "If you can tarry I shall do it this very afternoon."

Sensing a long alteration, Mae excused herself. "I've a letter to post at the tavern."

"Wait," Coralie said, gesturing to the discarded dress she'd worn to the shop. "Please post my letter as well."

To the lieutenant? Taking the sealed paper from Coralie's dress pocket, Mae schooled her dismay and went on her way to Day's Bridge Tavern. Despite the deep gray of the day, signs of spring snuck past lingering patches of snow. Snowdrops bloomed in green and white profusion along the riverbank and at the base of bare trees. But her mind wasn't on them nor the tethered horses indicating the presence of soldiers. Chatham's largest tavern was truly a second Continental headquarters, as some said.

By the time she'd walked into the tavern's entryway and past the noisy taproom, she'd made up her mind. She retreated to the small, empty room to the right of the stairs, stood by the hearth's fire, and silenced her guilt as she broke Coralie's seal. Why were her hands shaking? Because she felt this a reverse betrayal?

The letter began with all the usual flowery lovers' talk, making her feel the worst sort of intruder. Coralie described what she had been doing, the lack of goods in Chatham, deaths and illnesses of those he knew, news from church. Nothing that would frame her sister as a spy.

Perhaps Coralie had had second thoughts and never mailed the one incriminating letter telling Eben she'd report everything she could to help the British cause. Had Mae been wrong to suspect her sister? Yet why was Coralie returning to the hidden room to overhear conversations?

The fire's logs settled, shifting the interior's light and shadows. Stepping nearer a lit candle on a table, Mae gasped as Coralie's writing between the lines of the letter became visible from the candle's heat. Not a cipher or secret code . . . a sympathetic stain?

Forgive me for being so foolish as to not write discreetly previously. I will now do as you advise with ink as I continue to glean information from J and CS at home. To our loss, RH has returned to Lowantica Valley. Though essential, he was never glib.

I plan on attending a ball in Morristown hosted by none other than George Washington himself to see what can be had there.

You said your superiors are most interested in knowing troop movements, supply routes, etc. Now with so many rebels in the village, I will make it my ambition to learn more.

I trust that what I provide is of use and can help, in even a small way, to bring a halt to these turncoats ruining our very lives.

Further shaken, Mae lay the letter on the table, wrestling with the contents while wanting to throw it into the fire. What would

Coralie's punishment be if she was caught? Nathan Hale flashed to mind. She wouldn't hang like Hale, surely. The schoolteacher-turned-spy's death haunted. Was it just last September the young Patriot had met his demise?

"Miss Bohannon."

The low voice turned her around. Rhys?

He stood in the doorway, concern on his face as she shoved down her hurt he'd not used her forename. His gaze lowered to the letter. Surely he sensed her disquiet. He was as shrewd as his rifle was unerring. The room grew unbearably still, the ticking of a corner clock overloud.

For once she wished he was garrulous.

She pocketed the letter, then held out her cold hands to the fire's warmth, missing her wool mittens. "I came here on an errand but didn't expect to see you."

"I'm here regularly for meetings and mail."

"How are you faring at Lowantica Valley?" She took him in from his wool coat to his boots. When he'd resided with them all the lean corners of him had begun to soften, but now he appeared whittled down again. The time they'd been apart seemed an eternity, not days. "Are you warm enough? Well-fed?"

"Nay to both." He looked to his boots with a wry half smile. "And the company is decidedly lacking."

She made no reply, riven with frustration. He could remedy the situation between them in an instant. But he wouldn't. Though she didn't know him as well as she wanted, she was certain he wasn't one to change course. He was honest. A man of integrity. One who would keep his word. And it only magnified her feelings for him.

They were staring at each other in a most unseemly manner. Openly. Lingeringly. Longingly. He was the first to look away.

"I should go." She raised her cape hood and he started to say something more, but then, as if he thought better of it, let it pass. "Good day, General Harlow. Till we meet again."

fourteen

With regard to military discipline, it was safe to say that no such thing existed. . . . There were no regular formations, the formation of each regiment was as varied as their mode of drill dictated and which consisted only of manual exercise.

Baron Friedrich Wilhelm von Steuben

The ballroom of Arnold Tavern faced a village green fronted by several tall, south-facing windows. General Washington occupied the second floor and often used the ballroom for meetings. Early each morning, the general issued orders of the day in which he communicated daily passwords for sentries, troop movements, changes in policies, and commands that were the lifeblood of the army.

Rhys studied the tall, well-honed man who stood at the room's center. His officers were ringed around him, listening as he spoke about the most pressing needs of the army at this juncture of the war. They were preparing for the next assault, spies watching the movements of British troops in the northeast and Canada and maintaining a close eye on what was happening in the southern campaign. For now, Washington was most concerned about the British occupation of New York City.

Today, his jaw slightly swollen, Washington seemed even less talkative than usual. A dentist had arrived, hoping to bring relief. Washington's frayed temper likely had more to do with his dental woes than the war. Imposing even when smiling, he wasn't smiling today.

"We have strong reason to believe the enemy is on the point of making some push. What their objective is remains a matter of uncertainty," the general said. "They have lately been considerably reinforced in Jersey, and from a variety of accounts are meditating some blow. I am firmly persuaded that they mean to attempt to reach Philadelphia again, as I do not know what other object they have ultimately in view."

The creak of a door halted his words as an aide-de-camp interrupted. "An express has just arrived, sir, with urgent dispatches from Congress."

With a nod, Washington adjourned the meeting. The dinner hour was upon them.

"Let's go below for a toddy," Bohannon said hoarsely to Rhys and Sperry. He cleared his throat. "I need something warm before I ride back to Chatham."

"You should never have left Chatham to begin with," Sperry said, looking askance at him. "You're ill."

"Well, it's not the pox," Bohannon replied. "Simply an ague of some sort, is all."

They sought an empty table in the congested taproom, pipe smoke swirling like spent gunpowder above their heads, the reek of ale and spirits foremost. Toddies ordered, they awaited their drinks, taking stock of who came and went. A great many couriers, express riders, and townspeople served Arnold Tavern's incessant needs with an army in residence, and they made sure the place was never idle.

Just now a colorful delegation appeared at the tavern's entrance, made up of Oneida warriors and chiefs. They looked much like Rhys's riflemen in dress, the exception being the Indians' feathered beaver hats. No better spies or scouts existed.

Sperry followed his intent gaze. "So General Washington is hosting the Oneida?"

Rhys nodded. "They've recommended rebuilding Fort Stanwix in a bid to block the British invasion routes from Canada through the Mohawk Valley."

"The New York frontier is a powder keg, in other words." Bohannon grimaced. "And I have a feeling we're headed straight for it once we march."

"I can't keep track of all the posts north of us as they change hands and names so often." Sperry began reciting them as if testing his memory. "Fort Ontario . . . Fort Niagara . . . Crown Point . . . Ticonderoga . . . Fort Anne . . . Fort Edward. And a number of lesser garrisons."

Bohannon rubbed his brow as if his aching head denied him his memory. "What did General Washington say about our numbers?"

Rhys looked away from the Oneida. "We're four thousand strong, a force unequal to a successful opposition."

Sperry frowned. "The enemy's number before this last reinforcement was estimated from seven to eight thousand."

Uppermost in Rhys's mind was what the general had told him privately.

"All our movements have been made with inferior numbers, and with a mixed, motley crew who were here today, gone tomorrow, without assigning a reason, or even apprising us of it. In a word, I do not think any officer since the creation ever had such a variety of difficulties and perplexities to encounter as I have. How shall we be able to rub along till the new army is raised I know not."

"Those of us who remain support the general fully." Bohannon paused as a tavern maid served them toddies. "But once we do break camp again that old fear for his safety will resurface."

"Aye, he takes little care for himself in any action. His personal bravery and leading by example make him fearless of danger." Sperry took a sip, the spices turning the stale air pungent. "What did the chaplain say of him last service? That 'we shall continue to storm heaven, which has been his shield, to continue to guard so valuable a life'?"

Rhys took comfort that heaven could be stormed when all else failed. "We are none of us in control of our lives or the outcome."

He pulled the printed sermon given to all Jersey soldiers from his pocket. Entitled "For the Love of Our Country" and written by an army chaplain, it raised Rhys's spirits when his doubts surfaced. He'd begun reciting parts of the sermon around the campfires at night to his men who couldn't read. Along with a little fiddle playing, it seemed to bolster spirits.

Mae's gift of her father's instrument still surprised him, and he vowed to return it when the army broke camp.

Passing the sermon to Sperry, he said, "This reminds us of our mission. I've pretty much memorized it."

"Obliged." Sperry perused it. "What lines mean the most?"

Rhys took a long drink and weighed the question. "'If the love of your country is indeed the governing principle of your soul, you will give up every inclination which is incompatible with it; nor will you cherish in your hearts any rivals of the favorite passion.'"

Yet another reason why pursuing Mae was so ill-timed.

Bohannon studied him over his tankard. "My sister asks about you."

Heat climbed up Rhys's neck. A timely remark, given he was thinking about her. But he was always thinking about her. "Is she well?"

Bohannon winked. "That would depend on you, sir."

Sperry regarded them with wry amusement as he summoned the barmaid for another toddy.

"I leave for the saltworks tomorrow, as you know." Rhys leaned back in his chair, wishing Mae was as near as the hovering tavern maid. "The salt meadows near Mount Pleasant, if she's wanting details."

Bohannon's chuckle turned into a cough. "Women always want details."

Rhys felt the toddy do its mellowing work, bracing him for the ride back to Lowantica Valley and another long, lonesome evening without her. "Tell her to pray we encounter no enemy scouts nor spies."

★ ★ ★ ★ ★

The moon was blessedly full, their party of two dozen riflemen loaded with salt. Even with the British blockade of imported salt and the redcoats destroying saltworks along the Jersey shore and elsewhere, salt must be had. The newly named states needed to find ways to manufacture it with armed guards or suffer dire consequences. At twenty-six dollars a bushel, few could afford it yet few could live without it. Procuring it had been worth the toil and danger.

Rhys left his party at Day's Bridge Tavern and turned toward Chatham, where candlelight flickered in myriad windows like fallen stars. The clear night was bone-chilling, and his stomach gnawed an empty complaint after a few bites of jerked meat. What he craved was Mae's company and something hot to eat, though he reckoned he'd have one and not the other. Tonight his aim was to leave a bushel of coarse salt at her back door and be away without alerting her. The moon foretold nine o'clock. She'd likely be abed already on so bitter a night.

He turned down a back street, his plodding horse in want of feed after so many miles. Weary and hungry as he was, he rued his decision to trade the Bohannons' for Lowantica Valley. The luxury of a bath and a feather tick taunted him.

He dismounted, untethered the salt sack with numb fingers, and slung it over his shoulder as he made his way to the back door. Light framed the kitchen window. Nearing the back steps he slipped on an icy patch, then righted himself by grabbing hold of a porch post. The slight commotion brought a figure to the window. Mae?

Before he took another, steadier step, the kitchen door swung wide. "General Harlow?"

"Aye." Could she tell how elated he was to see her? "With a gift."

"Please come in. My prayers for your safe return have been answered."

He passed her and set the sack on the worktable.

Her face radiated joy. "What have you brought?"

"Salt."

"Praise be." She felt the sack, her hands roaming over it like it was gold. "James said you've been gone for several days."

"Salt making is a tedious process, aye."

"Let me pay you." She started for the mantel, where she kept a stash of coins.

"All I want is something to eat and drink." A bald-faced lie. All he wanted was *her*.

Smiling, she pulled a chair closer to the hearth. "Mrs. Hurst has made a delicious fish chowder that's still warm. And there's bread, butter, and applesauce if you want to wash before you sit down."

A feast. He leaned his rifle into a corner and set his hat atop it before washing, watching as she stirred a kettle. She poured him some cider and then disappeared out the back door into the night. He wanted to follow but decided he'd only slow her. A nicker from his horse and the opening of a stable door told him she'd seen to Copper too.

In minutes she'd served him enough for three hungry riflemen, including a refilled salt box. He bent his head and said grace, savoring the abundance of the moment. When she sat near him on a stool, her arms about her petticoated knees, he nearly forgot to eat, she made such a comely silhouette in the firelight.

"I'd planned to leave the bushel by the back door," he said apologetically.

"I'm glad you didn't."

"I thought you'd be abed, the night's so cold."

"I'm a night owl, since you didn't know." She looked to the mantel clock as he ate. "Lately I've been sewing late by the kitchen hearth. It's warmer here than the parlor."

He saw a stack of garments piled high in a chair, their pale folds indicative of a great deal of dedicated stitchery. Soldiers' shirts? "I haven't thanked you proper for mine. Your name sewn in the hem makes it as meaningful as it is practical."

"Sometimes it's the simplest things that mean the most."

"Like this meal." He took a drink of cider. "I miss many things about lodging with you Bohannons."

"I feared you'd forget about us, being so busy with drills and meetings and such."

"There's no forgetting you." He held her gaze. "Let that be clear."

Again her face softened into a smile, one that seemed to light up a dark room. It took the resolve right out of him. He fought the urge to set down his spoon and take her in his arms. But he kept to his meal, savoring the fire's warmth and her gracious presence, a world away from the war.

Her voice held a sudden sadness. "I've heard the army is about to break camp."

"Don't think beyond this night," he told her. He'd trained himself to do the same. "This very moment is what matters."

"'Take therefore no thought for the morrow: for the morrow shall take thought for the things of itself. Sufficient unto the day is the evil thereof.'" She voiced the Scripture seamlessly.

"And right now there's no trouble, at least in this kitchen. You even kindly saw to my horse."

"Copper brought you back to me. 'Tis the least I can do." She got up and went to the hearth. "I don't suppose you'll stay the night."

"Nay. I drill early and the moon's full. Plenty of light to return by . . . even if I don't want to."

She took the hissing kettle off the fire. "James isn't here but in Morristown. Something about helping Tench Tilghman compose correspondence for Congress."

"Aye, Tilghman is General Washington's most valuable scribe.

There's a frightful amount of paperwork and reporting that's ongoing."

"I don't know where Captain Sperry is."

"Probably at Arnold Tavern too." He looked toward the closed kitchen door that led to the hall. "And your sister?"

Mae pointed upstairs. "Writing letters or abed."

The kitchen grew quiet. Too quiet. He finished his meal, wondering if she still had the pearl heart he'd given her.

"Have you any inkling of your orders?" she asked as she cleared away his dishes.

"The general is keeping a close eye on enemy troop movements and plans. Spies and couriers fly back and forth daily. Everything could change in a trice."

"You'll tell me—before you go?" She turned round, and he saw the blue ribbon about her throat, the heart hidden beneath her bodice.

"Aye." His own throat knotted. "I'll tell you. I promise."

"Will you humor me for a moment?" Taking up her scissors resting atop the stack of finished shirts, she added, "I need a lock of your hair."

"The pearl heart won't suffice?" he teased, though he felt anything but lighthearted.

"Nay. And given I'm armed with newly sharpened scissors, I doubt you'll deny me." She came behind him and tugged at the leather tie that held his queued hair so it spilled free about his shoulders.

"Don't scalp me," he murmured, steeling himself for other reasons.

Her fingers combed about his head in the most maddening way possible. Her gentle touch seemed to reach from his scalp to his booted feet. Wooing him. Beguiling him. He nearly stayed her hand. And then the expert snip of scissors ended his momentary torment.

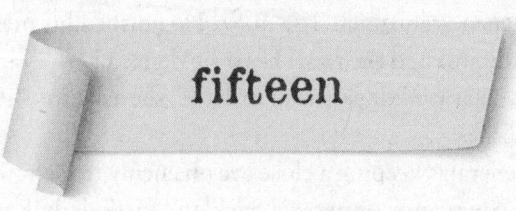

fifteen

I have not yet begun to fight.

John Paul Jones,
American naval captain

The quiet, firelit kitchen turned the moment more tender.

If he died in battle in some distant place, how would she find out? *Would* she? Or might it be her lot to forever wonder? All she had left of him was the lost token in the snow, worn day and night. She craved more of him, her unsettling need prompting her to cut a length of his hair. She held up the silken strand, admiring its gloss, wondering if he'd recently washed it. The question seemed too intimate to ask. A louse-ridden soldier he was not.

He held out a hand. She gave over the scissors and he stood, leaving her the chair he'd vacated. She held her breath, his lock of hair still in hand. More gently than his calloused hands warranted, he stood behind her and removed a pin from her hair. A coil fell free. He paused, then pulled at another pin and then another, tumbling half her hair down her back.

Somehow this seemed as romantic as a kiss. He drew closer as if breathing in her hair's scent, making her glad of yesterday's rosemary wash. With a decisive snip of the scissors he gained a long strand that lay like yellow ribbon across his palm. He looked . . . captivated.

"'Tis so fine it will fall to pieces unless I braid it for you." She took the strand from him, wove it together, and tied it off with a scrap of ribbon from her sewing kit.

He took it back and slipped it inside his coat, out of sight. But his eyes held hers as if by exchanging locks they'd exchanged some sort of vow. Hair might seem a small gesture to some, but she read meaning in his eyes, and in her heart she felt something significant had happened.

A foreshadowing of things to come, after he'd taken a step back?

He reached for his rifle. The long barrel looked menacing and shook her with all its grim implications.

He put on his cocked hat, his hair still hanging free. When she attempted to locate the leather tie, he smiled. "It's warmer left undone."

"Good night." Fisting his clipped hair in the folds of her petticoats, she watched him leave without fuss.

No tears. No more touching. No questions.

★ ★ ★ ★ ★

She put the pearl heart and his clipped hair beneath her pillow. It seemed to sweeten her sleep, which was long in coming. What would he do with her braid? Carry it with him? Into battle and beyond?

Lord, protect him. Let him not be hurt.

Her prayers seemed small, her hazy dreams beset with shadows and loss. The crow of a rooster awakened her along with Mrs. Hurst's movements in the kitchen below. She pushed back the warm nest of covers and dressed hurriedly, craving tea and toast.

"Morning, Miss Maebel," Mrs. Hurst greeted her as she made breakfast. "Where on earth did we get that bushel of salt?"

"From General Harlow. He brought it by last night."

"Thought so." The widow gave a rare smile. "We'll be careful and make it last as long as possible. I overheard Aaron say he's in need of some at the apothecary."

"We can share ours, then."

"Or maybe you can just smile at the general and get another bushel."

Mae laughed. "I'll have some salt on my eggs with some brown bread and molasses, if you please."

With a nod, Mrs. Hurst began heating a skillet while Mae made tea. When Coralie appeared, Mae pushed down the bruised feelings that lately always accompanied the sight of her.

Forcing a smile, Mae asked, "Care for herb tea or coffee?"

"Anything to warm me." Coralie approached the table as Mae took another cup from a cupboard, glad Mrs. Hurst had moved the salt to the larder so there would be no questions. Her sister, it seemed, had no liking for the general no matter his gifts.

Soon the two of them sat in the dining room, where a robust hearth's fire barely took the chill from the room. Toast and tea quickly grew cold as their talk turned to the coming ball.

"Though our gowns are ready, I lack suitable shoes." Yawning, Coralie buttered more toast. "A visit to the cobbler might help."

Would she not change her mind about going? Though she seemed a small threat, it was many like Coralie who could collectively spy and sabotage the American cause.

When Mae said nothing, Coralie prodded, "You're awfully quiet this morning. Are you feeling well?"

"I stayed up late sewing, is all."

"Mind your eyesight. Sewing by the fire is quite tedious."

Mae lapsed into silence again, though Coralie was clearly in a chatty mood.

"What are your plans for today? Staying home or sewing with the Liberty Ladies?"

"The latter." Mae took a sip of lukewarm tea, glad when Mrs. Hurst refilled the pot with hot water. "And you?"

"Hanna needs my help at the apothecary filling orders for villagers." Finished with breakfast, Coralie stood as the hall's case clock tolled eight. "I'd best be early. There's been so much business of late."

She went out, and Mae sat for several long minutes after her sister had left the house before going upstairs to her room. Finding Eben's letters was easy enough. Coralie had them tied neatly with the embroidered ribbon from Madame Jaquett in her desk. They were even arranged chronologically, the latest on top. Disregarding any guilt at trespassing, Mae pored over the letter and hung on one telling line.

Beloved, the war is all but won. The Continental Army, from every report, is a shambles.

Mae refolded the paper, slipped it inside the ribbon's confines, and returned it to the desk as anguish twisted inside her. Would her prayers come to naught? Rhys hadn't mentioned the state of the army's affairs last night. Because they'd been too busy being entranced yet distant with each other, a fact that hardly soothed her troubled heart.

She tried to lose herself in her tasks, finding some relief that afternoon amid the likeminded Liberty Ladies. She even accompanied Samantha on her rounds at the church hospital, though seeing the suffering firsthand rocked her hard-won composure. Together they dispensed handkerchiefs and tobacco among the ailing yet grateful men. The pox had taken a frightful toll, blinding some and disfiguring others, while the inoculation had saved many a great deal of misery. Mae gave thanks her own vision was spared. She'd made peace with her scarring.

They tarried in the church vestibule and studied a posted list of needs.

Wanted for the sick at Chatham. Sugar one barrel. Tea six

117

pounds. Chocolate twelve pounds. Wine fifteen gallons. Butter one firkin. Hogs lard. Port, if to be had, if not, Madeira.

Samantha sighed. "I'm beginning to forget what life was like before 1776."

"I'll be glad when the church becomes fit for a sermon again," Pastor Heath—Phineas—said. Having returned from a burial, he removed his hat at the entrance. "Now that spring is almost here, the worst of winter is behind us."

"The days are getting longer, thankfully. More daylight is welcome." Samantha turned to Mae. "How is that brother of yours?"

James. Should she mention the Morristown ball? "He's so occupied I rarely see him."

Nor I, Samantha's doleful expression implied.

"Thank you both for your time here today," her brother said. "Your presence helps immensely."

"I still need to speak with the nurses," Samantha told him. She gave Mae a hasty peck on the cheek before excusing herself.

Phineas looked to Mae, who shivered despite her heavy wraps. "Let me walk you home since it's almost dusk."

Mae thanked him, sensing that something other than her safety prompted him. They trod the slippery church steps that fronted the village green, his steadying hand on her elbow. The sunset behind Chatham's liberty pole glowered a vivid British red. Soldiers milled about the bridge and Day's Bridge Tavern along with townspeople bent on the warmth of their homes.

"So have you quite recovered from your illness?" Phineas asked.

"I'm still rather weak but much better, thank you."

"Odd how the variolation affects us individually. I scarcely felt it."

"Glad I am of that. You're too needed to be off your feet," she told him. "You'd make a fine army chaplain."

"I'm not soldierly material, I'm afraid. Hardy in soul, perhaps, but not body. I couldn't withstand the rigors of a campaign." He grimaced. "And the war, I believe, is almost done."

Again, panic pinched her. The newspapers were declaring the same. She opened her mouth to question him when he said, "I hesitate to broach a delicate subject, but you know how congregants talk . . ."

"Oh, I do indeed, being a pastor's daughter."

He kept his eyes on the path they walked. "I need to let you know you're being watched."

"Go on," she said, tamping down her impatience. Phineas never seemed to come directly to the point. It hadn't used to bother her. Had Rhys's candor influenced her?

"Two members said they saw a man leaving your house late last night."

So she was being spied upon? "We do billet soldiers, as do you."

"Indeed. But of late there have been none at your house, the concerned party said."

"A soldier brought us salt. At twenty-six dollars a bushel I wasn't about to deny him."

"Generous of him. Is that all?"

She looked at him in dismay. "What do you mean?"

"He is said to have tarried awhile before leaving."

"Well, he's a Continental officer, not a British one, if that helps," Mae said with more patience than she was feeling. "I fed him supper as he was cold and hungry. Would these gossips not do the same?"

His smile was wry. "Perhaps not. This teller of tales is not known for being hospitable but *is* concerned for your reputation as their former pastor's daughter."

"Nothing untoward has taken place, nor will it."

"I believe you, Miss Bohannon. I'm merely cautioning you about the eyes and ears of the community, which are especially watchful and wary given it's wartime."

Truly, everyone in Chatham seemed to be on the highest alert, when once it had simply been a sleepy hamlet of homes, sawmills, gristmills, a market, outlying farms, and little else.

Her attention fixed on the river. "Why are so many sentries at Chatham Bridge?" she asked.

"A British general sent word to Washington that he'll be dining with him in Morristown by tomorrow night, only to be told by Washington he'll be in Hades after."

"Oh my." She took her eyes off the sentries as they reached her residence.

"A bluff by the British, I sense." He looked west where the forest stretched black and thick. "These mountains surrounding Washington and his army are hard to breach."

Mae put a mittened hand to the door handle and didn't let her bruised feelings stop her from being gracious. "Thank you for escorting me—and reminding me Chatham has eyes and ears, wartime or not."

She slipped inside, shut the front door soundly, and bolted it with such force that it brought Coralie from the parlor. Her sister's relief was palpable.

"Thank heavens you're back safely! There's been an uncommon number of soldiers moving about today. Aaron saw me home from the apothecary. He and Hanna want to have supper with us tonight. I may tell them about Eben—but only if James isn't present. He's never cared for Eben, though Aaron seems more understanding."

Removing her wraps, Mae sought the parlor's hearth. "What about Lieutenant Gibbs, exactly?"

"He's unwilling to return to Chatham as we'd planned. He blames the village's Patriot leanings and feels he might be endangered. I might journey to New York instead, where we'll wed."

Mae listened, feeling a little tug that Rhys didn't care for her enough to make such a bold commitment. "Then that is where you should be. With your beloved."

"I can tell from your expression you think it a horrid idea."

Mae sighed. "'Tis a dangerous time to travel anywhere, is it not?"

Coralie's jaw firmed. "'Tis daunting, yes, but worth the effort. As you know, Eben believes there will be no more war, that the Continental forces are too weak and enfeebled to continue fighting. He's certain his land grant will enable us to settle somewhere in New York very soon."

"He told you this in his latest letter?" Mae asked, thinking of Coralie's fury if she knew Mae had read it.

Coralie nodded. "'Tis our new plan."

Horrid, indeed. Mae sat upon the sofa, her sewing basket near, and tried to think of better things. If the weather stayed clement, she'd take the wagon to Lowantica Valley and deliver another load with James once he returned home. Their shared trips had become treasured and made her feel useful.

Thoughts adrift, she hardly heard Coralie talk about a cousin's coming wedding in Perth Amboy. Instead her kitchen meeting with Rhys came to mind with sweet clarity despite Phineas's secondhand scolding. She kept the beloved memory close. It helped offset the shattering moment in the Lowantica Valley cabin when she'd seen his mutilated back.

Bittersweet—that was what their relationship was.

A path of peaks and valleys.

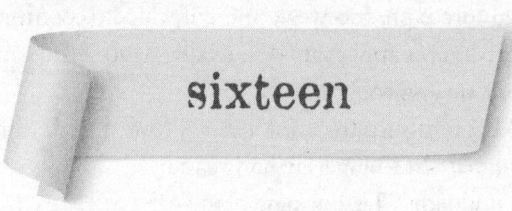

sixteen

I was a shoemaker and got my living by labor. When this rebellion came on, I saw some of my neighbors got into Commission; they were no better than myself. I was very ambitious. And did not like to see these men above me. These, sir, are my only motives of entering into the service; as to the dispute between Great Britain and the Colonies, I know nothing of it.

Lieutenant William Scott of the Continental Army

Supper was enlivened by Hanna and Aaron. As plates were scraped clean and dishes emptied, Mae sensed her brother and his wife had something to share. So far, Coralie had been less than forthcoming about her plans. Had she changed her mind about telling them?

"We've glad news and thought we'd tell the two aunts first," Aaron said, smiling at Hanna. "Come harvesttime we shall have the first arrow in our quiver, as Scripture says."

Mae felt her anxious mood give way. "Truly?" To be an aunt. To have a little one about. Her own womanly instincts surged like the Passaic in spring. "I'm overjoyed for you both—for our family." She looked at Hanna. "How are you feeling?"

"Topsy-turvy." Still, Hanna's reassuring smile said all was well. "Aaron often insists I rest when needed, or even be abed when I'm at my worst."

"We must celebrate," Coralie said, raising her glass of cider. "Mrs. Hurst has made a splendid pudding."

As their housekeeper brought in dessert, Mae heard the front door open and shut. James? She'd discarded any hope Rhys would be with him. As expected, Captain Sperry accompanied him instead. With wind-chapped, reddened faces, the men joined them at the table, offering congratulations at the happy news.

"You've come from Morristown?" Aaron asked.

"Aye." James sat down in his usual place. "Tomorrow is the Sabbath, so we've no drill or other duties."

Watching them, Mae sensed something amiss, though neither officer said another word. The men devoted their attention to their supper plates as talk turned to other matters.

"Pastor Heath is holding an outdoor service if the weather doesn't worsen," Aaron told them. "I hope you both can join us."

"General Washington himself might attend," Captain Sperry said between bites.

A hush fell over the dining room.

Mae grew more uneasy, wearying of the ongoing suspense.

"He's greatly indebted to Chatham and the benevolence shown to his men while here," James said as he poured more cider. "I sense he wants to express his thanks in person."

Was the army preparing to march? Mae pushed down her melancholy. "Speaking of benevolence, we've another wagonload of goods to be delivered when there's time."

"Monday morning, then, if the weather holds," James replied.

"We've been supplying a number of rheumatism remedies, which usually indicates a turn in the weather." Aaron's words weren't entirely in jest. Old, aching bones often foretold conditions when nothing else did.

"Just when we began to hope for spring." Hanna put a hand to her waist and made a face. "I'm afraid the babe is protesting my supper."

"Perhaps you should lie down," Aaron said in concern.

"I'll brew some mint tea," Mae offered, disappearing to the kitchen while Hanna and Aaron continued to the parlor.

As she steeped the fragrant tea, Mae counted the days till the ball—unless the Continental Army began to move again. Already she missed Rhys. How would it be once a greater distance separated them—perhaps once and for all?

★ ★ ★ ★ ★

By morning, Sabbath service was the furthest thing from their minds. A northeaster had swept in during the night, leaving an ice-edged blanket of snow, immobilizing all of Chatham and beyond, and surely sending spring back to wherever it came from. Leaning into the windowsill of her bedchamber, her warm breath fogging the icy pane, Mae wondered just how cold Lowantica Valley was.

As she dressed in the frigid dawn, she counted her immediate blessings. Quilted petticoats. Salt. Freshly milled flour. Firewood. From the kitchen below came the aroma of coffee and baking bread. Never mind that the eggs and milk would be frozen. They were snug, well-fed, and beneath a sturdy roof.

Mae let go of her disappointment at not seeing General Washington for the first time as the service was canceled. Any plans to decamp would also be delayed with the weather.

In the parlor where a robust fire was lit, she returned to sewing, which had become such a satisfying part of her days, and recalled Rhys's pleasure at finding her initials sewn into the hem of his shirts with indigo thread. What would fill the absence when her efforts weren't needed anymore?

As the Sabbath afternoon stretched long, Coralie played the spinet, the bright tones resonating to the rafters. After several cups of independence tea—though Mae didn't dare call it that to Coralie—they both planned to write letters, but the ink had frozen in the inkwells.

"I suppose winters in the New York frontier are just as frigid as here, if not more so," Coralie mused, cradling her cup in her hands. "Though Jon never complains when he does write from along the Hudson River."

Again, Mae wondered just where Lieutenant Gibbs was in so vast a territory. "If you do marry and settle in New York, you might see Jon far more."

"How odd to think there may even be another infant we've not met by now. I must say, Jon and Joanna seem as fertile as their fields."

They laughed, and Mae felt some of the tension between them ebb. "I do wonder where we'll all settle once the war ends."

"Perhaps you'll remain right here. Pastor Heath recently escorted you home. A fortuitous match, as Father hoped."

Fortuitous and far-fetched. But Mae said nothing.

Coralie regarded her intently. "For a time I worried you might succumb to General Harlow's attentions. I breathed a sigh of relief when he stopped billeting here."

Mae nearly bit her tongue in two. "Why do you find him so disagreeable?"

"Is it not obvious?" Coralie stared back at her in surprise. "He's but a farmer, a marksman. You're more gently bred."

"Farming is an honorable pursuit," Mae said. "Chatham is surrounded by respectable, prosperous farmers. Jon is even one."

Coralie rolled her eyes. "*Rebel* farmers, you mean."

"So? As for the one you loathe, the man is a *general*."

"But not a learned man like Father."

"General Harlow is even more admirable given he's self-taught. He owns a great many books." Mae hated that she had to defend him. Coralie would never be convinced. "General Washington is much the same."

"General Harlow is also of questionable lineage."

It was Mae's turn for eye-rolling. "His father is of Quaker stock, his mother Welsh. What's so brow raising about that? Our own ancestry is quite scandalous if you recall." She felt an almost venomous pleasure mentioning it. "Have you forgotten our mooncussers?"

Coralie recoiled. "What means you?"

"Mama's family who cursed the moon for foiling their plundering, as they could only steal on cloudy nights?" Mae had always found their family history fascinating if dark. Early on, their colonial kin had been naught but rogues and thieves and worse, lining up and hanging lanterns from their saddles along the Jersey shore to lure unsuspecting ships to their doom.

Coralie closed her eyes in a theatrical moment. "Thankfully we descend more recently from a respected pastor, not water bandits and land pirates."

"Besides, being a pastor's wife is not for the fainthearted. Mama was held to an impossibly high standard, as if people expected her to walk on water."

Coralie held fast to her dislike. "You would be a farmer's wife instead."

"I would be the wife of the man I love no matter his occupation, so long as it's honorable." Mae didn't miss Coralie's grunt of disapproval. "I don't care for Pastor Heath in that way."

"Many marry for practicality."

"Speaking of practicalities, what will your lieutenant do once there's no longer a war to wage?"

Coralie looked startled as if she'd thought no further than his epaulets.

"If he is awarded land by the British, he doesn't seem the sort to farm," Mae continued. "And New York is largely frontier, Jon told us, if you settle outside of the city."

"Perhaps we could lease the land he's to be awarded for his service and live in the nearest town. He could open a law office like his late father." Coralie shrugged, clearly done with the matter. "We shall soon see."

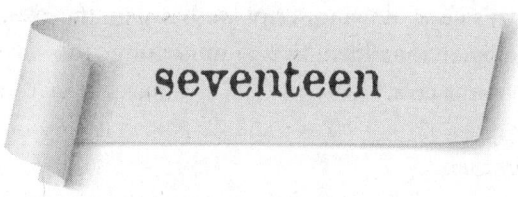

seventeen

I've neither reserve nor aversion to man. . . . But to keep my dear Liberty, long as I can, Is the reason I chuse to live single.

Hannah Griffitts

In the privacy of his own Lowantica Valley cabin, hemmed in by melting patches of snow, Rhys examined a borrowed frock coat with a critical eye ahead of the ball. His worn buckskin breeches would have to suffice. The finest shirt he owned had been made by Mae.

Rummaging through a small trunk, he found a clean linen stock that begged for ironing alongside some stockings atop a pair of shoe buckles that wouldn't shame him. There was a standing joke among Continental officers that they looked like threadbare scarecrows, but since the British weren't invited they needn't fret about their appearance.

He sat down in a chair by the fire, noting the time with his father's pocket watch that still ticked on as stubbornly as the old man himself. Charles Harlow showed no sign of stopping at sixty, able to wield an ax and plow a furrow like men half his age. He had never fought in a war, his Quaker beliefs forbidding it, though he handled Rhys's service well enough.

In the hubbub of the last few days brought on by the false alarm that General Howe was pushing through Jersey on his way to Philadelphia, Rhys had overlooked the latest letter from Virginia. With a swipe of his thumb he broke the blue seal. Liberty blue, his sister called it.

Bronwyn's clear, flowing script was easy on the eyes, though she'd developed a maddening way of writing crossways on the paper due to the cost.

Dear brother,

'Tis hard to believe we have survived our second winter without you.

Virginia has seen much snow, which turns the farm and fields a pleasing white. Father continues to split wood despite his rheumatism and keeps the fires hot while I keep him content by making cawl and Welsh pancakes.

We read your past letters so often that the ink is smudged and faded, and are very curious about this belle of Chatham you mention. Clearly she has your heart, which will crush your many admirers in the valley here when found out. Yet you make no mention of her feelings for you, so perhaps this Jersey lady will be left behind when you move on with the army. I hope not, for it is time you settled down, though I do wonder how she would like Virginia should she leave her home.

Soon I will put my hand to the plow to help Father in the fields. It is the least I can do with you away fighting for our very liberties. Our wheat and corn should be bountiful again this year, and my kitchen garden is wintering well. I am anxious to see how the bees and orchard fare come spring without your careful tending. Your house is empty but standing strong, a comfort to us when we look up the hill. I may plant you a kitchen garden of your own come spring.

Our prayers are with you, to protect and guide you wherever you go.

Your loving sister,
Bronwyn

One line dogged him. *Clearly she has your heart.* Though he had only mentioned Mae briefly, his astute sister had read the meaning within and summed up the dilemma of his moving on. Bronwyn said nothing about the man she loved who'd fallen early in the war. Micah Edmiston had been one of the Virginia line who'd died at the Battle of Great Bridge. Did she not mention him anymore because she knew how it grieved him? Or had she somehow moved past it? He doubted the latter.

Micah had been his childhood friend, more a brother, and Rhys still couldn't fathom he was gone. Nor had he much time to ponder his absence or the hole he'd left in the Shenandoah Valley, since Rhys had soon left to lead his riflemen to reinforce Boston's Patriots in 1775.

He folded the letter and put it in his dispatch case before reaching into his pocket. When he withdrew Mae's braid it lay like gold in his open palm.

Maebel Bohannon Harlow.

He tried picturing her in the valley, in the house he'd built. Of solid stone, it was a bare six rooms with a central staircase. A grand home compared to the log dwelling his father and mother built together and where his father and sister lived today.

But was Mae meant to be its mistress?

She could sew but barely cook. She played the spinet but he didn't have one. Her dresses were far above the simple linen and homespun of his Shenandoah world. Even the furnishings in the Chatham home were fine, far finer than any he owned. His house sat empty. His only pride was the beginnings of a library.

Still, stubbornly, he saw her there. But how would she manage?

Would Bronwyn be on hand or would Mae expect another Mrs. Hurst? Domestic help was beyond his ken. The nearest town was hardly the caliber of Chatham. Would Mae be willing to accept him on such humble terms?

Would anyone? He had no ties other than partnering with a woman for a dance or two at some local function where he'd been invited to fiddle. He'd had little time for amusements even before the war. And suddenly it seemed odd that he was still solitary at more than thirty years of age, as if he'd been waiting, keeping himself apart, his whole life till Mae.

His mind leapt ahead to children ringed round the table. Childish voices uttering prayers at bedtime. Mae's soft voice above them all. He hoped for a large family in time. He hadn't any inkling what she wanted. And it didn't seem to even matter as he might share Micah's fate. Above all the wonderings and imaginings and longings, he didn't want to hurt her by deepening their tie and making foolish promises he couldn't keep.

★ ★ ★ ★ ★

The temperatures rose and the northeaster was a dim memory when James readied the coach to journey to Morristown. Mae was glad to travel two days ahead of the ball as they'd need time to prepare their gowns and coiffures, to say nothing of their nerves. To be in the same room as General Washington and his lady was remarkable enough. But the possibility of being with Rhys again was all that truly mattered, and she was about to see if he danced as well as he fiddled.

His absence seemed a twelvemonth. She'd neither seen nor heard from him since he'd delivered the salt, nor had she asked James about him as Coralie was almost always present when they'd been snowbound. When she rode with James to deliver the last wagonload of goods to Lowantica Valley, Rhys had been elsewhere, thus she missed him again.

Expectant and somewhat heartsick, she pinned all her hopes

on the ball. After all, he was an officer, and all the general's officers in the winter encampment were invited, clear to Chatham and beyond.

As she and Coralie arrived at Morristown in a flurry of petticoats, capes, and baggage, their elderly aunt met them at the front door.

"Welcome, my dears!" The bent, wrinkled widow ushered them in with her usual peppery relish. "'Tis been an age! I've been hearing rumors that the British might storm Chatham any minute, then move on to Morristown. I'm more than relieved you're here safe and sound."

"I'm sorry the weather and the pox kept us away so long." Mae removed her cape. "Praise be 'tis spring and we can turn our minds to other matters."

"Indeed, a dance is most welcome after so much death. I've seen far too many soldiers and townspeople buried over the winter. For a time I feared there'd not be a friend left standing. There is simply no more room in the Presbyterian and Baptist graveyards."

"We're glad you're still breathing, Aunt Verity," Coralie said, kissing her pockmarked cheek. Their aunt had suffered the disease as a child long ago, so long ago she couldn't recall it, she'd said.

She helped them remove their wraps before resuming her vigil by her parlor window. "I've been wanting to catch sight of Mrs. Washington ever since she arrived. Such a tiny speck of a woman from what I've heard—and the general is as strapping as they come! Two hundred ten pounds in heft, 'tis said—and standing six foot three!"

"If you don't see Mrs. Washington—Lady Washington, some call her—beforehand, we'll tell you all about her afterward," Mae reassured her. "I understand she's very gracious and brings great cheer wherever she goes."

She and Coralie hurried up the stairs to the room they shared whenever in Morristown, conveniently situated on the town square.

Pale sunlight streaked the worn wooden floors of a space that hadn't changed since their childhood.

"Come down, dearies, when you've settled in and we'll have a dish of tea," Aunt Verity called from below.

A dish of tea took the chill off their seven-mile journey, though the tea table was positioned by the parlor window, which emitted a frightful draft. But their aunt's patrolling of Morristown wouldn't be denied.

"A great deal can be learned by careful observation." Aunt Verity began pouring from an ancient porcelain pot. "For instance, how many times the bakers and butchers service the tavern, how many laundresses are required, even how many times couriers come and go. The place is a veritable hive of activity at all hours of the day and night. I've become very fond of seeing the general taking a walk or riding about town, always in the company of his Life Guards and the like."

"Does this mean you're siding with the Continental cause, Auntie?" Coralie asked, taking a tea cake from a floral plate.

"Ha! I don't know that one can do otherwise, given Morristown is overrun with Patriots."

"Chatham too," Coralie told her, biting into the sweet.

"The army will soon be moving on," Mae said, careful to keep regret from her tone. "Everything shall return to normal—the churches ceasing to be hospitals, Lowantica Valley a field instead of an encampment, and our villages soldier free."

Aunt Verity turned away from the window. "Are you still billeting James and officers?"

Mae nodded. "Just James and Captain Sperry on occasion."

"Much as I miss them, I'm glad your parents didn't live to witness all this commotion. Their peace-loving souls would be torn in two." She spooned sugar into her tea. "And what of the lieutenant you mentioned last visit, Coralie? Is he still in New York?"

"Somewhere between New York City and the Hudson River Valley, I believe."

"How is he faring?"

"He's confident the conflict is over or soon will be. His letters are full of his assurances that the British will triumph."

Aunt Verity's thinning brows nearly touched her hairline. "He's *British*?"

"I may have forgotten to mention it," Coralie replied, finishing her cake.

With a reproving cluck of her tongue, Aunt Verity stole another look out the glass. "As for your lieutenant's assurances, he might change his mind were he to meet General Washington. The man oozes confidence and conviction. He gives no indication of surrendering whatsoever, I assure you."

Coralie smiled thinly. "Well, appearances are deceptive, as is said."

"Indeed," their aunt replied tartly. "In that vein, a great many British officers are blinded by their arrogance. I can only hope your Lieutenant Gibbs isn't one of them."

Mae felt a little thrill of triumph at her sister's set-down. Lately Coralie's own arrogance seemed to bloom, widening the chasm between them.

Coralie frowned. "Are you in danger of becoming a Patriot, Aunt?"

"I desire peace foremost, but if I had to choose sides, I prefer the Patriot cause, yes."

"Then that makes two of you," Coralie said, sending Mae a sore glance. "Though my sister says she is neutral, she is not."

"And why, my dear, are you attending a Continental ball if you are aligned with the British?" Aunt Verity turned the full force of her gaze on her youngest niece. "I sincerely hope your motive isn't to spy. I won't abide a spy in my house."

Mae's shock gave way to amusement. For a trice Coralie looked as if she'd swallowed a needle, so pained was her expression. "I— well, I simply crave a bit of merriment, and we were kindly extended an invitation."

"I doubt an invitation would have been forthcoming were your true allegiance known," their aunt continued, pinning Coralie with her shrewd, close-set eyes. "Let Mae have her shining moment. You shall stay here with me."

★ ★ ★ ★ ★

As Mae dressed for the ball, Coralie sulked in the parlor below. Mae could feel her sister's contrariness clear to the second floor. Undeterred, Aunt Verity helped her dress while humming a tune that sounded suspiciously like "Yankee Doodle Dandy."

Shift. Stays. Stockings and garters. Then the confection of a dress. Mae felt like a spring bouquet in such sumptuous, colorful silk. She splashed a bit of rose water on her wrists, stood back, and studied her reflection in the looking glass till a knock on the door curtailed her scrutiny. Aunt Verity returned, something in hand.

"I've been saving this for your wedding day, but now seems the right occasion." She opened a velvet box and removed a three-tiered choker of pearls. "'Tis your grandmother's necklace, given to your mother, her firstborn, on her wedding day."

Mae marveled at the necklace and its antique clasp, which Aunt Verity fastened at the back of her neck. The pearls were cool against her skin, the perfect pairing with her gown.

"Pearls suit you, as does silk." Aunt Verity stood back, her approval apparent. "Madame Jaquett's creation, I suppose? And in the polonaise style? Exquisite!"

"Coralie ordered the gown for me." Mae smoothed the looped-up skirt. "I've not danced since mourning Father and Mother. I hope I'm not stumbling rather than stepping."

"Nonsense. The officers will be so pleased to partner with you, you'll have no time to worry. Prepare for an onslaught of attention." Her aunt's admiring smile put Mae at ease. "Now, off with you. James is below to see you safely across the street in your pattens."

Mae's thoughts swung to Samantha. Had James asked her to come? Or had she declined?

Her brother stood alone by the front door, waiting.

"I'd hoped to see Samantha here," she said, not wanting to pry but wondering his thoughts on the matter, if only to set aside her own misguided hopes.

"I didn't ask her." He took her arm as they crossed the muddy, moonlit street. "We've decided a wartime courtship is as unwise as it is inconvenient."

"I understand," Mae told him. Only too well. Yet they could still dance and forget their momentary troubles, could they not?

As they neared Arnold Tavern's open front door, a great many guests cascaded about the steps and porch. Lanterns hung from the eaves, the din of the public rooms spilling through open windows into the quiet of the night.

Nerves taut, Mae looked discreetly about for Rhys, but the press of people was too great, and she was swept upstairs to the second floor in a breathless, petticoat-crushing rush. Even James got lost in the crowd.

Great pains had been taken with the ballroom. Shining windows, dozens of fragrant beeswax candles, and a polished floor met her glance before she noticed the chairs and sofas lining the wallpapered perimeter.

By the hearth at the ballroom's far end stood an exceptionally tall gentleman she knew at once was General Washington. He was resplendent in buff and blue and wore a blue moiré silk ribband as commander-in-chief, his backdrop the new American flag. As she'd heard, he shunned wigs and had simply powdered the front of his hair, leaving the back natural, a hint of russet sneaking through. Beside him was a tiny lady dressed divinely in saffron silk who didn't even reach his shoulder.

A line snaked about the large room. Officers' wives dressed in their finest, some with outlandish hairstyles, kept Mae riveted for a few moments. One woman's coiffure was a foot high and shaped like a cocked hat—a giant powdered pyramid atop her head. Some even sported red, white, and blue powder.

A few of Chatham's belles were here, and Mae smiled at those she knew. As she moved forward in line to meet the Washingtons, she looked back over her shoulder now and again and was rewarded at long last.

There, gracing the ballroom's entrance, stood Rhys. Clad in a handsome blue frock coat and buckskin breeches, he wore a stock, the first she'd seen him in, turning him more gentleman than rifleman. Did he have on the shirt she'd made him? He looked so fine, all the breath left her.

Would he dance with her? Or keep his distance?

The intimacy they'd shared in the Lowantica Valley cabin and then the Chatham kitchen faded in light of the fact they now stood so far apart. In fact, he seemed to not even be aware of her. The officer next to him claimed his complete attention.

As a trio of musicians began tuning their instruments, a woman touched Mae's lace sleeve with the tip of her folded fan. "What a lovely gown."

Murmuring her thanks, Mae realized she'd forgotten her fan. Despite the cool damp of spring, the room was warming rapidly. Once the dancing began she'd be berry red.

The line lurched forward, and she soon found herself curtsying in front of the general and his lady as if they were colonial royalty. Her face heating, she read admiration in Mrs. Washington's gaze— was it for her gown?—and earned a slight smile from General Washington as introductions were made. He even made mention of James's and Jon's service.

"Thank you for traveling from Chatham for the festivities, Miss Bohannon," Mrs. Washington said graciously. "I hope your evening is well spent."

Curtsying again, Mae moved on, her restless gaze traveling to Rhys, who now stood by a large window. If he hadn't noticed her, others had. One . . . two . . . three soldiers paid her a compliment and asked her for a dance in advance. She simply smiled, her gaze returning to Rhys and then hanging on the ballroom's entrance, where Coralie hovered in her wedding gown.

How had she escaped Aunt Verity?

Her sister spied her immediately and made her way across the floor and around guests till she reached her, eyes red. Had she been crying?

Mae tamped down her dismay. "You're supposed to be with Aunt Verity."

"I told her you'd need this." Coralie reached into her pocket and produced her lace-tipped fan, a sly smile on her pale face.

For a moment Mae's irritation eased. Thanking her, she extended the fan's painted folds with a flick of her wrist.

Coralie's gaze swept the room. "And now that I'm here I must step a country dance or two."

"A shame Lieutenant Gibbs is elsewhere. You look very pretty."

Flushing with pleasure, Coralie extended her own fan. "I'm ready to forgive these rebels everything if they provide a fine evening's entertainment." Her smile slipped. "I spy General Harlow."

"You make too much of him. We haven't even spoken yet." Now Mae tried *not* to look at him again lest she appear overeager. "I don't think he's noticed me."

"No matter. Others certainly have. Or perhaps it's me they're admiring." She laughed, suddenly the coquette.

Not even Coralie's British lieutenant could change that.

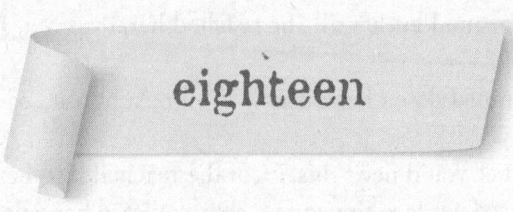

eighteen

*I dare say the Men would fight very well (if properly Officered),
although they are an exceedingly dirty and nasty people.*

George Washington on his own army

When Rhys saw Mae, all the other comely women in the noisy
room faded to the far reaches, and he drank in all the details like a
parched man at a well. Her garden-like gown held a lustrous sheen
in the candlelight, and the pearls encircling her throat reminded
him how far removed she was from his reach. Though their feelings
for each other contradicted the notion, doubt still riddled him.

Mae was without doubt the belle of the ballroom—and gaining
considerable attention. Jealousy, ever a poor companion, gnawed
at him, though he tried to put it down. No matter his doubts, she
was his in his most private thoughts, her lock of hair proof, and
no other man dare trespass.

Coralie, in a scarlet gown seeming to mirror her British loyalties,
doubled the sisters' attention once the music began. Two officers
claimed them for a country dance immediately. Rhys stayed where
he was, his back to a papered wall, content to bide his time—for
the moment.

If Washington's aim was to fool the enemy with reports of a

well-endowed fete, he'd certainly accomplished his mission. Morristown's residents had taken the ruse and risen to the occasion too. Decorations and confections abounded, even cake, and punch brimmed in a silver bowl that promised replenishing.

"Sir, with all due respect, why are you not dancing?" Bohannon's deep voice upbraided him from behind. "Rather, why not partner with my eldest sister?"

"Because I'll have to wait in line to do it," Rhys replied, now shoulder to shoulder with Mae's brother. "Besides, I'm content to simply watch the festivities and pretend all is well."

To his chagrin, Mae showed no sign of declining even one dance as she spun and stepped up and down the large room. When she passed by him, their eyes met briefly, ending his wondering about whether she'd seen him.

Overfull, the frolic pulsed with heat and high spirits. Soon the room turned stifling. Tugging at his snug stock nearly sprang the buckle at the nape of his neck. Rhys lifted a sleeve to dry his upper lip before turning around and tugging open a window.

After another heated quarter of an hour, an older woman fainted. For a few flustered moments, the dancing ground to a halt as someone revived her with a vial of something vile. The temporary lull brought Mae to his side. Standing close, she fluttered her fan and he was grateful for its wind.

"Do you not dance, sir?" she teased.

"I'd hate to wait in line for you," he half jested. "Or start a duel."

She smiled. "You Virginians are known for your fine stepping. General Washington and his lady are proof."

The two mentioned led out—the topmost couple—but Rhys stole a long look at an enthralled Mae instead. Half of her hair was caught in an elaborate knot at the back of her head, the rest loosed into a fall of pale curls that framed her shoulders. He fisted his hands behind his back to keep from touching her as she turned those chicory-blue eyes on him, her skin pink. Amid all the scents wafting about, not all of them pleasant, her rosemary essence reached him.

Bohannon excused himself and partnered with a Morristown miss, leaving the two of them alone—as alone as a couple in an overcrowded ballroom could be.

Mae leaned in, her words a caress near his ear. "I much prefer a firelit kitchen in the quiet of the night, General Harlow."

He could barely hear her above the raucous fiddles. "You're not supposed to make this harder, Miss Bohannon."

"I've missed you." She looked wistful. "Why not make the most of the hour given us?"

He turned toward her with a surrendered half smile. "Are you asking me to dance?"

She simply smiled back at him, further whittling him down like a knife on soft wood. In light of her willingness, he felt hard-hearted, miserly with his time and affections, living a lie when his feelings for her knew no bounds. His vow to keep his distance began to collapse. She put a hand to her bodice, and he knew his lock of hair hid beneath. He wanted nothing more than to hold her, enfold her in his arms. But a dance would have to suffice.

A country dance was struck, and it mirrored his emotions. Calm one moment, careening the next. When the dance ended and they were near the ballroom door, he took her hand and she followed without a word.

Mayhap his need of her would lessen if he kissed her. Just once. He knew better but was willing to believe the lie.

The adjoining rooms across the tavern's wide second-floor hall held couples in conversation, the doors open. No privacy to be had except a linen closet. He opened the miniature door, half expecting another couple to have gained the trysting place, but it was blessedly empty, one small window letting in moonlight.

Once Mae entered on his heels, he shut the world out. The music and chatter faded as her softness and scent filled his senses instead. She turned toward him and his hands spanned her waist. The punch he'd drunk utterly failed to inebriate him like she did.

"Mae . . ." Even saying her name made him woozy. The thud

of his heart was surely felt beneath her hands as she placed them against his waistcoat.

"Can we dispense with Miss Bohannon and General Harlow forever?" she whispered as her arms encircled his neck.

His lips met hers softly in answer and then more surely, hardly the chaste, hurried kiss he'd envisioned. Sparks seemed to fire, the tumult inside him intensifying. She had him, body and soul.

He lost count of their kisses in the crush of emotion he'd battled since he'd first crossed her threshold. It didn't help that her response was just as searing, lit by her own long denial. It took an iron will to rein himself in and simply hold her, her head resting in the hollow of his shoulder.

"Who thought a linen closet could be so"—her breathless voice held amusement—"beguiling?"

He kissed a loosened strand of hair by her ear. "Marry me, Mae."

★ ★ ★ ★ ★

Marry me, Mae.

The low words turned her from breathless to disbelieving. "Marry you?"

"When I get back from the war."

If he got back. *If* the war was won. A hundred ifs threaded her swirling thoughts.

"I'm yours," he told her. "I've made it clear. All that I have is yours, including the stone house built with my own hands in western Virginia. My father and sister live nearby. They'd like nothing better than to see me return with a bride."

"You have a sister?"

"Bronwyn, aye."

She let that fact settle. He continued to surprise her with how little she knew about him. Bronwyn—a lovely name. Welsh, perhaps. "Is she wed?"

"Nay. The man she was betrothed to died early in the war."

141

The pain in his voice bespoke much. Was that why he was so cautious with her? With their future? "A terrible loss to bear."

"He was like a brother to me."

"Oh, Rhys . . ."

"That's always in mind in regard to you—us."

All his reluctance regarding her became clear. Yet all he offered went deep. He loved her and would wed her upon war's end if it went in their favor. If it didn't, he'd face a traitor's death. Their life together in the house he'd built, its rooms waiting to be filled with children and a thousand heartfelt memories, brought unspeakable longing. And surely he felt it too, for he said, "I keep seeing you there, bringing beauty and peace to the passing seasons, always by my side. Or, when I'm away, waiting to welcome me home."

"Never doubt that I want to be that for you. Be there for you."

Slowly he released her and stepped back. "For now, needs be we consider how to emerge from this linen closet with our reputations intact." He straightened his stock, and their eyes met again. "You first, then I'll follow."

She hesitated. He was so handsome in his fine garments she felt half melted—and just as determined to have a final memory. "Not till you kiss me again, because I've no idea how long it'll be before the next time."

But he simply kissed her hands before taking hold of the doorknob. "The next time I kiss you I don't intend to stop."

nineteen

New lords, new laws. The strictest government is taking place and great distinction is made between officers and men. Everyone is made to know his place and keep it, or be immediately tied up and receive not one but 30 or 40 lashes.

A chaplain on discipline in the Continental Army

Coralie, from all appearances, had completely forgotten her British lieutenant. Nor did she seem to notice Mae's absence amid so many attentive rebel officers. The rest of the evening flew past, and then James escorted a yawning Coralie and Mae across the street to Aunt Verity's well after midnight. Once he'd left them at the door, Coralie wasted no words as they entered the house.

"I spied you dancing with the general more than once. What does that signify, I wonder?"

"Mind your own business." Mae was half tempted to remain in Morristown since Coralie so vexed her. "You best hurry upstairs."

"I'm quite worn out, but from the look of Auntie, we shan't go straight to bed," Coralie said with a hysterical little laugh. Clearly she'd drunk too much punch. "She's been at watch by the parlor window since we left, I'm willing to wager."

143

Their aunt called to them as soon as the front door closed. "I'm still quite put out that Coralie defied my order to stay home," she said. "Who is this general mentioned?"

"Mae's beau, General Harlow," Coralie answered, already at the bottom step.

Stifling a yawn and her dismay, Mae dutifully entered the parlor as her sister snuck upstairs, knowing she'd get no sleep without elaborating.

"Is this true, my dear?"

Mae began removing her white kid gloves. "General Harlow is the finest man I've ever met. A rifleman from Virginia."

"Is there an understanding between you?"

"If you mean, do we hope to wed once the war is won, yes," Mae told her with far more joy than certainty.

"I only wish your dear parents were here to witness it, God rest them. Your general must be rather extraordinary to have captured your attention."

Mae kissed her parchment-paper cheek. "I shall tell you more in the morning."

★ ★ ★ ★ ★

The next morning, General Washington showed no sign of having danced half the night. Rhys resisted a yawn as he stood in the commander's office awaiting orders. A number of other bloodshot-eyed officers filled the chamber, where maps covered tables along with troop rosters, military correspondence, and an abundance of paper, quill pens, and inkwells. A cheerful fire burned in the hearth, occasionally sending a puff of smoke into the room when the spring wind gusted.

Rhys had spent what little remained of the night after the ball reliving the linen closet. What had been said. Proposed. Weighing the past with the present. Did Bronwyn regret her and Micah's decision to postpone their wedding? He recalled they'd considered marrying before Micah enlisted.

What had Mae said? *"Why not make the most of the hour given us?"*

". . . If any man in action shall presume to skulk, hide himself, or retreat from the enemy, without the orders of his commanding officer, he will be instantly shot down as an example of cowardice."

Rhys yanked his thoughts back from Mae to the present. Washington was looking straight at him, his gaze ironclad, his legendary temper taut. Fortunately, his riflemen were not among the cowards Washington railed against.

"Harlow, if we hear of the enemy's advance, you and your men will go out and continue scouting, flanking, and harassing their rear guards."

Rhys nodded, knowing they must be able to march at a moment's notice. Everything depended on the enemy's movements and the intelligence arriving more than hourly of late. Spies were thick as gnats, and Washington placed great stock in intelligence. His own spy web was sticky and extensive.

Washington continued, "Keep the enemy's fear of you alive even as you and your men continue to be fearless. British officers taking ship for America are being warned to put their affairs in order lest they encounter American riflemen. Your unerring ability to hit an object incites terror among the Hessians especially."

Yet many British called their methods dishonorable—this skirmishing with and targeting British officers and their Indian guides. Though the enemy had their own rifle corps, they lacked the rebel's deadly accurate long rifles.

"I'm awaiting word of troop movements in Jersey as well as enemy activity in New York," Washington said. "The latest dispatches will determine our next campaign."

"I would propose, sir," Colonel Finley said, "that if we're to go north, the Rifle Corps would best serve by leading the advance."

Washington looked about the room. "What say the rest of you?"

Rhys had grown used to Washington's tactics during councils of war. He was adept at presenting ideas and inviting argument and opinion among his foremost officers, thereby arriving on the best course of action. He was decisive yet willing to consider all viewpoints till he issued an order. He lived by the Scripture "Where no counsel is, the people fall: but in the multitude of counsellors there is safety."

Rhys gave his own opinion about the matter as the clock ticked toward noon. At last the meeting ended with the arrival of the Frenchman de Rayneval. Leaving Arnold Tavern, Rhys set his sights on the silversmith down the street.

The sign of the crown and three pearls on Market Street was easily seen. Once Rhys was inside, the jeweler's shop made a muddle of a determined man. Medals, buckles, buttons, thimbles, broaches, and chains shone about the shadowed interior. Plenty of pinchbeck—faux jewelry—abounded but failed to impress. Mourning rings beckoned, adding a melancholy note to an otherwise joyously decisive moment.

"What do you buy, sir?" the jeweler asked, spectacles perched on the end of his thin nose.

Rhys continued to peruse all the wares inside a glass case. "A wedding ring."

"Ah. Over here by the watches."

Along a far wall was an astonishing selection for so small a village. Smuggled goods? Rhys's attention caught on a plain gold band with a small but glittering rose-cut diamond.

"You have a discerning eye, sir. This piece makes paupers of the rest." The jeweler reached into the case and took out the ring. "Imported in the last vessel from London before ports closed." As Rhys examined it, he added, "I'm also taking bespoke orders if nothing in stock suits, but 'twill likely be contraband, understand."

"The rose-cut band will do." Rhys didn't flinch at the price. He could afford it but didn't dare lose such a treasure.

Now, would Mae like it?

★ ★ ★ ★ ★

A warm April wind blew through Lowantica Valley's woods. Rhys sat in a pool of sunlight, cleaning his rifle outside his cabin, the ring in his pocket.

Opposite him sat Sperry whittling a pipe, wood shavings at his feet. "Seems like we've been shut up here four score and ten years. I'm more than ready to march even if it means battle."

"May, to my reckoning," Rhys replied.

"A month from now?" Sperry held the knife aloft. "For certain?"

"A bold guess."

"May means we're nearly done with spring and the damp. I imagine the enemy is as ready as we are."

"We're awaiting word on Howe's and Gates's positions, the strength of their numbers, and the like. Then General Washington will have us decamp."

"Speaking of the general . . ." Sperry left off, his gaze fixed on the valley floor below. "I'd know that fine mount anywhere."

"Blueskin or Nelson?" Rhys said without looking up. The chestnut gelding and white half-Arabian were known by many, friend or foe.

"Nelson."

They both stood, abandoning their tasks. Though it wasn't uncommon for Washington to leave Morristown and ride to the valley, Rhys sensed this visit had significance. He started down the hill, Sperry on his heels.

"Sir." Rhys raised his hand to his hat as the general came to a halt in front of the quartermasters.

Washington dismounted, a dozen of his Life Guards near, and gestured to a path that led to a makeshift chapel and graveyard. Rhys fell into step beside him.

Washington walked with head down and hands clasped behind his back. "Prepare to leave for Fort Montgomery within twenty-four hours of my order to march."

New York, hazy till now, came sharply into focus. Rhys digested the news without comment as the general continued.

"You're now in charge of a four-hundred-man corps of riflemen comprised of the Virginia and Pennsylvania lines, which will act as vanguard ahead of the main body of the army once it joins you for the next campaign."

"You've changed your mind about reinforcing Ticonderoga, then."

"For now the plan is to advance no further than the Hudson Highlands. If all goes as planned, you may be joining the northern army under General Gates as reinforcements against an expected British invasion from Canada. Once you reach Stony Point you'll be augmented by three hundred light infantry under Major Dearborn."

A well-thought-out plan. "Burgoyne has left England for Canada, then."

"Aye, the latest intelligence indicates he's expected in Quebec soon. Once he arrives, he plans to march south from there toward Ticonderoga, then continue down the Hudson River. His eye is on Albany, where he'll likely join forces with Howe and possibly St. Leger."

"Who mean to dominate New York and cut the supply chain between our northern and southern forces."

"Aye, by seizing waterways foremost. Their attempt last year failed, but they seem poised to try again. Their goal is to quell all rebellion in New England, which they hope will force the southern states into submission."

Rhys well knew Virginia's mood—every bit as volatile as Massachusetts's. "The southern states will never submit even if the northern front is brought to heel."

"My aim is to keep any separation from happening. To win this war we must make the conflict as costly to our enemies as possible and as long as possible, forcing any who want a hasty conclusion to retreat and thereby surrender." Washington turned a corner, trading the sun for shade. "That's not uppermost in my mind at the moment but Colonel Bohannon's request from the Hudson Highlands."

Rhys's mind veered to Mae. He'd heard from Bohannon that his brother—Colonel Jon—had written Washington about his sisters accompanying the army if they moved north into New York. Rhys was against it yet held his peace about the matter, which was in truth a family affair. If Washington approved the request, he'd deal with it then. Traveling with the army was a safer endeavor than if they ventured there in a small party.

"Two other ladies—both officers' wives—will be traveling north with the army to the Hudson. Colonel Bohannon's kin will accompany them." Washington turned to look at him. "You're acquainted with the Bohannon sisters, are you not? I saw you dancing with one of them the other night. In fact, I remember you billeted with them for a time."

Rhys nodded. "Aye."

"There's no better guard than your Rifle Corps. Given that, I would assign you to the Misses Bohannon once we decamp."

Rhys's resistance roared as his plan for Mae to remain in Jersey unraveled. Stoic, he kept walking, matching his long stride to the general's as Washington concluded their conversation.

"I would have you and your men as defense, especially if matters turn deadly. You know as well as I that the territory to be crossed requires supreme vigilance."

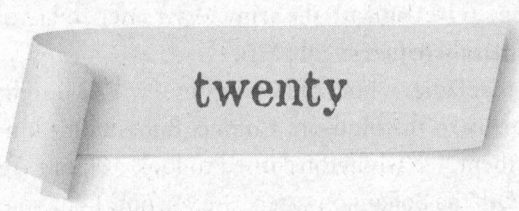

twenty

> *The hour is fast approaching, on which the Honour and Success of this army, and the safety of our bleeding Country depend. Remember officers and Soldiers, that you are Freemen, fighting for the blessings of Liberty . . . that slavery will be your portion . . . if you do not acquit yourselves like men.*
>
> George Washington

Coralie's decision to remain in Morristown with Aunt Verity gave rise to Mae's suspicions that something was afoot other than sewing. Coralie was gifted at Broderie perse, an appliqué using patterned India chintz that Aunt Verity was so fond of. But might her remaining have more to do with being near Continental headquarters instead?

Tight-lipped about his own orders, James returned Mae the few miles home, not even staying for supper. Clearly his mind was elsewhere, and Mae suspected it had to do with the army's imminent plans.

When Mae's solitary meal was over, Mrs. Hurst saved the remainder for Hanna and Aaron, who were working long hours at the apothecary. Wartime hours, Aaron sometimes said, concerning Mae as he'd begun to look more and more beleaguered of late. Until the church ceased to be a hospital they'd continue overworking, though Aaron was increasingly concerned about Hanna's condition.

Nearly out the door with the leftover supper, Mrs. Hurst looked aghast when Mae tried to go in her stead. "Not with so many men milling about and the threat of British invasion so high. Bolt the door behind me. I'll stay here with you tonight if your brother doesn't return."

Unsure about both James and Captain Sperry, Mae went upstairs to take advantage of Coralie's absence. She went through her sister's writing desk to see what, if anything, could be found to confirm she was spying even in the most insignificant way.

Only a few old letters from Eben and a few scraps of rag paper indicative of the British blockades were on hand. Nothing new, nothing incriminating. Torn between relief and dismay that Coralie remained in Morristown, Mae went below to play the spinet and try to quiet her nerves and every roiling remembrance of Rhys.

★ ★ ★ ★ ★

The next afternoon, when the ever-watchful Mrs. Hurst visited another widow, Mae stepped out to fetch the tavern's post. She took the river walk, a foot trail worn by countless soldiers and citizenry that followed the sweep of the Passaic. Many were outside on this mild spring day, including triple the sentries on the bridge.

Rather than be fearful, shouldn't she be reassured with so many Continental soldiers about? Were the British waiting till the Americans left Jersey to strike? Suspicions that they would indeed arrive on the heels of the Continental Army's leaving had begun spreading like wildfire. Would Chatham and Morristown be punished, even burned, like other Patriot-supporting villages and towns?

She'd seen so little of James and Captain Sperry lately that she'd begun to think they'd decamped already, though Rhys wouldn't leave without saying goodbye, surely.

Raising a hand to steady her straw hat, Mae waved to a couple she knew, intent on her destination. If Lieutenant Gibbs had written Coralie, she'd attempt to read the letter without breaking the seal. If she did break it, she'd burn the letter.

Lord, forgive me.

She stepped onto the tavern's long porch, smoke and spirits assailing her as she tried to rein in her hopes that Rhys might be here. She passed into the hall opening to the taproom and found herself seeking the corner table he preferred, only to find it occupied by someone else.

Just as well. Her business was the post. She sought the tavern keeper, who kept all the mail delivered by couriers in a cupboard behind his desk. The letter he handed her was worn and mud-flecked, though her brother Jon's strong copperplate hand wasn't diminished. A letter from Lieutenant Gibbs had fared less well—torn, the seal already broken.

Mae sought the small chamber off the entrance hall to read both. An elderly man smoked near the fireless hearth, a few empty tankards and handbills on a table. Sitting in a window seat, she read her brother's letter first.

Dear sisters,

I write to you hoping the distance between us will soon be shorter and you will be on your way north with a colonial detachment. I have it on good authority that Chatham will no longer be safe once General Washington removes to other parts. I cannot hazard you remaining there, though the journey before you is no small endeavor. I feel you need to be nearer us here in New York.

It was our parents' wish for us to be reunited, so we will see it done as safely as we can. Furthermore, Aaron is in agreement and may well join us in time.

Don't concern yourself with the details. I am arranging matters, and all that needs doing on your end is packing. And praying. Till we meet again.

Your loving brother,
Jon

"Miss Bohannon." The beloved voice brought her head up.

Rhys stood in the doorway, his return to formality a douse of cold water on her fiery feelings. Propriety, however, must be maintained, at least outside a linen closet.

He removed his cocked hat and gestured toward the open tavern door. "Walk out with me."

She went ahead of him as if responding to an order. "I didn't expect to see you in town, General Harlow."

"I had a letter to post to Virginia."

To his family there? She swallowed down her questions as they stepped off the porch together.

"I also have something to discuss with you based on a conversation I had with General Washington yesterday."

He sounded so grave she stopped walking. "Then by all means tell me here and now."

He met her eyes yet still managed to keep watch on all surrounding them. "At the behest of your brother in New York, you and your sister are to travel with the army."

She nodded and took out Jon's letter. "My brother has posted the same right here."

"You've been assigned a guard to the Hudson Highlands." His half smile was wry. "A four-hundred-man rifle corps at your beck and call."

"Fancy that, when all I need is one." Her amusement matched her pleasure. They weren't facing a looming separation after all. But he clearly wasn't as pleased as she.

"I wish it were that simple—and safe."

"Meaning you believe this entirely too dangerous."

"It's no secret what I think."

"There are rumors flying around Chatham that the British mean to make an example of Chatham's treasonous loyalties and reduce the village to ashes once you Continentals decamp. I'd rather accompany you and your riflemen."

He looked away from her to the alert sentries on the bridge, his expression grim. "Be that as it may, I've been through New York's neutral ground a time or two. It's lawless. Filled with Loyalist and Patriot raiders who terrorize local residents. The worst of it being something could happen to you and I would never forgive myself."

She fastened her eyes on the linen fringe of his shirt and tried not to think of the scars beneath. She'd not considered herself dying. Only him. Would she and Coralie become targets, moving with the army? Her chest was so tight she forgot she'd pocketed Lieutenant Gibbs's letter.

Still, she said firmly, "I'd rather be with you than away from you, hard as it is, dangerous though it may be."

The look in his eyes was anything but encouraging. "Start packing, then, as we're to leave with only twenty-four hours' notice."

★ ★ ★ ★ ★

Rhys walked her home, the turn of events silencing them, perhaps even building another wall between them. Their linen closet kiss seemed like it never was. She stopped at the front door without asking him to stay on for supper or even a drink. There was simply no time. Their leaving was imminent. With a terse goodbye he turned away, and she retreated to the parlor to read the remaining letter.

The contents were quite bland, with Lieutenant Gibbs complaining of the boredom of army life and the many Hessian soldiers at Fort Knyphausen, which she knew was located along the Hudson River in Manhattan, New York. At least she knew his whereabouts, an uncomfortably close twenty-five miles. She still lamented the capture of the former Fort Washington last fall. A great many Continentals had been taken prisoner and held on prison ships and in warehouses and other makeshift prisons in the area, all of them dire. But the floating hulk HMS *Jersey* was surely the worst, further depleting Washington's troops.

She lit a candle, holding the letter over the flame to see if Lieutenant Gibbs had used any sympathetic stain like Coralie had. But it simply seemed a benign, terribly unromantic post and nothing more. Coralie wouldn't miss it if she threw it away, but, conscience guiding her, Mae lay it on the hall table where her sister would see it once she was home from Morristown.

Restless, she wished James were here, wanting to share the news they were leaving soon. Or did he already know?

She went upstairs to her bedchamber to consider what needed packing and what would be left behind. What possessions from her six and twenty years would she choose?

Leaving Chatham suddenly seemed the most significant hurdle of her life.

twenty-one

The Army as usual is without pay; and a great part of the Soldiery without shirts; and though the patience of them is equally thread-bare, the States seem perfectly indifferent to their cries.

George Washington

Soon the Chatham house was turned upside down as their coming journey loomed large. The village seemed to shrink to pin-sized proportions as New York's wilderness opened up to them. Before returning Coralie to Chatham, James had informed her that she and Mae were to march with the army.

"How interesting we're to be on the army's coattails once they move—the esteemed Rifle Corps, anyway." Coralie's mocking smile held mirth. "A rather ironic turn of events, given I'm being escorted by the Americans to wed a British officer."

"About which they know nothing." Mae found it less amusing. "We wouldn't be going at all except at the behest of Jon."

"I'm sure in time Eben would have sent for me," Coralie said in his defense. "What are we to do once we reach New York? In my excitement I can't recall all that James told me."

"We're to go to Fort Montgomery first and reunite with Jon. His farm isn't far from there. Only a couple of miles distant."

156

"Fortuitous, that."

"For now," Mae said, folding a favorite apron, "we pack, hope, and pray."

"All I care is that my wedding dress is in my trunk."

"We're allotted two trunks if the baggage wagon has room. As for me, I'll take one trunk and rely on saddlebags. We'll both be on horseback, remember."

"I already envision being sore. You're a far better rider. Perhaps I should rely on the wagon instead." Coralie sighed. "How long will it take us to reach the Hudson Highlands?"

"I didn't ask." Mae bent to retrieve a dropped stocking and garter. "I suspect light infantry like General Harlow's moves fairly quickly, even a few hundred men. We don't want to slow them."

"I hope we're not mistaken for camp followers." Coralie shuddered.

"Pray that we're half as hardy." Mae checked her sewing kit to make sure she'd packed the lovely pincushion she'd suspected was from Lucy. "They provide a valuable service no matter what they're called or thought of."

"Doxies, Eben says, shouting and cursing with sluttish shrills—"

"Coralie, please!" Mae chastised sharply. Did she believe these women were prostitutes?

"They even loot the fallen after battle, thieving their personal belongings and then wearing their coats."

"Some, perhaps. But I feel the best of those who follow the army are indispensable and quite brave. Some risk coming into the line of fire, even taking their soldiers empty canteens and refilling them with water during the hottest parts of engagements."

Coralie rolled her eyes. "I shan't be doing any of that as an officer's wife."

So far Coralie hadn't mentioned Lieutenant Gibbs's latest letter, the one Mae had left on the hall table. She played along, asking, "Has he told you where he's stationed? You'll need to know if you're to surprise him with your sudden arrival in New York."

"At a captured fort along the Hudson River north of New York City," she replied. "I plan to post a letter to him right before we depart."

Mae listened absently as she sorted through her petticoats. Suddenly the redcoated officer was the furthest thing from her thoughts. Should she give her extra garments to Lucy?

"Do you have any regrets about leaving Jersey?" Coralie asked quietly.

"I worry about leaving Hanna at such a time."

"Why? Hanna has family from Morristown to Pequannock to help her." Coralie sat down on the bed's edge, brow furrowed. "I wonder what officers' wives do in the same condition."

Mae looked up from packing. "Once wed you may soon find out."

Her eyes widened. "Oh my stars and garters, imagine being far from home, thick as a brick, and not a midwife to be had in the middle of the wilderness!"

Mae smiled at her colorful phrasing. "Marrying often begets children, no matter where you happen to be."

"I try not to think of such . . . complexities." Coralie's gaze narrowed. "You've seen little of General Harlow of late, have you? I suppose he's extraordinarily occupied with preparations to decamp."

Mae chafed at the triumph in her sister's tone. "Given he has charge of so many men, I don't doubt it."

"Or has he finally realized you're far above his station?"

"I'm hardly the duchess of Chatham, Coralie." She skewered her sister with a glance. "Nor is the general a lowly lieutenant."

Coralie frowned and bristled all at once. "Venom doesn't become you, Mae."

"I've made little fuss over your alliance with Lieutenant Gibbs. I expect you to respect mine."

For a few moments silence reigned before Coralie said, "Alliance? Lately I wonder. Eben's last letter was rather terse. He hasn't been writing as often as he used to. I hope nothing has happened to him and he's not fallen ill. How I wish his family hadn't left Chatham for the city and I could keep better informed about him."

Below, the foyer clock resounded five times. Mae wished Rhys would happen by—or even James. She had so many questions ahead of their setting out. And she couldn't push down the notion that Rhys might be more right than Jon and staying in Chatham would be wiser.

Finished with her trunks, Mae moved on to her saddlebags. "What books shall we bring?"

"Books? As if we'll have time for reading on the trail?"

"Once we get there we shall. I want to bring Father's Bible. Also, *Poems by Mrs. Robinson* and the new novel Hanna and Aaron gave me for Christmas I've not had time for."

"*Travels for the Heart* by Pratt?"

"That, and *A Voyage Towards the South Pole* by Captain James Cook."

Did Rhys have these volumes? Mae meant them more for him, an addition to their future library. Thoughts of his newly built Virginia house, a firelit hearth, and two Windsor chairs on a snowy winter's night warmed her even now. Though they would be traveling the wrong direction, she held on to hope that the Shenandoah Valley was where they'd end up eventually.

twenty-two

To cash paid for saddlery, a letter case, maps, glasses, etc etc etc. for the use of my Command: pound symbol here 29, 13 shillings and sixpence. . . . To Mrs Washington's travelling expenses in coming to and returning from my winter quarters, the money to defray that taken from my private purse: pound symbol 1064, one shilling.

George Washington's expense claims to Congress

On the next Sabbath in Morristown, Rhys attended church. First Presbyterian's white spire, seen for miles, impaled a cloudless spring sky. General Washington entered first surrounded by his Life Guards, the pews filling fast. Rhys followed with Bohannon, his gaze immediately landing on Mae. She sat with her sister and an elderly woman. Her aunt?

"Careful lest Aunt Verity invite you to Sunday dinner," Bohannon murmured as they took the pew behind them.

"Our last civilized meal," Rhys replied. "I'm tempted."

But the only temptation for now was Mae, and if he had to weather Aunt Verity he'd be glad to do it. He'd been so entrenched in preparations to decamp he'd not had a moment to spare her. When she turned her head to acknowledge him, she smiled, easing his mind somewhat.

Bohannon had brought both sisters and their baggage and horses to Morristown day before yesterday. Tomorrow they would march. There was now no doubt they were leaving, nor any use praying they'd stay behind. Though Mae had no finer guard than the Rifle Corps, he still had grave concerns about her going, and that included her sister. Coralie was as fractious as Mae was amiable. He wanted no trouble on the trail. The enemy without was concerning enough, but an enemy within . . .

The service began, and the pastor's sermon about Abraham going into the wilderness was not far from the mark. Washington appeared thoughtful, his attention unswerving despite two hours passing. A special prayer was said for the safety and protection of the Rifle Corps, given their destination. When the final hymn was sung, all filed outside into the April sun, where Bohannon's prediction materialized as Aunt Verity descended like a hawk, fixing Rhys with a canny eye.

"General Harlow, I presume? You must join us for Sabbath dinner."

"Gladly," Rhys replied, replacing his hat as Mae came to stand beside him.

"My housekeeper has prepared ample dishes—a sort of farewell celebration. 'Tis not every day we have two fine officers joining us." She smiled up at her nephew, who dutifully leaned over and kissed her wrinkled cheek before offering her his arm, Coralie on his other side.

Mae lay a gloved hand on Rhys's extended forearm as they made their way down the congested street and slowed her steps so they were well behind her family. "Is all in order to leave on the morrow?"

"We depart at dawn." One look at her entreating expression and he remembered Bohannon's words. *Details*. Women wanted details. "You'll ride at the center of the column, such as it is. My men don't march in formation as do regulars and militia. There'll be the customary baggage train to slow us, but with fair weather, no breakdowns, and no enemy activity, we should arrive in a week or so."

The longest week or so of his life. She'd be closely guarded, and he'd not rest till she was safely in Colonel Bohannon's hands.

"A few days' march through the wilderness is doable if difficult," she said serenely. "As I've already mentioned, I'd rather be with you than without you, come what may."

Sabbath dinner proved a formidable feast. Rhys navigated Mae's aunt's probing questions with as much tact as he could muster while consuming large amounts of roast beef and all the early vegetables her garden could provide, as well as a great deal of wheaten bread and gravy.

"So, my dear nephew, promise you'll send word that my nieces have arrived safely? I want to hear all about Jon and his family too."

"I promise," Bohannon said, forking another bite of beef. "I'd feel bad about leaving you if Aaron and Hanna weren't near at hand. They asked me to relay their hope you'll visit them soon."

"If the village isn't rubble and ashes, you mean." She smirked. "Otherwise a visit to Chatham might suit, though neither village shall be the same once the entire army is gone. I won't know quite what to do with myself."

Thankfully the talk turned to crops, a local fair, the Sabbath sermon, and the birth of Morristown's triplets before circling back around to New York.

"Well, I must say, I'm confident that Maebel is in good hands, General Harlow." Aunt Verity's smile faded as she looked to Coralie with noticeable concern. "I wish I could say the same for my youngest niece and Lieutenant Gibbs."

A hush fell over the room. Rhys sensed Mae's unease even as Coralie looked abashed. What was afoot? At the opposite end of the table, Bohannon cleared his throat and set down his knife and fork.

"Lieutenant Eben Gibbs?" he asked, attention on Coralie. "I'm not sure what happened to him since he left Chatham, though I sense you do."

"We exchange letters on occasion," Coralie said, eyes down as she dabbed at her lips with her napkin. "Though his last letter was rather . . . lacking."

"Like the man himself," Bohannon muttered.

"James!" Coralie stared at him in reproach. "I'll not have you talk that way about an officer—"

"In the British army?"

Rhys sensed he'd stepped into a wasps' nest. Mae looked as distressed as Coralie.

"What are his intentions?" Bohannon persisted.

When Coralie failed to answer, Aunt Verity said, "Last I heard, he considers the war all but won. She hasn't shared more than that."

Another strained pause brought the housekeeper round with a berry pie, though all seemed to have lost their appetite. Dessert left on the table, the woman hurried out, surely sensing the ill feeling in the room. Mae took up a knife as if nothing was amiss and began to cut wedges as Bohannon and Coralie continued their wrangling.

"You know how Father felt about Eben Gibbs." Bohannon's intensity turned his features taut. "I refuse to call him lieutenant because unlike American officers who earn their rank through service and merit, British officers simply purchase theirs."

Coralie's high color reminded Rhys of her scarlet gown at the ball. Standing so abruptly she almost toppled her chair, she threw down her napkin and then fled the room. All eyes returned to Mae, who handed dessert around the table. Such serenity would serve her well in the wilds.

Or so he hoped.

★ ★ ★ ★ ★

Mae got little rest that night. Dismayed and fearing she'd be half asleep in the saddle the first day of the journey, she lay wide-eyed, wondering what to tell Rhys. *If* she should tell him. She'd almost convinced herself that Coralie and Eben Gibbs's correspondence didn't matter. But his last, baffling letter left her wondering once again if he'd been using her sister for information—intelligence— even of the most innocuous kind. How she wished Coralie would stay behind. What if she arrived in New York and found that the lieutenant didn't even want her?

The next morning Aunt Verity managed a tearful goodbye as James hefted their belongings to the wagon Coralie would ride in, her horse tethered behind. Mae mounted Orion as Morristown became a hive of riflemen and horses and wagons. Most of the Rifle Corps were on foot save the officers, Rhys leading on his chestnut gelding, Copper.

As Rhys said, she was at the center, two officers' wives ahead of her and Coralie. They'd been hastily introduced to Catherine Kersey and Alice Wentz, who were as unalike in physical appearance as they seemed in temperament. Catherine was as tall and spare as Coralie while Alice, shorter and plump, resembled Mae. From Boston, they seemed genteel, their husbands among General Washington's topmost officers leaving Morristown for Fort Montgomery.

Too excited to be tired, Mae ran a gloved hand down Orion's glossy neck as he tossed his head and shifted his weight from side to side, clearly wanting to move. At Rhys's command they finally began. All around her ranged riflemen, the bane of the British, their weapons ready.

These Rifle Corps were no strangers to the wilderness. All the accoutrements of war hung about them, down to the hatchets and knives at their waists, and they moved with the silence and stealth of Indians, though the wagons and followers raised a frightful din. Most men wore the shirts she and the Liberty Ladies had sewn, which were dyed with walnut hulls and chamomile leaves to a warm brown or a pale green like the woods themselves.

As the miles unfolded, towns and fields and pasture gave way to forests, the road shrinking to a skunk's stripe with barely enough room for the wagons to pass. Beneath her hat, Mae squinted as the sun burned down, turning her head and her riding habit itchy and damp. This was no leisurely jaunt from Chatham to Morristown. Every mile seemed to present a new challenge, and Coralie, already weary, exchanged her wagon seat for the saddle till Rhys halted for a respite.

Self-conscious among so many men, Mae all but ran for the cover of the woods to relieve herself, Coralie on her heels. Here there was no chamber pot or prim necessary at the back of the kitchen garden. Thick-waisted chestnuts and oaks and a screen of mountain laurel with blooms as big as dinner plates allowed them a moment of privacy instead.

They emerged from the brush batting at flies and yanking their petticoats free of briars. For a moment, Mae just stood and tried to get her bearings. A lack of breakfast and the heat sent her senses swimming.

"That wagon seat is hard as iron—much like General Harlow and his riflemen." Coralie dabbed her shining brow with a handkerchief. "We've only just begun, but it seems he means to kill us long before we see Jon—"

Mae silenced her with a glance. "If we're weak and haven't been beyond Morris County, that's hardly the general's concern. He cautioned me against coming in the first place."

"Why didn't you warn me, then?" Arms akimbo, Coralie set her jaw, which, Mae thought, might serve her better than limping along. "I might have stayed behind."

"Warn you? You seemed wholly set on Lieutenant Gibbs and past all reason." Fatigue sharpened Mae's temper. "What we've traversed so far is nothing compared to what's coming. James has warned of mountains that make the Watchung we've known all our lives mere anthills. Keep in mind that we're moving with an elite guard, arguably the most intrepid of men."

"Intrepid—or heartless?"

Mae refused to blame Rhys. If anyone, Jon was at fault. "Clearly we haven't the makings of a soldier, even a sunshine one, as Paine said."

"Sixty or seventy miles of torment and we've just begun." Coralie thrust her handkerchief into her pocket. "What did we bring to eat?"

"There's hard cheese, bread, and boiled eggs in my saddlebags."

"We shan't be resorting to the army's hardtack and parched corn, I hope."

"What we most need is water—and replenishing what we've drunk so far."

"What I'd give for a hot cup of tea in the quiet of our own parlor." Coralie smoothed her wrinkled skirts. "I must speak with James."

To complain? Or apologize for her part in their Sabbath quarrel? Mae prayed it was the latter.

They parted, and Mae passed groups of riflemen eating and drinking, some even napping, making her wonder how long their break was to be. Taking a seat beneath a sycamore tree near Orion, she rued the woolen blanket beneath her, a pretty trifle a true frontierswoman wouldn't require. Did she read amusement in Rhys's eyes when he approached? Or was it only her own insecurities?

"Miss Bohannon."

Such formalities frustrated her too. She held her temper by a thread as she removed her hat to ease her itching head. "Good day to you, sir."

He crouched down beside her and offered her something long and spiked. What on earth?

"Ginseng. The root of life. Chew it and you'll revive."

She took it reluctantly from his outstretched hand, remembering a ginseng jar in the apothecary. "So you sense me wilting from a distance?"

"I'm always aware of you, Mae, even when I have to be General Harlow."

"So you've not forgotten my forename after all." It felt good

166

to smile and tease him, to feel their tie was still intact. She took a tentative bite, rolling the root between her back teeth. To her surprise the bitterness mellowed to a mild herbal flavor.

"Need any for your sister?"

"Nay." She pulled the ginseng from her mouth and examined it before tasting it again. "Coralie's not one to sit on the ground and chew roots."

He chuckled then turned serious. "What's this about her tie to a redcoat?"

She spat out the root, feeling the most unladylike of her life. "I don't know where to begin."

"Later, then." He stood abruptly and left her side as they prepared to resume the journey.

★ ★ ★ ★ ★

That night they made camp in a wildflower meadow. A guard was posted, reminding Mae they'd entered contested territory. British patrols might be about, even spies, or marauders and their ilk. In the wagon bed, she and Coralie slept atop a mattress thin enough to be rolled up and stored away efficiently by day. Flat on their backs, they found rest for their sore bodies.

"Look how bright the North Star is." Mae's finger seemed to touch the clear sky as she pointed to various constellations. "Without the lights of town, I mean."

"Forget the stars," Coralie replied. "I hear wolves howling."

"At a distance." Mae had hoped to distract her. "We're surrounded by riflemen, so be easy."

"What do you make of the officers' wives?" Coralie whispered.

"I've hardly spoken with them yet."

"The one—Catherine Kersey—seems to regard us as no better than slatterns. I overheard her saying that unmarried women shouldn't travel with the army."

"Well, our being here *is* unusual. She must not know Jon arranged it."

167

"Who would have thought these city-bred wives would feel superior? They even have tents to sleep in with their husbands."

"James said we'll have a tent too if it rains."

"James also said 1777 is the year with three gallows in it."

"Meaning the sevens are gallows?"

"Rather ominous, if you ask me." Coralie's exasperated sigh hung over them like a dark cloud. "You know what the papers are printing, don't you? A great cry has gone up among Loyalists and Tories calling for American rebels to be hung."

"Rebels who are right this minute defending you."

Coralie yawned, too exhausted to continue her tirade, or so Mae hoped. "You are Patriot to the core, Sister."

She said nothing in reply, relieved when Coralie turned over. Soon her sister's even breathing indicated sleep. Mae continued to look at the stars, wondering if Rhys did the same. She wasn't sure where he bedded down, nor James, though like he'd said, he was well aware of her. Let that be her comfort.

The camp was quiet as a tomb despite their number, only an occasional snore or cough. Even the howling wolves grew more distant. She longed for a little music to sweeten the lostness she felt and recalled Rhys's earlier words.

"Will you play your fiddle on the trail?" she'd asked.

"Only if I want to invite the British and Indians to dance," he'd said.

A horrid thought. Homesickness carved a well-deep hole inside her, making her realize she'd never experienced this empty, melancholy feeling before. Yet it wasn't Chatham she wanted but a Virginia house she'd never seen and the man who'd built it. Now well beyond Jersey, she was ready to move past girlhood and embrace a different sort of life. And somehow this challenging journey seemed a gauntlet to get there.

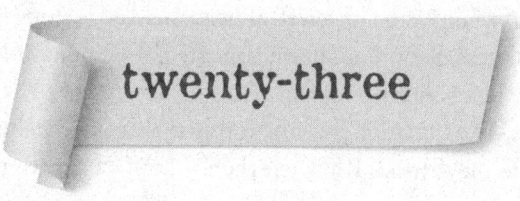

twenty-three

Stand your ground; don't fire unless fired upon, but if they mean to have a war, let it begin here.

Captain John Parker

On the third day, twenty-eight miles into the journey, the calendar seemed to turn back to winter and the heavens opened, unleashing a cold, drenching rain. Rhys ordered the party down an open, barren hill to lower ground where bushes and small trees offered some shelter. Egg-size hail rattled down in a ferocious wind, sending Copper into a frantic spin.

Rhys leaned low in the saddle, his firm commands lost in the barrage of rough weather. As he grappled for control, his gaze went wide and took in Mae, lost in her own battle with Orion, who had all but trampled two men in a bolt for the trees. At the sight of her frantic features, all his usual precautions flew from his head. Sliding to the muddy ground, reins fisted, Rhys tugged a panicked Copper in the same direction, his gaze never leaving Mae as the orderly army turned chaotic.

Orion half unseated Mae as he reared and shrilly screamed his fear. She gripped the saddle horn as her hat took wing, and its pale green veil caught in a branch. He caught her before she hit the ground and helped her beneath a big oak. A gash glowered on her cheek as she looked up at him, water dripping from her hairline and the tip of her nose.

He forgot his own soaked state as she dug for her handkerchief. Taking it from her, he removed the blood from her cheek as gently as he could while Orion lowered his head, his ears no longer pinned back in distress. Soon Bohannon appeared, took hold of his reins, and spoke in a soothing voice.

As quickly as it came the storm rolled away, hail pebbling the mud where they stood. Rhys felt the icy lumps beneath the soles of his boots.

"Thank heavens it wasn't the British and their Indian allies," Mae said, taking back the stained handkerchief. "I've never seen Orion so startled. But where's Coralie?"

"Underneath the wagon." Bohannon gestured toward the edge of the trees where it rested, their sister huddled there.

Her gaze returned to Rhys. "Are you all right? Your horse?"

"Copper bolted but he'll return." He took a few steps back and tugged her hat and veil free of the branches. "I'm all right, but I can't say the same about this."

"Thank you, but it's rather old and bedraggled, anyway." She wrung it free of water before replacing it atop her thoroughly wet head. "My late mother's, in fact."

He grew quiet, savoring the relief of the moment. "You're the only woman I've ever met who looks just as beautiful drenched as dry."

She smiled, but she was clearly shaken. Leaving Chatham had taken a toll. She wasn't made for this sort of roughness, though she was making the best of it. Her sister, on the other hand, had gotten into some sort of scrape with the officers' wives earlier, though he didn't know the details nor want to.

"We're nearly halfway there." Halfway stretched the truth, but he wanted to see the light return to her eyes.

"Miles are of little consequence to me. I'd go to Canada and

LAURA FRANTZ

back for you, General Harlow." With that, she moved past him to see to her sister.

★ ★ ★ ★ ★

The evening turned so chilly that fires were lit to dry them all out. Mae stretched her hands toward the feeble flames even as insects bedeviled her through the greenwood's smoke. A reminder of all the seasoned oak and hickory in their woodshed that burned brilliantly and hotly.

Coralie sat beside her, coughing amid the smoke. "I tell you, if the high-and-mighty Mrs. Kersey refers to us as camp followers again, I'm going to—"

"*Shush*," Mae replied under her breath. "What does it matter when we know we're not?"

"It still stings."

"Your pride suffers, you mean."

"And yours doesn't?"

Mae took a sip of tepid tea and swallowed down an answer. They'd run out of the victuals they'd brought, and her stomach rumbled for more than the soldierly ration of jerked meat and dried corn. Fort Montgomery's fare might not be much better, but Jon's wife was a seasoned cook, their bountiful gardens mentioned in letters. Mae pinned her hungry thoughts on that as Coralie stared into her cup with a wince.

"What is this strange root called again?"

"Ginseng," Mae told her. "Aaron keeps a supply of it at the apothecary, remember. Good for reviving the body."

"I don't feel revived. I feel enraged." Coralie looked around at the hunkered-down camp. "You would think we ladies, being so outnumbered, would band together and form some sort of bond."

"Why? We'll probably never see them again after this. Think of all that awaits you instead."

Coralie tossed her tea into the damp grass. "I can't think of the future when the present is so frightful."

171

"Frightful because we've spent so much of our lives living comfortably that anything else is a trial and temptation for us?" Mae pushed back a loose strand of hair. "So far it's been a bit of heat and dirt and discomfort. Thankfully the hailstorm has passed, which was the worst of it."

"I beg to differ. Did you see that serpent one of the riflemen killed? Two feet long and rattling like a box of bones. A timber rattlesnake, he called it."

"James told me to beware when using the woods as a necessary." Mae shuddered, feeling the pressing need to perform that now-frightening task once again. "We're moving into the mountains and out of the foothills. Even the air seems different."

"Harder to breathe, you mean. My chest *hurts*." Coralie looked as worn as Mae felt. "I wonder if we'll live to see Jon and Joanna and their children. Since we've not yet met them all, they're a muddle in my mind."

"They're easy as the alphabet to recall," Mae said with forced mirth. "Oldest to youngest, there's Alexander, Bennett, Cassandra, Dierdre, and Euphemie. Jon has plans to finish with Z."

"Six and twenty?" This elicited a rare smile from Coralie. "He'll have to build a fort, not a farmhouse! And we mustn't forget his long-suffering wife who's survived the ordeal five times now."

"Remember the Vassal family of New York has one and twenty children and the Fishers in Massachusetts have the same."

"'Twould be just like Jon to try and best them." Coralie waved away a mosquito. "Just so you know, I apologized to James for my outburst back in Morristown."

Had she? "I'm glad. Did you share your plans?"

"Not yet." Coralie looked at the ground. "Jon and James are a pair in their dislike of Eben. Neither will be pleased at my becoming Mrs. Gibbs."

"Be that as it may," Mae reassured her, "we want the best for you, and if you feel marrying him is what you want, then who are we to naysay the match?"

Oddly, her gracious words seemed only to nettle Coralie. Standing, she handed Mae her empty cup. "I'm too weary to talk about this anymore tonight."

Mae watched her return to the wagon at the edge of the woods. James took her place, sitting down on the same hollow log. He tossed a handful of moss and sticks into the struggling fire as if to coax it to life. Mae looked down at her muddy hem, the rock beneath her as uncomfortable as the saddle. She'd misplaced her woolen blanket. She regarded James through the smoke as he took out his pipe, trying to gauge his current temper.

"How fares you, Sister?"

"I'm well." *If I could just bathe . . . relax in an upholstered chair . . . have a proper cup of tea.* Suddenly even talking seemed to require effort. "And you?"

"Tolerable." He drew on his pipestem a considerable length of time, so like their father that Mae's eyes watered. "You're holding up well under the circumstances. Never a cross word. I can't say the same about our sister."

Had there been another spat she didn't know about with the officers' wives? "Coralie has always been the tetchy one."

"You've been her mainstay on this journey, which is no easy task. Thankfully we're nearing Fort Montgomery."

"We've come safely through New York's disputed territory so far."

"Four hundred or so rifles keep things quiet. I won't rest till you're within fort walls, though I'll not lie to you. All of New York is something of a powder keg."

And she'd thought them somewhat safe. "I'd rather hear the truth than lies or empty assurances."

"If there's any trouble, take cover as best you can." He stopped smoking and knocked the dottle into the fire. "The threat of ambush is at every turn."

twenty-four

I was more dead than alive, though not so much on account of our own danger, as for that which enveloped my husband.

Baroness Riedesel

They were pushing harder now despite the challenging terrain. The very air seemed to bristle with tension. Stops were briefer, talk terse. To anchor herself amid the rising heat and swirl of insects, the plunging valleys and pulse-pounding climbs, Mae kept her gaze on Rhys. He frequently rode at the head of the column only to circle back as rear guard. Though he claimed to be aware of her, how could he be? His vigilance seemed obsessively single-minded, so dedicated to the slightest aberration in his surroundings that even one look at her might spell ruin.

Her own mouth was slightly agape as New York's wonders unfolded around them. Jersey seemed rather tame with its subdued pastures and farms and wooded foothills. New York was raw, shocking wilderness, another world entirely, every mile imprinted in her head and heart in fresh ways.

On the next Sabbath, they halted in a forested area by a small river that bled into the more formidable Hudson in the Highlands region they sought. A chaplain gave a timely message that spurred them on to look ahead—not backward like the fear-ridden, faithless Israelites—with God as their guide. Mae sat with Rhys and listened apart from the rest, the rush of the water an unceasing song.

"Now seems the time to tell me about your sister and this British officer," he said quietly when the sermon ended, turning his cocked hat in his hands.

She paused, not wanting to worry him. "She's known Eben Gibbs since childhood, though his Loyalist family left Chatham for New York City some time ago. They exchange letters and plan to marry, but I wonder if that will ever happen."

"Because of the war?"

"Because Eben is rather like a weather vane, shifting this way or that, never able to stay the course with much of anything. I do wonder what my sister sees in him." She took a breath. "How far is Fort Washing—Knyphausen?"

"The captured British garrison? Fifty miles or so of hard marching from Fort Montgomery."

"I ask because Lieutenant Gibbs is there—or was."

"Hard to conduct any sort of courtship across enemy lines."

He said nothing more as one of his riflemen called him away to another matter. She watched him go, thinking how he carried the weight of the entire camp yet his shoulders stayed square, his outlook unwavering.

After supper, James sought her out. "Look for a black bear lying down and you'll have Bear Mountain," he said. "Fort Montgomery is below it. Fort Clinton is a bit to the south of Montgomery. Interestingly enough they're commanded by brothers. General George Clinton and General James Clinton."

"Rather confusing," Mae mused. "Isn't there a British officer named Sir Henry Clinton?"

"Indeed." James grimaced. "*That* redcoat is in New York City, waiting to join forces with General Burgoyne and capture the Hudson River once he and his men push south from Canada."

"Are we almost to the twin forts, then?"

"A few miles more, aye."

Neither she nor Coralie wanted to meet Jon disheveled and dirty, so a well-armed James escorted them downriver where they could bathe in privacy.

"I suppose our arriving alive is Jon's foremost concern," Coralie jested, eyes on the bushes and trees nearest the riverbank. "But at least I'll die clean if we don't reach him."

Mae gasped as she stepped into the rushing current, soap in hand. In a quarter of an hour they'd both scoured themselves head to foot, their long hair tangled about their hips. Quickly they brushed each other's hair into submission after changing into clean garments. And Mae wondered as she took in the wilderness around them, how one could feel gloriously alive yet terrified.

Night was stealing in, only slightly less sultry than day. They returned to camp only to find their drinking water in need of replenishing. Mae went back to the river gladly, for it was much cooler there. She knelt to fill her pail, riflemen milling about with their weapons. When she stood and turned around, she came face-to-face with Lucy Hawkes. Mae hadn't spoken to her since the march began in Morristown. Lucy kept to the rear of the column like most of the women and children and animals.

"Miss Bohannon." She held out a hand, something purple atop her palm.

Candied violets? How on earth did she come by them?

"Please, call me Mae." Overlooking the woman's soiled hands, Mae set down her water pail to take her offering. "You're so kind, Lucy."

"The Jersey woods were bursting with violets. I came by some sugar and made these before we left."

Mae ate one, a delicious reminder of home. "I've yet to thank you properly for your pincushion, the prettiest I've ever seen."

Lucy looked pleased, her sunburned, befreckled face the color of her hair. Had she no hat? Only a plain linen cap covered her disheveled head. "I made it with you in mind."

"I was in need of one. I've brought it with me in my sewing kit."
Mae ate another sweet, saving the rest for Coralie. "You're not just
a seamstress but an artist."

"My mother put me to shame. She sewed for a fancy Boston
woman before they both died of the pox."

"I'm terribly sorry. Were you just a girl?"

A stoic nod. "After that, Pa and I moved to Virginia to be nearer
kin. That's how I met and married Isham, who's General Harlow's
drummer. We don't have our own farm yet but will once we win
this war."

Mae looked around for Lucy's little mongrel dog, though she
was more interested in Isham, whom she'd not seen since that
snowy night he and Lucy visited the smokehouse. "Where's Petey?"

"He hardly leaves Isham's side, but that might change once we
reach Fort Montgomery." She reached for Mae's pail and began
carrying it back to the wagon where Coralie waited.

"You don't have to do that." Embarrassed, Mae followed, but
Lucy was well ahead of her, toting the full pail without spilling
a drop.

Thanking her, Mae watched her hurry off as if she was well
aware of Coralie's displeasure.

"Why are you keeping company with that tramp?" Coralie
asked when Lucy was out of earshot.

Mae handed her the remaining violets before swallowing a long
drink of water, hoping it would cool both her temper and her
thirst. "*That* tramp happens to be the wife of General Harlow's
drummer. She made that lovely pincushion you've admired many
a time. And she kindly carried our water."

Coralie ate the candied violets with little enthusiasm. "Why
would she?"

"I did her a kindness last winter." What would her sister's reaction be if she knew she'd given Lucy their mother's shawl? "She's
not forgotten."

"Have a care, Mae." Coralie frowned. "Your association with

her will simply lead the officers' wives to believe we aren't any better."

"We are no better." Mae took another long drink. "If you and Mrs. Kersey and Mrs. Wentz would stop turning up your noses, much can be admired in Lucy Hawkes."

With a final grumble, Coralie began preparing their bedding in the wagon while Mae set the water pail beneath it. Saying nothing to her sister about her intent, she threaded her way through the camp, searching for Rhys. Tents began sprouting like mushrooms among the camp followers to keep insects at bay, though Rhys and the majority of his riflemen slept in the open once all had settled for the night.

As the moon rose and the camp quieted, she finally found him. He stood beneath a pine tree. Was he on watch? At her approach he turned round and she saluted. His amused smile was a startling white in the dusk. James, usually near at hand, was missing. Did Rhys crave a moment of privacy, if such could be had?

"General Harlow."

"Miss Bohannon."

Greetings exchanged, she ached for him to take her in his arms, their first and last kiss never far from her thoughts. She moved nearer the pine, hoping it sheltered them from any gossip. What would the officers' wives say about this tryst? Coralie?

"Have you need of anything?" he asked quietly.

"You." The honest answer left her fisting her hands in her skirts to avoid touching him.

"Likewise," he replied, crossing his arms as if his intent was the same.

"James said we're almost to the Hudson River. I've been looking for Bear Mountain."

"Tomorrow should see us there, barring any calamities."

She stemmed a sigh. Every mile was fraught. Her gaze roamed his deeply tanned features, so dark against his fringed linen shirt. "You never seem to tire."

"I hide it well. Most nights I sleep with one eye open."

"Fort Montgomery will be a refuge for us all."

"It will be, though I'm in no hurry to see you leave for your brother's farm."

Because it was less safe? Or because he'd miss her? She leaned down and picked up a small pine cone. The earthy fragrance of the forest was something she'd miss. "You must come visit."

"Come courting, you mean?"

"Will there be time?"

"Sabbaths should be free, though once word spreads that the belle of Chatham has arrived, I'll be hard-pressed to stand my ground as you'll have so many suitors."

"You flatter me."

"Nay." He opened a flask and took a drink. "You don't know men."

She dropped the pine cone. "Nor do I want to, just you."

He sat down on a rock outcropping, rifle in one hand while he reached for her with the other. She took a place beside him, near enough to hear the river's rush, the silvery water shining in the moonlight. His fingers felt rough as the bark of white oak. Why hadn't she saved some candied violets for him?

Together they searched the gloom, where even the slightest breeze seemed a menace as it might mimic or hide a footfall. The enemy was out there somewhere, capable of striking any second. The thought chilled her to the bone despite the sultry night.

"Tell me about the twin forts, Montgomery and Clinton," she said quietly.

"The garrisons are new, built last year to defend the lower Hudson. The British have their eye on every American fort along the river with the intent to take it and wrest control from us. Once they combine forces this will be a battleground."

"How long will you be at Fort Mongomery?"

"Orders could change in a heartbeat, though I imagine I'll remain in New York for some time, mayhap move north to the upper

Hudson and Ticonderoga. New York is vast, and we're only in the southern part."

"And Jon seems to think Chatham is more dangerous." Suddenly Jersey seemed infinitely safer.

"This is hardly the conversation we should be having at dusk." He lifted her hand and kissed her fingers. "You'll get little sleep."

She felt a start, realizing she'd been gone long enough that Coralie might come looking for her. "Then I bid you good night, sir." She curtsied, their return to formality, this painful show of restraint, becoming a sort of game between them.

"Good night, Miss Bohannon."

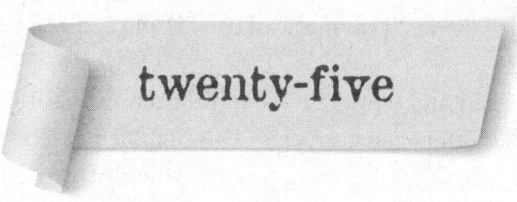

twenty-five

We must all hang together, or assuredly we shall all hang separately.

Benjamin Franklin

Fort Mongomery was perched high on a cliff overlooking the Hudson River, a plunge that made Mae's stomach drop even from a distance. The Rifle Corps and company approached from the west along a newly built road wide enough for artillery and wagons. All seemed to breathe a collective sigh of relief when the fort's main gates swung wide, rescuing them from woods that seemed increasingly hostile and dark.

Mae dismounted, leaving Orion to a fort farrier since the bay had thrown a shoe at the base of Bear Mountain. She took a moment to peer over one earth and timber wall to the river far below, relieved they'd arrived unscathed. For the moment, the garrison seemed more melee as several hundred riflemen swarmed the fourteen-acre fortification. Mae soon lost sight of Rhys but found Coralie in Jon's embrace.

Their eldest brother, aside from a few wrinkles she didn't remember, seemed much the same, both short and stout, his robust voice carrying. He released Coralie when he saw Mae, scooping her up into a bearish hug that seemed to erase all the years that had come between them. "You're here—safe—and I can finally give thanks."

"General Harlow and his men kept us from harm," she said, smiling. "And the Almighty, of course."

"We're clean but still hardly fit to be seen." Coralie smoothed her wrinkled skirts. "I cannot wait to sit down at a real table with real food."

Jon laughed and motioned them toward a two-storied timber building that resembled barracks. "Our humble quarters aren't as civilized as Chatham, but I can promise you plenty to eat."

★ ★ ★ ★ ★

That night they gathered in the officers' mess for supper. Coralie's dismay was evident as the two officers' wives and their husbands joined them. Had she thought they'd dine alone with Jon? To Mae's delight, Rhys sat across from her, with Fort Montgomery's commander, General James Clinton, at the head of the table. Tall and as physically imposing as Rhys, he wore a uniform of blue cloth with buff facings adorned with epaulets much like General Washington's. Mae wondered if his brother at Fort Clinton dressed the same.

Everyone sat and smiled through introductions before the meal was served by orderlies in the airless, candlelit room. Roast beef, vegetables, and hearty wheat bread as well as thick slices of Cheshire and Dutch cheeses filled pewter plates. The rigors of military life weren't discussed, as if there'd been an order forbidding it. Unsure of their surroundings and fort protocol, Mae kept quiet, listening to the steady hum of voices all around her, the officers' wives foremost.

Alice Wentz took out a fan and wafted it slowly, leaving Mae wishing she'd brought hers. Forts had few windows and fewer adornments.

"I don't mean to complain, but is New York always skillet-hot in spring?" Catherine Kersey asked as she dabbed her brow with a handkerchief. "I'm tempted to jump from the cliff top to the river below."

A rumble of amusement ensued from all but Coralie, who seemed steadfast in her vow to shun the wives' company and conversation. Eyes down, she continued eating, though her own skin shone from the heat.

"A sheer hundred-fifty-foot drop is not recommended even on the hottest of days." General Clinton took a long drink of Madeira, his own lip beaded. "There's a steep, narrow trail that weaves from the garrison's east sally port if you'd like to brave it and wade in the river."

"Come now, Catherine, perhaps a boat would be best," cajoled her husband.

"There are a number of bateaux, Durham boats, and canoes," Jon said with a glance at Mae. "But be advised, the water is deep with dangerous currents."

"Not to mention British patrols and their Indian allies," General Clinton added as dessert was served.

Mae breathed in the bitter aroma of strongly brewed coffee, glad when cream and sugar appeared. The sponge cake with violet jelly was delicious, returning her thoughts to Lucy's candied violets. She'd not seen her since.

"How soon will your sisters venture to your Highland Falls farm?" General Clinton asked Jon, who sat between Mae and Coralie.

"Tomorrow," Jon replied, looking to his sisters. "After you've had such a rigorous journey here, you'll be happy to know you've not far to go. The trail is downhill and into the valley, thankfully."

Coralie sent him a relieved smile.

"A fortuitous time to arrive." General Clinton leaned back in his chair, looking pleased. "All seems relatively calm at present."

Mae set down her fork. "We appreciate your hospitality, General, and the sacrifices and courage of everyone in this fort."

"You're most welcome, Miss Bohannon, but it is I who should thank you. Your presence here raises the spirits of countless men and reminds them of what they're fighting for—family, their very homes and lands. I hope you feel welcome here at Fort Montgomery however long you tarry."

★ ★ ★ ★ ★

Reveille awoke them. The drumming beat through the wooden walls and finally roused Coralie, who sat up atop her cot, rubbing her eyes as light seeped through the sole window. Mae yawned and began to dress in what she'd worn to dinner the night before, wondering if her leather shoes would make the journey to Highland Falls. A heel was missing, but she secured the dusty buckles, a dozen thoughts darting through her sleepy head.

Would Rhys accompany them?

After breakfast came her answer. Rhys waited by the fort's rear gate—but not only her beloved. Half a dozen Indians ringed their baggage wagon, two of them conversing with Rhys while James looked on. He'd told her Rhys had learned some of their language during his captivity in Canada. She tried not to think of his lacerated back.

"What on earth?" Coralie stopped walking. "I was expecting Continental soldiers, not—"

"The Americans' ablest scouts and guides are Indians." Mae continued walking despite her sister's nails digging into her forearm.

Jon came across the fort's parade ground, his pleasure evident at finding them up and ready to depart. At Coralie's questioning, he explained, "These are Oneida allies who'll accompany us to the farm before continuing further up the Hudson on a foray."

With a few last-minute orders, horses were saddled and brought round as everyone readied to ride out, Orion having been reshod. Only the Indian escort was on foot. The sun crested over the fort's eastern wall as the main gates were opened by sentries. The sole wagon carrying their baggage rolled down the sloped embankment into the forest behind the mounted riders.

No one spoke as birdsong pierced the dawn. Silence seemed the language of the woods, at least in wartime. Perhaps the sights and sounds of the Hudson Highlands were best savored in quiet.

Before they'd gone a quarter of a mile, Mae wished she could dismount and gather the bounty she saw. Grapevines clung to tree trunks while milkwood and moss grew in pink and green bursts. Blue and purple irises crowded creek banks while wildflowers she had no name for brightened the narrow, sunlit valley. Again, so different from Jersey, the only place she'd ever known. She could see why Jon had chosen to expend his labor and life here. Was Virginia's Shenandoah Valley as beautiful?

In a quarter of an hour she spied a stone house, a large fenced garden at its back. Children went about their chores to the barn and chicken house and stable. An apron-clad woman appeared on the porch, shielding her eyes from the sun as she faced the party coming toward her. Joanna?

"The Bohannon homestead," Jon said with pride.

Mae looked at Rhys, who'd come to a halt, the reins slack in his hands. Was he thinking of the house he'd built far from here? Rather, was he missing it and wanting to resume a normal life beyond the shadow of war?

With a start she realized their Indian escort had melted away into the woods. Rhys dismounted and helped her down as Joanna and the children hurried toward them—all flaxen-haired and green-eyed. Alexander, the eldest son, was now equal to Jon in height while Bennett, Cassandra, Dierdre, and Euphemie were smaller versions of their mother and eldest brother.

"Our Jersey kin, can it be?" Joanna hugged Mae and Coralie at the same time, her ample frame making Mae wonder about another Bohannon. "With all that's happening I despaired of ever seeing you again!"

The children eyed them shyly, unused to the notion of two aunts or an Uncle James. Mae couldn't recall if Joanna had family near. Rhys tousled the hair of the youngest boy while Mae fastened her eyes on tiny Euphemie. Phemie, they called her.

"And James? Look at you—a Continental officer!" Joanna said. She turned to Rhys once introductions were made. "General Harlow, we've just gathered the eggs so we'll have breakfast. Plenty of bacon, fried potatoes, and toast to go around."

Mae couldn't imagine feeding all the children *and* guests, but Joanna acted as though it was an everyday occurrence. The smallest of her brood skipped toward the house and held the door open wide, inviting them in. Mannerly, all of them. Even Coralie looked charmed.

Nay, this wasn't Chatham, but the house was spacious and well-kept. Folded quilts brightened an enormous cupboard, and one of the largest hearths Mae had ever seen anchored the main room, a framed if faded painting of a ship over the mantel. Jon and Joanna had done well carving a home out of the wilderness.

The table was made of the same boards as the floor, large enough for all of them to gather round. A pitcher of the flowers Mae had seen behind the garden fence graced the center. She met Rhys's eyes as a flush stole over her and left her wishing this was their table. Their children.

"We've a room ready for you two sisters," Joanna was saying as she began serving. "Top of the stairs. After breakfast we'll bring your belongings in and get you settled. I'm so thankful you're here. We keep hearing reports that Jersey is naught but a battleground."

"But is New York any safer?" Coralie asked as she buttered her bread.

"With so many newly built American garrisons along the Hudson, aye." Jon winked at her. "Were you loath to leave Fort Chatham?"

"True, we had no such defense there," Coralie admitted with a smile. "I do wonder how long General Washington will remain."

"He's just moved his headquarters to Middlebrook, south of

Morristown," James said. "Though by now he might be on his way north to join us here along the Hudson. The Jersey militia has forced the British out of the colo—state—as the British have failed in their efforts to win most residents back to the Crown."

Hopeful, Mae sat as quietly as the children. Might this be the time for Coralie to share her plans? Since she'd apologized to James and he her, perhaps the next discussion would be less charged. But Coralie simply continued to sip her coffee as talk turned to Jon's fields and the oxen he'd recently driven home from market, and what was happening in the valley.

Once they'd eaten, Mae helped with the dishes while the men went outside. When she emerged from the house, she found Rhys with Copper in the pasture ahead of his return to the fort. He approached her, hat in hands, the black cockade catching her eye with its decorative knot of silk ribbon.

"So, Miss Bohannon, may I see you the next Sabbath?"

"You may, General Harlow."

He studied her thoughtfully. "You seem . . . preoccupied."

"I'm just trying to come to terms with being here, so different than Jersey."

"You're missing Chatham."

"Is it so telling?"

"Only by someone who's made a study of you."

"I'm missing home, yet it's ceased to be that for me." She looked at him entreatingly, near tears. "I'm missing you too, even though you've not left yet."

Her emotional words dwindled as James approached, ready to return to the fort. Bidding them goodbye, she stood and watched them ride out, the entire valley at their back. Wooded hills to the west pressed close, teeming with bears and wildcats and snakes—and capable of hiding the enemy. The river to the east hemmed them in, a formidable crossing. All the frontier raids she'd heard of or read about in newspapers returned in a bloody rush.

What did tomorrow hold?

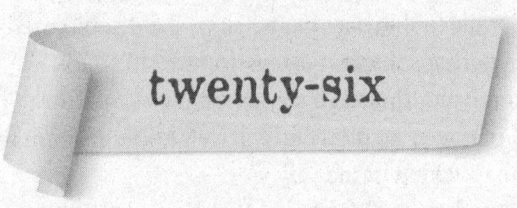

twenty-six

I only regret that I have but one life to lose for my country.

Nathan Hale

"Sister, it's time you learned to fire a gun."

Mae looked at Jon across the vegetable garden where she'd been gathering, her apron full of herbs. If he'd asked her to jump into the well she'd have been more willing. "Your flintlock?"

"Aye. I have two. One is with me at all times and the other is kept inside."

"Let me take these herbs to Joanna first." She hurried to the house and stepped into welcome shade as the early morning promised more heat. By the time she rejoined Jon, he was waiting in the open doorway to the barn, Alexander beside him with his own gun. Her thoughts flew to Rhys, who seemed so at home with his rifle that seeing him without it gave her pause.

Wary, she took the weapon from her brother, wincing at its weight. "I doubt I'm a fair shot."

Jon chuckled as Alex handed his father a powder horn. "We'll soon find out."

"You've never handled a gun, Aunt Mae?" Alex asked.

She paused, thrust back to a frigid night and smokehouse thieves who were now friends. "James showed me how to use Father's pistol before he left home. But a rifle is another challenge."

"Welcome to the wilds of New York."

She tried to smile back at him. "A far cry from Jersey."

"Ever heard of Margaret Corbin?" Her nephew's face wore respect. "When her husband fell at Fort Washington last November—I refuse to call it Knyphausen—she took his place at the cannon, loading and firing it against those redcoats till the very last."

Mae tried to imagine it. "Was she hurt?"

"Badly, aye. But she kept at it even wounded."

Margaret Corbin's mettle reminded her of Lucy Hawkes. She sensed that same underlying strength, the ability to withstand whatever life handed her. No doubt Lucy could fire a rifle *and* man a cannon.

"Mind the weight of the gun," Jon said, taking it back from her and tipping the muzzle upward. "Hold it like this. I'll measure out the powder this round, then you'll do the same next."

She watched as he poured a small amount of priceless black powder.

"Now, take the lead ball and patch and ram it down the barrel's length with this ramrod."

Her clumsy attempts led to her heated cheeks and Alex's half-hidden grin as he scratched his jaw.

"The flint strikes the steel frizzen and lights the powder," Jon instructed patiently. "Now cock the hammer."

She pulled back the hammer as Alex corrected her stance. "Stand with your feet as far apart as your squared shoulders."

Clearly enjoying the process, Jon gestured to a distant post. "When the gun is firmly in hand, aim at that target over there. Take a breath, then lightly squeeze the trigger."

She tried to keep the weapon steady as the sun beat upon her head and back and turned her sweaty. One, two, three, *pull*. The ensuing crack stole her breath as the rifle kicked like a mule and sent her back a step. Jon reached out to steady her as white smoke curled around them with a sharp, sulfurous smell.

"You nearly hit the target, Aunt Mae!" Alex's pleasure eased her awkwardness somewhat.

"Reload and try again," Jon told her.

Mae went through the motions a second time, finding the gun cumbersome at best. She was hard-pressed to school her astonishment when Jon said, "With enough practice you might best General Harlow's reloading in twenty seconds on the run."

Alex gave an admiring whistle. "Uncle James said his best time is five shots in under a minute."

"That matches the British army's three to four shots per minute with a smoothbore musket, which is far easier to reload than a rifle," Jon said as he helped Mae measure the powder.

Composing herself, Mae fired again, this time wide of the mark. The jolt to her shoulder left her wondering how Rhys managed repeated firings. "Coralie's turn."

Both Jon and Alex chuckled. "Coralie's refused. She said you'll make a far better markswoman."

Mae handed back the rifle, more than ready to return to the garden. "Can Joanna shoot?"

"Joanna won the last women's competition at the valley's spring gathering," Jon said with obvious pride. "She and Alex hold the farm when I'm away at the fort."

Mae mulled this over as Jon and Alex returned to the fields. She looked after them as they moved beyond the small, heavily leafed orchard. Wheat would soon be flowering, the maize tasseling and bending slightly in the breeze. She turned in a slow circle, still chary of the landscape.

"Mae, quit your woolgathering," Coralie admonished, coming up behind her. "There's far more to be done than firing a gun. I've been told to water the horses and turn them out to pasture, then feed the chickens. How I miss our hired help at home."

"This is a working farm, remember. Feeding chickens and helping with the horses aren't herculean tasks. We're not guests but family." Mae turned toward Fort Montgomery, wishing she could see its bastions. "Your attitude needs mending."

For once, Coralie seemed contrite. "I apologize for being fractious. I'm just impatient. Joanna said a courier rides through here, but I doubt mail delivery is reliable or timely. Long gone are the days we went to the tavern for the post."

"You wrote Lieutenant Gibbs before we left?"

"I posted a letter from Morristown the day before our departure, yes, but who knows when he'll receive it? Once he does, I hope he'll write back quickly, given we're both in New York."

"You still want to marry him, then."

"I do indeed, no matter how you or Jon or James feel." Coralie fanned her flushed face with her apron hem. "And I know what you're thinking. You keep waiting for me to tell them."

"Would you rather I do it?"

"I'll announce our plans once Eben replies and all is in place."

"Did you ever think the post might fall into the wrong hands? That by telling your whereabouts this farm and valley might be raided? Overrun by the enemy?"

"We're talking about Eben, a longtime tie from Chatham, not the British and their allies."

"We're talking about a redcoat officer determined to quash at all costs what he and his fellows call a treasonous rebellion. Do you deny that?"

"I refuse to think of Eben as the enemy!"

"Then are we the enemy, Coralie? Your family?"

"I don't want to take sides, Mae!" Her taut features bespoke her turmoil. "This madness must have an end. And *you* are mad if you think the Americans—outgunned and outnumbered—will win this ill-founded, misbegotten war."

"They may be outnumbered and outgunned, but this war is neither ill-founded nor misbegotten. General Washington and those committed to the cause will prevail." Mae spoke quietly lest they

191

be overheard, though anyone watching would realize their tense exchange. "Any man who will stake his very life on winning independence is not easily overtaken or undone."

Before she'd finished, Coralie turned and walked toward the barn, leaving Mae to the garden's weeding. But her thoughts were in a tumult, and she wondered again just how dire the American cause was. Her entire future with Rhys seemed to depend on it.

When the dinner bell sounded, they all gathered again, then spent the afternoon hours inside the house. Joanna spun on her Saxony wheel while Mae sewed and Coralie washed dishes and set the table for supper.

Dierdre, not yet ten, took out her own sampler to sit beside Mae. "What are you making, Aunt Mae?"

"Cockades." She held up a rosette fashioned from scraps of silk she'd gotten from Madame Jaquett before leaving Chatham. "Soldiers wear them on their hats. I noticed your father doesn't have one, so this is his."

Dierdre reached out a hand and stroked the silk. "I like this blue color best, not the scarlet of the redcoats."

"Would you like me to teach you how to make cockades? Your father would rather have one made by you, I'm sure. Or there's white silk if you'd rather."

At Dierdre's glee, Joanna smiled. "She begs a break from her sampler, I'm sure."

"'Tis better than carding wool." Dierdre cast a sympathetic look at her sister, the carding brushes in her hands moving swiftly to prepare the wool for spinning into yarn.

Mae reached into her sewing kit where the pincushion rested.

"Pretty!" Dierdre touched it with a careful finger. "Did you make this?"

"Not I. My friend who travels with the army did—Lucy."

"Lucy is a comely name. I should like to meet her."

"She learned to sew from her mother like you do yours."

"Is Lucy a lady like you?"

Mae smiled. "I don't consider myself a real lady, not like British aristocrats or even the genteel Bostonians and Philadelphians and such. As for Lucy, she and her drummer husband don't have a home yet and follow the army."

Joanna clucked from her corner. "Lucy sounds to my liking. Would she come to sup with us on a Sabbath, you think? She and her husband?"

"Do you really need any more to feed, Joanna?" Coralie's teasing held a bite as she finished setting the table. "I certainly don't want to wash more dishes."

"Mercy, living out here so far-flung, I always welcome company so long as they're honest, God-fearing folk. Our Lord tells us to practice hospitality, does He not?"

"I'd settle for a single letter." Coralie took a seat by a window, turning her face toward the breeze riffling the curtains.

Waiting for the post, no doubt. They'd been in the Hudson Highlands less than a week. Did Coralie think the post would be swift across enemy lines? Mae felt just as impatient. She'd not rest till this matter with her sister was settled.

"The post will come." The whir of Joanna's wheel underscored her certain words. "I recall the Seven Years' War. Even in the worst of times letters eventually found their way."

Mae gave silent thanks that Joanna was good-natured. She bore Coralie's complaints like a long-suffering older sister. As for this letter, when and if it came, would it be as terse as Eben's last? The unknown made the wait even more nettlesome.

"Soon Jon will return to the fort and leave the rest of us to manage the farm." Joanna continued her spinning with deft hands. "But before he goes, he'll have to tell you our valley's history."

Curious, Mae slipped outside and rounded the house to admire the early-budding rose she'd found climbing the house's south wall. Jon wasn't far, mending fences in the pasture where Orion grazed.

She walked toward him, glad to stretch her legs after so much sewing. "Is now a good time to tell me about the history here?"

"Joanna must have whetted your appetite." He struck a nail, driving it into the wood. "Her grandfather actually named nearby Buttermilk Falls."

"A true waterfall?"

"Aye, some seventy-five feet high and foaming like buttermilk." He gestured toward the foothills where a footpath was visible. "Grandfather Fowler was among the English who came into this valley and routed the Dutch, who'd routed the Lenape through fighting, failed treaties, and disease."

"A sorry tale much like Chatham's," Mae said.

"Chatham—what?" He grunted his discontent. "I cannot make peace with Day's Bridge being renamed Chatham in '73."

"Even if it's to honor the earl of Chatham who's been some-what sympathetic to our American cause?" At the firm shake of his head she said, "I think once the war is won we shall see a great many name changes. Perhaps Chatham will return to being Day's Bridge once again."

"If it's still standing, you mean."

They exchanged a grim look. "I fear for those who remain," she said. Hanna and Aaron especially were never far from her thoughts. "I pray the Americans prevail."

"You're as staunch in your belief they will win as Coralie is in her belief the war is lost."

"I hold on to hope. And I pray. 'Tis the least I can do when so many decent men are dying on both sides."

"Aye, pray. Without ceasing." He looked up from replacing a rotted post with one newly split.

"Any more valley history you want to share?"

"Aye." He winked while continuing his work. "Buttermilk Falls is known to be a comely place for courting."

Mae's sudden fluster left her tongue-tied. He knew?

He settled the log into place. "It's plain as print the both of you are thoroughly smitten, though General Harlow covers it better than you do."

"All right, then," she confessed. "I've not been the same since he first set foot in Chatham."

"You light up like a firefly around him. Joanna's noticed too."

"Do you give your blessing?"

"There's none finer than the general, unless it's Washington himself."

"But you've just met him."

He nodded. "The measure of a man oft happens before you reason your way through it. I've long heard about him even before he left Virginia, including his exceptional marksmanship, mayhap the best since Boone."

"Colonel Boone of the Virginia militia?" Mae thought back to countless conversations around Chatham's dining room table. "He and General Harlow surveyed together in the Shenandoah Valley a few years ago."

"As has been said, birds of a kind and color always flock and fly together." Jon winked again. "Maebel Bohannon Harlow sounds quite fitting."

Smiling, Mae pushed away from the fence, saying over her shoulder, "I hope we all live to see it."

twenty-seven

*The defeat of the Americans in Canada and the advantages gained
by the British arms in the Jerseys, and indeed for some months
in every other quarter, gave to the royal cause an air of triumph.*

Mercy Otis Warren

On the next Sabbath, Rhys rode into the valley with James, the
short time they'd been apart the longest of Mae's life. Suddenly
self-conscious, she smoothed her apron and hair while they dismounted and turned their horses to pasture. She wore her second-
best dress, the silk taffeta a pale sage green, an ivory sash about her
waist. Hardly the linen and homespun of the wilds of New York.

As the two men approached the porch where they waited, Mae
felt as excited as little Phemie, who all but danced atop the planks
beside her.

"Uncle James?" she echoed when Mae told her he was coming.
"And the giant!"

The giant, of course, was Rhys. With a little shout, Phemie
jumped off the porch and into James's arms. When he tossed her
into the air she erupted into giggles. Once they'd gone inside,
Mae faced Rhys, who'd removed his hat and eyed her like a long-
denied dessert.

Freshly shaven, he'd exchanged his rough trail garb for a respectable pair of breeches, shirt, and frock coat, even boots. He clutched his rifle in his right hand, reminding her of her shooting lesson.

"Walk out with me," he said.

Her heart leapt as she stepped off the porch. She'd thought they'd join the family and not have a moment to themselves the entire Sabbath.

Once they'd left the yard and moved toward the western edge of trees that hedged the valley, her petticoats swished and caught at the tall grass and brambles. The wind that sent her lace cap fluttering against its pins made her take a deep, steadying breath.

"Where are we going?" she asked as a wood thrush began singing in flutelike tones from a shaggy hemlock.

"Buttermilk Falls."

Had Jon told him? Or had his reconnaissance outside fort walls led him there?

They took a deer trail, the woods closing green and shadowed about them as they began a slight climb. In minutes Mae grew winded and Rhys swiped at the sweat beading his upper lip with a coat sleeve.

They heard the falls from a distance, their thunder muting the morning birdsong. When they came through the trees the falls' mist met them, stirring ferns and foliage as the cascading water poured into a mossy, rocky basin remarkably like an emptied pitcher of buttermilk. For a few moments they just stood hand in hand, awed.

Letting go of him, Mae discreetly turned her back and slipped off her shoes before removing her garters and stockings, then laid them in a little heap atop a rock at the rim of the pool. Already damp from the mist, she threw caution to the wind, submerging one pale, slim foot below water as shockingly cold as the day was warm.

His caution to mind her steps on the slippery bottom simply spurred her on, the chill felt clear to her spine. Holding her skirts to her knees, she took a look over her shoulder. Now barefooted and bare chested, Rhys waded in after her. His rifle leaned against a rock, the furthest thing from her mind if not his.

He came toward her at the pool's center, her breath catching at the strength of him, his shoulders and chest startlingly pale against the deep mahogany of his hands and face. In his shadow, she felt like a wildflower, as fragile as the bits of color clinging to the pool's rim.

He didn't touch her, but his tender gaze was full of a thousand caresses that left her lightheaded with longing. Still clutching her skirts above the water, she tipped her head back and took in the top of the falls, her voice barely heard above the water's rush. "I'll not forget this place."

He reached out and brushed her damp cheek with the back of his fingers. He was near but not near enough. Their linen closet tryst seemed faded as old cloth. Would he not kiss her again? Instead he removed something from his little finger and held it out to her. Sun and mist struck gold and turned it glittering.

"Will you marry me, Mae . . . for better or worse, richer or poorer, and all the rest?"

She stared at him, wondering if the waterfall had made a nonsensical mess of his words. He reached for her, sliding the ring on the fourth finger of her left hand. It fit slightly snug, but she didn't care. The ring, a miniature rosette, reminded her of the cockade she'd made for his hat.

His question hovered in the air between them. *Will you marry me?*

In answer she let go of her skirts. They pillowed atop the water before sinking as she studied the ring. Wonder turned to teasing. "I feel like I've passed some sort of test and been rewarded with a ring."

"Mae . . ." he began, his tone riven with regret.

Her voice shook with emotion. "You well know my answer, Rhys."

"Asking you was a long time coming." He swallowed, clearly as moved as she. "Not because I had any doubts . . . only because I wanted your best."

"I never doubted you. And waiting made me realize how impatient I am." Surely the Lord was teaching her in the waiting and making something more of her than she was.

She needn't even ask the question that burned the tip of her tongue, for he said, "There's a chaplain at Fort Montgomery, Israel Evans, who'll wed us at the farm or fort. I want it to be memorable for you, the way you want it. When you want it."

So she was to decide? Tongue-tied, she looked down at her soaked dress. She was up to her knees in water, the silk dark green now, as weighted as her spirits were soaring.

Taking her ringed hand, he tugged her toward the thundering torrent as it flowed over the rock face, only to take her in his arms and finally kiss her. So many kisses she lost count, the water running in rivulets off their skin.

She held on to him, her words half drowned in the deluge. "'Tis the sweetest moment of my life, even if I had to risk my life getting here."

Slowly she became aware that the sun, at high noon when they'd arrived, now slanted west. They'd missed Sabbath dinner and would have to answer for their absence and wet garments. Or would they? He seemed to read her thoughts.

"We need to make the most of the hour given us," Rhys said above the water's roar. "And we don't owe an answer to anyone."

★ ★ ★ ★ ★

Mae all but tiptoed into the clearing, aware of James and Jon smoking their pipes on the porch. The half-mile walk from the falls hadn't dried their clothes nor made them look any less bedraggled. Rhys seemed unconcerned, but Mae's embarrassment mingled with her joy.

"Here come the lovebirds now." James leaned forward with a

grin, pipe in hand. "We did wonder what other reason would have you two fly the coop and miss such a fine Sabbath dinner."

"Buttermilk Falls always wins," Jon remarked with a knowing smile. "And on such a fine day one can't help but enjoy the water."

Mae stopped just shy of the porch, Rhys coming up behind. She held out her ringed hand, then pressed it to her bodice as words lodged in her throat.

Rhys came to a stop by her side. "I've asked Mae to marry me, and she's said . . ."

She slipped her hand in his and squeezed his calloused fingers. "Yes—I do."

"Such glad news!" Jon called for Joanna. "You're welcome to hold the wedding here. We can have a small celebration—or a large one if you like, and invite all your riflemen."

Joanna appeared, Phemie on her hip. Smiling, she seemed to sum up the situation in a glance. "I knew there was something between you the moment I first saw you together, and I couldn't be happier."

James winked. "Better start baking a wedding cake."

"Not till I feed them. One can't live on love alone," she said, motioning Rhys and Mae toward the open door. "There's plenty of fried fish and garden sass left over, even pepper cake."

Mae started up the steps, her wet skirts dragging, and bumped into an open-mouthed Coralie.

Aghast, she stared at Mae's gown. "What on earth? Your lovely dress—"

"I'll change once I eat."

"*After* you eat?" She stepped aside as if not wanting to get wet. "What's this about a wedding?"

Not even Coralie could dim the moment. "We're to be married here at the farm."

"When?"

Mae looked to Rhys, then said, "As soon as Fort Montgomery's chaplain is free to perform the ceremony."

Speechless, Coralie turned and disappeared upstairs while Mae and Rhys took a place at the empty table. Joanna came in with two full plates, smiling and calling for Cassandra to fetch cider as Jon and James resumed their conversation on the porch and the children played outside.

With a wink, Rhys leaned across the table and took Mae's hand to say grace. "For what we're about to receive we give Thee thanks. Bless this meal's preparer, and please save us from our sins—and quarrelsome sisters. In Your name we pray. Amen."

twenty-eight

I hate to complain. . . . No one is without difficulties, whether in high or low life, and every person knows best where their own shoe pinches.

Abigail Adams

The wedding day dawned overcast, the May heat tempered. The floral chintz made by Madame Jaquett had been aired and ironed, none the worse after the journey from Chatham. With Coralie busy in the kitchen, Joanna helped Mae upstairs. Once dressed, her hair pinned beneath a newly made lace cap, Mae turned away from the looking glass as the sound of riders reached them.

Her groom—or the long-awaited post?

Joanna went to an open window, her voice high with excitement. "The chaplain is here with General Harlow and a few officers—and I spy another horse carrying a young couple. Lucy Hawkes and her husband? You were kind to invite them."

"I'd rather Lucy and her husband than four hundred riflemen," Mae teased, joining her at the window.

"We've never hosted a wedding before. The prospect makes me quite giddy. I suppose, had the entire Rifle Corps come, we would have simply rolled out kegs of cider and not all of them would have had cake."

Joanna had baked a lovely wedding cake four stacks high. It sat in the buttery, the house's cooler north corner. Early this morning, Phemie had snuck into the shadowed room and licked at the icing till Dierdre shooed her away. Now all three girls were in the garden picking flowers for Mae's bouquet while the boys helped Jon tend the roasting pig in back of the barn.

"My, how handsome General Harlow looks in his bottle-green coat." Joanna turned away from the window. "And you, my dear, are a very lovely bride."

"I'm certainly the happiest," Mae replied, hoping Rhys felt the same. "Though this is a far cry from the wedding I thought to have with Mother by my side, Father officiating, and Hanna and Aaron attending."

"How I wish we could all be together in one place. It seems something of a miracle to have a wedding in wartime, at least betwixt an officer and his lady." Joanna studied her wistfully. "We'd best go below. Guests are usually impatient—and hungry for the wedding feast."

Mae followed her down the stairs, a sudden shyness overtaking her. Was Rhys sure of today? She looked to her ring, a dozen memories resurfacing along with her doubts. But when she came to the porch and found him waiting, every bit as handsome in his frock coat as Joanna said, she read adoration in his eyes and let go any remaining fears.

For a moment they seemed at a mutual loss for words. And then he extended his arm and she took it as the girls rounded the house with her bouquet, exclaiming with delight at her gown. Giggling, they soon scampered away, their petticoats as colorful as the posies they'd picked. The wedding party waited in the shade at the side of the house where the climbing rose was trellised. The entangled vines wound up the stone wall, the first ruby blooms heady.

Chaplain Israel Evans was not the aged, silver-haired man she'd envisioned but young as she and Rhys, his amiable manner winning her over in an instant. As the ceremony began, James and Joanna stood as witnesses while the children looked on with Jon, Phemie in his arms. A smiling Captain Sperry spoke in low tones to Lucy and her husband behind them, and then came Coralie, head down.

Mae refused to let her sister's mood taint the day. She faced Rhys, their hands entwined, and listened to the vows she'd once thought she'd never hear him say.

"I, Rhys Harlow, take thee, Maebel Bohannon, to be my wedded wife, to have and to hold from this day forward, for better or for worse, for richer, for poorer, in sickness and in health, to love and to cherish, till death do us part, according to God's holy ordinance, and thereto I plight thee my troth."

She repeated his words, their gazes never wavering. The depth of such vows, meant to weather the years, shook her. *Lord, let it be for a long time, enduring through the war, reaching into the next century.*

Suddenly it was done, a prayer and benediction said.

She was his. He was hers.

Till death do them part.

★ ★ ★ ★ ★

Rhys escorted Mae to a table beneath a widespread oak where platters of roast pork and garden vegetables waited. The wedding cake sat at the center, fresh flowers and sugared almonds atop thick icing. Everyone was talking and laughing, the solemn ceremony already a pretty memory. Joanna and Jon were the perfect hosts, as if weddings were held every day of the week.

Rhys sat at the head of the long table with Mae to his right. She hadn't stopped smiling, nor had he, so the slight ache in his jaw told him. Nor could he take his eyes off her. The flush of joy turned her radiant. She darted loving, almost disbelieving glances his way, making him wish the meal over so they could be alone. But first, the feast.

The bountiful meal was washed down with punch, the taste of

rum and molasses and ground spices from the cake lingering. When the music began, the children flitted about like fireflies, dancing to Mae's father's fiddle once Rhys rosined the bow and began "Soldier's Joy," then struck "Haste to the Wedding."

"Come now, the groom can't be burdened with playing at his own nuptials," James said as Chaplain Evans took out an engraved fife.

The instrument's bright, clear sound pierced the air as everyone took a partner, even the children, and made merry till twilight. All but Coralie. She'd disappeared after the ceremony, but Rhys had given it little thought. Lucy and Isham were the liveliest dancers, their faces alight in the gathering dusk. He wondered about their own wedding. They'd married young and been inseparable since. Not even the war could divide them.

"I've been long enough at my fields and will return to the fort tomorrow," Jon said to Rhys as he poured more punch. "Your riflemen will no doubt offer a great many huzzahs and congratulations at your and Mrs. Harlow's arrival . . . though you might want to linger once you see the dower house."

"'Tis yours for however long you like," Joanna told them as Mae cast an appreciative look at her sister-in-law. "'Twas my late mother's and has sat empty for some time."

Rhys looked toward the path that would take them there, a quarter mile farther south along the river. He'd passed by on scouting forays and thought it a shame so comely a place sat empty. A fitting bower for a bride and groom.

He turned back to Mae with a smile. "Say the word, Mrs. Harlow, and we'll begin our honeymoon."

She smiled and set down her empty punch cup. "Let's begin then."

★ ★ ★ ★ ★

When Rhys opened the dower house door, it seemed a glittering of fairies had been at work. All was clean and tidy, a small parlor adjoining a bedchamber. Scattered across the white coverlet of the four-poster bed were rose petals. Joanna's doing? All the window curtains were drawn, touched with gold as the sun sank from sight.

Mae walked about slowly, delight stealing through her as she set her posies atop a table. Everything here seemed in miniature, the still air scented with pine and candle wax. Outside a dove cooed plaintively. Was it missing its mate?

Rhys barred the door and went about the room locking the shutters. Nearly all the light was snuffed. "This place casts quite a spell, though I think it's more the company I'm keeping."

They stood facing each other as his fingers moved to her lace cap and pulled the pins free one by one. Her hair tumbled about her shoulders, which stilled him a moment. He'd never seen it all unbound, and from the look in his eyes he found the shining length of it a glory, like Scripture said.

"You seem more angel, Mae."

"I'm no angel, just your adoring wife." Her own fingers found his linen stock and the back buckle that secured it. She let both fall to the floor, along with his frock coat and her own garments, till they both stood in their smallclothes, the hush of the room hallowed.

"Kiss me and make me forget about this war and tomorrow and all the rest," she said softly. "I'm yours and the night is ours, and for the moment nothing else matters."

twenty-nine

Join, or die.

Benjamin Franklin

The cooing doves woke her. Mae stirred, mindful of the man sleeping beside her, the coverlet and rose petals scattered. Closing her eyes again, she listened as the day dawned beyond the closed shutters. Thankfully the dower house lacked a clock. She could just lay suspended in a timeless tangle of pleasure and wonder as if tomorrow no longer mattered.

When he woke, his words were almost lost as he burrowed his head in her hair. "So, should we go on up to the falls again?"

In answer she pulled him closer, if that was possible, one arm anchored about his neck. "Mayhap in the heat of the day."

He chuckled. "This *is* the heat of the day."

She looked toward the window again as if to naysay him. "I thought it was dawn."

"It's nigh on noon." He kissed her again as time ticked on.

They were oblivious till a noise at the door finally roused them. Sitting up, Mae pulled free of his arms reluctantly, the rumble of his stomach a reminder that one couldn't live on love alone. She padded to the door on bare feet, unbarred it, and pulled it open.

A linen-covered basket sat on the stoop. Packed by Joanna, no doubt, and delivered by one of the boys. She grabbed the handle and retreated to the table as Rhys got up and barred the door again, moving his rifle nearer the fireless hearth.

Pulling on his wedding shirt, he sat down, watching her expectantly as she removed a flask of cider. By the time she'd emptied the basket the small table was completely covered. Cold roast chicken, pickled vegetables, cheese, still-warm wheaten bread, slices of wedding cake, and a small sack of raisins, dates, and almonds meant enough for supper too. They ate with their fingers as there was no cutlery, just a linen towel.

"When do you want to return to the fort?" she asked. "I'm sorry to say a wedding cannot put a war on hold."

"By dusk tonight would be wise."

She took a sip of cider. "You've room enough for me?"

"My quarters aren't large but ample enough. The other officers' wives live in the same building with their husbands. We share a common dining room. But if we want to be alone there's always locking ourselves in like this."

She took a bite of cake. "If I'm to ride Orion I've packed what's needed in saddlebags. My trunk can come later by wagon."

"I want you to be comfortable, as comfortable as possible. Living at a garrison, even a new one, is sure to come as a shock."

"I want to be of use, of service."

"Keep sewing, then. There's always a lack of the most basic of garments."

"Is there enough linen and supplies?"

"Hard to come by, though I've asked the quartermaster to save some cloth, even needles and thread, with you in mind."

Were the Liberty Ladies still plying their needles now that the army had left? Mae's attention returned to the rumpled bed and all its implications. Perhaps she'd soon be sewing more than soldiers' shirts. She felt both a thrill and a chill at whatever lay before them.

At their leaving, she promised to visit Joanna and the children as much as she could. Coralie turned tearful, though Mae felt nothing but relief that she'd remain behind at the farm.

"Please send word when you receive a post from Lieutenant Gibbs," she said in parting.

But Coralie just crossed her arms and said nothing in reply, her expression a strange mix of ire and sorrow.

★ ★ ★ ★ ★

Huzzahs erupted as the newlyweds passed through Fort Montgomery's open gates. General Clinton himself left his headquarters and crossed the expansive parade ground to greet them as Rhys helped Mae dismount. The sense she'd stepped into another world deepened as the tattoo sounded, the drum that signaled the end of the day. Roll call ensued and sentinels were posted. Scouts were sent out and lanterns lit.

Rhys's newly finished barracks still smelled of sawdust, the room holding few furnishings, making the dower house seem almost luxurious in comparison. Mac was glad she'd brought little with her from Chatham, her wedding gown stored away at the farm for another occasion. She did carry the books, presenting them to Rhys as a sort of wedding gift, and was pleased when he placed them on the mantel.

After evening devotions, they lay down and Rhys slept, but the novelty of the hour kept her awake as she adjusted to a narrower bed and the man beside her. Chatham had had its own distinct night sounds. The bark of a dog. Laughter from the tavern. The passing of a cart or horse. But here, where hundreds of soldiers were garrisoned, the expansive fort never seemed to rest. Doors opened and closed. Voices murmured. A distant wolf howled, followed by the deep-bodied hoot of an owl. She fancied she heard the river's rush far below.

Reveille woke them. Heat filled the one-windowed room like a woolen blanket, so she chose her lightest linen dress. Breakfast was a hasty affair of toast and tea at their spark of a fire, which had no business being lit given the weather. Already the yeasty aroma of the fort's beehive ovens competed with the roasting of coffee beans. Fort Montgomery was wide awake.

As Rhys resumed his duties, Mae tried to be as useful yet as unobtrusive as possible. Walking discreetly around the hive of a garrison amid all manner of soldiery proved a challenge as she familiarized herself. Barracks, officers' quarters, storage buildings, and magazines for ammunition spread across acres. A blacksmith made continual noise, but the stables were kept well away from the din of his hammering and forging, the officers' horses corralled at the opposite end. Orion was hobbled and left to graze in the near woods, awaiting Jon to return him to the farm.

As Mae rounded a corner of the fort one afternoon, she spied Lucy by the well. Mae approached her as she wound the creaking handle and brought the full bucket to the top, its wet sides shimmering in the summery light.

Lucy looked up, startled, then smiled. "Miss Bohan—Mrs. Harlow."

Mae smiled back at her. Would the delight of her married name ever fade? "Just Mae, please."

"All right. Where you headed?"

"I don't rightly know. I'm just trying to get my bearings. How about you?"

They fell into step together, walking toward the fort's open postern gates.

"Me and Isham and Petey live outside fort walls on what's called Sutler's Row," Lucy explained. "We only come inside these pickets if the danger's high."

They continued through the trees toward tents and makeshift shelters stretched in long rows beneath oaks and elms and maples. Crowded and industrious and colorful.

"You can get whatever you're lacking out here," Lucy said.

"We've sutlers and tinkers, trappers and traders, a cobbler and tailor, carpenters, and farm folk selling garden sass, even an old woman to tell your fortune."

Children and dogs ran about, even a squealing piglet and squawking chickens. Mae's attention turned to a break in the trees. Half a dozen Indians approached the fort, their garments a medley of buckskin and Continental linen and wool. One wore a black cocked hat dripping with vibrant beads and feathers. A chief?

"American allies?" she asked Lucy, who nodded.

"Oneida—or, as they say, Onyota'aka."

Mae repeated the unfamiliar word beneath her breath, finding it hard to look away till she stopped to admire handkerchiefs both plain and patterned strung on a line. She settled on one with embroidered indigo stars for Rhys. Lucy's workmanship? Mae plucked coins from her pocket.

"Thank you kindly." Lucy gestured to the flagpole inside the fort's pickets, clearly the inspiration for the design. The faded flag bore red and white stripes with thirteen white-pointed stars in a circle. "General Clinton's flying the American colors outside his quarters." They'd reached the end of a long row where a lone tent stood. "This here's mine and Isham's. Only he's fevered and in the field hospital."

Mae looked at her in concern. "How sick is he?"

"Sick enough that he doesn't ken if I'm afoot or horseback. The surgeon's been treating him with yarrow and willow bark. General Harlow's been by a time or two."

Had he? Fifers and drummers were no mere musicians but the heartbeat of the army, some said. Drummers communicated orders from superior officers through different beats and rhythms, even amid the chaos of battle. Mae had become accustomed to hearing their music in Chatham and Lowantica Valley. Often they were mere boys, though drum majors were men.

"Are you safe here on Sutler's Row, Lucy?"

"Safe?" Lucy whistled and Petey emerged from the tent. "I've

211

a mighty fine guard. He'll take a piece out of anyone who means me harm."

As if sensing her praise, Petey wagged his mottled tail and hurried to his mistress's side.

Looking past them, Mae noted the sinking sun, wishing she had a watch. "'Twill soon be suppertime. Please send word if your Isham worsens or if you need anything, Lucy. Anything at all."

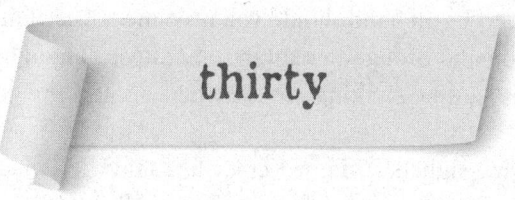

thirty

My Dear Son . . . remember that you are accountable to your Maker for all your words and actions.

Abigail Adams

The officers' mess, or dining room, was just large enough for a dozen around the trestle table. Rhys always sat at one end opposite General Clinton while the officers' wives sat interspersed with their husbands. Here there was an air of gravity that bespoke the precariousness of their mission, though the men seemed careful to not talk solely about the war. Mostly listening, Mae missed the easy talk and laughter at Jon and Joanna's table, especially their children's.

To her surprise, Catherine Kersey invited her for tea in future, though tonight she looked unwell and pushed the chicken pie around her plate, even declining the watermelon served for dessert. Was she ill or suffering the effects of hotter weather?

"I'm a bit queasy," she murmured, setting down her fork.

"I've a small tin of mint tea in my quarters, if you'd like," Mae told her quietly as the men withdrew to the room's opposite end to smoke near open windows.

"Thank you kindly, but nothing I've tried helps . . . and I may not feel relief for several more months." Catherine turned rosy. "My husband is determined to find the best midwife along the Hudson when it's time."

What? Mae's warm congratulations held concern. To birth a baby in such rustic conditions in the middle of the wilderness . . .

"I hope to be on hand should you need me." Alice finished her watermelon and brought a napkin to her lips. "Though Colonel Wentz has said he's taking me elsewhere should the danger be high."

Catherine sighed. "Major Kersey has said the same, though the nearest settlement resembling a town is Albany, some distance from here. I'm not keen on my firstborn making his or her entrance anywhere near a prison for Loyalists and the like."

"Perhaps you could stay at the Van Schaick mansion near there, owned by a Continental officer and far safer, given it's on a small island between the Mohawk and Hudson Rivers."

Mae listened, pondering all the possibilities. Her ongoing prayer was that Fort Montgomery would endure and remain the Hudson River's first line of defense—along with Fort Clinton opposite Popolopen Creek, a quarter of a mile away.

"And you, Mrs. Harlow?" Alice asked. "Where will you go if the British reach us?"

"Likely to my brother's farm in the valley, if that can be safely done."

"Is that where your sister is now?" Catherine asked. At Mae's nod, she exchanged a look with Alice. "She seems of a rather . . . temperamental disposition."

"Coralie is rather high-strung," Mae admitted, her longtime wish of an easier, more agreeable sister resurfacing.

How could she explain the rivalry that had existed between them since childhood, at least on Coralie's part? Wanting to be more like Mae and feeling as the eldest sister she got the best— even marriage—while Coralie herself got seconds in everything.

"Perhaps she'll find New York to her liking." Catherine dabbed at her brow with a handkerchief. "As for me, I've had quite enough of this terribly close room."

"So, ladies," General Clinton asked as they rose from the table, "what are your impressions of Fort Montgomery now that you've bettered it by being here?"

"The view is unsurpassed," Mae answered with a smile.

"My compliments to the cook and baker," Alice replied. "The fare is quite good, far better than we had on the journey coming here."

Catherine said nothing, just put a hand to her waist as if debating whether the delicious fare would soon reappear in the nearest chamber pot.

★ ★ ★ ★ ★

Rhys watched Mae rise from the table, outwardly serene though she'd been unusually quiet during the meal. If he'd had any qualms about her adjustment to fort life, he set them aside, though it was still early. She glanced at him as the ladies moved toward the door, her pale green gown trailing behind her on the plank floor. Did she sense he was wanting to finish matters and join her?

Excusing himself, he exchanged the stale, smoky air of the mess for the sultry night. "The view is exceptionally fine on so clear an evening."

It was time for the tattoo at close of day. She slipped her arm through his as they continued across the parade ground, the faint scent of gunpowder lingering from the day's exercises. Night thinned the soldiers and their duties somewhat, though sentries stood at their posts and patrols and scouts entered and exited the fort at all hours, a continual reminder it was wartime. A full moon shed ample light as they bypassed both guardhouse and powder magazine and walked up a slope to the highest point of Fort Montgomery, a giant earthworks and defensive embankment built the year before.

"'Tis aptly named the *Grand* Battery," she said as they came to stand where artillery crews, now absent, manned the great hulks of cannons above the Hudson River. "Enemy ships navigating the river, beware."

Rhys looked to the sky instead of the moon-silvered water below, wishing he had the Almighty's view. Only God knew where the British were on such a night.

"Is it true General Washington is on his way here?" she asked.

He nodded, his hands on the ledge of the battery's wall. "He's left Jersey and is expected soon. Our main concern now is General Burgoyne's advance south from Canada. We've just received intelligence that British forces have captured Fort Ticonderoga."

At her sharp intake of breath, he'd never been more glad Ticonderoga was so many miles north.

"So, Gentleman Johnny has struck a victory—though I doubt that describes Burgoyne fairly in wartime." She frowned. "I thought Ticonderoga was indestructible."

"Gentleman or not, Burgoyne mounted a bold advance that St. Clair wasn't prepared for. And now St. Clair and his three thousand men have gone missing. It's not known whether they've gone over to the British or been captured."

"Which weakens the entire northern campaign."

He couldn't naysay her. She was right. He'd always found her well-informed, though sometimes he wished otherwise. Most officers' wives preferred socializing to news.

"Will the British tarry at Ticonderoga or keep moving south toward us?" she asked.

"They'll likely try to take Forts Lee and Edward next, though General Schuyler is thwarting their advance by felling timber and destroying bridges. Once Washington arrives we'll have a better idea of what's happening and what our task will be."

"I heard General Clinton talking about the great chain right below us." She stared down through the dusk as if seeing the barrier the Continental Army had erected to keep the British navy from coming upriver. Sunk just below the Hudson's surface, the massive chain's iron links were forged one by one.

"The same chain is needed near West Point," he said. Another missed opportunity. The Americans were often plagued by them. "But with Burgoyne's advance that undertaking is now too late."

He sensed her distress, yet she regarded him as if he was her anchor, as starry-eyed as the sky. "I don't want to leave your side even if the danger is high." She spoke calmly as if she'd given it considerable thought. "I'd rather be here close by no matter what."

He looked down at her small hand lost in his large one. She was so . . . fragile. She'd never been beyond Jersey, never seen the frontier until now. She hadn't any idea what it was like to stare down an assault of bayonets nor hear the cries of the wounded and dying. He wasn't sure she realized he and his riflemen made it their mission to target the topmost British officers and their Indian allies. Their belief in the American cause made them ruthless. Relentless. Nor did she know he pored over intelligence like a madman to determine the threat to her here.

"The river is beautiful but rather chilling," she said, leaning over the wall.

"Look up rather than down, Mae." He moved behind her so she was in the protective circle of his arms. "Anything can happen here below, but the heavens are untouched. Mayhap the Almighty wanted to create something beyond man's destructive reach."

Together they looked up, rewarded as a star streaked across the blackness in an arc of light before extinguishing like candle flame.

"Some say falling stars mean good luck," he told her, though luck seemed too tame a word for what they'd just witnessed.

"Luck is simply a lesser name for Providence. God's hand moving across the heavens."

They were alone now on the battery, men withdrawing from their posts. His thoughts were far from here. Rarely did he let himself think of Virginia, but tonight he did.

"One day we'll stand on our porch in the Shenandoah Valley and witness the same."

"Our porch?" Her voice turned wistful.

"It's south-facing with a view." He well recalled the joists, beams, and posts, though his father had done much of the work while he was in the fields. "Since it's built on a rise, you have a view of both sunrises and sunsets. There's a creek running alongside."

"Whistle Creek. You said it passes through our milk house by way of a stone trough, then circles back again to stay fresh."

He'd not told her much, but what little he did she never forgot. "You remembered."

"I don't merely want to remember. I want to live it. Make it mine—ours."

"Soon, aye."

"Not soon enough," she said with feeling.

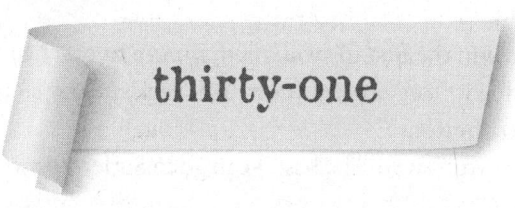

thirty-one

We hold these truths to be self-evident, that all men are created equal, that they are endowed by their Creator with certain unalienable Rights, that among these are Life, Liberty and the pursuit of Happiness.

Declaration of Independence

Days became weeks, and dispatches came bearing news that General Washington had entered New York and was moving toward King's Ferry a few miles south of them. A sense of jubilation threaded the air both inside Fort Montgomery and out.

Mae returned from visiting Lucy along Sutler's Row just as Rhys returned from the quartermaster's, James following, their arms full of indigo cloth. Entering their quarters, Mae removed her straw hat and hung it from a wall peg.

James set his burden down atop the table, which gave a little groan. "Your husband has volunteered you to make uniform coats for the foremost officers who need them."

She looked at Rhys, cowering at the very thought. "I beg your pardon?"

"I have full confidence in your and Lucy's sewing and am weary of seeing so many without. The 'apparel oft proclaims the man,' as Shakespeare said."

"And you riflemen? Might I relieve you of your fringed linen?" She ran a hand over the cloth atop the table. "Such fine wool seems quite hot in summer."

"By the time you're done it might be winter," Rhys told her with a wink.

"I'll fashion the first for you, then, if only to practice."

He nodded. "I've no objection. You've plenty of cloth. What you lack are buttons."

"Brass buttons would be best. I can go to Sutler's Row in search of some."

James regarded her in amusement. "Lately you've been more outside the fort than in it."

"I spend my time sitting in the shade with Lucy Hawkes, sewing and knitting for soldiers, especially those in the infirmary."

"Private Hawkes is improving," Rhys told her. He knew her concern for Lucy.

"Praise be, you'll soon have your drummer back." Mae eyed his wedding suit hanging on the wall. "Will you kindly part with your frock coat so I can use it as my template?"

"Whatever you need, aye."

"What I need is more thread, not only buttons."

"I'll ask the quartermaster, then." James looked at the small desk she used and her half-finished letter to Hanna and Aaron. Beside it lay a sealed one to Aunt Verity. "Homesick?"

"Only at first." She smiled. "There's far too much to fill the hours. Besides, we're to have Sabbath dinner at the farm with Jon and family tomorrow."

James looked at Rhys. "Jon has returned home as there's been talk of a raid in the valley."

Mae felt such a qualm she sat down. "What means you?"

"British Loyalists are known to be planning raids on Patriot farms." Rhys took a seat opposite her. "We've sent out scouts and patrols to alert residents up and down the Hudson."

"Does this mean we're not going to Jon and Joanna's?"

"I'll have a better idea when I speak with scouts come morning," Rhys said. "I may ride out myself."

★ ★ ★ ★ ★

The Sabbath came and went, keeping them at Fort Montgomery. Mae prayed there'd been no more talk of raids and the valley would remain undisturbed. Rhys returned with a peaceful report, bringing wool for knitting. Mae pictured Joanna at her spinning wheel, working despite any danger. At least a stone house was harder to breach and less likely to burn than a log one.

The next week a great commotion went up among soldiers and civilians alike. General Washington had reached the Hudson Highlands north of them in a place known as the Clove. A portion of his army was with him, the rest moving toward the British threat in Philadelphia.

Mae, feeling celebratory herself, danced a little jig with Lucy to a fife's joyful piping on Sutler's Row.

"I'm thankful for the army's safe passage but rather disappointed he's passed us by," Mae told her, resuming knitting in the shade of an oak tree. "I've not seen the general on horseback, just in a ballroom."

Lucy's snort turned into a sneeze. "If he rides as well as he dances, he's nothing short of a king."

"Yet another King George." Mae chuckled, finishing the toe of a sock. "Fancy that."

"Speaking of fancy, a high-and-mighty Frenchman's arrived to join the fight." Lucy's voice rose in mimicry of the French. "Some young marquis called Lafayette. He's on his way to Philadelphia to meet up with Washington in future."

"I'd rather talk about ballrooms than battles—and the general does dance divinely."

"He's not dancing now." Lucy scowled, the range of her expressions astonishing. "Not since Continental supplies got wrecked in Danbury. There's been a shortage ever since."

"Danbury?" Somehow Mae had missed this bit of news.

"The American army's stores in Connecticut. Isham's drum major told him redcoats ruined three thousand barrels of pork, a thousand of flour, several hundred barrels of beef, countless bushels of grain, rice, rum—all set on fire by raiders. The melted pork fat even ruined good folks' shoes in the street." Her needles flew fiercely. "Makes my hungry belly burn with ire."

"Are you hungry, Lucy?"

"I'm always hungry here lately."

"But the fort's bake ovens churn out bread continually."

"Sutler's Row doesn't see much of it."

"Then I shall do something about that. Talk to the fort's quartermaster or commissary officer. Or visit the baker himself."

"Losh, I don't want to cause trouble." Lucy's eyes rounded. "We get a ration of salted beef and such. And me and Petey forage what we can from the woods. Berries and nuts and the like."

"But that's hardly a meal. You must keep up your strength, even Petey, and especially Isham when he's on his feet again."

"Petey gets a steady supply of bones from the officers' mess. As for Isham, I've hoarded some to make broth."

"I'm hungry for fresh bread myself." Mae stood and gathered up her knitting. "I'll return shortly."

The clay and brick bake ovens near the fort kitchens were a source of wonder. They were stoked continually, the aroma of bread as prevalent as gunpowder. Night and day army bakers prepared dough and maintained the immense ovens, which required an endless supply of wood brought in by soldiers on fatigue duty.

Mae stood by, sewing kit in arms, and watched the head baker thrust a peel into the oven and remove loaves of crusty bread in rapid succession onto cooling racks. Memories of their Chatham kitchen rushed in, tantalizing if slightly hazy.

Oh, for a taste of Mrs. Hurst's blackberry jam.

The German baker, one of several from the Palatinate, grinned at her. "Hungrig, Frau Harlow? I can spare a loaf or two if you like."

"Much obliged, Mr. Helmer." She thanked him as his son, looking no older than Jon's Alex, bundled up two crusty loaves in a square of linen.

Mae felt she'd achieved some sort of coup. A fresh loaf would be a fine addition to Lucy's bone broth.

Head down, she skirted the parade ground past drilling, milling soldiers and nearly bumped into General Harlow himself.

"And what brings my bride begging bread?" he teased when she stopped right in front of him. "Let me guess. For Lucy?"

"And Private Hawkes and Petey."

"Petey?"

"Their dog."

"Ah." He ran a hand over his shadowed jaw. "Now I remember. What else do they need?"

"I'll find out. Lucy's promised to help me sew those indigo coats once more thread arrives."

He eyed the bread. "A fair trade in which we get the better deal."

"How was your foray?"

"Uneventful."

"Your one-word answers are rather unsettling, but I can't argue with uneventful." It was enough to stand here with him, her unassuming rebel in linen and buckskin, rifle slung across his back with a leather strap. Would he ever cease to make her heart turn over? "I'm relieved you're back. I prayed you'd be safe—and all those within and without these walls."

"Keep praying—and don't venture beyond Sutler's Row."

"I promise. Where are you headed now?"

"To report to General Clinton."

Bidding him goodbye, she watched him walk through the fort's gates, her questions lingering. Had he gone scouting alone? On foot, likely. He'd been away since daybreak. Now the sun foretold four o'clock.

Once she'd delivered the bread she would return to their quarters and ready for supper, perhaps have time enough to rest and finish her letters to Aunt Verity and Hanna. For once, thinking about home failed to bring the usual pinch. Chatham seemed less like home the longer she was away from it.

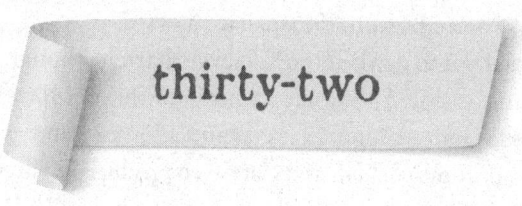

thirty-two

We recognize no Sovereign but God, and no King but Jesus!

John Adams

Four o'clock. How had she forgotten Catherine Kersey's oft postponed tea invitation? *That* set fire to Mae's heels. In her haste she all but flung the bread at Lucy before departing again. After returning to the parade ground, she hurried into the officers' quarters and their own small, shadowed room, wondering what to wear. Her sweaty linen garments wouldn't do.

A quarter of an hour later left her wishing for Coralie's help with her hair and stays. The small, cracked looking glass that had barely made it up Fort Montgomery's hill told her that her cap was in place even if her hair wasn't. But her dress was a pleasing lilac lustring, a nosegay of silk flowers pinned to her fichu. She even wore her wedding shoes. Wanting to contribute to the tea, she remembered the spiced comfits she'd brought from Chatham.

Just next door, Catherine Kersey answered at Mae's first knock. "Come in. Alice isn't here yet, but you're right on time. And please, call me Caty."

From somewhere in the parlor a clock chimed the hour. A small table stood between two open windows, three chairs waiting. The linen cloth and mismatched cups and saucers were a wee, welcome luxury in a temporary, disheveled life.

"I've brought sugared almonds and orange peel," Mae said, taking the tiny tin from her pocket.

"Truly?" Caty brought her hands together in delight. "I've not had the like since Boston. Please, have a seat."

Mae tried not to gawk at the Kerseys' quarters, though this was her first time inside. She wouldn't bemoan the fact they had two rooms to the Harlows' one. Lace curtains adorned windows, books rested on a decorative shelf, and Caty even produced a silver teapot.

"I see you admiring my mother's pot. She was a Boston silversmith's daughter and this is his creation, a gift when she wed my father."

"The floral engraving is especially beautiful."

"I weighed the wisdom of bringing it, but a touch of civility makes being here more bearable. And Alice has promised to bring some smuggled tea."

"Indeed, I have," Alice said as she pushed the door open. "The blackest bohea."

"It pairs well with the comfits Maebel brought." Caty gestured toward the empty chair. "I hope to weather our little tea party and the heat well."

A sudden breeze lifted a lace curtain but failed to reach farther into the room. Mae took out the fan tucked into her pocket. Alice did the same while Caty prepared the bohea.

"'Tis hard to believe August is upon us," Alice said to Caty, fluttering her lace-edged fan harder. "When is your lying-in, by your reckoning?"

"Christmastide. Heaven only knows if we'll be here then. I can't imagine a winter spent in this fort, what with the blizzards New York is known for. Summer is trial enough."

Waiting for the tea to steep, Caty launched into a litany of all she found wrong with Fort Montgomery. The privy pits smelled abominably. Well water tasted tainted. Rats had been found in a storehouse. Unruly livestock had overrun a kitchen garden while soldiers had broken into the rum supply and gotten falling-down drunk.

"But that's not the worst of it." Caty began pouring tea. "There's been a terrible tragedy upriver near Fort Edward."

Their fans stilled.

"Fort Edward upriver?" Mae ignored her cup of tea. "I heard it was controlled by Americans under General Schuyler."

"Not any longer." Caty shook her head, her features tight with distress. "It's since fallen to the British—General Burgoyne—after he took Ticonderoga."

Alice recoiled. "So the British are felling forts left and right on their way south? Will we be next?"

Mae looked from Alice to Caty again. "That isn't the tragedy you speak of."

At the shake of Caty's head, Alice urged, "By all means, tell us."

"'Tis quite . . . gruesome. And it might have been one of us instead." Caty took a sip of tea as if to steady herself. "A young woman named Jane McCrea was recently en route to her fiancé at Fort Edward, a British lieutenant serving with General Burgoyne's forces." Clearly rattled, Caty toyed with her cup. "Miss McCrea's lieutenant arranged for a party of British-allied Indians to escort her and a female friend to Fort Edward, where they could be married. They didn't make it far."

Mae resisted the childish urge to cover her ears, but she'd always been repelled by brutality. Once heard, such news tended to play over and over in her mind.

"Some blame a skirmish between American and British forces and a stray bullet. Others report it was her Huron guard who killed her after having an argument over who was to claim the reward for her safe delivery. Whatever happened, her scalp was delivered to her fiancé at Fort Edward."

Mae flinched as the bloodshed played out in her head.

Alice's gasp shook her further. "Are you sure 'tis true?"

"Intelligence came in today confirming the report. My husband rarely shares such things with me, but he felt it necessary that I be on my guard. And I tell you now so that you'll be on yours."

Mae's mind veered to Coralie. How alike Jane McCrea and her sister were. Both affianced to British officers. Both in New York. Jane's fate might have befallen her sister. Had Lieutenant Gibbs written as she'd hoped?

"Tragic," Mae murmured. "The lieutenant's life will never be the same."

"I imagine he's more than brokenhearted." Alice shuddered. "He's likely blaming himself for arranging her transport in the first place."

They finished their tepid tea in silence. What more was there to say?

★ ★ ★ ★ ★

That night Mae and Rhys retired early to bed. She washed first, the tubful of cool water refreshing. Rhys preferred the river, having found a secluded spot up Popolopen Creek. Once Mae had donned a nightgown, she took out her brush.

"This weather makes me want to snip off my hair."

"Don't you dare," he told her, taking her brush. "Your hair is your glory, like Scripture says."

Her thoughts took a melancholy turn. What color was Jane McCrea's hair? Would he not tell her about the incident as Caty's husband had done? Nor had he told her about the fall of Fort Edward.

Silent, he began braiding her hair, each finger a thumb.

Turning, she interrupted his clumsy efforts by standing on tiptoe and kissing his bristled cheek. She preferred him a bit scruffy, liking the way his roughened skin felt against hers. Sand against silk, he said. He kissed her back, driving all thoughts from her head, including the room's uncomfortable heat. For a moment, war and advancing armies—even Jane McCrea—seemed distant and less dark.

Once they'd said their nightly prayers they lay down on the too-small bed with the thin mattress, and he ran a finger down her flushed cheek. "Someday we'll have a thick tick filled with a great many goose feathers."

She shut her eyes, trying to envision it. "Describe our bedchamber in that house of yours. Every inch."

"'Tis a large room at the top of the stairs with a corner fireplace, with south- and north-facing windows overlooking what I hope to be gardens."

"A flower garden and a kitchen garden."

"Under your oversight, aye. I already have the seed."

"Tell me more."

"As for the finished bedchamber, there's oak floors and lime-plastered walls with raised paneling."

"No wallpaper?"

"Papered walls?" His amused voice held disbelief.

"A silver and blue trellis pattern, perhaps, with matching canopy and bed-curtains and coverlet."

"You'll make a poor man of me, Mae." His sleepy smile told her he didn't mind in the least.

"'Tis nice to dream, is it not?"

"You well know I can deny you nothing when you look at me like that." He stifled a yawn with his fist. "We rise early. Needs be we sleep."

She kissed him good night. Daybreak's reveille would come far too soon. Since his recovery, Private Hawkes often drummed at dawn, but tonight a fifer signaled slumber. Tomorrow she and Lucy would begin making coats, having gotten a new supply of thread.

Soon Rhys's rhythmic, even breathing told her he slept even as the dark denied her another look at him. Through the open window came the steady chorus of crickets and the distant, hollow hoot of an owl.

She dreamed of befeathered heads and fixed bayonets. A swarm of redcoats and menacing stands of trees. Their branches scraped like talons, tearing at her skin and dress. She lay on the forest floor atop the leaf-molded ground, dirt beneath her nails, and then a sharp tug to her scalp brought her head up, and she saw Coralie—a broken, bloodied Coralie—face down, her hair torn away.

The sharp cry was her own, banishing the dream if not the darkness. It brought Rhys upright as if he were poised to fight.

"Mae, Mae. Easy, my love." He took her in his arms, his mouth near her ear, one hand caressing her hair. "A bad dream . . . mayhap a nightmare."

"'Twas Coralie. I saw her in the woods—she'd been killed, scalped on her way to meet Lieutenant Gibbs. She lay upon the ground and I couldn't help her—"

His hand stilled. "You heard about Jane McCrea."

She buried her head in his bare shoulder. "Caty Kersey told us today."

"A tragedy—a casualty of war."

"What do you know about her?"

"She was a pastor's daughter. From Jersey. Affianced to a British officer."

Somehow the similarities made it all the more chilling.

"Would you like to go to the farm on the Sabbath?" he said quietly. "Be with your family?"

She did—and she didn't. "I'll only go if it's safe. I won't endanger myself or you or anyone else."

Yet even as she said it, she realized nothing was safe or certain here. Survival was ever in mind even within Fort Montgomery's sturdy walls.

thirty-three

Last Sunday the Rebel army was Mustered at the White plains, when it was reported amongst them that they have 20000, but the Friends to Government say if they be 14000 that is the outside of them. That the Women and Waggoners make up near the half of their Army.

British intelligence report, New York

How good it was to sit around the family table with everything just as it had been before she'd wed and left. Jon presided with a prayer, Joanna served, and the children chattered as Coralie sat beside Mae, Rhys and James opposite.

"Did you fort dwellers bring any news?" Joanna asked as she sat down.

Mae tensed, hoping Jane McCrea wouldn't be mentioned in front of the children.

"Little to report," James replied, buttering his bread, "except for General Washington encamping a few miles north of here."

"At the Clove, yes, in Ramapo Valley. On the other hand, I heard Ticonderoga and Edward have both fallen." Joanna's delight turned to dismay. "One hardly knows what to pray for from day to day."

"All changes hourly," Jon said. "This war is truly tit for tat."

"Be on your guard from every direction," Rhys told them, taking a drink of cider.

James nodded. "So far you've had nothing stolen or destroyed?"

"Nothing thus far." Joanna passed a basket of bread. "Word is there's activity on the other side of the river, though. Something about a Loyalist spy hiding in a cave between raids on Patriot farms."

"We have more to fear from that Ramapo Valley gang, horse stealing for the British and all else," Jon told them between bites.

"Claudius Smith?" Rhys looked up from his plate. "He goes by the alias of James Reed and John Wright."

"That's the one." Joanna grimaced. "Evil by any name."

Jon met her eyes. "We've had militia on watch in the Ramapo Mountains because of him and his fellows. We don't want trouble come the harvest."

"Wise," Rhys said. "I'd also recommend the militia assist in bringing in the valley's wheat, if only to stand guard once the harvest is underway."

Jon nodded. "All the farms could be covered that way."

"Now that Washington is at the Clove I doubt there'll be much trouble."

Mae listened, yearning for Virginia. Yet how could one pine for a place they'd never been? Rhys gave her a glimpse of his farming life as he talked, but try as she might, she couldn't see him trading his rifle to get behind a plow or planting seed or even haying, scythe in hand.

"So how is life at Fort Montgomery, Mae?" Coralie asked as she poured more cider.

"Never dull," Mae replied, having lost count of time. "I've finished making cockades and am now sewing garments again."

"And the officers' wives?"

"We met for tea recently. And we usually have dinner together with the officers."

"I'm glad you're not the only woman there," Joanna told her, taking Phemie on her lap. "Though I know there are plenty of women followers on hand. I've even thought of taking some produce to sell on Sutler's Row myself."

As the heaping contents of the dishes dwindled, Mae stood. "Let me tidy up. 'Tis the least I can do after so fine a Sabbath dinner."

"I'll make no objection," Joanna replied with a grateful smile.

Mae plucked an apron from a wall peg and tied it around her waist while her oldest nieces began clearing the table. How good it felt to do the most mundane tasks and be among family again. Seeing Coralie hale and hearty dispelled the lingering taint of her own nightmare.

As the men rose from their chairs and left the house, Mae looked up from scrubbing dishes. "I thought I heard a horse."

Joanna brightened. "The post rider, likely, though he's not been by for some time."

At that, Coralie rose from the table, hastened out the door, and bypassed the men on the porch. Might it be too much to hope Coralie would have a letter?

Going to a window, Mae saw the rider slow and greet Coralie. He came to a full stop near the barn before rummaging in a saddlebag. Mae could sense her sister's tempered hopes, ready to be snuffed like candle flame, and all but held her breath. At last the rider leaned forward and extended a letter. For Coralie or someone else?

Coralie's smile answered as she turned back to the house. Good tidings or ill? As he was an officer, the whereabouts and fate of Eben Gibbs were ever in question.

Lord, let it be good news, please.

Mae returned to her dishwashing while Joanna sat down in her favorite chair, both of them waiting. Coralie returned on catlike feet, reading as she walked. She came to a stop by the hearth, and the room grew more hushed. A sudden cry rent the quiet kitchen, shattering Mae's hopes. Coralie hurled the letter into the low fire, then fled upstairs. Drying her hands on her apron, Mae watched the paper curl as flames licked the edges, ending in embers and ash.

Joanna looked perplexed. "What on earth?"

Coralie had held tight to her secret. Would it be left to Mae to tell them?

"My sister had some sort of understanding with a British officer stationed in New York," she began quietly. "Lieutenant Eben Gibbs was originally from Chatham, but his family left for New York City at the start of the war, given their Loyalist stance. He and Coralie kept corresponding . . ."

Joanna sighed. "I pray the man's not ill—or dead—though I never thought I'd be saying that about a British soldier."

"I'll go up to her." Mae hung the dish towel on a peg, trying to summon the right words before climbing the stairs with a weight like a cold iron on her heart.

Coralie was in her room beneath the eave, sobbing so hard she struggled to breathe.

Mae sat beside her and placed a hand on her shuddering back. "Sister, what has happened?"

Long moments ticked past as Coralie continued crying. "Eben wants nothing to do with me. I've come all this way only to hear him say his feelings have changed—that he refuses to marry into a family of Patriots."

So he blamed them and their loyalties? "Are you sure you read it rightly?"

"He was quite clear." Her embittered voice broke, and she shook Mae off. "You and James and Jon and Aaron are to blame!"

Schooling her tone, Mae forged ahead. "Best you find out now rather than later if he's a wastrel and a rogue."

"Oh? He's neither, though I well know how you feel about him." Coralie dug in her pocket for a handkerchief. "Leave me be—right now. I want to be alone."

Mae stood, feeling helpless in the face of such an emotional storm, and returned to the kitchen. Her nieces had finished washing dishes and gone outside. Joanna waited, seated by her spinning wheel, her face full of questions.

"Lieutenant Gibbs has decided to end matters between them."

"Jilted, then." Joanna's distress mirrored Mae's. "She's talked of little else since you left, forever waiting for a letter."

Mae stood by as James entered the kitchen, returning his empty cider mug. "Why is Coralie crying?"

"You don't know the whole story, but in a few words, Coralie has just been jilted by Lieutenant Eben Gibbs." Mae gestured to the hearth's fire. "She burned his letter she was so distraught."

"I can't say I'm surprised." James looked at the dwindling flames, where only a blackened corner of the letter remained. "But I'm truly sorry for her misery, if nothing else."

Jon entered next as sobbing was again heard on high. "All is not well, I take it."

"A matter of the heart," Mae told him, explaining it all over again.

"I wish she'd told us there was more to their arrangement than letter writing." Her eldest brother took a seat at the empty table. "As for Coralie, she always did have the worse end of the staff."

Guilt pricked Mae. That was the short of it. Coralie had always been in her shadow, the least of the sisters, or so Coralie said and believed. Less comely, less capable, less well in body. It had been a thorn betwixt them since childhood. And now this . . .

James looked at her in concern. "Although you may want to stay on and comfort her, we need to return to the fort."

"I understand." Mae removed her apron, feeling as much relief as sorrow. "In her current mood, my being here will only aggravate. My place is with Rhys."

★ ★ ★ ★ ★

Rhys mounted Copper and extended a hand to Mae as she stepped from the mounting block. She swung herself into the saddle and smoothed her petticoats, keeping them free of the stirrups.

235

With her arms anchored around his waist, he let James lead, Jon in the rear, all of them watchful with nary a word spoken.

Though he rued Coralie's hurt, he was glad Mae wanted to return with him. Between anticipated raids on valley Patriots and the British advance down the Hudson, the farm was less secure than the fort. He was hours away from ordering his riflemen out to harass British patrols and scouts, including their supply lines. Washington's latest orders had been clear. "Wear down, disrupt, distress, but avoid engaging in full-blown battle."

He leaned out of the saddle far enough to snatch a wild rose. Mae took it, the delicate bloom fragile in her hand. He sensed her wordless pleasure as she leaned into him like a caress, her softness pressed to his straight back.

When the fort's main gates appeared at the end of the rutted, dusty road, he let out a pent-up breath. Helping Mae dismount, the sun catching in her pale hair, he tried to push aside the nightmarish happening with Jane McCrea. He knew details few did. How violent the last moments of her life had been. How her hair had touched the ground, a yellow-gold torrent like Mae's. News of her death had begun to spread like fire, many blaming the British for such brutality.

For now, Mae stood looking up at him, a light in her eyes that bespoke relief at their safe return. Yet he read sadness there too, a concern for her sister, who hadn't the happiness they had.

"Where to now?" she asked as they cleared the front gates.

"Once I return you to our quarters, I'll meet with Clinton and hear the latest intelligence."

"Please don't ride out on a patrol without telling me."

"Never," he vowed. "And you?"

"I shall finish that letter to Aunt Verity and see if Lucy is ready to begin cutting more cloth for officers' coats."

He pushed open the door to their quiet, spare barracks room, wanting to join her, a headache pulsing at his temples. "Till supper then."

thirty-four

[That person] will be the best Soldier, and the best Patriot, who contributes most to this glorious work, whatever his station, or from whatever part of the Continent he may come.

George Washington

Mae inked her quill and wondered if she should share Coralie's heartache with Aunt Verity.

Since you asked about Coralie and Lieutenant Gibbs, I will tell you that Coralie has just received word from him ending their engagement. She is understandably distraught and even threw his letter into the fire. I tried to comfort her to no avail. Please pray that her heart will mend and she will recover from being spurned in time. For now, she remains on the farm with Jon's family, though she may want to return to Chatham—

A knock sounded on the door. Lucy?

"Come in," Mae called, setting aside her letter once again.

Lucy appeared, Petey on her heels. She made the adoring dog stay at the door, then shut it, sewing kit in hand. "I saw you come

237

in with General Harlow and your brothers and thought you might want to begin those coats."

"I'd rather sew than write," Mae told her, leaving the desk to fetch some of the waiting wool. "How's Private Hawkes?"

Lucy smiled her tea-stained smile. "Tip-top and drumming again."

"So I hear." Mae turned toward the window, where it seemed the drummers were intent on storming the gates of Hades. Though she wouldn't tell Lucy so, Mae preferred the more lilting fifes of the fife and drum corps. Drums sounded ominous, but fifes reminded her of bright, piercing birdsong.

"He's learning a new call—a drum signal—for battle. Though he's been missing, he's top drummer now, his major said."

"Is it true the fifes are heard over the chaos of battle, like drums?"

"Aye." Lucy took out newly sharpened scissors. "There's a new lad who's joined the corps by the name of Nathan Futrell. Only seven years old."

Mae's heart twisted. "So young."

"Been playing since he was wee, like my Isham."

"Where are his parents?"

"He's orphaned."

"How sad. Think of the danger."

"Plenty of that." Lucy sighed. "Especially when they happen to be standing in the middle of the battle with no protection, not even a musket."

Soon the snip of scissors took hold as they cut the woolen cloth into pieces, their goal one fine coat. Next came the linen lining.

"I'm a sorry tailor," Lucy said as she coated linen thread with beeswax. "Feminine garments are more to my liking."

"Hopefully I'll improve over time." Mae studied their efforts, having used Rhys's wedding coat as a pattern. "'Twill be a fine way to winter."

"If we're still here." Lucy eyed her warily. "Burgoyne is fighting his way toward us, though he's been slowed some at Fort

Edward. I fancy he prefers a fort to plowing his way through the wilderness."

Fort Edward again. Had Jane McCrea been buried there? "With General Washington and several thousand Continentals near at hand, I'm feeling rather comfortable."

"Don't get too snug. Washington may be heading another direction."

Mae stopped snipping. "Truly?"

"He's torn between staying here in New York to rout Burgoyne or stomping on Howe in Pennsylvania."

"How like a game you make it sound." Mae resumed snipping. "You hear a great many things, far more than I do."

"Sutler's Row is always abuzz. And I mostly keep my mouth shut and my ears wide open."

"Perhaps I should do the same," Mae said, examining the linen. "Shall I use a backstitch or running stitch to sew the lining together?"

"Take your pick, just make your stitches clean and tight."

"Aye, General Hawkes," Mae teased.

★ ★ ★ ★ ★

At week's end Jon came to the fort from the farm. At their quarters where she and Rhys were having a simple supper alone, he appeared with James in tow. Though Mae welcomed them warmly, she sensed something amiss, as did Rhys.

He looked up from his plate and the tough cut of meat beneath his knife. "I sense a council of war."

With a hoarse chortle, Jon sat down at the table while Mae got up to serve her brothers small beer. James looked more serious as he downed his drink in a few gulps and asked Mae for more. She grew more uneasy as her brothers exchanged a fretful glance.

"I bring news from home," Jon began. "All continues calm in the valley, thankfully, as far as raids and such. But Coralie is wanting to move here to the fort."

"Here," Rhys repeated tersely, continuing his meal with a look at Mae.

James stirred as if uncomfortable in his chair. "Joanna said she's cried since you left and claims she needs her sister."

"Her sister is now my wife and has no time for theatrics," Rhys told them, to Mae's astonishment. "She's busy being of benefit here and can't play nursemaid."

"Agreed, sir," James said, clearing his throat.

Mae looked from her brothers to Rhys. A headache had turned him cross. He'd become especially protective of her since she'd been unwell lately. Yesterday she'd even been abed, unable to sew with Lucy. Rancid meat or vegetables, likely, given the stifling weather.

"If Coralie can return safely to Chatham, that might be best," Mae told them quietly. "Hanna and Aaron and Mrs. Hurst will welcome her, and she can help with the baby once it comes."

"I said the same." James sat back, arms crossed. "But there's little to no travel to Jersey at present."

"Would that there was." Jon took another drink. "I'm sorry to say that Coralie and Joanna don't see eye to eye. Having her on the farm is proving more hindrance than help."

"Joanna has been most patient and obliging," James said. "The fault is not hers."

Mae wanted to moan in dismay. She'd sensed the tension between Joanna and Coralie and pinned the blame on Coralie, who hadn't fared well with the officers' wives either. A heartbroken, homesick sister was unendurable. In truth, her own anger toward Eben Gibbs still simmered since he'd left them to deal with the difficulty he'd caused.

Finished with supper, Rhys pushed back his plate. "If she comes here, she'll do so by working as a laundress or nurse where help is needed. If she refuses, she's welcome to find a way back to Jersey on her own."

"I'll relay that to her," Jon said. "And bring back her answer."

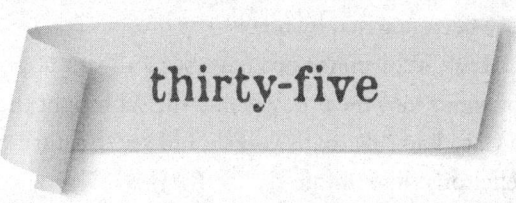

thirty-five

She drew her rations as other soldiers did.

Pension information for Mary Cochron,
camp follower

The next day, Coralie appeared and all but fell into Mae's arms. Embracing her at the door of their quarters, Mae ushered her inside, where she'd been about to make mint tea.

"Hot tea? In this weather?" Coralie asked.

"I'm rather unsettled from the heat and bad rations." Mae eyed her warily, noting her wan color and bloodshot eyes. Was she not sleeping? Still crying? "How are you faring?"

"I've just come from fort headquarters, where your husband read me the riot act about my being here."

"Meaning?" Mae prodded.

"He said I'm to contribute to the fort by working in some capacity, either as a laundress or nurse. Imagine! I'm no better than a camp follower like Lucy or—"

"You helped at the hospital in Chatham." The memory was suspect. Had her sister been gleaning information to pass to Gibbs instead?

"That was different. This is so . . . *lowering.*"

Mae began measuring tea leaves from the tin into a creamware teapot. "Helping the fort run more efficiently is hardly lowering. We must all do our part or become, as General Washington said, 'a clog upon every movement.'"

Coralie sat, drumming her fingers atop the table. "And to think I might have been married by now!"

"Being Mrs. Gibbs might not have been all you hoped." Mae poured hot water into the pot, wishing she'd brought theirs from home like Caty had. "Perhaps you should see this turn of events as more felicitous than unfair."

"How glib you are, Mae. And how easy it is for you, being happily married to an officer and cozily sharing this spot, rude as it is." Coralie's restless gaze roamed the room. "This fort's pickets feel more prison, but 'tis better than the tents and shacks I spied outside fort walls."

"Sutler's Row is colorful and full of life," Mae said, setting down sugar and a spoon. "Where will you lodge?"

"James showed me my quarters, a dreadful hovel near the sally port shared with two decrepit nurses. I left my belongings there and pray they're not stolen."

Mae sat opposite her, patience thin. "Sister, if you don't take yourself in hand, no matter your heartbreak, you might well be turned out of this fort."

"What means you?"

"You're here at the mercy of General Clinton and my husband. If there's trouble from you in any quarter, you'll be sent packing. Surly attitudes often end in the guardhouse. These men are fighting for their lives—our lives—and the future of this country. Think on that rather than your own small struggles."

Coralie continued her fretful table tapping. "If I had a guide I'd employ him to return me to Chatham."

"'Tis a very dangerous time to be traveling, even more so than when we came."

"So I've heard." Coralie made a face. "Given that, I'll be working as a laundress starting tomorrow, though my duties include mending washed clothes and the like."

"I've seen the washing area on the riverbank below and up Popolopen Creek. The women toil hard to keep the men clean and trim."

"At least the view of the Hudson River and surrounding hills is astounding." She looked past Mae's shoulder. "I suppose I'll soon be laundering officers' coats like the one behind you."

"We've finished the first and have several more started."

"*We?*"

"Lucy Hawkes is a marvel with a needle. Remember the pincushion she made me?"

"Vaguely."

"Her husband is an excellent drummer, both of them contributing a great deal to this garrison."

"Drumming? I loathe all that noise just as I did in Chatham."

Mae bit her tongue, wishing Rhys back and her sister already at work on the riverbank. But would she wrangle with the laundresses too?

"I'm not to take my meals with you either but in the common mess like the other help."

"Since you didn't get on well with Mrs. Kersey and Mrs. Wentz, that would be wise."

"And how are the high-and-mighty wives?"

Mae opened her mouth to share Caty's glad news, then thought better of it. Doing so might stoke her sister's discontent and usher in another rant. "They're making the best of being here."

"Seems like an age since we left Chatham." Sighing, Coralie took out a handkerchief and dabbed away the sheen on her brow. "I want nothing more now than to return and be an aunt to Hanna and Aaron's firstborn if I'm not to be a wife and mother myself."

"I'm sorry," Mae murmured. "Truly I am."

"I suppose I might meet someone here, though many officers

are already married and there's precious little time for any frolicking."

Precious little, indeed. The Arnold Tavern ball seemed more like a fable she'd read long ago. "Every moment here is dedicated to the cause. The celebrations will come later."

"Here we go again." Coralie rolled her eyes. "How on earth can a ragtag group of the worst sort of rebels and ruffians triumph over the most highly trained fighting force in the world? I don't even recall how all this madness started."

"Let me remind you." Mae took a steadying breath and glanced at the teapot with distaste. "Have you forgotten the Stamp Act? Or the Townshend and Tea Acts? Then there's the Intolerable Acts and countless restrictions of American colonial trade, all continual violations of our rights. Because of these and other offenses, these ragtag rebels and ruffians, as you call them, have been forced into a ferocious fight they'll undoubtedly win even if takes a decade to do it."

Coralie stared back at her with red-rimmed eyes. "I cannot imagine another conflict like the Old French War that dragged on seven years."

"Nor can I," Mae said, sensing they'd found common ground at last. "Two wars in one lifetime are more than enough."

★ ★ ★ ★ ★

Mae looked at Lucy, whose head was bent over a coat sleeve as she plied her needle tirelessly. Sunlight filtered through the oaks overhead, a welcome breeze rustling the leaves like silk petticoats. Mae pressed a discreet hand to her queasy middle, half frantic to find relief. She could no longer blame the victuals she'd partaken of days ago being rancid. Nor could she blame it on Coralie's cantankerous presence or Rhys's increasing forays away from the fort.

Taking a deep breath, she began piecing together another linen coat lining while wishing for candied ginger or chalk-and-oyster-shell lozenges. The memory of Aaron's apothecary and all those handsome blue and white delftware jars lining his shelves, promising relief, taunted her.

"How's your sister faring?" Lucy asked without looking up. "I spied her hefting a basket of soiled linens on her way to the river this morn."

Spied. Mae winced at her wording. Thankfully Lieutenant Gibbs was long gone, and Mae's suspicions with him, or so she hoped. Yet she still felt the sting of Coralie's perfidy and her own complicity in abiding it.

"She's been at work awhile now and seems to have settled in." Did Lucy hear the relief in her voice? "I think the generals scared her a little. She's been on her best behavior."

Lucy chuckled. "Clinton and Harlow are scary, aye. The Brits think so too."

"Yet you knew my general before all of this started," Mae replied, "since you're from the Shenandoah Valley too."

"'Tis a big valley. Folks don't often crisscross, though everybody knows everyone else by name—or reputation."

"What do you miss most about Virginia?"

Lucy grew thoughtful. "The Blue Mountains. They're bigger than these foothills here and all ablaze in the fall." She paused and looked up at the quaking leaves overhead. "Maybe these will turn fiery if we're here long enough to see them."

"Do you ever regret following the army?"

"Nay, but Petey does." She gave the little dog gnawing on a bone beside her a loving look. "He misses his barn bed and all the critters he used to chase."

"Will you come visit me, Lucy, once we're back there? Or can I come see you?"

"I'd like nothing better. We'll sit down when the war's won and have us a proper cup of English tea."

They laughed till all of Sutler's Row looked their way. As Mae's stomach gave another lurch, she rued giving the rest of her mint tea to Caty.

Why had she not thought of searching for wild mint here? Surely somewhere in the woods it grew, likely along Popolopen Creek. Best to gather it of a morning, Mama had once told her, once the dew was off and before the sun robbed it of flavor. Even the hope of it brought relief.

Tomorrow morn, then, Lord willing.

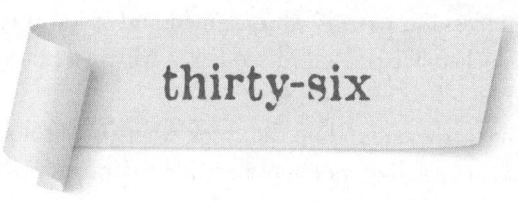

thirty-six

In every human breast, God has implanted a principle, which we call love of freedom.

Phillis Wheatley

A fife broke through the stillness of August, sounding reveille. Mae rolled over atop the lumpy mattress, missing Rhys. He'd gone north days ago on another foray with a select company, the best of his riflemen. When the hours grew hollow without him, she dwelled on all she missed. His smile. His touch. His clean habits in a fort naturally given to filth. The prayers he said morning and evening, the most beautiful she'd ever heard, an echo of his Welsh ancestry. His low, slow playing of her father's fiddle.

Somehow he seemed to sense how the wilderness struck a woman who'd never been beyond Jersey. His tenderness and patience in the face of her fears and uncertainties made her all the more smitten. The belle of Chatham, as he liked to call her, seemed a far better woman with him by her side.

Once roused, she dressed slowly, pulling at her front-lacing stays and feeling a pinch. She let out a bit before tying them at her waist. How could she be more stout when she'd eaten so little of late?

Ignoring the question, she donned a light indigo linen dress, her white apron and cap freshly washed.

Since she tasked herself with her and Rhys's own laundry, her return to Popolopen Creek was familiar. She arrived ahead of a dozen women who manned the kettles and fires and lye soap, Coralie among them. For now, the gravelly bank was mostly empty save the guards and patrols who roamed and stood watch. One doffed his cocked hat and addressed her as Mistress Harlow when she passed by.

She went farther inland up the creek where water flowed over mossy slabs of rock like stairsteps in a spirited journey to the river below. Amid the ferns grew wild masses of mint with long, lush stems and dark green leaves. She stripped a stem clean and crushed the leaves between her palms, breathing in the heady scent till her stomach quieted.

She gathered more for tea, already envisioning laying it out on the windowsill in their quarters to dry, and continued till her apron was full. The rising sun dispelled the river's mist, then the queasiness struck hard again, almost sending her to her knees.

Why this foot-dragging fatigue? Frequent naps when she'd never napped before? Feeling ravenous when she wasn't nauseous? Being near tears for no apparent reason?

She refused to admit what stared her squarely in the face.

She lowered herself to a log and closed her eyes, allowing her mind to roam where it had never been before. She braced herself for the pain of childbed . . . the possible fall of this very fort . . . traveling from New York to Virginia . . .

What would Rhys's reaction be?

She'd sensed a change about him lately. A tenseness, even a terseness. While still gentle and considerate of her, he seemed increasingly preoccupied. He didn't confide in her like the other officers did their wives. Did he want to shield her from the worst of the conflict? The ugliness and brutality of the fight?

"Maebel Bohannon Harlow."

She startled, though the beloved voice was rich with mirth and affection. She opened her eyes. Rhys stood a stone's throw away, his shirt and leggings besmeared with mud, his battered hat missing the cockade she'd made, a telling bruise beneath his right eye.

A thrill of relief coursed through her. "You look like you had a tussle with the wilderness—and lost."

He sat down beside her as a grouse flushed from hiding and careened overhead. "Is that all the welcome I get?"

Smiling, she scooted a bit farther away. "Till you bathe, it is."

He removed his hat and flung it into the water that pooled below them. His moccasins followed, then all the rest of his tattered garments. He pulled himself to his feet and waded into the creek, water frothing about him in its musical rush to the river below.

Long minutes later he emerged, his wet skin glistening, his dark hair plastered to his tanned neck and shoulders. Half drunk with delight and wonder, she watched him as she would a captivating sunset or sunrise.

"You'll need clean clothes," she called, getting up and forgetting her apron full of mint. It spilled to the bank in a green torrent, but she left it, hurrying up the nearest trail hugging the hillside.

When she returned, he sat behind the screen of a sprawling laurel bush. Once dried and dressed, he began helping with her mint, picking up what she'd dropped in her haste to help him.

"I don't recall you being overfond of mint."

She lifted her shoulders in a shrug and lowered herself to the log again as wooziness got the upper hand. She'd not eaten yet, nor had he, she guessed. Toast and coffee, eggs and bacon were what he needed. She even had a few potatoes to fry. But the very thought of cooking . . .

His eyes roamed over her as if he'd been gone a month. Their eyes held, his so sharp they felt cutting. And somehow she sensed he knew what she was about to say.

★ ★ ★ ★ ★

Rhys studied her, finding her somewhat different—more beautiful than she'd ever been, as abloom as a wild rose. Her skin reminded him of the fine porcelain cup Bronwyn treasured. Only a few faint pockmarks remained. Simply put, Mae glowed. As he stared at her, a hitch of concern dented his awe.

Women looked that way for a reason.

"I'd thought to tell you this in Virginia once we were settled, not here in the wilds of New York. Naive of me." She took a breath, her eyes entreating. "I'm—we're—"

"With child," he finished for her.

She looked surprised and relieved all at once.

Father. Soldier. The two words seemed contrary. For a trice a soaring elation got the upper hand, then it came crashing down. He wanted to hear "Father" with all that was in him. Just not now.

His throat tightened as he swallowed. "I don't know what to say."

"Say we'll manage this together." Her eyes glittered. "I have to believe that whatever happens, for whatever reason, this is meant to be now and not later."

"We'll more than manage, Mae." He knelt before her and took her hands in his. "There's no better news."

"I know, but I never thought . . ."

"You thought all our lovemaking would come to naught?" He regarded her with an amused tenderness.

Color pinked her cheeks. "Say nothing to anyone. Not Jon nor James."

"Why?"

"'Tis too soon."

"When will it be, by your reckoning?"

"Early spring, perhaps."

"You're well. Strong. You were meant to be a mother."

A sigh. "I'm actually quite unwell at the moment."

A commotion on the bluff above brought them to their feet. The washerwomen were coming downhill, baskets on hips, singing a familiar tune.

"Let tyrants shake their iron rod,
And Slav'ry clank her galling chains,
We fear them not, we trust in God,
New England's God forever reigns."

Mae was certain Coralie wasn't singing along. How galling did she find their show of patriotism?

Rhys touched her cheek, and she looked back at him. "I have a report to give Clinton. Then I'll head to our quarters and break my fast with you there—if you can manage it."

"I'll fix you a fine breakfast."

"Have some mint tea first."

Once all the laundresses were on the riverbank, Mae and Rhys started up the hill. Coralie raised a hand after setting her load near a washtub. Mae waved back in reply, having seen little of her in recent days. She'd seemed to settle into the humble routine better than expected, walking round the parade ground in the evening, talking and playing cribbage with other women and soldiers. She'd even ventured onto Sutler's Row. Rarely did she come to Mae's quarters.

Dare she hope her sister would find some measure of peace and purpose, after all?

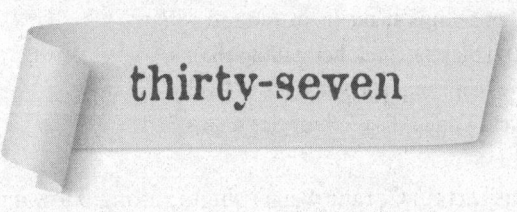

thirty-seven

Every post is honorable in which a man can serve his country.

George Washington

Inside headquarters, General Clinton looked up from the map spread across his desk, anchored with one-pound cannon balls. Rhys entered the room and the aides scattered, leaving them alone.

"Welcome back, Harlow." Clinton looked haggard, the half-moons beneath his eyes indicative of a commander with too much on his mind. "Good news?"

Rhys hesitated, wanting to report the British were in full retreat. "News, anyway."

"There's no slowing Burgoyne's advance, in other words."

"They remain at Fort Edward for now, organizing and preparing for the next campaign. It helped that St. Clair crippled Fraser's troops near Ticonderoga." Rhys approached the desk, damp hat beneath one arm. "As for us, I've returned with all forty of my riflemen, having harassed their patrols and scouts for two days and nights without rest, stalling supply lines and doing whatever mischief we could to those outside Edward's walls."

"Word is the British are having considerable trouble with Indian allies since the murder of Jane McCrea."

Rhys nodded. "Burgoyne has issued orders to restrict their actions. He's even alienated many Mohawk by trying to make them fight like English soldiers and abide by European military discipline."

"A Pandora's box." Clinton gestured to the map. "Once Burgoyne leaves Edward, how long do you think it will take for the enemy to reach here?"

"The march will be slow and taxing even with fair weather and no opposition." Rhys traced a finger down the black line of the Hudson. "Their progress is sure to be slowed by terrain and Orange County's militia patrolling fifteen miles of shoreline."

"Burgoyne's numbers?"

"No more than eight thousand."

"To our eleven thousand spread across the Highlands." Clinton frowned. "Washington is weighing whether to remain here or move elsewhere."

"Benedict Arnold has been ordered to join forces with Schuyler to halt Burgoyne's movements here, I heard."

"True. But whether or not that occurs is another matter entirely. Washington believes the bigger battle may well be Philadelphia, and he could order our troops to counter General Howe's advance there. If so, he's willing to sacrifice men here along the Hudson to that end."

Sacrifice. Rhys withheld a wince. The entire war seemed about extinguishing the biggest fires on every front while lesser conflicts were left to fend for themselves with whatever fighting force could be had. Fort Montgomery might be one of them.

Picking up a letter, Clinton said, "Washington states, 'I consulted those best acquainted with the strength of the passes, and they all agreed that about two thousand men at Peekskill and Fort Montgomery would be sufficient to repel any force that would probably be sent against you.'"

Rhys held his tongue. He sensed the greater threat might come from the south if Sir Henry Clinton advanced from New York

City. Surely Washington had considered this too. Who was he to naysay him?

Clinton continued, "He feels we have overrated enemy forces in New York, further reason to draw part of our army away from the Hudson Highlands toward Pennsylvania."

"Has he indicated where the Rifle Corps might go next?"

"Not yet." He continued studying the highly detailed map. "For now, he's issued orders that all farms, barns, and crops within a twenty-mile radius be destroyed lest they provision the enemy. Patrols and militia have been sent out to inform those settlements. If the settlers don't do as ordered, we're to confiscate or destroy what's left standing."

A harsh order. Rhys's mind swung to Jon, both soldier and settler. "Better that than the British." Still, his mind churned along with his gut. Years of toil turned to ashes overnight. Few settlers would welcome that, even if they were on the American side.

"Enough hard news." Clinton's smile was thin. "Be at your ease. I would have you and your men rested and ready for the next foray."

★ ★ ★ ★ ★

Rhys entered his and Mae's quarters quietly, finding her asleep. His breakfast was on a pewter plate atop their trestle table, the mint she'd picked on the sunny windowsill. He set his weapons aside and tied his still-wet hair back with ribbon before eating. His exhaustion seemed bone deep, his eyelids leaden.

Completely still, Mae slept on. He still hadn't come to terms with her being his bride, bearing his name, even following him here to a hazardous outpost. Rather than unsettle him as she'd done when she'd been Miss Bohannon, she steadied him. Because of her he was a better man. A better soldier.

Removing his coat, he lay down beside her as quietly as he could. The room's heat soon lulled him into the black oblivion of sleep, then wonder tugged him awake. He was a father even though he'd not yet held their child in his arms. Come spring, where would the three of them be?

He couldn't rest long with his mind crammed full. He swung his feet to the floor, got up, and pulled on his boots, then reached for his hat before heading to Sutler's Row.

Half an hour later he arrived, delayed by countless side conversations as soldiers and civilians came and went. Finally he found Lucy sewing by her tent. As he approached, her wee dog wagged its tail then barked, alerting her.

She started to get to her feet, but he put out a hand.

Tucking away her sewing, she gestured to a stump near her cook fire. "What brings you, sir? Mrs. Harlow's not ailing again, is she?"

Did Lucy know the reason?

He sat, reaching out a hand to scratch the brindled dog behind its raised ears. "She's asleep."

"She's been poorly lately. Sick to her stomach and sluggish."

"Aye, so she told me." He rested a hand on one of the pistols at his waist. "I've come to talk to you about what to do if this fort is besieged."

She nodded like they were merely discussing the weather. "The redcoats are still coming, then."

"Aye, though we're making it as troublesome for them as possible. The question is which direction they'll come from first."

"'Tis like chess, this conflict."

He nodded, somewhat amused. She played the game with Private Hawkes, who'd learned from an officer who'd carved them a set. She often won. Lucy was as smart as she was stalwart.

"Checkmate is the goal." He cleared his throat, hating the harsh details. "If the enemy nears, our pickets will give a warning of impending attack. At the first sign of danger, find my wife and flee in the safest direction. If you can't get to the horses, go on foot. Keep to the heaviest brush and out of sight as much as possible." He unbelted his leather money pouch and handed it to her. Next came two pistols. "This should see you both to the Shenandoah."

She took hold of everything, then hid the pistols in a near basket before belting the money around her waist and out of sight. It gave him some ease but not enough. There was no guarantee they'd get away. If any survived the first assault, a thousand other things could go wrong. Astride horses made them a target. Afoot meant other dangers. They could be killed, captured, or worse.

God preserve them. All three.

thirty-eight

Three things prompt men to a regular discharge of their duty in time of action: natural bravery, hope of reward, and fear of punishment.

George Washington

Another week passed, with Oneida spies and scouts appearing more frequently at the twin forts. The lush landscape held a brittleness, the hardwoods showing the first signs of color. Mae felt a change in the very air. Would autumn come early? Chatham was especially beautiful in the fall, the foothills and mountains afire. New York would be the same, she sensed, once the dog days of August were behind them.

She dressed for dinner, wearing her loosest gown, her stays less tightly laced. Seated in the officers' mess, she smiled when Rhys's fingers found hers beneath the table as they sat side by side.

Caty Kersey's chair was empty. Ill again, she kept to her quarters, attended by a midwife from the Hudson Highlands. Major Kersey had excused himself too. He was a doting husband, the prospect of a family reinforcing his desire to fight.

"I suppose there's one benefit of being childless—I shan't leave your side," Alice told her husband fondly. "And it's all a matter of perspective, is it not? I've only come from Boston, while some officers' wives follow them across an ocean."

"You speak of Baroness Riedesel, traveling south with Burgoyne and the British," Colonel Wentz said. "She even has her young children in tow. Three to be exact, including an infant daughter."

Alice's astonishment mirrored Mae's when she'd first heard about the noblewoman in Chatham. "Those Hessian wives sound as fierce as their husbands."

"Her husband, General Riedesel, is an upstanding officer, though he's joined the enemy," Colonel Lamb told them. "He served with distinction in the Seven Years' War."

"And you, General Clinton?" Alice asked as dinner was served. "Is it true you have children at home?"

Clinton smiled from his position at the head of the table. He was clad in one of the finished indigo coats, brass buttons gleaming, the fringed epaulets glinting with the metallic thread Lucy had worked. "Cornelia and I have four daughters and an infant son, George Washington Clinton—a fierce Patriot since birth."

They laughed as two orderlies served dinner, though Mae thought it sad the war had taken Clinton away from his family at such a time while also plunging a German noblewoman and children into the thick of it.

She listened to Rhys and the officers talk about the books and writings they were reading before circling back to the rebellion. Stomach settled, she helped herself to heaping dishes of beef, salat, wheaten bread, and a great many vegetables from valley settlers selling the last of their garden's bounty on Sutler's Row. If she wasn't careful she'd reveal her condition to everyone at table.

Rhys eyed her with amusement as her nausea gave way to ravenousness. His momentary shock along Popolopen Creek had since faded to a quiet, steadfast joy.

"The Mohicans are proving invaluable to us. There are no better scouts or intelligence in the northern campaign," Rhys was saying as the men discussed Indian allies.

"It doesn't hurt that you can speak their tongue," James told him with a knowing smile.

"Can you now?" Alice asked, appearing as surprised as Mae.

"Only because two Mohicans were held captive with me in Quebec. It was either learn their language or languish from loneliness," Rhys replied with a touch of drama. "Some of our allies speak better English than I do."

The others chuckled, and conversation continued as an orderly served apple tarts.

"When are the prisoners in the guardhouse being transferred?" Colonel Lamb looked to General Clinton, who gestured to Rhys.

"Harlow is the one who apprehended them near the Clove, where General Washington is encamped with troops. He'll be escorting them to a court-martial shortly."

The Clove. Lucy had told her it was a twenty-mile stretch where a few taverns stood, a region terrorized by Loyalist outlaws often in league with detachments of British regulars.

"We were able to get confessions from two of the fugitives exposing the rest." Rhys set his knife and fork on the edge of his empty plate. "Smith claims to hold a lieutenant's commission in a Loyalist regiment, but I have my doubts. General Putnam will decide their fate since he's the authority on military justice."

Clinton's relief was obvious. "Putnam warned that their gang has been promised a considerable reward if they seize American officers and conduct them to the British."

Mae felt a qualm and looked to Rhys. "You'll go with a guard to deliver the outlaws, I hope."

"Rest assured, Mrs. Harlow." Clinton smiled as if to cheer her. "Your husband will lead the party, which will be heavily guarded. He and your brother are far too valuable to risk capture or any violence along the way."

When supper was finished, she and Rhys, the officers, and Alice walked to the Grand Battery. Though she'd been several times, she was continually awed by both the cannons and the view. Who would believe amid all this wild beauty that armies were advancing? Everything looked so sunlit and serene, forests and mountains hemming in the river as it glided north and south.

A detachment of guards changed positions outside fort walls just as Mae spied Coralie. A basket of laundry on her hip, she spoke with a soldier in the shade of the powder magazine. Their animated talk and laughter drew more than Mae's eye. Rhys glanced at them, surprise on his usually stoic features.

"And who," Mae all but whispered, "is my sister talking to?"

"Captain Sinclair of the 5th New York Regiment."

"Perhaps she's forgotten Lieutenant Gibbs."

As Rhys turned to answer a question from Colonel Lamb, Mae descended the battery toward her sister. It wasn't the first time she'd seen Coralie with Captain Sinclair. Sometimes in the evenings they'd play cribbage on the common. Card games were popular, though gambling wasn't allowed.

Coralie turned away from him and faced Mae. "You've not come to remind me I should be about my work, have you?"

"Nay, I thought you might introduce me," Mae replied as Captain Sinclair returned to duty.

"You're a minute too late," Coralie replied, hefting her basket to her other hip and walking away.

"Say you'll come for tea soon," Mae called after her. They had little time together. She spent more time with Lucy than anyone. Did that nettle Coralie?

"'Tis too hot for tea," Coralie replied with a wave of her hand, moving toward the sally port. "Perhaps once the weather cools."

Mae watched her go, the heat causing her to itch as sweat dampened her back and bodice. But at least today she wasn't nauseous, and mint tea awaited if she was.

She tarried in the shade of the magazine till Rhys joined her. Would he leave again soon on a foray or to transfer the prisoners? The fear that he might walk out those gates and never come back bedeviled her night and day.

"What is it, Mae?" he asked once they were in their own quarters.

"I'm forever missing you. Even when you're right beside me I'm already anticipating you leaving again, which robs me of the joy of this minute." She couldn't put into words how she felt. Strangely empty and a bit lost. Homesick for a place she'd never been—or was it the feeling of safety and security she craved? "But I won't bemoan your duties. I'm simply . . . touchy lately."

"With good reason." He took her in his arms so gently she felt more fragile.

She lay her head upon his shoulder, wishing she was more like Alice. Alice, ever outspoken, who never flinched at war talk and even seemed to relish it. Alice had some of Lucy's mettle.

"You're the finest wife I could ask for," Rhys murmured, stroking her hair. "And you'll be the finest mother too. Remember all this is fleeting. We seem to be walking through fire now, but it has an end. When you feel at a loss, remember the Shenandoah and our home there. One day this fort in the middle of the wilderness will be all but forgotten."

thirty-nine

Happiness depends more upon the internal frame of a person's own mind—than on the externals in the world.

George Washington

At daybreak, Rhys and a company of riflemen set out with Claudius Smith and three of his fellow renegades. Smith wore leg irons, the rest bound with rope. The journey took Rhys farther from Fort Montgomery than he wanted, Mae uppermost in his mind every step. He was beginning to rue being away from her. If she became ill or needed him or lost the baby . . .

They halted briefly midmorning to dole out water and jerked meat. Used to traveling on foot thirty miles or more a day with the army, farther on horseback, Rhys chafed at the delay. The surly prisoners walked surrounded by riflemen both afoot and astride horses as the sun baked the stony path hard as granite. No wind stirred, turning the march suffocating beneath the humid trees. Even the birdsong seemed muted.

Smith, their foremost prisoner, glared at his captors and cursed his irons. Rhys paid him no attention except to note the powder burns beneath his right eye and his unkempt beard. He'd murdered several men—all Patriots—since his rampaging began and deserved hanging, but punishment needed to be quick lest he escape like he'd done before.

"What do you think Ol' Put will do to Smith?" Bohannon asked Rhys, refilling his canteen at a creek.

"General Putnam has little patience for renegades," Rhys replied as he checked his rifle. "I doubt Smith and his cronies will live to see the sunrise."

They finally reached King's Ferry. Heavily guarded by the Americans, it was a strategic point where Continental Army troops, supplies, and communication between New England and the southern colonies—now the thirteen states—continually crossed. Signs of their passage were everywhere. Several thousand men couldn't move through the wilderness without scarring the land. Trees had been felled to widen the way, underbrush trampled, streams diverted, and makeshift bridges built to ease their passage. The smell of freshly cut timber hung in the humid air.

Rhys surveyed the ferries and flatboats and oarsmen that had hauled an entire army with artillery and horses and wagons over water. The distance from the landing at Stony Point to the landing at Verplanck's Point was about half a mile wide.

"What did General Clinton say about Verplanck's Point?" Bohannon asked, tilting his cocked hat further forward.

"He wants a report on the fortifications there." Rhys trained his spyglass on the eastern shore. "Entrenching tools have been sent from West Point, but I see little from this side in the way of defense."

They dismounted and led their horses onto the waiting ferry as the incoming tide licked the transport's edges. Rhys glanced back at the remainder of the riflemen who waited with the prisoners for the next crossing.

"How goes it upriver at the twin forts?" the ferryman asked. "Any sign of Burgoyne and his lobsterbacks?"

Rhys faced the wind. "In the words of General Washington, the enemy keeps us in a state of constant perplexity and conjecture with their extreme inactivity and delay."

"Crivvens!" The ferryman spat overboard. "Washington certainly can't be accused of dithering, moving south then ordering Lord Stirling's division on toward Peekskill."

"You've been busy," Bohannon jested.

"Aye, and I hope to heaven we're not soon seeing General Howe heaved in sight with armed sloops and gunboats. The Americans have none and are no match for the Royal Navy."

Rhys withheld a groan, though Bohannon didn't. He hadn't any doubt Howe had in view a strike against the Highlands and the forts there, like Burgoyne. Their prime goal was control of the entire Hudson River.

"Take care lest ye be caught between the two—Burgoyne by land and Howe by sea." The ferryman stuffed more tobacco in his cheek with grimy fingers. "The loss of the Highlands will be a sore loss indeed."

They disembarked at Verplanck's Point, only to be met by militiamen more intent on the renegades than the fortifications they were building. Bohannon spoke with them while Rhys oversaw the second ferry's landing. Once all the riflemen and prisoners were across, they set out again toward the place of military justice, a former trading post now the command center for the Hudson Valley.

Five barracks and two redoubts were soon in their sights atop a hill overlooking the bay, along with a great quantity of rebel stores. One dwelling lodged American officers, and a humble tavern supplied food and drink. Parched and hungry himself, Rhys knew his riflemen needed a reprieve. But first, the prisoners.

General Putnam met them near the guardhouse, his bulk considerable, his weathered face a stark red beneath his remaining white hair. A respected officer from the French and Indian War, he wasn't one to mince words. "Good to see you, Harlow, even if your company is lacking." He gave an order for his second-in-command to oversee the prisoners, then turned back to Rhys. "Come inside and we'll discuss matters."

Rhys's plan to return to Fort Montgomery by nightfall was discarded as he followed the general into headquarters with its sweeping territorial view.

Noting his admiration, Putnam said, "I'm always alert for British sails. We're constantly on guard, awaiting intelligence from every direction."

"As are we at the twin forts." Rhys stood by the window, the water a blinding blue in the afternoon sun. "I've heard two American frigates are being built for these waterways."

"Indeed. Congress has approved both the USS *Montgomery* and the USS *Congress*. I pray they aren't scuttled to avoid capture. There are also two galleys, *Shark* and *Lady Washington*. But I digress." He poured them both a drink. "My heartiest congratulations on apprehending and transporting these cutthroats. I understand they've recently stolen and corralled a considerable number of horses near Ramapo Pass, which you've returned to their rightful owners."

"Aye. I'm glad to finally rid the Highlands of them." Rhys took the glass he offered. "A word of warning. Smith has a knack for escaping and helping others do the same. He nearly fled Montgomery."

"They'll be tried immediately by a general court-martial according to the articles of war, given they belong to this state and owe allegiance to it." Putnam moved to the window, his lined face grave. "Washington agrees that the speedy execution of criminals is absolutely necessary to the preservation of the army."

"Agreed." Rhys took a long drink. "Edmond Palmer comes to mind most recently."

"Yet another officer in the enemy's service, lurking within our lines. He's since been tried, condemned, and executed as a spy here at headquarters." Putnam looked at him, eyes narrowing. "You don't suspect anyone at the twin forts."

"We're always wary. British deserters happen by regularly, but there's little of substance or suspicion so far."

"Good to hear. We cannot afford a breach. Be especially vigilant." He smiled, the tenseness suspended. "You and your men need a hearty meal at the tavern before your return. I won't delay you any longer."

forty

If this be treason, make the most of it.

Patrick Henry

Mae poured tea in her quarters, the chipped cups reminding her of the lovely porcelain china back in Chatham's cupboards. She tried not to make comparisons, but as the days unspooled along the Hudson with all their sameness and smallness, the crudities of the fort were increasingly felt. She seemed caught between one life and the next, the old of Chatham and the not yet of the Shenandoah.

Seated by an open window where rain smeared the pane, Coralie leaned nearer her cup and inhaled. "What on earth is this?"

"Independence tea—sassafras leaves, mint, bee balm, red clover, and chamomile flowers." Mae sat down and pushed a wayward strand of hair beneath her cap. "Lucy showed me how to blend it."

"Lucy again?" Coralie made a face. "I've seen several officers wearing the new uniform coats you two have been making. 'Tis a wonder you have any time for blending tea."

"We've run short of buttons again, but the coats are quite dashing, don't you agree? Indigo is such a handsome color." Fitting Rhys out for his had been one of the little thrills of her married life. "General Harlow looks splendid."

"Far better than those rustic hunting shirts he and his riflemen usually wear, though I suppose their garments keep them safe in the woods."

"Far more so than scarlet. I daresay the British are ruing their red as it makes them such targets."

"I'd not thought of that till this war." Coralie stirred sugar into her tea, her sunburned features drawn in a frown. "Speaking of red, being outdoors all day, even wearing a hat, spoils my complexion. Autumn should be cooler, according to some of the militia from this area."

"You're making quite a few soldierly friends," Mae said, adding sugar to her own cup. "Is there a favorite?"

Coralie looked pleased. "Well, Captain Sinclair plays a fine game of cribbage . . . Private Jenkins is well-read . . . Major McTavish is as dashing as his name . . . and Captain Etienne Lefevre from Fort Clinton is très beau."

"No favorite, then."

"All four help relieve the sheer drudgery of being here."

"I don't suppose," Mae dared, "that you've become any less a Loyalist and more a Patriot given the company you're keeping."

"Ha!" Coralie reached for a berry tart and took a bite, spilling crumbs onto her bodice. "All I'll say is that these Continental soldiers help me bide my time till I can safely see Jersey."

"If troops are ordered south, you could return in the same way you arrived here, accompanied by the army."

"We've had quite a comedown since Chatham." Coralie's eyes roamed the rough-cut walls with distaste. "No better than slatterns."

"'Tis only temporary, remember. Once this is over, we'll go home."

"Home will never be the same." She took a second tart. "I never thought I'd miss Mrs. Hurst, but . . ."

Mae laughed. Coralie and their housekeeper had never seen eye to eye. "I wrote Mrs. Hurst a letter, then remembered she doesn't know her letters. Hanna and Aaron will read it to her, I suppose."

"I haven't written anyone." Coralie looked back at Mae. "What's there to write about? 'Dear whomever, I washed fifteen bushels of breeches and hung them out to dry, then mended one too many officers' shirts.'"

"'Tis not easy being a laundress when you've not done that before."

"I'd thought to be far from here by now—in New York City with Eben or his family." She looked down at her lye-battered hands. "I'm glad they can't witness *this*."

"We all have a part to play in this war, no matter what side we're on."

"You've always been sunny, Sister, making the best of the moment. Would that I were more like you."

"Sunny? Not always. But lately I've prayed to be the person the Almighty wants me to be. Let challenging circumstances change me for the better."

"Noble of you." Her voice held a brittleness that set Mae on edge. "I'm simply the belle of Chatham's younger sister and always will be."

"I'm sorry if you feel you've lived in my shadow. I never wanted that to happen."

"You're not to blame. You can't help your appearance, though I do wonder why God makes so many of us plain when He could just as easily make us pretty."

"Probably because man looks on the outward appearance, but the Lord looks on the heart, as Scripture says."

They fell into an uncomfortable silence that weighted Mae sorely. Would they never be friends, only contentious sisters? How she longed to share that she was expecting, that Coralie was to be an aunt three times over. But her sister would resent that too.

"I should go." Coralie finished her tart and tea. "I don't want your husband returning and finding me here."

"Whyever not?"

"He's never cared for me, nor I him. Do you deny it?"

"He's never spoken an ill word about you."

"Yet I've shunned him ever since he appeared in Chatham. I'll grudgingly admit, however, he's an able commander and has the respect of a great many men." She stood, staring down at her soiled apron. "Back to the river. The head laundress is a termagant about work."

"Not before I give you some salve Joanna made that Jon brought by recently." Mae went to a cupboard and retrieved a small ceramic pot. "Rub this on your hands nightly, especially when they feel chafed."

To her surprise, Coralie took it and embraced her. Rarely did her sister show affection. Their stoic, studious father had been the same. Murmuring her thanks, Coralie bade her goodbye and went out, and Mae watched her sister's tall, spare figure cross the parade ground to the sally port. She suddenly realized Coralie had some of Aunt Verity's vim and vinegar.

Would her sister ever be settled? Settled in spirit and in a home of her own? She didn't ponder it long before a familiar tread sounded on the wooden floorboards outside their quarters, and she opened the door she'd just shut.

Rhys appeared, hat in hand. His clothes were begrimed—his indigo coat more dusty brown than blue—and his half beard turned him more handsome. She melted into a puddle where she stood. When he caught her up in his arms and swung her around she forgot everything else, even the brokenness with Coralie.

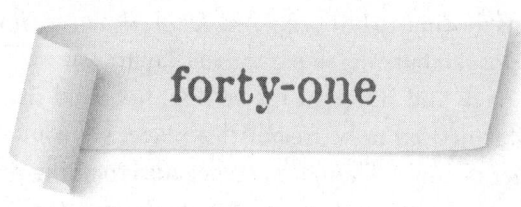

forty-one

I desire you would Remember the Ladies, and be more generous and favorable to them than your ancestors.

Abigail Adams

Sleepless, Rhys turned over atop the bedsheets, cursing the heat beneath his breath. His ire faded as he saw Mae undisturbed beside him, the faint whistle of her breath reassuring. Dawn broke through the window, outlining her flushed features and the faint shadows beneath her closed eyes as she lay on her back.

Gently, not wanting to wake her, he placed a hand on the thin linen of her nightgown where the slight rise in her middle showed. He'd memorized every curve of her, and the change was noticeable, at least to his discerning eye. Her child. *Their* child.

He'd still not written to his father and Bronwyn to tell them the news. He could only imagine their joy. His mother's death had cast a long shadow, and then the war had brought another when Micah died. A Scripture he'd recently memorized rolled through his mind with the realization the timing of their child's birth was no accident.

To every thing there is a season, and a time to every purpose under the heaven: a time to be born, and a time to die; a time to

271

plant, and a time to pluck up that which is planted; a time to kill, and a time to heal; a time to break down, and a time to build up; a time to weep, and a time to laugh; a time to mourn, and a time to dance; a time to cast away stones, and a time to gather stones together; a time to embrace, and a time to refrain from embracing.

Now was the time to be born. *Lord, let me live to see it.* His full heart felt close to bursting in part anguish, part joy.

He lay back and stared at the ceiling, his hand still on her middle. Mae needed to be free of this place. He could no longer send her to Jon's. Though the renegades roaming the Highlands had been hung, there were a hundred more dangers. Even the safety of this fort was in continual question. Nothing was a refuge along the Hudson any longer. Not with Washington withdrawing most of the army from the region, leaving only a few hundred men.

Mae stirred, and her soft fingers covered his own. "Soon you'll be able to feel the baby move."

He swallowed down the words he wanted to say. *I hope I'm here for it.*

"We've not talked about names."

He brought her hand to his lips, kissing her fingers. "Names . . ."

"If a daughter I'd like to call her Mahala."

"Mahala Harlow." He liked that it echoed Maebel. "And if a son?"

Her sleepy smile brightened. "You decide."

"Gerard after your father, mayhap. Or Charles after mine."

"I'm unsure." She looked thoughtful, even sad. "I'd rather something fresh as befits a new life."

He pondered that. "Rhion."

Her brows arched. "I've never heard the like."

"Wyn . . . Madoc. Welsh names, all."

"But none so fetching as Rhys."

He kissed her brow, overcome by the sweet herbal scent of her. "Mahala for certain."

"You wouldn't mind a daughter first? So many want sons."

"I want whatever God gives us."

She kissed him as if seconding his answer. Outside, reveille sounded, turning his thoughts from any intimacy. He was to ride out this morning on reconnaissance upriver and didn't know when he'd return.

"If you sew with Lucy today, bring her inside our quarters instead of going to Sutler's Row," he said. "I don't want you outside fort walls any longer."

"All right. Is there something you're not telling me?"

He sat upright, running both hands through his untethered hair. "Mayhap."

She sat up too. "Wouldn't it unburden you to tell me?"

"Nay, it would double my burden, burdening you." He left the bed, went to a basin on a table, and all but dunked his head into the tepid water. A clean shirt hung from a nearby peg. He began dressing as she plumped their pillows and smoothed out the coverlet.

"I should return by nightfall."

"And if you don't?" Her quiet question hung between them, begging for a reassuring reply.

"Think nothing of it. Sometimes I'm waylaid."

She reached for her stays. "Is this foray today especially dangerous?"

"All of New York is dangerous, Mae." He expelled a breath. "The latest intelligence says much of New York is on fire. Fort Ticonderoga fell first, then Fort Edward, and now Fort Ann. Fort Stanwix to the west is under siege as we speak. Burgoyne seems to be delayed, mayhap at Fort Edward or some unknown point upriver, so we're waiting, gathering more intelligence, all the while suspecting a strike from the British below us."

He'd confided in her at last, but it made him all the more knotted.

"Might the British leave us alone? Take the fight elsewhere?"

273

"Not when they want complete control of the Hudson River. Their aim is to cut off rebellious New England from the rest of the states and thereby stamp out all treason."

England, once the mother country, wanted to crush the American spirit that had birthed Bunker Hill and the ferocious battles of Lexington and Concord. Other battles, too many to name—including White Plains and Lake Champlain and Trenton and Fort Lee—had brought a frightful loss of life and further irreversible division.

He knew Mae had read about past engagements in newspapers, every last detail. But here, newspapers and broadsides new and old were kept at headquarters and not as widely circulated. Not all soldiers could read. Drill books and military manuals ruled the day instead.

Once dressed, they sat down together as was their custom before beginning the day and breaking their fast. He opened their Bible, the family Bible she'd brought from Chatham, and read aloud from the Song of Solomon. He hoped his low, steady voice assuaged her despite the present turmoil. "Set me as a seal upon thine heart, as a seal upon thine arm: for love is strong as death."

★ ★ ★ ★ ★

While the afternoon wore away, Lucy worked her intricate stitches on General George Clinton's coat. As Fort Clinton's commander across Popolopen Creek, he'd admired his brother's new garment and wanted one for himself. The highest compliment, Mae thought. She stopped her own stitching to marvel at the decorative work Lucy had wrought on the cuffs and lapels in silver thread.

"He promised to keep us in pewter buttons henceforth. I do prefer pewter to brass against all that indigo blue." Lucy never seemed more content than when her needle was in hand. "We're about out of cloth, though. A sorry thought."

"Perhaps another supply train is coming."

"The last was ambushed by the King's Men."

"Oh?" Lucy was a fount of information, but whether it was fiction or fact Mae didn't know. Rumors were thick as flies in a fort.

Lucy stopped sewing long enough to heave a sigh. "And Petey's been mighty restless."

Petey? Mae bit her lip lest she laugh. The faithful cur lay in the half-open door as if guarding his mistress, giving a throaty growl on occasion.

"You might have heard of General Howe's fox terrier?" Lucy said. "Follows him everywhere, Lila does. Word is she delivers messages between enemy outposts. Even has a collar marked with Howe's name."

Mae stared at her in disbelief.

"General Washington has his own hounds at home if not in the field. Sweet Lips, True Love, and Venus are said to be his favorites."

Mae burst into unladylike laughter. "You jest!"

"God's truth," Lucy said reverently, looking heavenward. "What's more, General Lee has his Spado. He even ordered the hound onto a chair to present his paw to Mrs. Abigail Adams last spring."

Clutching her sides, Mae grew sore and slightly nauseous from amusement. "Petey is in good company, then."

"I pay attention when he gets tetchy."

"I don't blame you," Mae said, suddenly serious.

"Dogs don't lie. Even the horses on Sutler's Row are acting a bit fey and off their feed." Lucy returned to her stitching with a frown. "Mark my word, the enemy will soon be at our door, and they will show no mercy."

forty-two

The British are coming.

Paul Revere

The day began like any other. Hot as the inside of an iron skillet and just as sticky. Rhys had returned, only to go out on another foray after a few hours' sleep, a meal, and a long meeting inside headquarters. Mae noted the activity, Lucy's words earlier in the week an unwelcome refrain.

"Mark my word, the enemy will soon be at our door, and they will show no mercy."

Unable to sleep, Mae got down on her knees and prayed as if it was the last prayer she would ever say, until her knees and back protested. She pleaded for an end to the war. For Rhys's safe return. For all the soldiers and camp followers at the twin forts and beyond to go home peacefully and whole. She even prayed for the British to make peace.

As the fort came awake, she breakfasted alone, just toast and tea at her own hearth. Rain was needed, and when she heard the first drops of a deluge she rejoiced. The air smelled of dampened dust that would soon become churning mud, though the heat was already easing.

Bible reading took the next half hour of her time. She pondered writing another letter to Hanna and Aaron but had received no reply. Best wait till she did.

Midmorning there came a sudden knock, and Mae opened the door to see a wet, bedraggled Lucy standing there, Petey by her side. Behind her the gray parade ground dripped with rain. "Please come in."

Lucy entered and went to stand by the low fire burning in the hearth from breakfast. She said nothing—odd for Lucy. Petey snuck in before Mae could close the door, then sat and cocked his head.

"Would you like tea?" Mae asked her.

"Nay." Lucy swallowed. "General Harlow isn't here?"

"He's gone out on another foray but should return soon. Is there something the matter?"

After some hesitation, Lucy shoved a hand into her pocket and brought out a piece of paper. Mae set down the teakettle and took what Lucy held out. A letter? The handwriting was as familiar as her own.

Coralie.

Her long, loping script was in cipher, sending Mae's stomach somersaulting again.

"Where did you find this?"

"Up Popolopen Creek there's a willow with a hollow in it." Lucy stared at the letter as if it was tainted. "Your sister put it there while I hid and watched. It wasn't long before a soldier come and took it from the tree once she'd gone."

"A soldier?"

"Aye, dressed as a Continental. But he's not familiar to me from either fort."

Mae's chill belied the room's heat. Her thoughts tumbled one after another, trying to make sense of the matter. Restless, she sat down, only to stand up again.

"I've seen your sister go up the creek before, but I thought she meant to relieve herself." Lucy's eyes were grave. "When I followed her, I found out otherwise."

"Then we must tell General Clinton straightaway." Even as Mae spoke, dread pinned her to the plank floor.

Heaven help us.

They went out, Petey on their heels, all three of them trying to stay beneath the parapets to avoid the deluge. The guards had no such refuge, their garments soaked, their cocked hats waterspouts. And Rhys, out there somewhere . . .

Mae stopped midway, fearing she'd lose her breakfast.

Lucy reached out a comforting hand. "Are you all right?"

"Nay." Mae took a breath and continued on.

She'd never been to headquarters, just watched from a distance and thought it resembled a beehive with all its comings and goings. At Lucy's knock, an aide-de-camp admitted them to a sizable room spread with maps and weaponry. Dispatches lay like fallen leaves on an immense desk, leaving no doubt a war was ongoing. Between narrow windows facing the parade ground a large flag hung, its stars and stripes a pleasing pattern.

She saw no sign of General Clinton, but his aide-de-camp soon remedied that. Had they interrupted his breakfast?

He appeared, smiling but clearly surprised when he saw them. "Mrs. Harlow and Mrs. Hawkes, what brings you through the downpour to my quarters?"

Lucy handed him the letter without speaking. Was her throat as tight as Mae's?

"Cipher?" He examined it in the light of a hanging lantern since the room was shadowed. "Where did you get this and whose handwriting is it?"

Lucy told him how she'd found it, and Mae swallowed past her wooziness to confirm it was Coralie's.

"Bring Miss Bohannon here," he told a waiting lieutenant. He called for another officer to decipher the letter, though from his expression, Clinton knew well enough what it contained and wasn't pleased. Was he merely seeking confirmation?

Time ticked on as she and Lucy took the chairs the general offered. Mae kept an eye on the open door, the eave dripping water. The laundresses wouldn't be working in such weather. They'd wait till the rain passed before going to the river.

What would Coralie say when confronted? Moreover, what did the confiscated letter say?

Sister, Mae wanted to scream, *what have you done?*

Her mind whirled as her suspicions came hard and fast. Coralie had never stopped her spying. And Mae had never stopped her sister from doing so. Oh, there had been half-hearted attempts to intercept her letters. But how many had Coralie posted from Chatham and then here without Mae's knowledge? And now she knew . . .

Coralie's supposed parting with Eben Gibbs was naught but a ruse.

By the time the lieutenant returned, her heart pulsed far too fast. She felt its frantic tick in her wrist and neck. She wanted nothing more than to flee this room and her shame and any potential blame.

The young officer looked distressed. "Miss Bohannon is gone, sir. Her quarters are empty, her belongings missing. No one has seen her since late yesterday. The laundresses didn't wonder as she usually spends her evenings with the soldiers on the common, retires late, and is awake early."

Mae felt the burn of shame. Coralie had been gathering information from first one soldier and then another. Making the rounds till she had enough to pass on. Talking, flirting, deceiving. Was that it?

Lucy looked at her in sympathy as the general said, "I commend you both for coming to me. I suspect this has been going on since Miss Bohannon first arrived in the Highlands."

Lucy spoke, but Mae barely heard her. The nausea she'd tried to tamp down bubbled up in the back of her throat till she tasted bile. Murmuring an apology, she bolted toward the open door and barely made it outside.

"May I be of help, Mrs. Harlow?" a concerned soldier asked as he stood to one side of the door.

Mae dug for a handkerchief to wipe her mouth, fearful she'd be sick a second time. "I need to lie down."

"Here, let me escort you." He took her by the elbow and slowly guided her back toward her quarters, which seemed as far as Jersey.

Stomach still swimming, she murmured her thanks, wondering why Lucy remained at headquarters.

Betrayed. By her own sister.

Though she needed to lie down, anxiety kept her moving. How would Jon and James react?

She stopped her pacing to look out the sole window to the parade ground. Thunder boomed like cannon fire, one volley after another, raking her nerves. Rain still slashed down, nearly obscuring her view of Rhys as he crossed from headquarters to their barracks.

Finished with his latest foray? Her usual joy fled. When he pushed open the door she realized he knew. Unsmiling, he looked at her, then leaned his rifle against the wall, removing his powder horn and belt. His hatchet and shot pouch and knife were next.

Never had he looked so worn. Or so wet. His hair, blackened by rain, fit his scalp like a snug hat. Water puddled beneath his moccasins. His clothes clung to him, but he didn't undress. He came farther into the room and stopped at the table.

"Where is your sister?"

The question turned her to ice. She lifted her shoulders in reply.

"How much do you know, Mae?"

Feeling she might be sick again, she pressed her hands to her stomach. "What do you mean?"

"What do you know of your sister's spying?"

"Very little . . ." She swallowed hard. "I suspected, is all."

"You suspected." His tone was flat. Leaden.

Another round of thunder shook the room, and she heard

horses whinnying outside in distress. It mirrored her own inner turmoil. The ire in his expression terrified her.

His gaze was sword-sharp. "Since when did you suspect?"

"Since . . ." She fisted her hands in her skirts, her voice a whisper. "Chatham."

"*Chatham?*" he roared, striking the table with both fists as he leaned forward. The teapot perched precariously at one end fell to the floor and shattered.

She jumped back, colliding with the windowsill as pieces flew. "Please, let me explain. I never thought her posting letters from Chatham was any kind of threat."

"How many letters?"

"I don't know." Tears stung her eyes. "I destroyed those I could."

"Destroyed them." He hadn't moved, his hands splayed atop the table, leaning in like he might lunge at her. How she longed to see understanding in his eyes. A speck of sympathy.

"One of them was in cipher like Lucy found today. The kind that's made visible by candlelight." She winced as all the implicating details rushed back. "I caught Coralie listening in on your and James and Captain Sperry's after-dinner conversations in Chatham—she hid behind a wall in a small room once used in times of Indian attack—"

"Yet you told me nothing." His face hardened further.

"There are numerous Loyalists and spies all over, so I've heard." Her voice shook. "I thought one woman mattered little."

"It matters!" he fired back. "Every deceitful action and word matters!"

She bent her head, trying to dry her tears with her apron hem.

"You chose your sister over me. By saying nothing, you made your choice."

"Nay. You were *always* my choice, then and now."

"Yet your actions say otherwise."

She looked up, tears still streaming. "I thought coming here would mean an end to the matter."

Disbelief scored his features. "You never realized the ruse of her failed engagement was just that. A means to get inside the walls of this fort and wring what she could from flattered soldiers who drink and talk too much."

"I truly believed Eben Gibbs had abandoned her. She seemed heartbroken—"

"She's a skilled deceiver bent on destroying all here, and that includes you and your brothers. No doubt she's run off to this Gibbs now that she's been found out."

"How do you know?"

"Because it makes sense. Are you blinded by your family bond? If not for Lucy and her hawklike eye, your sister would still be carrying on her sham."

The blame in his voice made her want to hide her face in her hands. He was looking at her as if he didn't know her, as if she was a stranger—as if he *hated* her. The realization almost buckled her knees.

He pushed away from the table. "I should turn you out of this fort."

"I didn't betray you, Rhys. I've always been faithful to you— loyal." She was crying so hard her words came out in breathless snatches. "I never—ever—meant you harm."

"I trusted you once." He turned his back on her. "And I can trust you no longer."

forty-three

Stand fast, my brave grenadiers!

General Charles Lee

The entire fort seemed to regard her differently now. Since Coralie's discovery, Mae moved about as if she wore a scarlet letter, a *T* for treason. Traitor. As summer bled into autumn, she kept to their quarters, even shunning the officers' table at meals. She'd not seen Rhys since their confrontation. His absence, now days long, not only cut her, it haunted and bespoke a finality she feared. He hadn't told her where he was going. For all she knew he had taken up quarters elsewhere in the fort. Only Lucy told her differently.

"He's gone." Lucy sighed when she said it. "General Washington ordered him to reinforce General Gates north of Albany. Isham and most of his riflemen have gone with him. Colonel Bohannon too."

At least Rhys wasn't shunning her within these walls but from a distance. Yet even that left her feeling half alive. He was too far to make amends. Too far for her to say she was sorry. Her brothers as well. James hadn't bid her goodbye, nor Jon. Did they blame her too?

"You'll be bone-dry if you keep crying," Lucy cautioned, handing her a clean handkerchief. "'Tis not good for the babe."

Mae cried harder. "How did you know?"

"You're rarely weepy or sick to your stomach. And now you're both."

Mae blew her nose, a horrid sound that made her feel all the uglier. "I've not told anyone about the baby but the general."

"Well, glad I am there's that betwixt you. It'll help mend the rift."

"I don't want him to forgive me because of the baby. I want him to forgive me because . . ." Mae couldn't grasp the right words. *Because he loves me. Trusts me. Because he believes I didn't think to harm him or the fight.*

"He'll come round." Lucy patted her shoulder as Petey looked on. "He just lost his head for the moment."

"I've never seen him so angry." The memory made her shudder. "In fact, I've never seen him angry at all."

"Isham has." Lucy's full lips twitched. Whether grimace or grin, Mae didn't know. "And 'tis not a pretty sight."

"What's more, he has reason to be angry with me. I fear he'll never trust me again."

"You meant no harm. That I know full well."

"I should have told him back in Chatham." Mae took a seat at the table. "I'll regret that to the day I die."

"There's spies aplenty from here to Georgia, though I think it goes harder when one's your sister." Lucy sat down across from Mae. "But it's wrong to judge her harshly for where her loyalties lie. She's not a criminal. She's a Loyalist. She feels you—all of us—are committing treason and she wants to stop it."

Mae dried her tears. "Nor are we criminals, just people who want to live free and independent of England."

"But in the end only one side will win."

Mae stared at the cocked hat Rhys had left hanging from a wall peg, the colorful cockade she'd made faded by the sun. "Worst of all is wondering if I'll ever see him again. I might not have a chance to make amends."

That was unendurable. If he sickened or had an accident or fell in battle, would their heated row be her last memory of him?

★ ★ ★ ★ ★

In the September forenoon, Rhys stood with other American officers atop a wind-blasted bluff along the Hudson River behind defenses thick with artillery, twenty-two cannons extending a mile. The Continental Army's nearly nine thousand men, including his own, ranged over a large area. Save the river, dense woods surrounded them on every side, a single rutted road all that allowed passage from north to south.

The morning's scouting reports were clear. Burgoyne and eight thousand men were advancing to attack, sending General Benedict Arnold into a fighting frenzy.

"Burgoyne has sent out a reconnaissance to test our defenses," Arnold told General Gates as he joined them on the bluff. "General Fraser and Baron Riedesel and his Germans are at the forefront a few miles from here. There's no time to delay."

Gates nodded. "They're approaching Freeman's Farm in three columns, according to the latest reports. The left flank is led by Riedesel along the river, the right by Fraser inland through the woods, and the middle by Burgoyne himself."

"Then they'll meet with General Harlow's riflemen and the Mohicans." Arnold looked at Rhys. "Take to the woods and cause confusion in their ranks. Don't allow Burgoyne to advance through the farm's clearing. His aim is to break through American lines here and proceed on to Albany."

Rhys raised a hand and turned north. Several hundred of his riflemen followed on foot, their faces set with purpose. This would be the last he'd see of some of them, but there was no time to be wasted. No time for mawkish thoughts.

"Scour the woods."

His terse command dispersed the elite corps and their Indian allies into dense trees, their rifles ready. He gave a last hard look at Private Hawkes. The man was hardly as wide as his snare drum, its leather strap encircling one thin shoulder, his brown woolen coat wrinkled and bloodstained. Painted on the instrument was an American rattlesnake and "Don't Tread on Me." The hickory sticks in Hawkes's tanned hands began a tight cadence communicating Rhys's commands. For now, the drummer would stay above the fray on the hillside.

Rhys led, the dry woods and uneven terrain a cauldron of color and confusion sure to slow the British's advance guard as they approached Freeman's Farm. They stirred the dust of the road three men abreast, their own drums sounding at the center of the formation. Their foolish line fighting did them no favors. In their flaming red coats, they made as bright a target as Virginia's cardinals.

At the crack of his rifle a hundred more weapons followed, dropping redcoated officers from their saddles onto the hard ground. Choking smoke whitened the air as the first British column began to break under such an intense surprise attack. Some regulars bolted toward the woods for cover while wounded and dying men cried out, their orderly ranks bedlam.

Rhys reloaded again and again, moving through the underbrush at will, aiming again and again, refusing to dwell on the fact that this unknown enemy had a name, a face, a family. Heads split like melons. Chests burst with blood. He'd never know who he brought to a final, fatal end. He only knew his own dead.

Kill or be killed.

Bedeviled by a swarm of flies, he stumbled, and his moccasin caught on a tangle of mountain laurel. Nay, one of his own. A body lay face down beneath the sprawling bush, the listless hand gripping his rifle. John Skelly. Steeling himself against the regret of it, Rhys kept moving, leaping over brush and rocks and a creek, firing and reloading as he went. Finally he realized the British light infantry had nearly routed them.

"We've been outflanked from the west!" he shouted as his men scattered.

A second column of redcoats surged through the trees as the British main force arrived at the farm's clearing. Rhys could hear the cadence of Hawkes's drum above the melee as more redcoats rushed over a grassy rise like ants on a hill.

Still shouting, he ordered what Rifle Corps he could into the woods south of the farm. "Protect the line's right flank!"

To his right, Hessians were advancing as cannons fired from both sides, bodies and earth shattering. He dropped down on one knee, rifle raised. Burgoyne was in his sights as he rode toward another officer atop a fancy saddle. Sweat streamed into Rhys's eyes, stinging and blinding him as another shot rang out, close enough for him to hear the whistle of the lead ball as it spun past and felled an unknown officer.

Everywhere he looked chaos reigned. Swiping his forehead with his sleeve, he aimed again and fired, reloaded and fired again, never missing a mark even as he became a prime target moving from forest to field. Winded and so parched it hurt to swallow, he continued amid the blood and screams as men fell.

Artillery officers and crews lay in heaps about their armaments, allowing a few frantic moments for the Americans to capture several cannons. And then the enemy rushed in to take the cannons and turn them against the Continentals once again.

Where in heaven's name were Gates and the Continental main body? Held back at Bemis Heights, unwilling to venture out? Though they'd started strong, reinforcements were needed lest they all die in a desperately undermanned fight. Arnold had led the action, and now his own riflemen were ferociously forcing the British back even as the enemy rode in with more cannons to halt the American advance.

"Let it never be said that in a day of action, you turned your backs on the foe; let the enemy no longer triumph."

Washington's words ricocheted through his mind, driving him

on despite a flesh wound to his shoulder. His hunting shirt was torn, scarlet soaking the linen in a warm rush.

"They brand you with ignominious epithets. Will you patiently endure that reproach? Will you suffer the wounds given to your country to go unrevenged?"

Dizzy, he blinked as two of his riflemen pitched forward, felled like trees, before the crushing roar of cannon fire that shook the earth left his ears ringing.

"Will you resign your parents, wives, children, and friends to be the wretched vassals of a proud, insulting foe? And your own necks to the halter?"

Taking cover behind a tree, he aimed at an advancing Hessian. The expected crack of gunfire faded to a choked fizzle. With no time to check the flint or clear the barrel, he swung the rifle like a club as the Hessian ran toward him, bayonet fixed. The wooden stock struck the side of his helmeted head, knocking him to the ground. A kick to the enemy's musket sent the weapon into the brush as Rhys moved past him to an oak. His back to the trunk, he heaved a breath as his bloodied hands took hold of his rifle's ramrod and dislodged the fouling from repeated firing.

"Nothing then remains, but nobly to contend for all that is dear to us. Every motive that can touch the human breast calls us to the most vigorous exertions. Our dearest rights, our dearest friends, and our own lives, honor, glory, and even shame, urge us to the fight."

He returned to the field as Burgoyne pressed reinforcements forward, threatening to overrun his Rifle Corps position. Sick to his stomach, head splitting, he was reaching the end of his tether. Back and forth, bluecoats and redcoats ebbed and flowed, a tide of men battling to the death amid choking smoke.

"And my fellow soldiers! When an opportunity presents, be firm, be brave; shew yourselves men, and victory is yours."

More glaring redcoats, more Hessians tearing through the woods, bayonets flashing, Indian allies shrieking above the smoky fire and clash of weapons.

How much longer? How many had they lost?

Toward dark, the British held the field, but the Americans had pushed them back till they begged for reinforcements. Finally the smoke cleared and the fifes and drums quieted.

He hadn't once thought of Mae.

★ ★ ★ ★ ★

In the bitter aftermath of battle, Rhys wanted to shut his ears to the groans of pain and cries for water or medicine from too many Americans. He emerged from the field hospital tent, his thoughts straying from Bemis Heights to Mae.

Jon Bohannon waited outside, his beleaguered face grim, battered hat in hand. A hole from a musket ball only added to its condition. "You all right?"

Rhys ignored the pain that tore through his bandaged shoulder. "I'll mend."

"How many Continentals dead?"

"Ninety all told and two hundred forty or so wounded. The British lost thrice that, mayhap more."

There was no triumph in his words. Though the enemy proclaimed it a victory simply because they'd held their lines, it came at a frightful cost. A tactical draw, Howe said. Burgoyne was hemorrhaging troops and in dire need of reinforcements.

"God rest them all." Jon shut his eyes as if uttering a prayer. "And preserve those suffering and still standing."

The burial detail had been at work since both sides had withdrawn from the field. Bodies were retrieved ahead of prowling wolves intent on the carnage, but identification was often impossible due to the sheer numbers and savage condition of the lifeless soldiers. As it was, the battle had raged from noon till dark, finishing many who might have been saved had they had proper medical treatment. Mass graves were dug for both sides.

"If I hadn't seen James fall, I'd remain uncertain," Jon said as they walked toward Gates's headquarters on a bluff. His voice broke, and he swiped at his eyes with the back of a grubby hand. "But there's no surviving cannon fire."

Bohannon had, unlike many, been killed instantly. Mae would be undone. Rhys pushed the thought away, only to have it circle back again. Outside the heat of battle he couldn't *not* think of her. Think of her he did, in equal parts ire, regret, and desire. It didn't help that a group of fifers burst into "The Girl I Left Behind Me." The jaunty tune did nothing to soothe his ragged spirits.

Maebel Bohannon Harlow.

What was she doing this very moment?

Nearby, General Gates's tent glowed with pale light. Rhys sat down to warm himself at one of many glittering campfires scoring the heights as Jon stretched out battered hands to the flames, his voice rising above the fifes.

"Did you hear the latest reports of the enemy pushing toward the twin forts while we sit here awaiting Burgoyne's next move?"

"Aye." The terse word carried a bushelful of angst. The miles between him and Mae had never seemed greater, every inch a powder keg waiting to ignite.

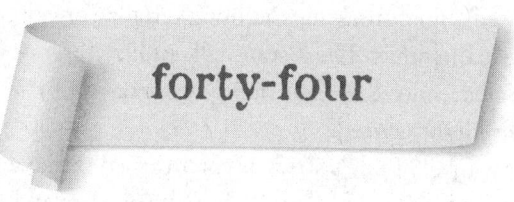

forty-four

Remember officers and soldiers, that you are Freemen, fighting for the blessings of Liberty.

George Washington

Fog hung over the Hudson River like a veil, lifting only slightly as the morning wore on. Mae ventured to the riverbank to wash her garments, continuing up Popolopen Creek and away from the laundresses who reminded her of her sister. But nowhere could she escape Coralie. Further up the rocky bank stood the willow that had held her secret letters.

Kneeling, she took out her turmoil on her soiled petticoats and shifts and stockings, soaping and rinsing them with a vengeance. What was happening with Rhys, Jon, and James? More than a month had passed with little word. Now October, summer's green had faded to autumn tints. Even the river seemed changed, not the silken blue ribbon of before but a gritty pewter gray. Birdsong erupted from the trees, but it seemed a muted and melancholy music, the wood pewee particularly plaintive. Her own thoughts twisted with sorrow.

Rhys, Rhys. I'm sorry. Stay alive. Come back to me.

Straightening, she looked down the creek where it emptied into the river below, her hands moving to her bodice. Spring seemed so long in coming. Time blurred and left her wondering exactly when the baby would arrive. No longer so sick, she still tired from the simplest of routines. She prayed that it would soon pass lest she be accused of laziness in addition to aiding and abetting a spy.

She rinsed a final stocking and hung it to dry on a bush beside her other smallclothes. The distant talk and laughter of the laundresses chafed. Since Rhys left she'd forgotten what it was like to laugh or feel lighthearted.

"There you be!" Lucy's strident voice turned her around. Lucy hurried down the steep bank's trail, her face pinched and red, Petey on her heels. "We've no time to waste."

"What means you?"

"The pickets report the British are just upriver—the redcoat Clinton and his men!"

Flummoxed, Mae looked to her wet laundry. "So there's to be a battle? Right here?"

"Not on my watch!" She grabbed Mae's hand and began pulling, Petey between their petticoats.

"But my laundry!"

"Laundry be hanged! We needs care for our very lives!"

"But we can't run south and meet up with the enemy."

"There's another way. I promised General Harlow—"

"What?" Hearing Rhys's name grieved her yet filled her with hope.

"There's no time to tell you. Hurry!"

They were at the top of the bluff now, winded but still at a half run. Mae put a hand to her head, dazed and dull-headed after little sleep.

"Hurry and gather a rucksack of belongings." Lucy issued orders like an officer. "Wear your sturdiest shoes and pack a second pair. Bring the general's belongings too, as we might need them, as many as will fit. Meet me in Sutler's Row as fast as you can."

With that, she disappeared as Mae stared after her.

Once inside Fort Montgomery, Mae found it much changed as officers barked orders and soldiers swarmed in every direction, preparing to defend the garrison. Where were the officers' wives? Would they remain?

In her quarters she did as Lucy bade, filling an empty rucksack with the best of her meager belongings while loathing leaving garments behind on the riverbank. Would they go far? Perhaps to Jon and Joanna's farm? Or the nearest Patriot refuge, wherever that might be?

Sutler's Row was emptying, carts and wagons, people and animals fleeing in every direction. Lucy was waiting near her dismantled tent, holding the reins of two horses, one of which Mae had never seen. Petey's head was visible from an unclasped saddlebag. Orion nickered when he saw her, but there was no time for affectionate greetings or to ask why he was here and not at the farm.

Ignoring the chaos around them, Lucy helped Mae into her saddle before climbing atop a stump to reach her own. She then led them into woods that seemed ready to erupt in light of the latest news. Their horses, well-fed and rested, seemed equal to the task.

Mae felt a sudden, almost dizzying bewilderment. She had no idea which direction they were headed. Here the woods were so dense the sun was blocked, blanketing them in shadows.

When Mae realized they'd missed a familiar trail, she backtracked. "This is the way to the farm—we're almost there."

Lucy slowed and looked back at her. "Nay."

"But isn't the farm our refuge?"

Lucy kept moving, but Mae went the other direction. She'd not leave the valley until she'd seen Joanna and family. Who knew when she'd have that chance again?

"By heaven, you're a stubborn woman," Lucy called in sharp exasperation, riding after her. "You'll see for yourself why we can't go there. 'Tis better you remember it as it was."

Was?

At the head of the valley they halted. Mae looked out on what had been green and fertile, fenced and thriving. Now there was nothing but scorched earth, a blackened reminder of Jon and Joanna's life and labors. No barn. No outbuildings. Just a gutted house, the walls still standing and open to the sky, the chimneys tumbled. The wheat and corn were no more. The fenced garden with its showy flowers and delicious vegetables was a memory. Only an acrid stench remained.

Mae gave a little cry. "Did the British and Indians—"

"General Washington gave orders all was to be burnt up and down the valley lest it fall into enemy hands."

Stunned, she looked from Lucy to the ruins. "Where are Joanna and the children? Did they move from here safely?"

"Only your brother Colonel Bohannon knows. I've not heard anything other than Washington's grim order."

They returned to the trail they'd been taking, Mae numb to all that was enfolding around her. Lucy's speed showed confidence, but Mae became more addled. Her internal compass was broken. If not for Lucy she'd be utterly lost. Had Rhys known that? But did Lucy know where she was going? As they continued, Mae's doubts swelled.

What were they but two small souls and a dog in the wilds of a war-torn territory that was as vast as it was terrifying?

★ ★ ★ ★ ★

When a wall of darkness forced them to dismount, they found shelter at the mouth of a shallow cave. Free of the saddlebag, Petey did a wild dance through fallen leaves and lapped up water at a trickle of creek. Supper was jerked meat and parched corn, the fare of soldiers. Mae gave half of hers to the little dog.

Too weary to talk, she still managed the burning question that had bedeviled her all day. "What did you promise General Harlow?"

"He told me to take you south." Lucy leaned back against the rock wall, Petey in her soiled, aproned lap. "To the Shenandoah."

"If the fort was threatened, you mean."

"Aye. He gave me two pistols and his money belt." Setting Petey aside, Lucy dug in a saddlebag for what Mae assumed were the weapons. She took out Mae's mother's shawl instead. "'Tis freshly laundered. I want you to have it back."

For a moment Mae felt choked. The woven butter-colored garment brought back a hundred beloved if bittersweet memories. Admittedly, she needed the comfort more than relief from the cold, and somehow Lucy knew. Mae took the shawl and draped it around her shoulders, never more thankful for the wool's warmth. "Did he tell you to take me south before he found out about my sister's spying or after?"

Somehow that mattered. Mae prayed it was after.

"Before," Lucy said. "But he never countermanded the order, so it still stands."

Countermanded. Such a complicated word in light of their predicament. "I don't know that it still stands, Lucy. He was in a fury with me when I last saw him, remember."

"He's not an unreasonable man. I misdoubt he's still angry weeks after."

So she'd been counting. Marking the time away from her husband too. Mae sighed, worn down by the possibility Rhys didn't want her, that he might divorce her. That she'd return home in disgrace to Chatham with their child.

"He wants you safe. Sound. On his land and in that handsome house he built."

Mae pulled the shawl tighter around her. "How are we going to make it so far?"

"Clear to Virginia?" Lucy looked undaunted as she stroked Petey's head. "Mile by mile. It won't be easy, but it's not impossible. The further south we go the safer it'll be. My aim is to get shed of these woods as quick as we can with the Lord Almighty's help."

Mae wasn't thinking of the Almighty but Jane McCrea. She

shrank back against the rock wall, cold and uncomfortable as it was. There were British and Indians in these very woods, perhaps some who'd witnessed the murder—or even caused it.

"If we keep moving we'll see the Shenandoah before the weather turns bitter." Lucy's calm continued. "Autumn is chancy here in New York but should get milder come Pennsylvania. For now, we'll have to ride hard to clear this wilderness but can let up later on once it's safer."

Already Mae's body ached, and it was but the first day. Her tenderest concern was how the baby fared. But she wouldn't complain. She would hope. Pray. Some things you just had to get through. Pondering trouble overmuch spawned a hundred fresh fears.

"With Petey between us we'll try to keep warm." Lucy handed Mae a thin blanket, put the little dog beside her, and rolled up in her own. "At least this rock ledge will keep the dew off."

"What do you think is happening behind us—at the twin forts?"

Lucy worried her bottom lip. "There's no doubt the British were at hand when we fled."

Mae wondered about the youngest drummer, Nathan Futrell. She'd seen him standing on the parade ground at the last. By now both garrisons were riven with the British. Would the Americans stand firm or would they fall?

Rather, had Coralie's duplicity contributed to any of it?

Amid the night noises, they eventually slept, Lucy's slight snore drowned out by the hoot of an owl and a chill night wind.

Toward dawn, Petey roused them, pulling at Lucy's blanket like a pup. She was first on her feet, producing Rhys's guns.

"Take this pistol. That way we'll both have one." Lucy examined hers like a soldier. "It's loaded, so have a care."

Mae took the weapon, hiding her reluctance. It lay cold and heavy in her hand, making her miss the gloves she'd mistakenly left behind at the fort.

"Good thing General Harlow gave us these pommel holsters." Lucy showed her how to place her pistol in the leather attached to the saddle on one side of Orion's neck. "You can draw it quick if you have to. I'll do the same. It's not only the enemy we're chary of but cougars and wolves and the like."

And snakes, Mae thought. Like the timber rattler Coralie had seen on the trail coming here.

forty-five

General Howe is certainly gone to New York, unless the whole is a scheme to amuse and surprise.

General John Cadwalader

The Continentals remained at Freeman's Farm. Both Burgoyne and his troops and Gates and his Americans were entrenched above the Hudson River's west bank, recovering and awaiting reinforcements ahead of their next engagement.

Though time hung heavy on his hands, Rhys was never idle, drilling his ablest men, visiting the injured, reorganizing and replenishing ammunition. He knew Burgoyne was growing desperate even before reports said the same. Outnumbered and ill-supplied, he would soon be forced to advance or retreat.

Drenching rains, frosty nights, and half rations failed to dim the American spirit. The Continentals were camped close to the British, their merriment heard far and wide. Their sentries soon complained about the revelry lest they fail to hear above the noise and give a warning should the British strike. General Gates ordered an earlier curfew at once, then called for a few of his officers.

At the summons, Rhys fell into step with Jon. They'd already discussed what might happen in the coming days. Now that seemed to be at hand. Would it take him nearer to Mae?

"Come in," the general told them, clearly in command inside the marquee-style tent. Aides and officers came and went as he gestured for the two to be seated across from a large table burdened with maps and charts and field glasses and more. "I trust you've recovered from the last action and can be sent further afield."

Rhys nodded while Jon uttered, "Aye."

"We've received a report that the twin forts are in need of reinforcements, especially given fresh intelligence that the enemy does indeed plan to come upriver just as Burgoyne came down." Gates retrieved a paper and perused it for a quiet moment. "I want you to take fifty of your ablest riflemen, Harlow, and a company of Bohannon's militia there. Leave as soon as you're able and be extra vigilant, given we expect the enemy will attempt to land troops south of here ahead of a strike on both Montgomery and Clinton. You'll proceed by water for speed's sake."

Further orders were given, including letters to both forts' commanders, and within an hour Rhys had his riflemen at the river's edge as Jon's militia joined them. The journey aboard the bateaux proved silent and somber. Alert to Loyalist militias and Indian allies, even British blockades the farther south they traveled, Rhys prayed there'd be no storm as a damp northerly wind pushed them along, recent rains swelling the banks.

Rather than the dust and blue skies that had seen them to Fort Montgomery in spring, all was mud and damp. River travel was slow, even hazardous, in the best of conditions. They had to sleep in snatches, eat, pay heed to the banks for any sign of the enemy.

The farther south they came, the clearer the memory of Mae was. The way they'd faced off inside their quarters—the hard looks and shouted words—had lingered and festered the time they'd been apart, his high regard of her tainted by her sister's actions. Coralie's deceit seemed to undermine their marital bond and make him question everything. He had thought Mae trustworthy. Loyal. Above reproach.

Didn't she realize the depth of his dedication to the cause? His willingness to be branded a rebel and die for independence?

As they neared Bear Mountain, he smelled smoke. Campfires? Something seemed different and he tensed, signaling his men to be extra vigilant. His gaze raked the bluff where Fort Montgomery's ramparts once impaled the sky. For a trice his mind roared with denial even as his gut roiled. No ramparts nor bastions. No sign of any Continentals atop the bluff or patrolling the riverbank below.

They landed at the undisturbed bridge across Popolopen Creek, then began the upward climb through familiar woods that seemed strangely empty yet heavily trod. Heart heavy, Rhys went at a half run, slipping on the mud and nearly falling backward as a gnawing need propelled him forward.

The bitter, charred smell, mingled with the overpowering stench of decay, grew stronger the closer he came. Once he was atop the bluff, the destroyed fort was in blackened relief in front of him, a tangle of burned beams and twisted timber, the destruction total. Countless fallen Continentals lay everywhere he looked. Fort Clinton across Popolopen Creek was the same.

He stood inside the main gates as riflemen and militia fanned out around him, some moving toward what had been the parade ground and Grand Battery, its stone foundations visible. Walking the fort's perimeter, Rhys grappled with the horror of finding Mae among the fallen, which made him want to retch.

God, help us.

The conflict here was hours old. Rebel scouts and patrols were likely only now reporting it, American troops having fled. The battle looked to have been brief but intense.

"You told Lucy to leave with Mae ahead of time, at the first sign of trouble," Jon said, coming up beside him. "I pray they're well on their way south."

Rhys hadn't told Jon about Coralie or his ensuing confrontation with Mae. If James had known about Coralie, he hadn't heard it from Rhys. His conscience was clear there. He wouldn't add turning brothers against sisters to his tally of regrets.

He simply said, "I'm thankful Joanna and the children are out of the fray and behind fort walls further west."

Still, the terrors of what had happened here while they'd been entrenched upriver at Bemis Heights seemed an unnecessary tragedy. Washington's moving the bulk of the northern army away from the lower Hudson, while understandable, had reaped irreversible consequences.

Jon cleared his throat. "We've lost James, but I don't sense we've lost Mae."

Rhys looked at the blackened ruins, trying to hold on to hope. "She may have been taken prisoner if she didn't get ahead of them with Lucy."

The very thought gutted him. Swallowing hard, he resisted the urge to pound the air with his fist and rail against heaven itself as Jon lifted a cocked hat off the ground with the tip of his rifle. Oddly intact, it was a muddy mess, the cockade a reminder of those Mae had made.

Woodenly, Rhys walked alone toward the remains of the Grand Battery, where he'd stood with her on countless occasions. The view was untouched, the Hudson rising and falling with the tide, true to its Lenape name, Muhheakantuck. The river that flows two ways. Today the beauty was blunted.

Below, the great wrought-iron chain and log boom that had blocked British ships on the Hudson had been dismantled. What the enemy had done with it he didn't know, but it seemed a further nail in the coffin of their cause.

Yet that was merely iron, not flesh and blood.

Mae, where are you?

His guilt at leaving her with so many loose ends at the last all but brought him to his knees. They might never meet again nor make amends. If he left New York to go search for her he'd be branded a deserter. For now, he was a soldier first, a husband and father, son and brother, second.

Till the war was won.

★ ★ ★ ★ ★

Rain smeared Mae's view of the woods and slicked the saddle, making it harder to stay seated. Her soaked skirts grew heavy and cold as she fought to stay upright and awake and not lose track of Lucy. Her Franklin hat, wet and soiled beyond recognition, sat heavily atop her head. They'd been traveling for days now, so many she'd lost count, and they'd still not come free of the green blur of woods.

Mile after mile pummeled her with the dreadful possibility that Lucy had lost her way. The tightening knot in the pit of her stomach told her they were traveling in circles. Even worse—what if something happened to Lucy? Ahead of her, Lucy bent low in the saddle, trying to avoid rain-soaked branches that tore at her hair and garments, only to rake Mae next.

If Lucy died, so would she. Cosseted and softened for years in Chatham, unwise to the ways of the wilderness, she now realized beyond a shadow of a doubt she had none of Lucy's mettle. She was not only untrustworthy, she was weak. Wholly unfit to be a seasoned general's bride. Even now Rhys was likely ruing he'd ever set eyes on her.

Her heart bled at every thought of him. Was he still alive? Had he been in a battle? Might he have been taken prisoner and put on one of the hellish prison ships in New York's harbor? The dire possibilities were endless. Her tears mingled with the rain.

Toward dusk, they searched in vain for a dry spot to make camp, finally deciding a widespread oak meant shelter. Utterly spent, Mae slid from the saddle, her cold fingers barely able to unbuckle the girth and rest Orion for the night.

Petey stilled and gave a growl. Across from her, Lucy dismounted then froze, her eyes big as brass buttons.

Mae's own knees buckled. Through the darkened woods came a long, silent line of Indians in single file, armed to the teeth and headed toward them. Painted black and vermilion, the tall lead warrior continued sure and steady. American allies or enemies?

Mae dropped down behind Orion while Lucy did the same with her mare. When Petey gave a throaty growl, Lucy hissed a panicked rebuke. Mae simply bent her head, rain trickling down the back of her neck, and prayed.

Heavenly Father, let Your creatures neither neigh nor nicker nor bark.

Would she live to laugh at the ludicrous prayer?

The procession of men clad in linen and buckskin seemed unending, their identity unknown. Their hair was dressed with eagle feathers, two up and one down. Oneida?

Mae's heart beat loud as a drum, and still they came on, an entire war party from the look of them. Her own pistol was still in the pommel holster. She'd not used it—didn't want to use it.

Hide us, please.

Orion stepped back abruptly, snapping a twig. The sound seemed to echo in the dripping forest. Hunkered down, she and Lucy watched as the party suddenly swiveled away from them. A bend in the trail? They now stared at the Indians' retreating backs. At the rear of the column, the last warrior paused. When his steady gaze pivoted in their direction, Mae's head grew so light she grabbed Orion's stirrup to stay upright.

And then the warrior moved on, catching up with his companions as they continued their silent journey. The drip of the forest resumed and a few bursts of birdsong pierced the gloom, but neither Lucy nor Mae moved. Long minutes ticked past till Mae's shaky legs would support her no longer. She sank down into the mud and leaf litter, so cold she couldn't feel her toes or fingertips.

"We daren't kindle a fire," Lucy murmured, thereby shooting down their hope they'd go to sleep warm if not dry.

Wrapping her arms around her stomach, Mae simply nodded,

empty of all strength yet filled to the brim with fear. How could she take another step? It would be one thing to push toward something certain, but she was heading toward a home she didn't know would be welcoming and a possible reunion with a man she was unsure of.

If either of them lived to see it.

"Here," Lucy said, looking as bedraggled as Mae felt. "I'll see to the horses. Let's get you in dry garments and tucked in a dry blanket with Petey."

As quietly as she could, Lucy settled Mae before unsaddling both horses and hauling their saddlebags beneath the sheltering branches. Next came their rations, the jerked meat and corn dwindling but their canteens full of water.

"I pray the Indians are gone for good." Mae's whisper held profound relief. "I don't know if they're friend or foe."

Lucy's voice dropped to a whisper. "I heard tell the Seneca wear one feather, the Onondaga two, and the Mohawk and Oneida three." She looked perplexed, still scanning the woods. "How we hid in plain sight with two horses and a growling dog befuddles me still."

"I've never prayed so hard."

"Well, the Almighty answered. 'In the time of trouble He shall hide me.'"

"How far do you think we've come?" Mae swallowed a bite of jerky. "Perhaps the better question is, how far do we have to go?"

"I've lost track." Lucy pushed back a limp strand of fiery hair. "We'll just continue south till we finally come to a farm or village, then we'll rest a bit before moving on."

"I don't know south from north nor east from west." Mae ate with filthy hands, the prospect of a bath ever before her. The thought of vermin crawling atop her scalp made her squirm. "A tavern of any sort would be welcome."

"Hmm." Lucy was looking at her as intently as an owl in the near dark. "Where's your wedding ring?"

"Strung on a ribbon around my neck." Feeling chastised, Mae

looked down at her bare finger. How in the midst of the jumble had Lucy noticed so small a detail? "I don't feel worthy to wear it."

"Worthy? Well, as hard as we've been traveling, I'd feel a sight better with it around your finger than around your neck."

"All right." Mae unknotted the ribbon and slipped the ring back on her finger. She didn't want Lucy worried. Her concern suggested she feared Rhys would hold her responsible for its loss. "Do we have funds enough to get to Virginia?"

Nodding, Lucy patted the money belt at her waist. "General Harlow is more than generous. But he said to stay out of Jersey. They're still fighting there."

Mae reluctantly abandoned the thought they might pass through Chatham. At the moment she wanted to lie down right here and die, not weather another mile. If it was only her, she might. But for her baby—and Lucy—she'd fight her way forward to a better, safer place.

Praise be she wasn't in the back of beyond with Coralie.

As the last of daylight gave way to full dark, a distant wolf howled. Petey settled against Mae's side, warming her in one spot, at least. She fell asleep praying for Rhys. She'd still not brought herself to pray for her sister. Coralie seemed nothing more than a distant stranger.

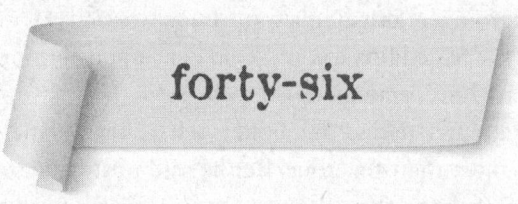

forty-six

If Ole England is not by this lesson taught humility, then she is an obstinate old slut, bent upon her ruin.

General Horatio Gates

Beneath overcast October skies atop Bemis Heights, Rhys faced General Gates's adjutant, Colonel Wilkinson. Down the road, the Freeman Farm was oddly quiet, the September battle there momentarily forgotten. Now it served as the marker dividing the British from the Americans. Behind it was Burgoyne's reconnaissance force of some two thousand troops, ready to test the Americans' positions and strength.

"General Gates is keen to act, sir. He said—" Wilkinson hesitated, clearly aware of the immensity of the moment. "Order on Harlow to begin the game."

Game.

Rhys gave a nod, his demeanor calm though his heart sprinted so hard he felt its tick in his neck. His Rifle Corps stood around him, hundreds strong, their weapons ready. They were well-versed on what to do. Target officers. Disrupt the chain of command. Drive the infantry back with all their firepower and force a retreat.

From a distance, the British drummers began to beat "To Arms."

With a wave of his hand, Rhys signaled his men to disperse. They started down the hill and skirted a wheat field just as the British began their advance from the north. Rhys entered the adjacent woods and took position, his heart now at a gallop.

The first to appear, General Simon Fraser anchored the enemy's right flank atop his gray horse. The Scot seemed especially bold, riding before his troops to rally them like General Arnold was doing with the Continental line on the opposite side of the field.

Tense moments ticked by. Timing was critical. Rhys's order to fire was followed by thunderous volleys into the British lines. Through the smoke he watched as Fraser stiffened then fell from his horse to the ground. The Scot's line broke and scattered while others made a harried run to carry him from the smoking field. Redcoats began to retreat, running pell-mell across the dry grass, desperate to flee the Americans' fire.

Flanked by his men, Rhys pursued the redcoats into the open, reloading on the run till they came to another wall of Germans. Standing their ground by firing repeated volleys, the Rifle Corps finally drove them into retreat. In every direction, bluecoats and redcoats lay thick as autumn leaves. For those still standing there was little time to think, only react, as the fighting turned more ferocious.

Captured British cannons and the wounded and dying didn't halt the Americans, who kept coming. When the British fell back behind a redoubt on the Freeman Farm, General Arnold wheeled his horse and advanced with another brigade against the Germans.

Dusk fell and it seemed they were fighting shadows. Barely able to see or even breathe past the smoke, Rhys watched Arnold fall from his saddle. His wounded horse also tumbled, pinning the general's leg beneath its bulk. A bayoneted British grenadier tried to thrust him through, but a shot rang out, blowing his attacker back. Moving forward, Rhys covered Arnold with rifle fire as his men ran to remove him from the field.

At last the fifes and drums fell silent.

★ ★ ★ ★ ★

Beneath General Gates's sodden marquee tent, a cluster of American officers gathered just as they had for nine long days since the last battle. Hanging lanterns pushed back the mid-October gloom, a double posting of sentries outside. Rhys stood shoulder to shoulder with Generals Poor, Lincoln, Learned, and Colonel Wilkinson. Only Benedict Arnold was missing, confined to the field hospital a stone's throw away, his left leg shattered. Would he live?

None but General Gates was sitting in the camp chairs provided, all of them as tightly wound as clocks, ticking toward another imminent fight—or Burgoyne's surrender.

The ruddy-faced general, spectacles perched on the end of his nose, turned bloodshot eyes on his adjutant. "How many British casualties all told?"

"At last tally, over eleven hundred, sir," Wilkinson replied, breath pluming in the cold air.

"Burgoyne's forces are significantly reduced," Poor said. "Our numbers are far superior, with more militia arriving by the hour."

"As for us," Gates continued, "Arnold suffered the loss of over fifty men. Our combined losses number three hundred, though more are dying as we speak."

Rhys listened to the conversation, wearied to his bones. It didn't feel like a victory or a celebratory moment. Not with so much suffering on both sides, not to mention untold widows and orphans at home. As for himself, he felt James's absence keenly. He should have been here to witness this. It wasn't the same without him.

"Tomorrow will be the tenth day since the last engagement, and Burgoyne's reinforcements have failed to appear." Gates reached for a decanter and poured them all brandy. "With so many militia arriving on our behalf, the British's depleted numbers make a future engagement suicide. Even their horses are dying for lack of forage."

Poor removed his hat and set it by the brazier to dry. "They're on reduced rations, both soldiers and camp followers, and the woods where they're holed up are nothing but a swell of mud, misery, and excrement."

"They can't last in such conditions, especially given foul weather." Even as Gates spoke, sleet tapped at the tent's top. "Disease alone will drive out those left standing." He gestured to the filled cups. "If a fire won't warm us, brandy will."

"We have them surrounded, unable to retreat and too weak to fight." Rhys reached for a drink. "There's nothing for them to do but lay down their arms."

Gates's gaze swiveled back to him. "Which you're in charge of, Harlow, if that time comes."

Rhys caught his uncertainty. *If?* For now, every soldierly instinct he had pointed to Burgoyne's surrender.

"What are we to do with six thousand British and Hessian prisoners once that happens, sir?" Lincoln voiced the question they'd likely all been pondering silently. It would be no easy march with so many, and a great number wounded with winter coming on.

"That remains to be hammered out in negotiations." Gates expelled a breath. "I suggest returning them to England, but Congress will likely have other ideas."

Learned frowned. "Prison ships are out of the question with so many Loyalist women and children, to say nothing of Baroness Riedesel and her brood."

"Enough war talk." Gates poured himself more brandy, his good humor prevailing. "Here's a story worth sharing." He winked as he continued. "General Howe, bless him, couldn't leave England without his pet fox terrier—"

"Lila," Poor interjected with a half smile.

"Aye, a smart one, Lila. Even though all was fog and confusion at Germantown and Washington suffered a defeat, somehow Lila managed to get herself lost and wander into Washington's camp."

Lincoln chuckled. "Are you telling tales, General?"

"Truth." Gates was obviously enjoying a bit of levity. "Washington, ever the gentleman, returned Lila to the British with a note that read, 'General Washington's compliments to General Howe. He does himself the pleasure to return him a dog, which accidentally fell into his hands, and by the inscription on the collar appears to belong to General Howe.'"

Chuckling ensued, which sounded a bit grim to Rhys. He finished his brandy. "A lesser man would have shot the dog and refused the courtesy."

Lincoln nodded. "Lucky for Howe, Washington has a fondness for dogs, even the enemy's."

The officers continued to talk in low tones and savor their drinks, but Rhys's thoughts were far-flung. His widening distress over Mae was unendurable. If she and Lucy had gotten away safely from Fort Montgomery, how far had they gone? And the baby? Were they well? The gnawing uncertainty knotted him like rope.

If they'd not parted so badly, would he be so torn up?

There'd been talk he and his Rifle Corps might be sent south to bolster the simmering if stagnant southern campaign, but Rhys took no comfort from hearsay. Being nearer Virginia seemed a hollow move. Would Mae be waiting? Again, the uncertainty tore at him.

Had he shaken her enough with his outburst that she'd return to Chatham instead?

forty-seven

We fight, get beat, rise and fight again.

General Nathanael Greene

'Twas cold enough to snow. After a second hard frost, Mae and Lucy began to see signs of civilization once they broke free of the woods and found the Old York Road. Their mutual relief was as profound as they were bedraggled and dirty. Since Orion had thrown a shoe, they searched for a farrier, finally finding one who reshod the hardy bay.

As they were low on strength and supplies if not specie, their new challenge was to avoid Loyalist strongholds. Two strangers traveling alone garnered considerable attention, so they tried to be as discreet as possible, finally coming to a Quaker-owned boardinghouse on the outskirts of British-occupied Philadelphia. Quakers were safe, sound. Being pacifists, they welcomed one and all.

The unadorned clapboard house in the midst of an orchard seemed more castle. Once inside, Mae stood by the common room's hearth while Lucy arranged lodging, securing them separate rooms. A hot bath followed, and then the two of them met again to have supper. Their Quaker hostess brought the latest broadsides and newspapers at Mae's request. Despite her neutral stance, Widow Wistar was astonishingly astute when it came to the conflict, but why wouldn't she be, with the war at their very door?

Mae's heart picked up in rhythm as their hostess said, "Though the British won at Brandywine and Germantown and now hold Philadelphia, they've lost New York. The redcoats are said to be surrendering there as we speak."

Lucy looked at Mae, understanding dawning. "Our men are near Saratoga—or were."

So many men. Rhys, Jon, James. And Lucy's Isham.

"'Tis reported a great many lost their lives on both sides, but there are more Americans than Brits still standing," the widow told them, pouring them freshly milled cider. "Now both armies will likely withdraw to winter camps and there'll be no more fighting till better weather."

Mae wrestled with the heartless uncertainty of it all. "Where is General Washington at present?"

"North of Philadelphia, though some suspect he's readying to move his men to Valley Forge."

Supper was served, heaping bowls of chicken stew, warm bread, cheese, and butter that neither Lucy nor Mae could get enough of. Still famished, they partook of dessert—apple dumplings with custard sauce. Murmurs of the other diners swirled around them as the great hearth's robust fire warmed the entire room.

"I'm tempted to stay another night and rest the horses as well as us," Lucy told her, clearly exhausted. "But with the weather worsening we need to press south as fast as we can."

"How far have we come?"

"One hundred fifty miles, the farrier said, and another one hundred fifty to the Shenandoah."

Halfway. Mae's spirits plummeted to her worn shoes.

Lucy seemed undaunted. "At least there's no more wilderness bristling with animals and Indians, just hostile Loyalists."

"Do you know the way?"

Lucy finished a second cup of cider before she said, "Of a sort."

"Are we still seeking the King's Highway south?"

"The widow warned us away from British-patrolled areas like the King's Highway. We're to keep to Ridge Road, which is less traveled and intersects with Tulpehocken Path, an old Indian trail that leads to the Susquehanna River. If we continue southwest to the Cumberland Valley we're nearly there."

Mae regarded her with admiration. "General Harlow was wise to put his trust in you, Lucy. I'd probably have led us to Canada by now."

"You're good company even befuddled." Lucy smiled at her fondly. "Bear in mind the days are short and the nights long. We mustn't slacken our pace."

They went upstairs, their steps dog-tired but their stomachs blessedly full. 'Twas strange to see Lucy without Petey about her petticoats. The little dog remained with the horses in the stables. Did Lucy miss her faithful companion?

Once in her room, Mae readied for bed—a real bed, not stony ground. If only she could simply revel in being clean, well-fed, and safe again. She donned a nightgown from her saddlebags before snuffing the solitary candle in its stand. Sinking down atop the feather mattress only allowed a fleeting peace before her biting worries beset her.

All she could think about was Rhys. Where he was. How he was. *If* he lived . . .

She forced herself to reckon with the thought. Was he still in New York? Where would he be sent next? Into another winter encampment rife with disease and death? As days and events unspooled, would they ever be reconciled? He was, he'd said once, a soldier first, a husband second. War had a way of lasting years.

Dry-eyed, she lay down. She'd cried herself to sleep more times than she could count since he'd gone, and now it seemed she had no more tears left.

★ ★ ★ ★ ★

At three o'clock in the afternoon on October 17, as the fifes and drums struck "Yankee Doodle," Continental troops lined both sides of the road upon which the defeated British army would pass. Shoulders back, gazes forward as if undergoing inspection, the Americans showed no emotion, their ranks still. No hatred or mockery or malicious pleasure at the enemy's defeat marked their faces. Rhys felt a beat of pride as he stood near Burgoyne and Gates atop Bemis Heights. Having surrendered his sword to General Gates, Burgoyne stood nearly shoulder to shoulder with him to watch the grounding of arms below.

"The fortune of war, General Gates, has made me your prisoner," Burgoyne said with the dignity befitting an officer and a gentleman.

Gates gave a sympathetic smile. "I shall always be ready to bear testimony that it has not been through any fault of Your Excellency." Turning toward Rhys, he said, "Proceed with the grounding of arms, General Harlow."

Rhys returned to his riflemen by the sodden field where the weapons were to be laid down. The British went first, followed by the Germans, and then their Loyalist followers. Redcoated officers surrendered their swords, and then the rest of Burgoyne's tattered, beleaguered troops moved past the Americans to lay down their captured artillery and small arms. Rhys and his men had charge of this, though it would take days to sort through the weapons and relay what had occurred to the Continental Quartermaster Corps and Ordnance and the chief of artillery.

The mile-long procession shuffled past, and the stacked weapons swelled as the enemy began their march to Boston per surrender terms. Most looked like whipped dogs, their rain-soaked faces downcast, the wounded carried by wagons and carts.

Baroness Riedesel's calash came through, its wheels bumping her and her children this way and that on the battle-scarred road.

Her husband, the general, stood with uniformed British officers to one side, all in mourning since their revered Scots general, Fraser, had died of his wounds.

At the very end of the column came the struggling, straggling women and children, even babies, sure to soften the hardest man's heart. Some were barefoot, so small they were tied on horses or in knapsacks on their mothers' backs.

Mae leapt to mind again—and their child—and his gut turned to gravel. A knifelike wind sent gold and bloodred leaves to the ground as his thoughts flew across the river to the twin forts—what was left of them. They'd buried all the dead that day when they'd returned to reinforce the ghostly garrison. He was still thanking God there'd been no women among them. Mae was still out there somewhere . . .

He turned back to the procession, wanting it done. His gaze hung on a woman on foot and better dressed than the rest, her face half hidden by a sopping bonnet. Something about her—something like Mae—rattled. As she walked past she turned the full force of her gaze on him. Her face was set like granite, loathing in every line. When she stumbled on her dragging hemline, she snatched her skirts up in fisted hands and kept walking. For a trice she seemed as stunned to see him as he her.

Coralie Bohannon.

Somewhere near was Lieutenant Eben Gibbs, he'd wager, if he'd not been felled in battle. Did she know about James? Rather, did she even care? Did Jon, wherever he was in the throng, recognize Coralie too?

The end of the procession neared, the sound of so many shuffling steps something he'd never forget. He took a deep breath as wind gusted from the northeast and muffled the sudden crack of musket fire. Turning toward the sound, he felt something hard and sharp buckle his knees and send him to the ground. A blinding, breathless burning made him cry out as his riflemen surrounded him. Screams erupted from the women and children still passing by, some scattering in fear of continued fire.

Sprawled upon the ground, Rhys looked down and saw the brown of his breeches redden, the mounting pain making him grind his jaw. A hubbub ensued and someone shouted for a surgeon, but it was a single winsome image that cut through his shock before his world went black.

Mae.

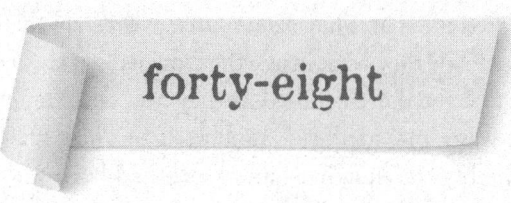

forty-eight

*The buffalo, elk, deer, bear, panther, wildcat, wolf, fox, beaver, otter
. . . were abundantly plentiful.*

Simon Kercheval, on the Shenandoah Valley

Breathless and disbelieving, Mae reached a rise overlooking the Shenandoah, a great bowl of a valley rimmed by mountains that were a peculiar shade of blue. She'd nearly despaired of ever seeing it, but here they stood, having come through a high gap. She literally stood on the cusp of her new home and life. New York and Jersey seemed a world away, if not their raw memories. Even the usually practical Lucy seemed overcome. Despite frequent stays at ordinaries, the both of them were weary, wrinkled, and emotional.

"Just a few miles more," Lucy said.

"Is there an ordinary near where we could stop first?" Mae looked down at her muddy skirts and begrimed hands. "Mightn't morning be a better time to . . . um, arrive on my in-laws' doorstep? They don't even know I'm coming, and it will be quite a shock."

Dusk was drawing in, not as cold and damp as in the north, but still calling for a warm hearth or a hot toddy. They'd ridden especially hard of late, finally ferrying across the south fork of the Shenandoah River. Even the horses were beleaguered.

Turning away from the view, Lucy finally said, "There's a decent place not far from here. We've plenty of coin left to see it done."

Plenty of coin. If not for Rhys's foresight . . . Mae felt stark relief as they rode past scattered farms to a two-story log structure puffing smoke. Once The King's Arms, it now boasted "Rebel Arms" on its trade sign. They dismounted and a stable hand saw to their horses while they went inside the crowded but clean ordinary.

The rest of the day dwindled as they ate, and Mae made use of the hot water provided, ridding herself of every speck of filth and thoroughly cleaning her hair, which had been wadded into an untidy bun for weeks. She laid out a clean if wrinkled chintz gown, hoping it wasn't too fancy. Lastly she washed her mother's shawl and let it dry by the fire, though it was still damp the next morning when she wrapped herself up in it again.

Revived if still skittish, she and Lucy took to the trail for the last time. Fog whitened the valley floor, wrapping round flaming maples and golden oaks like a tattered coverlet that bespoke November. Following a deer path that branched off the main road into dense woods, Lucy led while Petey trotted between them.

This wasn't the way she'd intended to meet her new family. Her dream had been to appear alongside Rhys, triumphant, the war won.

What could she possibly say?

Good morning, I'm Mrs. Harlow. I haven't any idea if Rhys lived through October's New York battles or if he's wounded, sick, or imprisoned. When I last saw him we quarreled and never spoke again. He may not return home, but here I am, carrying his child, and feel Virginia is where I should be.

"What is General Harlow's family like?" she said to Lucy's back.

"His father is well-thought-of all over the valley," Lucy called over her shoulder. "One of the Friends—Quakers. A farmer and woodworker. His sister, bless her, had her heart broke when the war started. And his mother, God rest her, was akin to a saint, always doing good, ever generous to any in need."

Mae fell silent. She was walking into a house of heartache that had nothing to do with her own. Nor was she akin to a saint. Suddenly she was questioning the wisdom of coming here and how far she would have to travel to return to Chatham. If not for Lucy . . .

Already Mae felt the wrench of separation. "Promise you'll come visit."

"Aye, once you've settled in." Lucy reined in her horse as they traded the trail for a clearing. "If you hear Petey bark you'll know I'm near."

Petey gave a sharp yip as a few grazing cows came into view. Fenced pastures reminded Mae of Jon's farm—or what once was. Here everything still seemed lush if autumn-tinged. The sun had dispelled the mist, shining down on tidy outbuildings and not one but two handsome houses, the farthest atop a hill. Her heart leapt. The home Rhys had built with his own hands? Lucy's father lived farther up the valley, as did Isham's kin.

Mae watched a tall man emerge from the smaller of the two houses, so like Rhys in height and gait she felt a little start. Lucy headed straight for him while Mae lagged behind, a fit of shyness overtaking her.

"Shush your yipping," Lucy scolded Petey in a rare rant as another cow ambled into sight. She slid from the saddle and snatched him up lest he set off on a chase.

When Lucy halted suddenly to let her go first, Mae balked. Gathering what little grace she possessed, she dismounted and walked Orion toward the man she sensed was Rhys's father. He turned toward them, axe in hand. Neatly stacked firewood filled the open shed behind him.

Oh, how like Rhys he was.

An older version of the man she loved, stockier and fuller of face. He didn't smile as she approached but continued stoic, even wary.

"Sir . . ." She stopped a stone's throw away. To come any nearer felt too familiar. "I'm Maebel Bohannon Harlow of Chatham, New Jersey . . . and I'm married to your son."

319

After a slight hesitation, his stoicism broke like the rising sun. Turning toward the house, he called, "Bronwyn, come and greet your new sister-in-law."

At once a young woman appeared on the porch, wiping her hands on her apron. She took in Mae and Lucy at a glance and broke into a half run toward them. Catching Mae up in her arms, she hugged her hard, turning Mae teary. This was the homecoming she'd hoped for. Warm. Welcoming.

"Can it truly be you?" Bronwyn's tanned features shone with pleasure. "Rhys wrote about you in his letters and told us you'd married, but we never thought to see you so soon, at least not without him. And riding horseback all that way?"

Lucy approached, Petey in arms. "He ordered me to bring her here shortly before the fort was attacked."

Mr. Harlow's features tightened. "Montgomery?"

"Fort Clinton too. We fled when Patriot pickets shouted the redcoats were coming."

"Earlier, Rhys had gone north with his riflemen to a place near Saratoga," Mae added.

"You haven't heard? The Americans won the battles there," Mr. Harlow said. "We got the news day before yesterday, though we've not heard from Rhys himself since he left Montgomery. That fort fell along with Clinton."

Mae drew a surprised breath. They'd left in the nick of time, then. Still, her heart hurt. Those she'd known there might have fallen with it or been taken prisoner.

"And you?" Bronwyn turned to Lucy. "I recollect you married one of the Hawkes up on North Mountain."

"Aye, my Isham is General Harlow's drummer." Lucy let Petey loose. "He went with him to fight near Saratoga."

"And you've come all the way from New York—two women alone?" Respect rode Mr. Harlow's lined features. "With a fine pair of horses and a little dog."

"I would never have attempted it without Lucy. And Petey's been quite a comfort," Mae told them with a small smile. "Especially on cold nights."

"The north is frigid this time of year. We've had a beautiful Indian summer, though it's frosted a time or two." Bronwyn gave her father a worried glance. "Mercy, how we rattle on in light of your exhaustion."

"Here, let me see to your horses while you sit down for breakfast. Bronwyn's a fine cook and her biscuits and gravy are about ready." With that, Mr. Harlow took the reins of both mounts and led them to the barn, which stood on the other side of a split-rail fence. Petey ran after him as if wondering where he was taking his faithful companions.

Mae and Lucy followed Bronwyn inside, the aroma of coffee strong. Spacious yet spare, the log home bespoke peace and orderliness. Bronwyn invited them to a long trestle table where Rhys must have sat countless times. Mae's eyes moved from the chairs at both ends to the side benches and tried to picture him there. Fronting the table was a huge hearth. Large enough to stand up in, it covered an entire end wall, the long mantel home to books and a clock and myriad candlesticks, even a landscape painting of a castle. In Wales?

"Once our home was an ordinary," Bronwyn told them. "Father was the owner, and this was the public room. He and Mother decided to close soon after I was born, though folks still happen by who once lodged here."

She placed overflowing platters before them and filled large mugs with coffee enriched with sugar and cream. Lucy looked as pleased as Mae felt. They'd not had so ample a meal since the Quaker tavern outside Philadelphia.

Bronwyn finally sat, her hands cupping a steaming treenware cup. "I don't know where to begin," she said, eyes on Mae. "I have a hundred questions, but perhaps it's best I talk while you eat and then you can answer."

Mouth full, Lucy nodded, while Mae had to slow herself down lest she appear half starved or, worse, rude.

"Rhys grew up in this house, but the one he built up the hill is finer—fit for a bride. You can see it plain now that the trees surrounding it have lost their leaves. Since the war called him away Father and I have tried to finish and furnish it, but there's still plenty that needs doing."

Mae could only imagine the hole Rhys's absence left. "He told me about starting with rock from your quarry here." Those memories, at least, were happy when he'd shared his pride in the details.

"He started between planting and harvest. It took years, but the house is finally habitable." Bronwyn's smile held relief. "I'm sure I speak for Father when I say you're welcome to stay here with us till Rhys returns if you don't want to live alone on the hill."

Mae put down her fork. "Actually, I'd welcome moving in ahead of his return." Should she tell all? "With a baby coming, I want it to be home. I want to help make it a home."

Bronwyn's eyes went wide. She reached across the table and squeezed Mae's hand. "A baby?"

"In spring, Lord willing."

"You came all that way . . ." Bronwyn's hazel eyes glinted. "So much traveling must have taken a toll."

Mae's free hand moved to her waist beneath her mother's shawl, where she felt a slight flutter even as she shared her joy. On the trail she feared the baby wouldn't thrive. How hard it would have been to meet Rhys with sad news when he returned.

"You're clearly worn to ribbon, the both of you." Bronwyn looked at Lucy, then back at Mae. "We can move you up to the house once you've rested. My raspberry leaf tea should help you recover your strength, among other things."

Was she an herbalist, then? Memories of Aaron's apothecary, hardly thought of on the journey here, came rushing back.

"We'll have to acquaint you with the midwife not a mile from here. She's birthed half the babies in this valley." Bronwyn looked thoughtful as if trying to come to terms with being an aunt. "Father will be so pleased. He'll make a fine grandfather."

Might the baby help fill the emptiness left by Mrs. Harlow and possibly Micah Edmiston? Perhaps in hindsight, Mae would realize that despite her rift with Rhys, her coming here was not happenstance but heaven-sent.

"There's a cradle in the attic." Bronwyn's excitement was palpable. "We'll move it in with you. I can make new bedding and line it with wool if you like." She gestured to a spinning wheel by a window, a basket of wool beside it. Rhys had told her they had a large flock of sheep.

"You're very kind," Mae said. "I'm sorry I've brought so little with me. Only what fit in a saddlebag."

"No matter. We'll soon have you settled with all that you need. If anything's lacking there's a store further down the valley, though the owner has enlisted like so many. His wife is managing business while he's away."

All across America were homes and farms and businesses abandoned or turned over to women and kin instead. Sad and sobering to think many men would never return to resume the lives they'd left. Mae could hardly bear the thought.

Bronwyn began gathering their empty plates. "It'll be good to see lights up on the hill while we wait for Rhys's homecoming together, all four of us."

Mae got up to help her sister-in-law, so sleepy she'd nearly nodded off in the midst of the meal. Bronwyn's graciousness was all the more poignant, given she'd been denied so much.

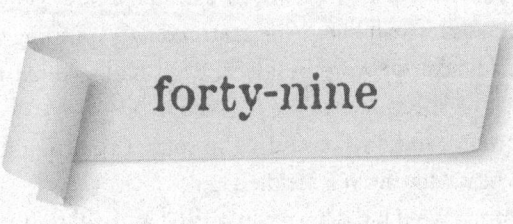

forty-nine

The women of America have at last become principals in the glorious American Controversy.

Benjamin Rush

Lucy left, and Mae, unable to wait a moment longer, went up the hill to the new house. Though Rhys had told her much about it, he'd hidden details and embellishments as if wanting to surprise her. Artfully arranged corner fireplaces, elegant wainscoting, tall casement windows, and paneled oak shutters greeted her. A straightforward stair in the hall with a few turns and a finely crafted balustrade had her hurrying upstairs.

All six rooms were sparsely furnished, but the furnishings were well-made. The parlor's settle reminded her of theirs in Chatham. A long, unscarred table with six ladderback chairs dominated the kitchen. Handsome cupboards and wardrobes and chests were upstairs and down. Carpets and curtains would soften the austereness in time. Lord willing, the echoing house would soon be filled with a baby's cry.

Soldier, rifleman, and farmer, Rhys was also an accomplished builder, his craftsmanship on display everywhere she looked. Some-

324

how that made her feel closer to him, cocooned by the work of his hands.

Over the next few days as she rested and recovered, life began to settle into a pleasant pattern. Between dawn and dusk's many tasks they took meals together downhill. Nightfall found Father Harlow making the rounds to the barn and outbuildings before Bronwyn snuffed the house lights. Mae snuffed the lights uphill. Never had she been so glad to lie down each night. A working farm was not for the faint of heart, even in the dwindling days of November.

Two weeks passed. Newspapers carried details of the battles near Saratoga, though there'd been no list of Continental casualties as of yet. British prisoners taken in New York were marching to Boston—more than two hundred miles of misery, 'twas said.

"'Tis a good time for Rhys to return home," Bronwyn said as she set jars of applesauce and preserves on the kitchen table. "Most of the fieldwork has halted till spring, though there's always clearing and splitting timber to be done. Cidermaking is finished and the larder and cellar stocked. Butchering, soapmaking, and candlemaking are next."

Mae didn't tell her she'd done none of that, having relied on Chatham's butcher, general store, and chandler, to say nothing of Madame Jaquett. But neither did she sit idly by and let her sister-in-law do the work. She marveled at all Bronwyn accomplished, but as the Quakers said, where work is shared, the burden is halved.

Standing in the large kitchen she was now mistress of, she felt at sea. But she could learn, could she not?

"I want you to teach me how to cook," Mae began somewhat hesitantly. "I don't want Rhys returning and having me make a mess of this beautiful kitchen he's built."

Bronwyn smiled, no stranger to Mae's hearth mishaps down the hill. "If you make messes it's only because you relied on Mrs. Hurst. Why don't we start with cornbread?"

"That's fine. But I don't just want to make cornbread," Mae told her earnestly. "I want to master corn pudding, fried corn, creamed corn, hominy, and anything else I might have overlooked."

"Corn is king here, truly." Rhys's sister was as patient as she was amused. "You northerners rely mostly on wheat, I take it. We do grow wheat but prefer maize." She began poking around in the cupboards. "Let's start at your own hearth then. Maybe you'll feel more at home right here and we can partake at your table on occasion."

"Of course," Mae replied with some trepidation.

"If you truly want to impress, you should master my brother's favorite, lemon cheesecakes."

And so they began, crossing the untrod pine floor to stir and bake and fry countless meals, as Mae's bespattered aprons soon proved. The bake oven built into the hearth was much like Chatham's, though it took time to get the wood and heat in harmony.

Weaving between patience and exasperation, Mae burned most of what she baked but pressed on. When Father Harlow pronounced her venison stew delicious, she wanted to rejoice. He even rigged a clockwork spit in the hearth, complete with drip pan, but this required skill and attention too. Never had Mae appreciated Mrs. Hurst so much. Or Bronwyn.

"I don't think I'll ever be the accomplished cook you are, but I've learned a lot in a short time," Mae told her.

"I've never seen anyone try harder. You're making great gains. Let's leave the kitchen for now and sew." Bronwyn led the way, trading the sunny kitchen for the parlor across the hall. "Your stitching needs no instruction. Rhys mentioned how much he appreciated you and the Liberty Ladies in a letter."

Had he? Mae took out her sewing kit with her newly sharpened scissors, thankful it had survived her journey. "When we met last winter, I began sewing for the army encamped at Lowantica Valley. Shirts, mostly. Once we arrived at Fort Montgomery I moved on to cockades and coats."

"Ambitious," Bronwyn said, admiring Lucy's pincushion. "I've heard the Continental Army is hoping to have blue uniforms with colorful facings for different regiments."

"Rhys and his riflemen mostly rely on linen hunting shirts and leggings, though Lucy and I did make him a handsome blue coat in New York." Mae tried to push away a darker memory. Their quarrel had come on the heels of finishing that coat.

Bronwyn looked up at her briefly before continuing work on a baby's cap edged in lace. "I sense a sadness about you when you speak of him."

Mae's needle stilled. Bronwyn was as perceptive as she was capable. How much should she confide?

"My last memory of him is a quarrel we had which seems to overshadow everything."

"I'm sorry, Mae. I don't mean to pry—"

"You're not prying but caring." Mae looked down at the tiny linen gown half finished in her lap. "The quarrel came about because of a family situation. I have a younger sister, you see, named Coralie . . ."

Even saying Coralie's name dredged up details and hurt feelings that were best forgotten. With a resolve to not besmirch her sister but simply state the facts, Mae let the whole story spill out, every miserable drop, and she felt both relieved and ashamed in the telling.

"So, your Loyalist sister chose Lieutenant Gibbs, and your family didn't take kindly to the matter," Bronwyn said as she stitched. "Don't judge yourself too harshly. You wanted what was best for everyone, including Rhys. You acted out of love and a desire to keep the peace, not from wrong or deceitful motives."

"I never thought her letters and loyalties would cause harm, but now I wonder if they didn't play into the downfall of the twin forts in even a small way. Both garrisons were well prepared but terribly undermanned. Perhaps my sister relayed their situation to the British and they seized the moment and attacked."

"You'll likely never know." Bronwyn gave a rare sigh. "'Things without all remedy should be without regard: what's done is done,' as Shakespeare says."

"I can't change any of it, though I wish I could. And I can't stop thinking about it."

"Try to dwell on Rhys and his homecoming instead."

But what if there's not to be one?

So far Bronwyn hadn't shared her own heartache. Mae had only heard the barest scraps from Rhys that Micah Edmiston had fallen in one of Virginia's first battles. Had Bronwyn moved past his death and locked that part of herself away?

"I hope and pray there's some word from Rhys soon," Mae said. "And more news from New York."

"Father has gone to market today so will hopefully return with a newspaper or broadside. I'm uneasy too. What little we do know is that General Washington is moving the northern army to winter quarters."

"Our Quaker hostess outside of Philadelphia mentioned Valley Forge near the Schuylkill River as a possible encampment."

"Hopefully once Rhys is settled we'll hear. He could still be somewhere along the Hudson River. New York is a vast territory, and mail is oft intercepted."

Mae withheld a wince. Fleeing the wilderness with all its hardships was something that would never leave her, nor would the memory of Jon's farm, burned beyond recognition. "Has the Shenandoah Valley escaped the conflict?"

"We've not escaped the war entirely," Bronwyn told her. "We've a few Loyalists here, though most of this valley are staunch Patriots. Several regiments are serving in the Continental Army all over the united states. Our foremost worry has been raids by the British and their Indian allies."

"Have there been any?"

"A few skirmishes so far—stealing supplies from farms and the like. We now have Patriot patrols to warn us." Bronwyn looked up and smiled. "I'd rather talk about tomorrow's Sabbath service."

Church? Mae sat back, hardly aware of time. Her days seemed as scattered as dandelion seeds.

"Our pastor is something of a firebrand, one of the so-called Black Robe Regiment who preach independence from the pulpit."

"Like Colonel Muhlenberg from Virginia. Rhys spoke highly of him. He actually forsook preaching to join the Continental Army."

"He did, indeed."

"Our own pastor in Chatham wasn't so bold." In hindsight, Mae saw how ill a match they would have made. "Tell me more about your congregation."

"On the third Sabbath of the month we gather for a community meal." Bronwyn smiled again, the dimple in her cheek unnoticed till now. "Best prepare yourself. You'll break a few hearts appearing as the new Mrs. Harlow."

★ ★ ★ ★ ★

Clad in her second-best dress that had finally been ironed, Mae sat with Father Harlow and Bronwyn in a back pew at the Presbyterian church. But being inconspicuous didn't seem to stop all the whispering behind hands, especially among the congregation's young women. Lucy's appearance bolstered her, though she sat upstairs in the loft with her kin.

"This morning we have with us General Harlow's new wife from Jersey," the pastor announced at service's end as countless heads turned in her direction. "I hope everyone will greet her kindly as we continue to pray for her husband's homecoming, as we do all the defenders of freedom from this valley and elsewhere."

Flushed, Mae tried to shake off her shyness and remember the names of those who greeted her.

The communal meal was held inside the church itself, plentiful southern fare that bespoke a rich harvest. Smoked hams were in abundance and numerous cider kegs were tapped, the Hewes Crab and Taliaferro quite different from Newark cider in Jersey.

Mae looked over the room, the pews pushed back, the talk and laughter deafening. Though Bronwyn had kept close to her side, she now drifted toward her female friends just as Father Harlow gathered with men outside the open door. Several older women peppered Mae with questions, and she felt stark relief when Lucy made straight for her.

"Fancy seeing you at church and not the middle of the wilderness," Lucy jested, squeezing her gloved hand. "How are you faring?"

"I've missed you, though Rhys's family has been so very good to me. I'm even living in the house he built. Soon you'll have to visit and we'll share some of Bronwyn's sassafras tea."

"I knew they'd welcome you proper-like, though I can't say the same for the unmarried misses who've long pinned their hopes on being Mrs. Harlow." She winked as if Mae had won at a game and outfoxed them all. "But he never paid any of them much mind other than a dance or two."

Mae mulled this, wondering if he now regretted his choice. Doubts continued to bedevil her, making her question everything, including their all-too-tenuous future.

"You've not heard anything about what came after Saratoga? Where our men might be?" Mae knew the answer before she asked. Lucy would have run to her house if she had.

With a shake of her head, Lucy shot down the notion. "All I know is that both New York battles were brutal. I'm sure my Isham was right there with his drum. The Rifle Corps fought ferociously, 'tis said, but not all stayed standing."

Mae felt as dependent on the unreliable post as Coralie had when she'd hoped for letters from Lieutenant Gibbs. Waiting and wondering seemed another sort of torment. No letters. No casualty lists.

If he lived, what if Rhys chose not to write because he'd not forgiven her?

fifty

Live free or die; death is not the worst of evils.

General John Stark

In the November twilight, Mae stood by the window of her upstairs bedchamber and took in shadowed outbuildings, fences and fields, and the long rutted road that wound in and out of their portion of the valley.

From which direction would Rhys come?

Cold seeped through the panes and turned her away from the window. Barefooted and nightgowned, she crossed the room to replenish the fire. Above, the mantel clock seemed to be ticking her life away without him.

Was she a wife or a widow?

The heirloom cradle rested to one side of the hearth, lined and softened by Bronwyn's bedding. Father Harlow had carved a remarkably lifelike toy lamb from willow, which rested at the cradle's foot.

Would their baby ever know his or her father?

Every day seemed to bring new changes. No longer nauseous nor so tired, she still felt different. She certainly looked different—fuller of face, not only rounder of body. Her dresses had to be let out at the waist, her stays loosened or remade. Though she'd seen countless expectant women over the years, she felt she was the very first.

"You look lovely in your new quilted cotton," Bronwyn had told her. "My brother will be blessed indeed to find you waiting."

Would he? Bronwyn, despite her deep loss, held on to hope in the face of the unknown, while she herself waged a private war between hope and despair. Lately she even dreamed of Rhys. Troubled, restless dreams that left her shaken and half sick.

Might he still be fighting or wounded? Or a prisoner, taken to one of the hellish prison ships in New York's harbor? 'Twas a fate worse than death. And then there were James and Jon, whose fate was just as uncertain.

Nights were the hardest, when the distraction of the day ground to a halt. In the silent, dark hours, so much loomed that left her feeling powerless. Her love for Rhys had not waned, but had his for her? All she recalled was his fury at the last, which tainted all that had been before. It made a poor bedfellow, leaving her to grasp hold of whatever assurance she could as she lay awake and awaited the dawn.

I will both lay me down in peace, and sleep: for thou, Lord, only makest me dwell in safety.

★ ★ ★ ★ ★

Autumn's chores set in as frost rimmed forest and fields. Mae found soapmaking tedious, while butchering involved a blood-bath that turned her squeamish. But candlemaking was a soothing if time-consuming task, especially on a fair, chilly December day.

"You've not dipped candles before?" Bronwyn asked, careful not to look too incredulous, Mae thought. "Rather delightful, actually."

"We always bought them from a chandler in Chatham."

Together they donned plain aprons and set about the work,

melting wax and preparing the flax wicks in the dyeing shed, where vats and candle ladders awaited.

"I can't abide the smell of tallow and it smokes abominably," Bronwyn told her, stirring the wax with a long-handled spoon. "So we indulge in beeswax and bayberry instead."

With Bronwyn's guidance, Mae handled the candle tree. She dipped multiple wicks into the wax again and again between their cooling, all the while breathing in the honey-spice fragrance.

"Last year we burned a hundred fifty-two candles, by my tally in the household account book," Bronwyn told her. "We'll double that amount this year since you're up the hill."

"Candlemaking is one of your favorite tasks, you said."

"It is—or was. Now it brings back that terrible December day in '75 when Micah fell. I was candlemaking then too when I heard the news."

"The battle at Great Bridge." Mae looked at her with sympathy, hearing the pain in her voice. "Rhys told me."

"A great loss to us both." Bronwyn bit her lip as she hung hardening candles on a candle ladder. "We were betrothed for a short time, but it was not to be."

Mae hesitated, wondering the wisdom of asking her question. "What was he like?"

"As fine a man as Rhys. Birds of a feather really do flock together. Strong. Steady. Dependable. In fact, Father's getting in hay with his father this morning at their farm. I rarely visit now. 'Tis still too painful, though I do see his kin at church."

"I understand." Mae fell silent as the sound of wagon wheels on the rutted road took her attention.

"A tinker perhaps." Bronwyn looked out the shed's open door and wiped her hands on her apron. "They do happen by, though not as regularly with the war on."

A gust of wind threatened to bang the door shut, so Bronwyn propped it open with a piece of firewood. Mae continued dipping candles, her mournful thoughts so full of Micah they crowded out Rhys. She paid little attention to the wagon halting in the yard beneath the biggest oak or the brief exchange of voices after Bronwyn left the shed. Hearing her startled cry, Mae nearly dropped the candles she'd just dipped.

She hung the candle tree from a hook and hurried outside toward the wagon. Bronwyn was already climbing into the wagon bed, her face drawn with alarm. What on earth? Mae leaned over the side panel, and her whole world flipped. There, atop a scattering of wet hay and a tattered blanket, lay Rhys in the blue coat she'd made, filling up the wagon with his height, his eyes closed and oblivious to their shock. Dead?

"Rhys?" Mae's hand shot out to smooth the unkempt hair from his unshaven face. His dry skin seemed to sear her palm.

With a groan, he thrashed about as Bronwyn pushed his coat back to expose his wounds. His right thigh was cocooned in layers of bloodied, dirty cloth that carried a sickly smell even in the open air. Beside him lay his rifle, which had likely kept him alive on the field. How it had made the journey seemed a second miracle.

The wagoner frowned. "He was transported by ship to Alexandria. The man with him sickened and died of a fever once they docked but paid me handsomely to bring him here before he did. I know little about General Harlow, but there's no doubt we're at the right place."

Mae clasped her husband's cold, dirty hand, her stinging eyes telling her she was crying before the realization struck. When Father Harlow rode into the yard on his gelding, Bronwyn called for him to come. The next minutes were a dizzying mix of panic and movement as the men carried Rhys from the wagon to the house and laid him out on a narrow corner bed. Mae hovered, unsure of what to do next.

Voice low, she looked to a clearly distraught Father Harlow, his usual stoicism scuttled. "Is there a doctor nearby?"

He nodded and, without another word, left on the horse he'd just ridden home, the wagoner departing in his wake. Mae and

Bronwyn began stripping off Rhys's filthy garments, top to bottom. His breeches were so threadbare they fell apart.

"Bring the washtub nearer and we'll fill it with warm, soapy water and bathe him as best we can," Bronwyn said as she tugged off a torn stocking. "His garments are beyond saving so we'll burn them, all but his boots."

Mae did as she was told, fetching hot water they'd meant for their own baths from the hearth till the tub was half full and sudsy. She looked him over in all his humbling barrenness but kept returning to his face, trying to reconcile who he'd been with the gravely wounded man before her, his only movement the slight rise and fall of his bare chest.

Cleaning a man so begrimed was not for the fainthearted. And Mae felt both faint and sick at heart. Where was the man she'd fallen in love with? Had he returned not to reunite with her as she'd hoped and prayed but to be buried instead?

"Look away, Mae, while I bathe the wound," Bronwyn told her quietly. "I would spare you that."

Mae took a cloth and bathed his face instead, then fetched a basin to wash his shoulder-length hair as he lay there. Soon she was as soap-spattered and damp as he was, but the task helped ground her. When he stiffened then flailed, his arm hitting her middle so hard the baby moved, she pulled back.

"He's feeling the pain of the wound, which seems to be festering, and I fear—" Bronwyn's whisper faded, then she continued. "Fetch the whiskey in the medicine cupboard."

Mae did so, knowing what her sister-in-law had been about to say but didn't.

Festering. She'd heard Aaron say it with dismay and finality. It usually meant the loss of a limb. Or worse.

fifty-one

For my part I have but one object in view, and that is the success of the cause. God can witness how cheerfully I would lay down my life to secure it!

General Hugh Mercer

"We know little about how he came to be here," Father Harlow told the doctor. "The wagoner merely said he was well paid at the Alexandria dock to bring him to the valley."

"Wounded in battle, likely. He may have been alert at first, then worsened on the journey." Dr. Hardy's voice continued calm as he examined Rhys, the whiskey they'd dosed him with riding the air. "My guess is that he came to Alexandria by ship from Boston, given New York and Philadelphia are under British control. Wounded as he is, he cannot fight, nor would he likely survive a winter encampment in such a condition. Whoever sent him south was wise indeed."

Mae wondered about his companion who'd died of fever. James? Jon? Or Isham?

As if reading her thoughts, Father Harlow continued, "Rhys may have no memory of who accompanied him."

"Memory is often lacking when one is gravely injured or ill," the doctor replied. "Perhaps in time . . ."

That night Mae stayed with him, trickling water past his cracked lips as he lay slightly upright on a bank of pillows. A woolen coverlet was pulled back from his wound, which was now bound in clean linen. Dr. Hardy had prescribed a poultice to be applied twice daily, charcoal in the morning and comfrey at night. She'd sensed a reserve about the skilled physician that she feared was hopelessness, though he'd said little other than they must draw the poison out.

Sitting near the head of the bed, she couldn't keep her hands to herself. Her need of Rhys whole and hearty again rose up and left her breathless. It was no small victory he was home. His washed hair felt like corn silk beneath her fingertips. She traced the sharp line of his cheekbone to his bearded jaw, wondering if he wanted her to shave him, frightened that he hadn't the voice to ask.

Leaning in, she kissed his rough cheek. "Rhys, you're home . . . and I'm here." Her voice broke. "Please keep fighting . . . if not for me, for our child."

Though he'd come to them almost lifeless, then restless—from pain, she guessed—he was now frightfully still. Smoothing her voice if not her emotions, she sang a low hymn, careful not to wake Bronwyn and Father Harlow upstairs. A Scripture came to mind, then fled her thoughts like mist.

The Lord will strengthen him upon the bed of languishing.

When her eyes wouldn't stay open, she joined him ever so carefully on the pallet, close enough to lay her cheek against his shoulder. She could barely hear him breathe. The fire's pumpkin-orange flames gave a pop as the logs shifted and cast light on all the crags and valleys of him, turning him older than his years. Suffering aged one. Suffering and war and wounds and hovering on the precipice of death.

Would he never get up again? Would she never see him trade his rifle for a plow or scythe in the Harlows' immense fields? Would she not sit with him at their new table up the hill? Show him the cradle or the tiny garments she'd made? Beg his forgiveness? Doing so seemed a privilege she'd never possess.

Where did the Harlows bury their dead?

★ ★ ★ ★ ★

Morning came and so did the doctor. There was talk of amputation, but the notion was quickly discarded. Angry red streaks extended from the wound like spokes on a wheel. As Bronwyn tended Rhys, Mae finished the candlemaking abandoned the day before. She could hardly bring herself to look at Rhys's torn-up flesh.

When she returned from the dyeing shed, his eyes were open and he'd found his voice.

"Where," he said haltingly, "is she?"

The three words brought the room to a standstill. Mae froze in the doorway, the cold December day at her back. Bronwyn motioned to her while the doctor and Father Harlow stood at the foot of the pallet. Pinched with unease, Mae felt all eyes on her as she stepped nearer and met those eyes that had been ice-gray at Fort Montgomery. They held hers for a few unfathomable seconds before closing again and shutting her out.

She stood as awkwardly as a scarecrow with everyone watching till Bronwyn pulled up a chair and gestured for her to sit down. The men moved toward the hearth, talking in low, rumbling tones. Mae felt more at sixes and sevens when Bronwyn disappeared.

"Rhys." Words hung in her throat. It had been easier to whisper to him in the dark of night than in broad daylight. "We're all waiting for you to get well. Your father is even making you crutches."

Eyes still closed, hands fisted on the sheets, Rhys gave no indication he heard her. Yet she felt the need to unburden herself and tell him of the time and events that had come between them, even if he couldn't take them in.

"I'll start from the beginning." She hesitated, gathering her thoughts before leaning in and speaking softly. "When you left the fort to go north to Saratoga, it wasn't long before the British came. Pickets alerted everyone ahead of their arrival, and Lucy and I were able to leave with the horses."

She still felt the fear and bewilderment of it all, the gnawing hunger and relentless unrest. "It took us days and days to clear the woods. We were lost a time or two. We even came across Indians, and it seems a miracle they didn't see us. Your money pouch stood us in good stead, and we never needed the pistols except to kill a panther following us. When we neared Philadelphia, we realized it was still held by the British, so we went another direction."

She stifled the urge to reach out and touch him as she had last night, her hands knotted in her lap. "We stopped at a tavern a time or two." How many times blurred in her memory, though she'd never forget the gracious Widow Wistar outside Philadelphia. "We finally arrived here on an early November morning, Lucy and I—and Petey."

She studied him, this husband of hers. He gave no indication he'd heard, yet she sensed he had in some ineffable way—if only the emotion behind her words, this painful recounting of all the hollow, harrowing weeks without him.

And now that he was here, would this be how she would remember him? On his back, the world shut out, unable to discern the extent of his suffering or summon a smile? Broken in body, he seemed to be shrinking before her very eyes, unable to eat, unable to even drink without help, withdrawing from the world and her in particular. This perilous, precarious dance between life and death clawed at her night and day and gave her no rest.

"*Where is she?*"

Would those be the last words he'd ever speak?

★ ★ ★ ★ ★

Somehow Mae's hushed words penetrated the pain and the anguished haze that held him. He rode the tide of illness, rolling in and out of consciousness, barely able to keep his eyes open.

Everything required herculean strength, even swallowing, but he knew he needed to eat—or die. This constant dribbling of water and tonics down his throat sustained no man.

"It took us days and days to clear the woods . . . We finally arrived here."

Mae's melodic voice tickled his ears and made him want to reach for her. But his hand seemed a lead weight atop the bedding, keeping him from it. His parched throat and reeling head still bespoke fever. Yet another deeper heat burned through him—ire over their unsettled past, their last confrontation needling him and demanding to be settled. But even this ebbed and flowed like the pain.

Night came. Mae left his side. He was awake now—as wide awake as the hooting owl outside in the trees. A full moon shone on the floorboards. He rolled over and gritted his teeth as he lifted first one leg then the other to the floor with his hands. Weak as a newborn foal, he was. Crutches rested at the foot of the bed and seemed a mile distant. He felt a wild, pulse-pounding resolve to reach them, even if he had to crawl to do it. And crawl he did.

By the time he grabbed hold of them, his shirt was damp with the sweat of sheer exertion. His wound seemed on fire, shards of glass embedded in his thigh where the musket ball had been. Swallowing, throat dry, he took a last look around the moonlit room.

No Mae. Had he dreamed her up, then?

His desperation to see her got him to the front door. He'd need to navigate the porch next and the now formidable stoop. *Breathe, step, breathe, step.* His wound screamed in protest, but he went slowly. One crutch made it across the worn planks to the stoop, only for the other to collapse, spilling him onto his back across the moonlit, frost-hardened ground.

Had he yelled? Something brought Bronwyn out the door, their father following. In their nightclothes, fright scored across their faces, they rushed to raise him, dispensing with the crutches altogether.

"We must get you back inside." Bronwyn's shock and exasperation were plain. "What on earth made you leave the bed?"

"I'm . . . going up . . . the hill," he replied breathlessly, expecting her next rebuttal. "I don't care that it's after midnight. The moon's full enough to light my way."

"It's a long climb for a man in your condition." His father's arm undergirded him as Bronwyn supported him from the other side.

"Where's Mae?" His voice, rusty from disuse, cracked.

"She's been by your side night and day since you came back to us. I told her to return uphill and rest. It's not good for her nor the baby to nurse you like she's doing."

So he hadn't dreamed of her, or the baby. And should he make it up this infernal hurdle of a hill, he would wake her.

"You've all but risen from the dead," his father said. "Though I wish you'd have done it in daytime."

Rhys tried to smile. For now, all he could manage was a wince. "I need to eat. Is there any food?"

"You've been unable to eat till now." Bronwyn eyed him warily. "Mae made a fine soup for supper, and there's some left."

Mae cooking? He chuckled. Not the Mae he remembered, who could char anything she set her hand to. He smelled the smoke of a chimney fire, mayhap his own.

Halfway up the hill, his body balked. He collapsed again, fighting pain and dizziness and exhaustion. His father left his side and returned with a wheelbarrow.

"You're lighter than when you left or I'd not be able to do it," he said as they helped him off the ground and lowered him inside the contraption.

Up the hill they went, slowly but teeth-rattlingly. His next hurdle was the porch steps he'd crafted with his own hands. The house, though just as he'd left it, looked strange to him, he'd been away so long. Or was it because he'd changed, no longer the man he'd been when he built it?

As the three of them climbed the steps clumsily, the front door swung open. Mae stood there, her nightgown falling to her bare feet. Her face lit up like the lantern in her hand. Their eyes locked and held, making him forget everything and everyone else. When he looked past her to the broad hall and the seventeen steps he must climb, his resolve shattered.

"Come inside." Mae stood to one side of the door. "We've moved the bed downstairs into the parlor so I won't have to risk the steps ahead of the baby's coming. But now I think it was meant for you."

"She slipped and fell partway down them the other day." Bronwyn's words made him forget his own misery. "Thank heavens it did her no harm."

He looked to Mae again as if to determine the truth of it, but she was studying him with such alarm he sensed she knew he was near collapse again. His ordeal was almost over.

Feeling like a man thrice his age and supported every step, he made it to the parlor, where the outline of a bed he didn't recognize—his father's doing?—dominated the room. Soon he was in it, the feather tick sinking with his weight.

"Soup," he said. But by the time Bronwyn brought it, the tide of pain had returned and the only way he could escape it was to ask for whiskey. Before he fell into a restless slumber he managed two more words. "Fetch Lucy."

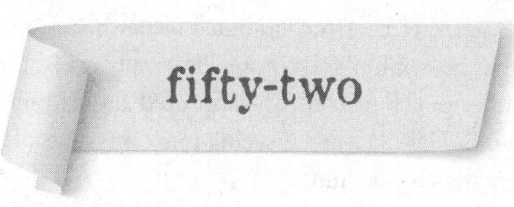

fifty-two

The flame is kindled and like lightning it catches from soul to soul.

Abigail Adams

Lucy appeared that afternoon, a ray of sunshine in the wintry landscape. While Petey remained outside, gnawing on a bone Bronwyn provided, Lucy hastened into the parlor, looking about in wonder. Her gaze landed on Rhys, who sat by the fire in a Windsor chair.

"Mercy, General." She eyed him nervously, coming to a stop by the settle. "I came as quick as I could but am sorry to see you brought low."

"For now, aye." Rhys shifted in his seat. "I bring good news. Private Hawkes is well—or was at our last contact—and will winter with General Washington in Pennsylvania at a place called Valley Forge."

Lucy's wariness turned joyful. "Glad I am to hear it, though I wish he was home like you."

"If he was he'd be injured or a deserter. You don't want that."

"Nay, sir. But I miss him something fierce." She took a seat on the settle, hands in her lap. "Who's in charge of the Rifle Corps with you here?"

He paused, so divorced from the army it seemed he was talking about another entity entirely. "They may have a new commander by now, or will have once they break camp next year. I haven't heard nor can I recall since Saratoga."

"Did you come by your injury in battle, sir?"

"Nay, after."

Her eyes narrowed. "After" sounded somewhat suspicious, he admitted, but he wouldn't elaborate. He simply called for Mae to bring a leather pouch of coin. She appeared almost immediately, pouch in hand. Her pleasure at seeing Lucy was mutual and lessened the soreness inside him.

"Private Hawkes wanted you to have a portion of his pay." He wouldn't say that the entire amount Hawkes had entrusted to him had been lost in his delirium on the way here—or stolen—and he'd had to ask his father for reimbursement.

Thanking him, Lucy took the sack and looked to Mae, who offered refreshments. "Sassafras tea, not proper English tea, or coffee or chocolate, if you'd rather. *And* iced ginger biscuits. Not burnt, I promise."

"Coffee and biscuits, then," Lucy said with a chuckle. "Will you be joining us, General?"

"Nay," he replied. "I've other business to take care of."

★ ★ ★ ★ ★

Lucy followed Mae into the kitchen, reminding her this was the first time Lucy had been inside. "Losh, but this house makes Fort Montgomery seem a hovel in hindsight."

Agreeing, Mae began brewing coffee, glad for company. "I'm fond of the kitchen especially. So very bright and airy. Father Harlow made an abundance of cupboards that even bests my former Chatham house."

"And such a handsome hearth!" Lucy held her hands out to the flames. "You'll be snug all winter, the babe too. How are you faring?"

"I've recovered well, thanks to you, and look forward to my

lying-in come spring. I'll be able to bring Mahala outside into sunshine and fresh air like my mother did me from the first."

"A girl?" A smile softened Lucy's freckled face. "A comely biblical name."

"I could be wrong . . . but sometimes one just knows."

"That's what my ma used to say."

"Do you want children?" She'd never broached the tender subject before, nor had Lucy.

"I don't suppose everyone is meant to have them. For now, Petey's plenty." She took a bite of a ginger biscuit and proclaimed it delicious. "I'll just borrow Mahala every now and then."

"Then we'll call you Aunt Lucy."

"I like the sound of that." Her smile widened, then faded as she saw Mae's sewing basket by the hearth. "A uniform coat?"

"Yes. Bronwyn gave me the wool cloth and I dyed it blue. The one we made General Harlow was ruined on his journey here."

"So you're making him another."

"For Christmas, yes. I thought I might ask you to finish it in silver thread like you did the Clintons' coats."

"You think he'll return to the army, then." For a few seconds Lucy fell as silent as Mae, then said, "The general's poorly. I've never seen him so. What happened?"

Mae poured them both coffee, her voice low. "He won't say."

"Well, it's clear he's had a grave injury. I pray he's out of danger."

"The doctor seems to think he'll be all right. For a time we feared blood poisoning."

"Poisoning's buried many a soldier." Lucy shuddered. "Now that he's mending, fatten him up and keep him off his feet."

"Sage advice, Lucy, but I doubt he'll agree to it."

"Well, 'tis clear he's glad to be home. He adores you, he does. I see it plain when he looks at you."

Mae reined in her surprise as she stirred sugar and cream into her cup. "He's rather . . . cantankerous of late."

"Men make poor patients. When he's himself again all will be well."

But he won't ever be himself again, she thought. *Nor will I.*

★ ★ ★ ★ ★

Mae missed Lucy the moment she left Mae alone with Rhys in a too-quiet house. His midnight feat of coming uphill and then meeting with Lucy seemed to set him back, though for a moment she'd grabbed hold of hope again.

She wasn't a widow. Nor the mother of a fatherless child.

Just the wife of a broken-down soldier who must be rebuilt bit by bit with food and care and kindness. For now, he could manage only a few spoonfuls of soup before his stomach cramped and he heaved it up again.

"By far the best medicine is his being here at home near you and the baby," Bronwyn had told her.

But Mae doubted she was the medicine he needed. There'd been no true conversation between them since he'd been back. Now he simply slept and ate by turns as if the sheer effort of living wore him out.

When another day passed and he slipped into a profound sleep, she feared his rallying was a ruse. Still, Dr. Hardy smiled for the first time since she'd met him as he examined Rhys and pronounced the infection lessened.

"Continue with the poultices and keep the wound clean. Do as much as you feel like doing, but don't overtax yourself," he advised Rhys. "Try to get up and navigate with those crutches I spy in the corner." Looking to Mae he added, "Fatten him like a prize calf before market."

And so Mae set to work in the kitchen, turning out apple tarts, thick stews, and endless cornbread and wheaten loaves. The aroma alone was enough to strengthen a man, Father Harlow said. Mae felt a small flicker of pride that she'd conquered the kitchen and become something of a cook, though she still doubted she'd ever rise to the heights of Bronwyn or Mrs. Hurst.

At week's end the doctor told them he wouldn't return unless they needed him. To celebrate, Bronwyn and Father Harlow carried a prized firkin of their best cider up the hill. Once the wooden bung was removed and the cask tapped, Mae poured them all a drink, including Rhys. He took his with an unsteady hand.

Once he'd seemed unstoppable. A force. She paled at his patriotism, his devotion to the cause. It had outweighed his devotion to her. She'd tested that devotion and come away the loser. As they toasted his return to health, she wondered . . .

How would their frayed tie weather his return to the fight?

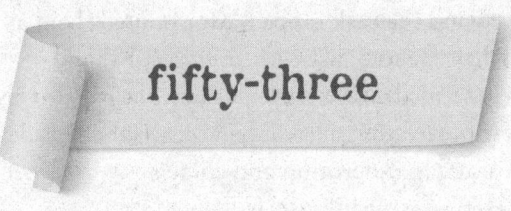

fifty-three

Why can I not fight for my country too?

Deborah Samson

Rising early the next morning, Mae made her way downstairs to the kitchen to find a fire already kindled. The sight stopped her cold. With a glance back across the hall to the parlor's open door, she saw another hearth snapping and leaping merrily, a most welcome sight.

Rhys's doing?

A beat of hope stirred her into action. As she prepared a breakfast tray in the kitchen, her culinary mishaps fewer and fewer, she prayed for their day. Toast, eggs, and bacon soon crowded the pewter plate, though she doubted he'd eat half of it. Sometimes she finished whatever remained.

Taking a steadying breath, she traded the warm kitchen for the parlor, expecting to find him sleeping as she so often did. Instead, he was leaning back against the headboard, his fingers trellised behind his head.

"Morning, Mae."

She tried to smile as she served him, unable to meet his gaze for fear of what she'd find there. "Thank you for tending the fire."

"It's the least I can do."

LAURA FRANTZ

Breakfast served, she started to leave the room, as addled as when she'd first met him, but his voice stopped her at the threshold.

"You're angry with me."

Was she? She turned toward him, all her fears gathering like storm clouds. Would he relapse and die right here? Or return to the fight and fall on some distant battlefield, shattering her heart all over again? Leaving her with countless regrets? The feeling between them was strained, anything but amicable.

"And you're still angry with me." Her voice wavered when she said it, all the pent-up emotion of the last months without him weighting her words.

He didn't deny it. He simply looked at the tray and made no move to eat. She sensed how much he hated being off his feet, an invalid, waited on hand and foot and unsure of the future.

"I'm angry with myself . . . our circumstances." She tried to express what tore at her. Failed. "But I cannot undo anything about all that happened no matter how much I want to. I live with the regret of it day and night."

He set the tray aside. Though far from agile, he reached for his crutches and began to get up. "I'll eat in the kitchen. There's no cause to be bedrid."

She followed him with the tray, his breakfast no longer hot. The house was big enough that the hearth's warmth failed to reach farther into the room than a few feet. She glanced at the kitchen windows in dismay. A light snow was falling, which might well lock her in with him and his smoldering fury and her own haunting regrets.

Jerkily, he sat down at the head of the table and leaned his crutches against a cupboard. She busied herself at the hearth, beginning the soup for their noon meal and wishing Bronwyn or Father Harlow would walk in. Rhys was often brusque with them too, saying little, mostly listening and protesting any attempts by them to turn him into a slabbering milksop, so he said. She vowed to not be one of them.

When the silence turned taut as a fiddle string, she murmured, "You miss your Rifle Corps."

"Aye." He continued his breakfast as she busied herself grating corn into meal for bread. "I miss being on my feet, hale and hearty."

A twist of resentment needled her. "You're married to the army . . . not me."

"You knew that the day I wed you."

His matter-of-factness made her want to throw the bowl of corn at him. As it was, she grated her knuckle and blood stained her clean apron. She took a handkerchief from her pocket, wrapped it around her finger, and kept grating. "You're sorry you wed me."

"Nay, Mae." He set down his fork. "I'm sorry you did what you did, but I'm not sorry you're my wife."

She felt the intensity of his gaze but couldn't bring herself to meet his eyes. "Do you forgive me?"

"I do," he said with feeling, reminding her of the hallowed vows they'd spoken at Jon's farm. "Why won't you look at me?"

"Because I still see anger in your eyes." Her voice shook as she met his gaze. "You're regarding me as you did at Fort Montgomery that dark day, only you're no longer shouting."

"I'm sorry it came to that." His voice held telling regret. "Do you forgive me?"

Did she? The hurt she'd carried ever since had festered into a bone-deep rankling. Their blissful beginning had soured that day, tainting her every thought of him since. The words that could never be taken back or undone played in her mind like a broken melody.

"You chose your sister over me . . . I should turn you out of this fort . . . I trusted you once, and I can trust you no longer."

She couldn't answer with any truthfulness, at least not the answer he wanted. Nor did she believe he'd truly forgiven her. She'd never felt less like a wife since he'd come home. This didn't feel like her home. She felt like an intruder despite the ring on her finger.

Something pulsed between them in this kitchen that was anything but harmonious. Lest she add more shards to the brokenness, she abandoned her task and fled out the back door.

*　*　*　*　*

Rhys pushed away from the table and his unfinished breakfast and reached for his crutches. By the time he'd hobbled to the back door, Mae had disappeared, well beyond reach. Snow was coming down again on a raw December wind, blowing into the kitchen. He leaned into the doorframe and looked past the plot of frozen ground meant for the kitchen garden to the wall of woods behind the house.

Where had she gone?

"Mae!" His aggrieved shout brought Bronwyn, which aggravated him as much as Mae's absence.

"Mercy, Rhys!" His sister hurried into the kitchen. "Shut the door before we all freeze to our roosts like chickens."

"Mae just left," he told her, refusing to shut it as if somehow Mae might take that as him shutting her out.

"Left?" She stood to one side of the hearth, her back to the dwindling flames. "What means you?"

"We had . . . words." He bent to a stack of wood near the door and heaved a piece of oak onto the fire from where he stood. "A misunderstanding."

"Oh? I don't want to get in the middle of it, but I am concerned." She looked to the cornmeal Mae had been grinding. "Father and I have tried to leave you be, let you both come to terms with being together again."

"Obliged," he said, sitting back down at the head of the table, appetite gone.

She looked toward the open door. "Do you want me to go after her in your stead? She may be in the pasture where the sheep are kept. I've noticed she likes to walk there."

"Let her return in her own time," he said, resigned. Still, she'd worn no cape or coat, and he was always mindful of the baby. "She won't be out long in this weather."

"What can I do to help?"

"Stir the soup and finish grinding the meal."

She gave the pot a stir, then resumed Mae's work at the table. "The miller, bless him, has decided to dress the millstones, so we've not had any corn ground lately. Being so aged he's quite slow—and quite stubborn. He refuses any help."

The miller had a rebel son who'd been cut down at Brandywine Creek. How Rhys ached to ride to the mill and insist on dressing the stones himself. Taking a drink of lukewarm coffee, he felt the thunder return to his head. Fevered again?

Looking at him warily, Bronwyn made short work of the rest of the corn and took a seat. "Have you told her about how you came to be injured? What brought you home?"

"Nay."

"Why not?" Her forthright questions were always broached gently, which made them more agreeable. "I'm sure she wants to know. I sense she's trying not to rush you but letting you recover first."

"I'm still mulling the wisdom of saying anything at all."

"The truth is always better than secrecy, especially between husband and wife."

How would she know? Though she'd been denied the wedding she wanted, she was wise to the ways of marriage. She should be in her own kitchen and not his, with children around her skirts, their small hands keeping her from her work or trying to help her as children liked to do. And yet here he sat, in a tangle of turmoil, with a wife and child, and had it all instead. Guilt nicked him like a wayward knife.

"She's a good woman, Rhys." Bronwyn's eyes shone with unshed tears. "She means to be a good wife. And whatever is wrong between you can be righted."

He got up, made his way to the back door again, and stared into pines and leafless oaks and maples bedecked white. What he'd give to go in search of her. If she stayed out much longer . . .

He heard the front door open and close quietly. Bronwyn brightened and his heart gave a leap. Footsteps sounded lightly on the stair, and he finally shut the back door, wanting to follow her yet realizing she wanted to be out of his reach. He might have mastered the front steps, but he hadn't attempted the second floor yet.

Perhaps the time had come to do just that.

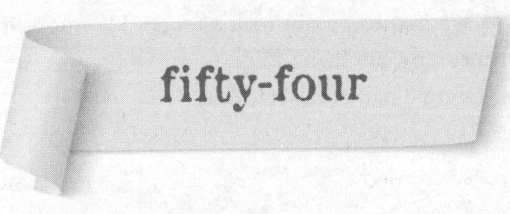

fifty-four

Truth will ultimately prevail where pains is taken to bring it to light.

George Washington

That night, despite Bronwyn's worries about the steep steps, Mae slept upstairs on a trundle bed Father Harlow had made, her ears tuned to Rhys in the parlor below. She'd not shared his bed since he'd first returned home, fearful of disturbing him. But she missed him and his warmth, the whole-bodied man he'd been. She hardly knew what to make of him now.

Bronwyn and Father Harlow had come up the hill for supper again. After they'd eaten, her father-in-law took out a violin, making her wonder where the one she'd given Rhys had gone. Perhaps her father's instrument had been lost along the way. But that seemed a question best left unasked, at least for the moment.

So many questions.

Rhys played briefly, a few tunes from the war. She recognized "The Girl I Left Behind Me" and "Yankee Doodle Dandy." Rather than brighten her mood, the music left her downcast, though she worked hard to hide it as she listened, sewing more swaddling from linen Bronwyn had spun and woven.

There was no heart to his music like before. Though skillfully played, it seemed flat. Forced. And then her in-laws had hastened down the hill as the snow robed the valley in deeper white.

She turned over, wishing she was nearer the fire. Snow light made it seem dawn, not midnight. Was Rhys warm enough? She'd given him an extra blanket but hadn't checked the parlor fire before bed, just gone upstairs to wash and say her prayers. Of all they'd lost, it was the prayers that bookended their days that she most lamented.

Had he stopped praying?

The thought nettled her till she slipped into oblivion, a cold, restless sleep where five blankets weren't sufficient and her pillow slip felt like ice. Unwillingly, she returned to the bewilderment of the north woods in her dreams. Muddled, distressed dreams where Lucy was missing and there was no sign of Rhys. She awoke shaken and half sick at first light.

Eyes open, she sensed another presence that brought her bolt upright. Shaking off her dream, she startled at the silhouette of a man in a Windsor chair. Rhys. His crutches made a skeletal shadow against the wall behind him. Somehow he'd gotten upstairs. The bedchamber's grate roared with light and warmth.

He was looking at the empty cradle, and she felt another start to find him freshly shaven, when he'd been bearded since his return. She brushed back her own unraveled braid, drawing her knees to her chest and hugging them, the blankets surrounding her like petticoats.

"Mae, there's something that needs saying."

His intensity troubled her. Terrified her. His low words held far less heat than when they'd faced off before but still shook her. She couldn't even gather the wherewithal to ask him how he'd managed to come upstairs. What if he turned her out like he'd threatened to do at Fort Montgomery?

"Rather, I need to tell you some things." He set his jaw, and she sensed his unwillingness to say what he must. "Much happened after I left you at the fort. It seems dishonest to keep it from you."

She looked at the leaping fire rather than his face, bracing herself for whatever was to come. Did he sense all her unasked questions?

"We moved up the Hudson, south of Fort Edward where Jane McCrea was killed." He paused, and she felt the horror of hearing Jane's story all over again. "Then the Rifle Corps joined General Gates and the main body of the American army near Saratoga. We battled the British twice there in September and October . . ." His eyes were aglitter. "James fought like the true Patriot he was at Freeman's Farm."

Was.

Her own eyes filled as the weight of his words pushed past her disbelief. Her beloved brother . . . gone. For some reason she'd rarely considered the possibility James or Jon might fall, only Rhys. She wiped her tears away with the sleeve of her nightgown as he continued quietly.

"He's buried near where he fell. James died quickly—didn't suffer long."

The fury of battle was beyond him. James, as firm in his faith as he was his Patriot convictions, was at peace.

"Did he know—about Coralie?" Somehow she couldn't bear it if he did.

"If he learned about Coralie it was through someone else, not me, though he never mentioned it. He didn't even know you and I quarreled."

Relief pulsed through her—and respect. Rhys was above besmirching family members, even angry as he'd been. "And Jon?"

"Jon is well, though he took a bayonet wound to the shoulder in the second battle. After that, he left to winter with his family and recover. He never mentioned Coralie again once she'd left the fort."

Jon would heal, she hoped, and one day rebuild all he and his family had lost.

"There's more." He leaned forward in his chair, hands fisted between his knees. "When Burgoyne surrendered, hundreds of

British soldiers and their followers gave up their weapons and walked past Continental troops. I was overseeing the British arms when I saw your sister."

What? She tried to imagine it, surprise trumping her shame. She'd thought Coralie was long gone. Where to, she didn't know. She'd never expected her to be near a battlefield.

"I saw her walk by," Rhys continued matter-of-factly. "She even looked my way."

And none too kindly, Mae was sure. "Where did she go?"

"She was among the prisoners taken to Boston. There was talk, per surrender terms, about putting both troops and Loyalists on ships to England."

England, a place Coralie had never been, though she remained loyal to the mother country. "She said nothing when she walked past you?"

"Nay." He paused again, and she steeled herself for something else—something worse. "As I stood on the field where they were laying down their weapons, a shot rang out from the trees on the hill behind me." He put a hand on his thigh, so near the wound she winced. "I was struck by musket fire and fell. The shooter was Eben Gibbs."

She drew in her breath so sharply it became a cry.

"He meant to kill me, he said. Muskets make miserable arms, or he might have done so. As soon as he misfired, he ran but was soon rounded up by the New York militia. After his court-martial, he hung."

Stung, she looked to the cradle as if it could anchor her. Her thoughts were dashing in every direction, trying to come to terms with James's death, Coralie's capture, and Gibbs's execution. And how Rhys had suffered the consequences.

The tears she thought checked began to fall again. "I'm so sorry."

"I'm sorry too." He looked to the cradle again absently. "I'm sorry in ways I can't fully grasp or express."

Sorrow washed through her, along with a burning ire and suffocating regret. She wanted to run out the back door again and escape her unruly emotions. As it was, she could only get up and grab her smallclothes and go downstairs to make breakfast. But that made her feel she was abandoning him when he needed her. Only he might not need her but push her away if she tried to comfort him or seek comfort.

In the kitchen, her hands fairly shook as she ground the coffee beans she'd roasted the day before, her mind grappling with all he'd told her. She'd never see James again, her beloved brother who had served so faithfully without complaint. Who had loved to tease and never bore a grudge. Who had introduced her to the man she loved best.

Once again she felt she held part of the blame for Eben Gibbs's final, dishonorable act, no doubt nurtured through Coralie and her loathing of Rhys and the American cause. Though it hadn't killed him, Rhys would carry the effects of it to his grave. As would she.

Woodenly, she went through the routine of frying bacon and toasting bread and brewing coffee, her hands busy but her head elsewhere. The tap of crutches brought her round. Though everything in her wanted to, she resisted the urge to hurry into the hall and help Rhys down the stairs.

When he finally came into the kitchen he took a seat at the head of the table. His bowed head and closed eyes brought another knot to her throat. She served him wordlessly, her own appetite gone. Would she ever be able to get past their confrontation at the fort? Did she misconstrue his intensity, his dark looks of late, for something else entirely? Might it have been the burden of keeping secret all that he'd just told her?

She wanted nothing more than to wrap her arms around him and return to the way they'd been at first, when even the roughness of a fort in the middle of the wilderness hadn't mattered with him beside her. But there was no going back. Only forward.

When he thanked her for breakfast it rent her already broken heart. As he ate, she stood by a window, staring out at the snowy landscape the wind had sculpted with deep drifts and pockets, the glare making her squint.

Only the pop of the fire sounded. And then she heard the scrape of his chair as he got up from the table. She hoped he might hobble toward her, perhaps put his arms around her as he used to do. The ache in her chest and throat grew unbearable as she held back her tears.

When she looked again he wasn't there.

fifty-five

The greatest and completest revolution the world ever knew, gloriously and happily accomplished.

Thomas Paine

Days passed, the brilliant snow now old and muddied. Though he was getting around on crutches with more ease, his pain more manageable, Rhys was not the man he'd been, neither in body nor soul. Because of it, he forced himself to tend to chores his father or Bronwyn could easily have done. He fell down more than once, even sliding on ice and getting bloodied all over again when he collided with the side of the barn.

Christmas loomed but none of the festive feeling with it, though Harlow House, as neighbors called it, overflowed with the aroma of gingerbread and beeswax candles and pine boughs. Mae seemed determined to decorate their home top to bottom as if staying busy could keep her grief over James at bay.

When he wasn't in the house he went downhill to his father's workshop, forbidding Mae to follow. Bronwyn was often uphill, keeping her company, so he didn't feel guilty absenting himself. By the workshop's fire, he and his father crafted a rocking chair from maple. Though his thigh was mangled, his hands were not. Using a drawknife, he shaped the spindles and backrest and legs while his father assembled the frame. It required both of them working if they were to finish by Christmas.

Anticipating Mae's pleasure spurred him on. Losing himself in something to benefit someone else seemed a tonic, a means to heal. The deadness he'd felt since New York began to lighten somewhat.

"So, are you ready to be a father?"

Rhys continued carving, shavings at his feet, surprised by his father's candor. He had always been a taciturn man, and Rhys seemed to mirror him since his harrowing return from the war.

"I misdoubt anyone is ready for the most important task of one's life aside from being a husband. And I'm a poor one at present."

"You're still healing."

Only physically, he thought. In other ways he seemed as far as the east from the west from the one that most mattered. Mae seemed untried territory, a wilderness with no compass, and he didn't sense a way through. "I can't seem to find my way back to her."

"To Mae."

Rhys swallowed, suddenly at sea. That was how he felt. Adrift. Unable to return to what they'd once had. "Much has changed."

"But not your love for her."

"Nay."

"Then you need to tell her." His father bent to join the chair seat to the frame. "It will do you both good. In hindsight, I didn't tell your mother near enough."

With that, he left to see to the horses, leaving Rhys alone. Leg aching, he took a stool by the hearth to continue his work. Long minutes passed, and he heard Bronwyn calling the cows for the evening milking. Dusk gathered at the windows, reminding him supper would be waiting. He stood, preparing for the long, slow journey uphill, his father's words accompanying him.

He hadn't told Mae he loved her since their wedding day. When had he decided it didn't need repeating? Mayhap it needed saying now most of all.

★ ★ ★ ★ ★

Mae cleared the supper dishes, waiting for Rhys to cross the hall and go into the parlor like usual. She usually joined him afterward. Sometimes he read to her by candlelight or they'd discuss something printed in the newspapers. Neither of them had mentioned Coralie again. They steered around anything personal, even the baby, and held each other at arm's length, a distance that tore her heart in two. But what was she to do? Was he waiting for her to reach out to him first?

Finished washing dishes, she carried a lit taper to the parlor, remembering the letter from home in her pocket. *Home.* Would she ever stop thinking of Chatham as home? Home was here. With Rhys and their coming child, despite a tangle of heartaches and setbacks.

He sat in one of the twin Windsor chairs fronting the hearth. He'd once jested that while their backsides were ice, their fronts were aflame. Tonight he had no book or newspaper in hand. Lately he'd kept up with war news less, perhaps because the army was in winter quarters and fighting had ceased.

"'Tis a momentous time," she said, "the day Congress has proclaimed we should stop and give thanks to God for blessing our nation and troops in their quest for independence and peace."

"I'm feeling far more grateful here at home than far afield," he murmured, reaching for his pipe.

Sitting down in the empty chair beside him, she took the letter from her pocket. "Hanna wrote us a letter."

He nodded and lit his pipe as she began to read aloud.

Dear Sister and Brother-in-Law,
    We are overjoyed to announce the arrival of Claire and James . . .

Twins? Mae stopped reading and Rhys raised an eyebrow.

"I mayn't have mentioned there are twins on Mother's side of the family," she said, thankful all was well. The pronounced flutter inside her and her increased girth challenged her to consider two Harlows. "I'm glad they've named him James, and Claire is especially pretty."

> . . . *born 26th October. They joined us around midnight during a full moon and have turned our home upside down with happiness.*
>
> *Their safe, healthy arrival tempers the loss of James somewhat. We have heard from Jon and they are rebuilding. What matters most is that they're all together and Joanna and the children are well.*
>
> *Your letter telling of your coming through the wilderness seems a womanly version of Robinson Crusoe or Gulliver's Travels. We thank God still that you and Lucy are all right. We pray daily that General Harlow's return to health is swift and he is on his feet again. For pain relief, Aaron advises an infusion of willow bark or Valerian root. Ample rest is essential.*
>
> *Perhaps once the twins are older, we can venture south to your new home. We are counting the days till spring and your confinement. You never know the wonder and joy a child brings till you experience the miracle yourself.*
>
> *We have moved into Father and Mother's house and let our apprentice live at the apothecary shop. Mrs. Hurst sends her regards to you both. She seems quite content to be with us now as she gets on in years and needs a remedy or two. She says the children will keep her young.*
>
> *Jon has told us of seeing Coralie from a distance at the New York surrender. We are sad that she has chosen to side with the British and is now a prisoner of war. We are even more grieved that her loyalties returned her to Lieutenant*

Gibbs and somehow influenced his heinous actions at the last, including his own death.

Mae paused, wishing she'd kept that part from Rhys. He sat stoic, still smoking, as she continued.

Please write as soon as you are able. The Shenandoah Valley sounds lovely, and we are comforted knowing you may be far from Chatham but are surrounded by loving family there. Again, give General Harlow our best. We pray for you and yours daily.

> *Your ever loving,*
> *Hanna*

Mae folded the letter back up and put it in her pocket. Somehow it assuaged her the Chatham house didn't sit empty and was near enough to the apothecary that Aaron wouldn't have far to walk.

"Do you miss home?" Rhys asked, drawing on his pipe.

"Only family and the apothecary, even the scent of it."

"We could go visit, in time."

"I'd rather they come to Virginia." She took up her knitting. "Since it was so hard getting here, I'm in no hurry to leave."

He chuckled, which lightened her spirits a little. "If you're wondering why I've been spending so much time in the carpentry, it's for a good reason." His pipe smoke purled between them, a richly spiced aroma that rivaled her gingerbread.

"Seeing you occupied does my heart good, though ample rest is essential, like Hanna says." Already they were sounding like a seasoned married couple, or nurse and patient. It chafed her and left her longing for the passionate tie they'd once had. "I'm guessing you're working on my Christmas gift."

"I am, aye."

"I've been working on yours too, in spare moments."

"Honestly, we should be done with such. Your company is all the gift I need, Mae."

She let that settle as she worked her needles, tears burning at the backs of her eyes. Fears and tears. That was what life had become lately. Tears over death and betrayal and what couldn't be undone. Fears that Rhys would return to the war. Many injured, wounded men returned to active duty, even limping ones.

"You do believe me when I say that, don't you?"

His careful question drew her out of her dark thoughts. She didn't look at him but continued her handwork. "Believe you?"

"That your company is all I need."

"I'm not very good company lately, mourning James." To say nothing of Coralie.

James especially was much in mind lately. Even the joys of the season couldn't shake her sadness or her ongoing worry that the man sitting beside her wouldn't fully recover but carry a grudge to his grave—or would return to full health only to fall again in some distant field.

"We're mourning together, then."

She looked over at him, thinking he had far more to grieve than she. In the flickering light she detected a few new lines in his face, carved by pain and disappointment and all she wasn't privy to. He rarely complained. And he seemed to be extending some intimacy to her now when they'd not been truly intimate for months.

Her answering unease brought her to her feet. "Would you like some hot chocolate?" Suddenly she craved the cocoa Father Harlow had gotten her at Hough's store. A luxury. For his coming grandchild, he'd jested.

At Rhys's aye, she went to the kitchen. She grated cocoa into the chocolate pot, then went to the spice cupboard, which stopped her. The finished uniform coat hidden there made her reconsider their drinks.

When she returned with the coat, holding it to her chest, he was standing by the hearth looking robust. His recovery of late had been nothing short of miraculous, though he would likely always bear a limp. She had prayed unceasingly for his health with every stitch, surrendering her own hopes and plans for their future.

What if he was meant to return to the war, after all?

Standing in front of him, she held the coat out to him with a tentative smile. She didn't miss the flare of surprise in his eyes. He took it and admired the fine blue fabric, the tailored epaulets and double row of buttons.

"I lined this one with silk, not linen," she said softly. "And Lucy managed the silver thread embroidery on the collar and cuffs."

He swallowed, visibly moved.

Her own throat was so tight her words sounded half choked. "Please, try it on."

He shrugged on the garment in one seamless motion, his arms sliding into the fitted sleeves as the coattails fell to the backs of his knees . . . so handsome her heart gave an almost forgotten flip.

"Well done, Mae." He smoothed the lapels with a sharp tug. "And Lucy."

The accolade fell short. If he would only take her in his arms and kiss her. It had been so long she'd nearly forgotten that too. Biting her lip, she simply admired him instead, reaching out to brush away a speck of lint on his sleeve.

He was so handsome it *hurt*.

He held her gaze in a way he'd not done in weeks. "Is this my Christmas present?"

She nodded, unable to look away. Something soul deep made her say, "When the winter is past and you return to the fight, I'll stand behind you."

The sudden hush was so fraught she felt near tears again. Had she misspoken? Resurrected some old wounds or poked at a new one?

Sparks flew past the andirons onto the newly scrubbed pine floor, and he ground them out with the heel of his boot. "I'm not leaving, Mae."

Her stomach lurched. "Why?"

"I'm most needed here." He began removing the coat. "But it's more than that. There's a toll that killing decent, misguided men takes."

So many men. Fathers. Sons. Brothers. Husbands. War was no respecter of persons. The lament in his voice wasn't lost on her.

"You sound like a Jersey Quaker—or your father."

"I'm no Quaker." He hung the coat on a wall peg. "Not with the men I've taken down."

The lament in his tone grieved her, yet she understood.

"Most of all I can't bear to be away from you and our child."

His low words narrowed the distance between them. This was what she most wanted. To hear his heart. To know he still cared for her, despite all her missteps and regrets—and his.

"You're my world, Mae." His arms slipped round her, as strong and warm as she remembered. His lengthy, searing kiss rivaled the linen closet of long ago. "I can't fathom being without you or living like we've lived lately—separate rooms, separate beds, withheld words. I love you with all that is in me. Nothing will ever come between us again save death."

Epilogue

APRIL 1778
SHENANDOAH VALLEY, VIRGINIA

The spring day dawned bright, befitting a baby's birth. Sunlight broke across the pine floors of their upstairs bedchamber, reaching all the way to the waiting, empty cradle.

"If you dinna put that bairn down ye'll nae get a speck o' rest," the midwife fussed good-naturedly. "Four hours old and not yet oot of yer arms."

Rhys smiled at the Scotswoman from where he sat beside the bed. "I suspect it will be a good while longer still. Why don't you go down the hill to summon my father and sister. They're probably awake by now, if they slept at all."

"Aye, General Harlow."

She went out, her tread catlike on the stair. Rhys looked at Mae rather than the baby, but she was so besotted she didn't look away from their firstborn. Watching them both, he marveled at what the night had wrought.

Labor had been amazingly swift, starting at the stroke of midnight. Father Harlow had ridden for the midwife while Bronwyn stayed by Mae's side till she arrived. Rhys had paced through the house and prayed, expecting childbirth to be something like battle.

The Belle of Chatham

Dangerous. Uncertain. Requiring an endurance and focus and intensity like little else.

Now new concerns clouded his joy. He studied his warrior of a wife for any sign of discomfort or distress. Her color was high, her eyes bright. All that had unraveled was her braid, but Bronwyn would soon set that to rights. Mae looked anything but beleaguered. She looked . . . radiant.

Overcome, he finally said, "You soldiered on so admirably I didn't hear so much as a cry."

"If it had dragged on any longer I might have." Mae looked up at him, wonder in her expression. "Perhaps all that exercise from New York to Virginia last autumn stood me in good stead."

He didn't doubt it. Tentative, he pulled back the baby's swaddling, revealing a rosy, dimple-cheeked face capped by a wispy halo of hair the color of his own. "She's as beautiful as you are."

"More so." She kissed the tiny silken cheek. "And still nameless."

"Mahala?"

"Nay."

"You've changed your mind?"

"*She* changed my mind. I knew it as soon as I saw her." Carefully she passed their daughter to him, though he felt all thumbs. "Mahala shall be saved for another day, Lord willing."

He settled the baby against his chest, cradling her feather lightness for the first time. When she opened her eyes and gazed back at him, the knot in his throat rivaled the sting in his eyes. Blue eyes. Chicory blue like Mae's.

"Meet America," Mae said quietly but assuredly.

"America"—he struggled to speak—"Harlow."

Leaning nearer, Mae kissed his damp, bewhiskered cheek. "I knew you'd treasure all that it means like I do."

Author Note

This novel was, without a doubt, the hardest I've ever written, though it may be the most rewarding. The American Revolution was so incredibly complex that it's difficult to capture a hint of it in four hundred pages of fiction. It even has its own vocabulary and terminology. History is subject to interpretation, and accounts vary as to what happened, why, and sometimes even when. I was continually torn between leaving important history in the story and letting it go. Though I pored over this novel at every stage of production, it is an imperfect, shortsighted work. How I wish I could ask those heroic Patriots my remaining questions and correct any unintentional errors.

Despite the challenges, researching and writing *The Belle of Chatham* fueled my admiration for the American colonies becoming states and then an independent nation. The war was long, enduring almost a decade—a time riddled with disease, despair, and death. How George Washington and his troops went from near defeat to victory against the world's foremost fighting force—Britain and their allies—is truly miraculous. France played a critical part. Gilbert du Motier, Marquis de Lafayette, is a memorable figure for a reason.

This novel was originally inspired by my editor Rachel McRae's ancestry after she graciously shared her family history. Jane McCrea was of Scottish descent and the daughter of a pastor, had siblings on both sides of the conflict, and journeyed from New Jersey to New York during the summer of 1777 to meet her fiancé, a British officer. She literally changed history after she was caught in the crossfire and killed that July. The precise circumstances of her death are conflicting, but posthumously she became a key figure in the fight for independence. News accounts of the time elaborated on her beauty, describing her as "lovely in disposition, so graceful in manners and so intelligent in features, that she was a favorite of all who knew her," and that her hair "was of extraordinary length and beauty, measuring a yard and a quarter."[1] Oddly, other reports described her as plain. Though she's only a shadow character in this novel, she left a memorable legacy.

Daniel Morgan, the renowned Virginia rifleman, shaped the character of Rhys Harlow. Early on, Morgan was a brawler but became a highly respected American commander. Men like Morgan and his riflemen made an enduring mark on the American Revolution and were among the chief reasons the war was won. Saratoga and the battles there are said to be the turning point, which is why I chose that setting and historical marker. For a closer, in-depth look, *Don Troiani's Campaign to Saratoga—1777* by Eric H. Schnitzer and Don Troiani is an excellent work.

Though the war was agonizingly long, Washington and his men made merry when they could. The ball Mae and Coralie attended in Morristown did happen historically. The ticket price was astoundingly high and rose even higher—to $400—by the second winter encampment there in 1780. We know Washington was as splendid a dancer as he was a horseman. At that later ball, Kitty Greene, wife of General Nathanael Greene, attended. It was

---

1. "Jane Macrae, Murdered on the Way to Her Loyalist Lover," New England Historical Society, accessed August 12, 2025, https://newenglandhistoricalsociety.com /jane-macrae-murdered-on-the-way-to-her-loyalist-lover.

reported that Washington "and Mrs. Greene danced upwards of three hours without once sitting down."[2]

Followers of the army like Lucy Hawkes make for fascinating storytelling. Though George Washington had strong feelings about these camp followers, as they came to be called, they were an indispensable part of the American army (and the British) wherever they went. Some of these intrepid women even fought in battles, like "Molly Pitcher," thought to be Mary Ludwig Hays. The American solider Joseph Plumb Martin wrote of her valor in his diary: "A cannon shot from the enemy passed directly between her legs without doing any other damage than carrying away all the lower part of her petticoat. Looking at it with apparent unconcern, she observed that it was lucky it did not pass a little higher, for in that case it might have carried away something else, and continued her occupation."[3] Insightful nonfiction about all those who helped wage and win the war is Holly A. Mayer's *Belonging to the Army: Camp Followers and Community During the American Revolution.*

I've included a few real names in the novel like Israel Evans, who was a wartime chaplain, and Nathan Futrell, the seven-year-old drummer boy. On the British side, General Burgoyne wasn't known as Gentleman Johnny until a later century, but I chose to keep the colorful sobriquet. It's kinder than his reputation for being pompous when he lived.

Though there were many noteworthy men and women on both sides of the conflict, one figure is so remarkable she deserves mention here. Frederica Charlotte Louise Riedesel was a baroness who traveled from Europe to North America to accompany her officer husband, General Riedesel, on campaign, taking her young daughters with her. She kept her children safe at Saratoga and became a

2. Philip G. Smucker, "Washington on the Dance Floor," George Washington's Mount Vernon, accessed August 12, 2025, https://www.mountvernon.org/george-washington/athleticism/on-the-dance-floor.

3. "Molly Pitcher," American Battlefield Trust, accessed August 12, 2025, https://www.battlefields.org/learn/biographies/molly-pitcher.

prisoner of war afterward. I highly recommend *Baroness von Riedesel and the American Revolution: Journal and Correspondence of a Tour of Duty, 1776–1783* by Marvin L. Brown Jr.

Though I've always admired George and Martha Washington, my admiration reached new heights after I researched them more thoroughly. Washington was truly a lion and Martha a lioness. Without them both I doubt the Americans would have been victorious.

I've also gained new insight and a far deeper appreciation for those first founding troops, the many who served and the many who died. It was no small feat to become a Patriot—synonymous with traitor—back then. Families were at war over their colliding allegiances in what became a very personal, brutal fight on every level.

I joined the DAR (Daughters of the American Revolution) because of their ongoing commitment to preserve and honor our nation's history and its veterans. My Kentucky chapter—Berea-Laurel Ridges—is one of the most dedicated. How I wish I could thank my own Patriot ancestor, George Hightower of Virginia, as well as my Hume ancestors from Virginia via Scotland who served in the Continental Army.

Other inspiration comes from friends like Dave and Linda Thomas, whose own family roots run rich and deep. Recently Linda took four generations of her family to the Mohawk Valley and to Ontario to trace their family stories, both Patriot and Loyalist. This is how history is preserved and passed down.

I wrote this novel with our nation's 250th anniversary of independence in mind. My hope is to give a tiny glimpse of what life in war-torn early America might have been like, a far cry from the comforts and liberties we enjoy today. I also want to recognize our current incredible military and their families, who continue to keep us free. My son and new daughter-in-law are among them.

The American Revolution was an unparalleled feat of faith, vision, and endurance. May we never lose sight of what those first founders and Patriots gave us.

Acknowledgments

This novel would never have come to be without Revell, a remarkable publisher who has a team of extraordinary people who create book after edifying book. We're now at novel seventeen, beginning with *The Frontiersman's Daughter* in 2009. Publishing and the market change continually, but Revell's quality and dedication do not.

To my agent, Janet Grant, thank you for your faithful guidance and help in all things publishing. It's truly priceless. Rachel McRae, you have rich roots! Your Jane deserves to be the heroine of her own novel. Thank you, Jessica English, a master at fixing timeline glitches. Your eye for detail at the galleys stage is noteworthy. And to excellent proofreaders like Julie Davis and Amy Tol. Rachael Betz, I knew you were special when I met you as a young reader years ago, only to discover you're a wonder of a marketing manager all grown up. Karen Steele feels as much a friend as a publicist—you make promotion a privilege and joy. And I couldn't have asked for a better cover to become the face of this novel. Heartfelt thanks to Laura Klynstra's stunning design. And to the savvy sales representatives and all those not named here, I'm deeply appreciative.

Thank you to readers who keep spreading the word about my novels and enabling me to write more. God gifted me writing and He gifted me you.

Laura Frantz is a two-time Christy Award winner and the ECPA bestselling author of seventeen novels, including *An Uncommon Woman*, *Tidewater Bride*, *A Bound Heart*, *A Heart Adrift*, *The Rose and the Thistle*, *The Seamstress of Acadie*, and *The Indigo Heiress*. She has also written *A Matter of Honor* and *A Fierce Devotion*, companion novellas to her longer works. She's the proud mom of an American soldier and a career firefighter. Though Kentucky will always be home to her, she and her husband live in Washington State. Learn more at LauraFrantz.net.

--- MEET ---

LAURA FRANTZ

Visit LauraFrantz.net to learn more about
Laura and her books!

enter to win contests and learn about what
Laura is working on now

tweet with Laura

see what Laura is up to

see what inspired the characters and stories